MW00567993

CARELESS WEEDS

Six Texas Novellas

SOUTHWEST LIFE AND LETTERS

A series designed to publish outstanding new fiction and nonfiction about Texas and the American Southwest and to present classic works of the region in handsome new editions.

GENERAL EDITORS: Kathryn Lang, *Southern Methodist University Press;* Tom Pilkington, *Tarleton State University.*

CARE-
LESS
WEEDS

Six
Texas
Novellas

Edited and with an

Introduction by

Tom Pilkington

Southern Methodist University Press / Dallas

Copyright © 1993 by Southern Methodist University Press
All rights reserved
Printed in the United States of America
First edition, 1993

Except for a segment of *Second Lieutenants of Literature* first
published in the *Missouri Review,* the novellas in this volume
have not been previously published. These novellas are
copyrighted by their authors and may not be reprinted
without their authors' written permission. For information,
address Rights and Permissions, Southern Methodist
University Press, Box 415, Dallas, Texas 75275.

Cover illustration by Barbara Whitehead
Designed by Whitehead & Whitehead

Library of Congress Cataloging-in-Publication Data

Careless weeds : six Texas novellas / edited by Tom Pilkington.
    p.   cm.—(Southwest life and letters)
    Contents: Wayfaring strangers / Jane Gilmore Rushing—Hardship /
Margot Fraser—The sun gone down, darkness be over me / David
Fleming—Summer seeds / Clay Reynolds—Bluebirds / Pat Carr—
Second lieutenants of literature / Thomas Zigal.
    ISBN 0-87074-338-4—ISBN 0-87074-339-2 (pbk.)
    1. American fiction—Texas.   2. Texas—Fiction.   I. Pilkington,
Tom.   II. Series.
PS558.T4C36   1993
813'.540809764—dc20   92-53613

To the memory of

SUZANNE COMER

THEY GO BY many names, but to those of us who know them, who have fought them in the sandy fields of West Texas and seen their encroachment into the cracked cement alongside the highways leading up onto the Staked Plain and beyond, they bear but one name: careless weeds. Their spores are carried on the capricious winds, and as they wave back and forth in the heat of high summer, they remind those who have worn a laborer's calluses that they are harbingers of hard work, small reward.

Novellas begin with the promise of a tight short story or a fully blossomed novel, and they ripen quickly; but unless they are "cultivated," reduced or expanded, they often become little more than pernicious pests for the writer, harbingers of hard work, small reward. This book comprises such fictional weeds, novellas, stories that are too long for short story collections and magazines and too short to be bound and published on their own.

Clay Reynolds

Contents

Introduction

*There is, it would seem, in the dimensional scale of the world a kind
of delicate meeting-place between imagination and knowledge, a point
arrived at by diminishing large things and enlarging small ones, that is
intrinsically artistic.*

—Vladimir Nabokov, *Speak, Memory*

THE FORM HAS no universally accepted name. Editors of
popular magazines, especially in England, once called it "the novel-
ette." Katherine Anne Porter insisted on the term "short novel."
Henry James preferred *"nouvelle"*—"the shapely *nouvelle,"* in Jame-
sian parlance. The most common, though far from unanimous, desig-
nation is "novella." Porter dismissed "novella" as "a slack, boneless,
affected word that we do not need to describe anything." The Library of Congress classification system solves the problem by declin-
ing to acknowledge the form's existence under any label.

One critic recently referred to the novella—the term I find most
useful—as "that slippery form." Though perhaps amorphous in
form, the novella is nonetheless a venerable genre of prose fiction.
Literary historians trace its roots to fourteenth-century Italy, to
Boccaccio's *Decameron*. Literary works recognizable as novellas can
be found in French, German, and British literatures beginning in
the eighteenth century. In the nineteenth century several of the
great Russian fiction writers made good use of the form. For reasons too obscure to speculate on with confidence, the novella appears to have reached its zenith in popularity and quality in the
United States during the past hundred years or so.

Some of the best-known works of American fiction from that period are novellas: Herman Melville's *Billy Budd*, Henry James's *Daisy
Miller* and *The Turn of the Screw*, Kate Chopin's *The Awakening*,

Mark Twain's *The Man That Corrupted Hadleyburg* and *The Mysterious Stranger,* William Faulkner's *The Bear,* Nathanael West's *Miss Lonelyhearts,* Katherine Anne Porter's *Noon Wine,* Saul Bellow's *Seize the Day,* Flannery O'Connor's *Wise Blood,* and James Baldwin's *Sonny's Blues.* Even certain famous works published as novels—I am thinking, for example, of F. Scott Fitzgerald's *The Great Gatsby* and Ernest Hemingway's *The Old Man and the Sea*—seem properly to belong to the novella genre. The list could be extended, but these titles indicate the novella's prominence in modern American fiction.

Defining the genre is difficult. The novella, as one anthologist has put it, "is prose fiction of intermediate length," usually between 10,000 and 40,000 words, perhaps 40 to 140 pages in length. Length imposes on the novella much of its peculiarity as a literary form. Since the novella exists on the peripheries of the short story and the novel, commercial demand for it is slight. Editors of periodicals and publishing houses ordinarily spurn novellas as too long (unless serialized) for magazines and journals, too short (unless stretched to fit with large type and wide margins) for publication between hard covers. It seems safe to say that few writers set out consciously to compose novellas.

The novella, then, is a "careless weed," an oft-heard phrase in rural Texas that Clay Reynolds uses as a metaphor for this inconvenient form. The novella is a scorned growth, often sprouting unbidden from the pen (or keyboard) of the fiction writer, a circumstance the hapless writer must view with dismay or even alarm. Yet there is an inevitability in the unwanted development: certain characters and events find their most suitable frame within the confines of the novella. Could Porter have telescoped the career of Royal Earle Thompson into a tidy short story? I doubt it. Could O'Connor have expanded the life of Hazel Motes into a lengthy novel of manners? It's not likely.

Usually fragmentary and suggestive, the short story centers on an "epiphany" that projects into a character's future but cannot show what lies ahead. The novel, on the other hand, frequently resembles narrative history, or biography, in its leisurely march through time and a dense thicket of detail to a more or less definitive conclusion. The novella partakes of the characteristics of both genres, but it maintains an autonomy of its own.

Henry James claimed that the novella is essentially an "anecdote," "something that has oddly happened to someone." In this aspect the novella displays its affinity with the short story—and, interestingly, with drama. The requisite economy of style and sharply focused narrative make the novella sometimes seem little more than a longish short story. The genre's typical unity of action and of effect allows for ease of adaptation to the stage, or, more recently, to film or television. (Novellas by American writers such as Melville, James, Porter, Willa Cather, Edith Wharton, and Carson McCullers have been successfully adapted to drama.) Still, the novella is lengthy enough to show the passage of time, to describe not just the illumination of an epiphany but actual change in a character's motivation and behavior. In this aspect it reveals its kinship with the novel. The novella, blending qualities of the short story and the novel, is a hybrid form both new and different. Its "main merit and sign," said James, "is the effort to do the complicated thing with a strong brevity and lucidity—to arrive, on behalf of the multiplicity, at a certain science of control."

In his essay "Composition and Fate in the Short Novel," the poet and novelist Howard Nemerov observed that most novellas (or short novels) "announce and demonstrate" their "intention . . . of becoming sacred books." Because of its brevity, Nemerov explained, the novella often scants social documentation. The author's message is conveyed by means of symbolism and an evocative probing of psychic depths. Meanings may stand out in such bold relief that the work takes on the coloring of parable or allegory. But commentators and critics from Nathaniel Hawthorne to Richard Chase have told us that these are qualities of American fiction of whatever length. Perhaps this is at least one reason so many American writers have excelled in the genre of the novella.

A survey of the published fiction of Texas writers in the twentieth century suggests Texans have *not* excelled in the novella form. They have turned out dozens of important novels and scores of compelling short stories, but aside from a handful of excellent "short novels" by Katherine Anne Porter and an occasional maverick such as William A. Owens's *Look to the River* or R. G. Vliet's *Rockspring,* they have not written novellas. Perhaps, however, given the difficulty of getting novellas published, these writers simply tossed their novellas into desk drawers and dismissed them from thought. That likelihood, at any rate, launched Suzanne Comer and Clay Reynolds on a search some years back for novellas by Texas writers that, in turn, resulted in the present volume. Their search did not provoke the suspected flood of unpublished manuscripts but, after much winnowing and sifting, did yield a promising harvest: a half-dozen memorable novellas by acclaimed contemporary Texas writers. Except for a segment of Thomas Zigal's, none of these novellas has been previously published.

It strikes me that, while any novella considered in isolation tends to be short on history and thin in the social dimension, these six novellas, taken together, provide a rich chronicle of the evolution of culture and society in Texas over the last six or seven decades: a chronological sequence, then, supplies the principle of arrangement in this volume. Characters in the tales encompass a diversity of race, class, gender, and age. Thematically the novellas cover a wide spectrum: growing up, war and its aftermath, racial conflict, the relations of the sexes, the American dream. Their tonal range is broad, from the comic to the somber and to points in between. Finally, these are works of imaginative literature, not of history or of sociology; their purpose is to disclose the way the human condition (to use a cliché) manifests itself in individual cases.

Jane Gilmore Rushing's *Wayfaring Strangers,* the longest work in the collection, moves at a slower pace than the other novellas. Rushing's prose, as in all her fiction, is lucid and precise. The narrator of *Wayfaring Strangers* is a woman looking back on her youth, a woman who now perceives a wider world than the one she experienced growing up in her native town. Set in the West Texas community of Perdue Springs in the early 1930s, the novella subtly establishes an undercurrent of fear created by economic hard times and the onset of the "dust bowl." Introducing ethnic and cultural difference into a town that is still a frontier village—ingrown, suspicious of outsiders—results in a potentially volatile situation. The quiet and sympathetic telling of the story, however, removes much of the possibility for bitterness and rancor.

Wars have always engendered adversity for Americans—not just for the men and women who served in the armed forces, but also for those who remained home. Margot Fraser's *Hardship* powerfully dramatizes the destructive effects of World War II on a family of ranching Texans. The mother, whose story this is, has no choice but to keep going—enduring emotional as well as physical hardship—as she watches her family disintegrate. Yet the governing message of the novella affirms the resiliency of the human spirit. The harsh, awe-inspiring beauty of the Big Bend country of West Texas is a fitting backdrop to the woman's persistence and courage.

The Sun Gone Down, Darkness Be Over Me, by David Fleming, takes place in East Texas, the part of the state with the closest ties to the deep South. It is set in the late 1950s, shortly after the start of the civil rights movement, a social upheaval that rocked the entire South, an upheaval even backwater East Texas could not evade. Fleming's story focuses on two people, a black man, William Temple, and his "niece." The novella depicts the ubiquitous and ironic nature of prejudice and the deformed and stunted soul of a man who has chosen emotional and spiritual isolation over contact with other human beings. Related in luminous prose, *The Sun Gone Down* is a haunting tale of lost love—agape, not eros—and of love regained.

The events of Clay Reynolds's *Summer Seeds* occur in the early 1960s, a time when children—males, in particular—routinely roamed the Texas countryside carrying weapons. This practice seems to have been in part a vestige of the state's frontier heritage, in part the result of its martial tradition, a tradition intensified by the seething frustrations of the "cold war." Throughout the twentieth century Texans have enthusiastically supported American military intervention in a variety of foreign adventures by signing up for military service in record numbers. The question is, Where do all those budding Audie Murphys come from? *Summer Seeds,* an initiation story with a twist, offers a provocative answer to the question. By means of a comedy of errors that turns to horror, it builds to an explosive and startling conclusion.

The setting of Pat Carr's *Bluebirds* is Haskell, a town north of Abilene, in the late 1970s or early 1980s. The novella concerns the problems of returning Vietnam vets. Amy, the focal character, is a victim of those problems through her two marriages to scarred veterans. Amy's decision to cast off passivity and dependency and to assume control of her own life, to become an autonomous and fully functioning adult, is movingly and dramatically portrayed.

Second Lieutenants of Literature, by Thomas Zigal, is a wicked and hilarious send-up of the literary lecture circuit and of the lower levels of the creative writing industry. On a broader canvas the tale is a fable of life in contemporary America and of the vanishing American dream of success. The narrator is a latter-day Willy Loman who loses his nerve and goes slightly berserk. For the narrator there is always tomorrow, a new venue with a new start and new "students," but his long-range prospects are ever-bleaker assignments and shrinking funding. Both *Bluebirds* and *Second Lieutenants of Literature,* the two novellas in this collection with the most contemporary settings, take place in small West Texas towns. Both could as easily have been set anywhere in the United States. Probably this is the collection's final comment on life in twentieth-century Texas: Texans now live in a homogenous national culture, and the things that, for better or worse, once distinguished us from other Americans are rapidly passing away.

I WANT TO acknowledge the substantial contributions of Clay Reynolds and Suzanne Comer in transforming *Careless Weeds* from a concept into a reality. The idea (as well as the title) for the collection came from Clay. Suzanne, to whose memory the book is dedicated, did much of the spadework to unearth these—and other—novellas by Texas writers. I salute Clay and Suzanne for their indispensable efforts on behalf of the collection. Thanks are due the two dozen and more writers who submitted proposals or manuscripts for consideration for inclusion in this volume. I wish also to thank Kathryn Lang, senior editor of the Southern Methodist University Press, for her patience and encouragement in guiding the project to its completion. Her advice and editing skills have made this a significantly better book than it otherwise would have been.

Tom Pilkington
Stephenville, Texas

Wayfaring Strangers

Jane Gilmore Rushing

I

THE DAGO came to Perdue Springs in the late summer of
1931 and camped down by the baptizing hole. He traveled in a
Model T truck, onto which had been built a low little flat-topped
house, its walls made of broad upright planks painted alternately
blue and yellow.

Rosie and I saw him when he first got there. We were lying on
our stomachs across the bed in the front bedroom at my house,
looking out the open east window at nothing but pale blue faraway
sky and mesquite brush sunbaked a pale brittle green. We heard the
truck before we saw it, rattling along slow like an old wagon. It was
coming from the south: probably, the driver had turned off the state
highway when he saw the sign that said "Perdue Springs, 3 miles."
Why he would was a mystery.

When we saw what kind of outfit it was, we called Grandma
from the kitchen and all three of us rushed out on the porch to
watch it go by. The man at the wheel was dark—some kind of
foreigner, we had to think. He had thick black hair that curled
down onto his neck and he wore an old-fashioned bushy mustache.
He had a blue bandanna tied around his head—for effect, I
thought, but Grandma said to keep his hair out of his face. On the
seat beside him sat a big woolly dog with a yellow scarf around its
neck. Above the housetop, on a tall stick, hung a blue and yellow
pennant, fluttering a little as the truck rolled through the still,
shimmering air.

"Now what in the name of time can that be?" said Grandma.

3

Using that expression showed she was overcome, because she was opposed to what she called "bywords," no matter how innocent they might seem. She had a little lecture she used to give me on that subject. Heck is the same as hell. Darn is the same as damn. Gosh is the same as God. People who use those words are cursing, and cursing is a sin. I used to wonder what the name of time really was, and if it could be a sin to speak it.

As the truck reached the crossroads, nearly every man, woman, and child in Perdue Springs must have been watching and expressing amazement in various more or less sinful ways. The driver came nearly to a stop, looking in all directions as if uncertain which way to proceed: westward, toward Hodges' general store and the tabernacle; eastward, to Mashburns' store and the schoolhouse; or straight ahead, past Grandpa's blacksmith shop and the gin, down to the thick willow growth that showed where the creek ran.

While he looked at Perdue Springs, Perdue Springs came out to get a better look at him. Mr. Hodges appeared on one side of the road, Mr. and Mrs. Mashburn on the other. After looking the newcomer over and bestowing quick glances on each other, they hurried back into their stores, not wanting to appear idle, as though suggesting business might be slow. Grandpa and the domino players came forth and stood awhile in front of the blacksmith shop, a little unpainted step-fronted building blackened by soot and age.

The seven Tadlock children came along after the truck, from their tumbling-down old house at the top of the hill, strung out raggedly from the middle-sized boy, running at full speed, to the two little ones, crying and calling out "wait," to the big boy, George Earl (the one between Rosie and me in age), who as the oldest was supposed to keep an eye on them all.

Seeing us on the porch, he turned and came through the yard gate. George Earl was a brownish boy, with the kind of skin that always looks dirty whether it is or not. He nearly always needed a haircut and wore faded blue overalls with a shirt that needed patching. I never thought much about whether I liked him or not. In the pattern of Perdue Springs, he belonged with Rosie and me, and to a certain extent we accepted him.

4

"What is it?" he asked.

We all said we couldn't imagine.

"He's going on down toward the creek," Grandma said.

We kept watching, and he never did go up the hill on the other side, so we guessed he had stopped to camp for the night. There was a broad, open stretch of ground sloping down from the gin yard to a pool that we called the baptizing hole, where travelers would occasionally stay overnight; but it was rare to see anyone camping there because no one ever came through Perdue Springs on the way to anywhere else.

"What could he be doing here?" Rosie asked.

"He must be lost," Grandma said.

We decided that must be the answer. George Earl called his brothers and sisters together and led them back up the hill. Rosie said it was time for her to go home and help cook supper.

I walked a piece with her, as I had been in the habit of doing nearly ever since the Fargos moved to Perdue Springs. Friendship had not blossomed between us at once, because in the beginning each of us thought the other was stuck-up. We were in the same grade at school, but I was two years younger, having started to school early and been put ahead a year—not an uncommon practice in our country schools in those days, but she thought it made me a smart aleck. As for my feeling toward Rosie, it was pure envy, because she was so beautiful. There is no other word to describe her. She had long, dark, softly curling hair; I had a plain brown windblown bob with straight-across bangs. She had fair, delicately colored skin that reminded me of an old china doll Grandma kept put up in the chifferobe; I had more than a sprinkling of freckles. No use going on with comparisons: she had dark blue eyes with thick black lashes; she had even, milk-white teeth; she walked like a princess.

How could I expect to be friends with a girl who looked like that? As it turned out, though, we got over our first impressions and learned we had things in common. Or did we? Looking back, I can't say what they were, but we had been chums for half a dozen years as the fall of '31 was approaching. She was fifteen and I was thirteen.

I always walked with Rosie as far as Mr. Goodacre's gate.
Mr. Goodacre was a farmer whose land lay for a short distance
along our east-west road. His house was located across a small,
mesquite-grown pasture, fenced off for cows so that anyone going
to Goodacres' had to open and shut a heavy plank gate. Their
house, a steep-roofed white frame with a veranda, was thus not
exactly part of Perdue Springs, although Mr. Goodacre made his
presence felt there. He was a little like the squire in old novels, and
the rest of us were the lowly villagers; my grandfather and some of
his friends often called him Squire Goodacre.

The wide top board of Mr. Goodacre's gate was where Rosie and
I liked to sit and talk awhile before our final parting after a visit at
either my house or hers. But this day, as we paused at the turn-off
and looked toward the gate, we saw Mr. Goodacre standing just inside it, watching us approach.

"Well, here's Rosie and Mmmm," he said. He always remembered Rosie's name, but never mine.

"What's going on in town, girls?" he asked as we approached.
Though he was not a tall man, his words seemed to come from on
high, like a preacher's from the pulpit.

It was easy to think of a preacher—the gently pious sort—in
connection with Mr. Goodacre. Or an angel. With his fine blond
hair curling softly across his forehead, he brought to mind pictures
in big Bibles or Sunday school books.

"I don't know, sir," I answered. "A man in a truck with a house
on it drove through and stopped at the creek."

"To camp, we think," said Rosie.

He didn't respond the way everybody else had, unless a subtle
hardening of his angelic features meant surprise and curiosity.

"We'd better see about that," he said.

I walked a little farther with Rosie, to say goodbye, and when I
went back by the gate he was gone.

At supper Grandpa told what he knew about Mr. Goodacre's visit
to the stranger. He had heard it round-about but believed it to be
the truth.

"Squire went down to the campground," he said, "and talked to that Dago."

"Is he aiming to stay long?" Grandma asked.

"They say he told Squire he didn't have any plans," Grandpa said, "and Squire said maybe he ought to make some. Then the Dago wanted to know if that was public property and if we had any laws about how long anybody could stay there."

"And of course it is, and we don't," Grandma said. "But I guess Cornelius thinks being justice of the peace makes him the law in Perdue Springs."

"He tried to make the Dago think he was. Said his welcome might run out if he didn't watch his step."

"Where did the man come from?" Grandma asked.

"South Texas, maybe," Grandpa said. "He's got Texas tags on that truck."

"What's a Dago?" I asked. I had heard the word before, but it wasn't clear to me whether it referred to race, nationality, or—as I understood to be the case with gypsies—simply a way of life.

Grandpa looked amused, as he often did at my questions. "Well, to tell the truth, May," he said, "I don't just exactly know. I reckon it's somebody pretty dark complected."

"Dark complected" covered a wide range, but the way Grandpa said it suggested someone alien and apart. There had never been anyone very dark or different in our village; it would scarcely be an exaggeration to say we thought the whole civilized world looked like us, or ought to. We knew better, of course; but our folklore taught us that different meant sinister or comic.

"Dago's not anything then," I said.

"Could be Eyetalian, maybe, or Egyptian," Grandpa said.

Dago, in my mental dictionary, went down as a person dark and flashy, unidentified as to nationality or race.

"What about the dog?" Grandma asked.

"Oh, he's a bear," Grandpa said, and began to laugh.

It was so much fun to watch Grandpa laugh at his own jokes that anything he said could seem witty. He would try to hold back, out of modesty I assumed, while he grew redder and redder, even to the roots of his sparse white hair, until at last he would let it all out like a balloon that got away before it was quite blown up. Then he would just sit and shake.

George Earl Tadlock walked in while he was laughing (no one knocked at doors in Perdue Springs) and sat down at the table to wait till Grandpa got through.

"Eat them taters, George Earl," Grandma said, seeing his eyes on them.

"I done eat supper," George Earl said.

"Well, eat 'em if you can," Grandma said. "They'll go to waste if you don't."

She would have made potato cakes out of them for dinner the next day, but she knew the Tadlock kids were always hungry. George Earl ate them out of the serving bowl.

"I been down to the campground," he said when he had finished. "And you know what, that feller's a fortune-teller."

"I never heard of a man fortune-teller," I said. "Did he tell you that?"

"I didn't even see nobody, but there's a sign on that little old house."

"I didn't see a sign."

"I guess he put it up since he camped. It's yeller with blue letters. It says RAVEN SEES THE FUTURE."

"Is that his name—Raven?"

"Must be, don't you reckon?"

"I would've got my fortune told," I said, "if I'd a been there."

"You might not," George Earl said. "The sign says twenty-five cents for a reading."

"What's a reading?" I asked.

"I don't know," he said. "But I'd a got one, if I'd a had a quawter."

"Ain't nobody around Perdue Springs got money for fortune-telling," Grandma said. "If you talk to the man, you tell him that."

"Yes'm," George Earl said.

I went to bed soon after George Earl left, but I didn't go to sleep very soon. I thought of all I'd heard about fortune-telling, and I wondered about the Dago and his readings. Would he read your palm, or the stars, or what? How much would he tell? I didn't know when I'd ever have the money for a reading, or whether I'd dare have one if I did, but I made up my mind to go to Rosie's next morning and get her to go to the creek with me. I didn't expect us to talk to the Dago, but I reckoned we could find out something just by looking around.

Rosie and I seemed to know already what our future would be. We had planned it together: it was more than a schoolgirl dream. We knew our goals wouldn't be easy to reach, but we meant to work hard. High school graduation. College. Then teaching together in some town or city. Rosie had not thought she would want to be a teacher until Nancy Brock, our schoolteacher's wife, told her about public school music as a career. In our one-room school, no one studied music, but Nancy said in big schools there was one teacher who taught music in all the grades and nothing else but music.

I had dreamed it all over so often it was like a scene remembered: the big old house we'd find to live in, the great long narrow book-lined room, a black grand piano in one end, the windows hung (oh yes, I went this far) with stiff silk purple curtains. And maybe—this came and went, I could never quite get the image clear—a white marble bust above the door.

Sometimes as I was falling asleep I could see that room as plain as if my bed stood in the middle of it.

Just so, sometimes in recent years, in the minutes between waking and sleeping, have I seen the village of my childhood spread out around me, all true and clear in one glimpse, and I almost believe it could take shape again.

II

THERE is a story about a village in Germany—cursed and godless it was—that vanished from the earth only to reappear one day in every hundred years. Once in a century the cracked church bell rings, gaily dressed young folk dance in the public hall, and the dead bury their dead. When the clock in the old church tower strikes midnight, a thick mist closes round the village and it sinks back into the swamp.

Whether our village was ever truly cursed, I cannot tell. Probably, it was just another victim of time and technology. I only know it vanished, and I do not think I wish it back again. Still I have these visions, glimpses only, like previews flashed too quickly by on the motion picture screen; and it seems to me that some day when the time is right, if I should live so long, I may find myself driving down the old highway and notice a sign that says "Perdue Springs, 3 miles." I'll turn off and drive along the red, rocky road past cotton fields and a peach orchard, and when I round the end of a long, flat hill, I'll see in a little valley below me a collection of houses, mostly unpainted, with trees and friendly windmills in their yards. I'll drive down nearly to the crossroads and stop at a little white house with a wire fence around it and a red rose blooming by the porch steps.

I may see myself coming out the front gate and hear the clang of the metal catch closing. I think I'd rather be younger, though, than I was that morning I set out for Rosie's house to tell her the Dago was a fortune-teller. I think I'd rather the season were spring. I'd want Perdue Springs itself to be younger—already then it had grown a little sad and sere, like the weeds and grass along the roadside.

But in spring the grass was green and the weeds were flowers. I'd run out of the house—free on a May morning, because in those innocent happy days the school term ended in mid-April. I'd be heading for Rosie's house, but I'd have some stops and pauses to make along the way.

First, the rocks. On the crossroads corner nearest our house they lay, hunks of sandstone more or less geometrical in shape, scattered at random as though flung by the hand of some baby giant suddenly tired of using them for building blocks, yet close enough together that an ordinary little girl could leap from one to another, making the sort of magic that city children do when they avoid stepping on cracks in the sidewalk. Most of them were fairly flat on top, so that, on a good-sized one, two or three children could sit comfortably, dreaming together. Some of the rocks held within them brilliant flecks of something that sparkled in the sun like diamonds. As a young child Rosie used sometimes to scratch them out with a nail. She would get a double handful, she said, and put them all together to make the biggest diamond in the world. That's what she was doing the day George Earl showed us his penis. She gave it a glance and went back to her work.

We always suspected there were rattlesnakes among the rocks, although Old Man Snodgrass the snake-hunter cleared them out twice a year. You could scare the little children off by talking about the snakes, if you didn't want them hanging around.

I was not afraid among the rocks, but I felt some magic there, as though they represented a casting up of secret power objects from the bowels of the earth. One way or another, I made contact with them every day, perhaps with some unconscious need of sharing in that earth-force.

Actually, their presence was easily explained. They were dumped there when the roads were built in Perdue Springs, having been blasted out of the hillside. Grandma, who had come to that area as a small child, had seen the road-building and she described it to me. Even so, I could feel the rocks' magic.

From the rocks, across the road to Grandpa's shop. That was magical, too. I would have awakened to the ringing of the hammer on the anvil, a call to come and watch the fire in the forge, see metal shape-changed by the force of Grandpa's hammer. Grandpa himself seemed transformed. He was big and tall, but I never thought much about his size at home. Here in the shop, wearing his tawny leather apron, he was a mighty man, just like the smith in the poem by Longfellow that Grandma liked to recite.

A pause in the wide, open doorway of the shop, a glance into the dimness and a wave to Grandpa, and then I'd be on down the road toward Rosie's. In that half mile, I'd pass Mashburns' store, which was also the post office and thus as close to being the town center

11

as we had. Two or three more houses, Mr. Goodacre's gate, the teacherage, and then the schoolhouse, a two-roomed frame building in need of paint, set on a broad bare plot of ground sloping down toward the creek, with the boys' toilet on the western boundary and the girls' on the east. It was a pleasant little walk to the toilet and back, a nice change from the schoolroom. I used to have to go a lot.

Finally, Rosie's house, just where the road curved up out of the little creek valley. It was one of the oldest houses in Perdue Springs and had been vacant for several years when the Fargos moved there. They had come when Mr. Fargo got his job as precinct overseer with the county road system. I don't know where they had been living before, but they all seemed to think this bare old house a great improvement.

It had been a pretty good house once. There was even paper on the walls, all its colors faded to a pale, faintly reddish brown, as though ready to crumble into the dust of our roads and fields. But the outside walls had never been painted, and almost everything about the place that could break or wear out was in need of repairs. Even so, they were all so happy about this change in their lives that in those old springtime days it was a joy to go there.

They owned one thing I had always longed for. A piano. A monstrously ugly, dark-varnished, curlicued old upright that seemed to take up half the space in what they called the front room. On a morning like the one I'm dreaming of, I could hear it long before I could see the yellow roses blooming along the falling-down picket fence. Two or three of the children might be playing it at the same time, banging out chords, one adding a tinkling melody played with one finger. Or a bunch of them might be gathered around singing, while one of the big girls "seconded." They were what we called a singing family, and they had somebody to take every part in the harmony. It seemed to me that something out of the air would come over them and suddenly everyone in the house would be standing around the piano singing. Mrs. Fargo, a still-faced woman with large, unwondering eyes, would come in from the kitchen, with a dish towel in her hand and a baby on her hip. And when she started singing her color would rise and her eyes would sparkle.

But on this day in 1931 when I went down to Rosie's, I did not hear any music. They had sold the piano months before, when they saw they would run out of money. The county had abolished the position of precinct overseer when they cut the road budget by more than half. All the Fargos said how lucky they were that Mr. Fargo got to keep a job running a road grader, but he could only work when the commissioner decided a road was on the verge of becoming impassable. I hated to see the road grader in the ditch out in front of their house, because I knew it meant Mr. Fargo was sitting in the front-room rocking chair, staring out the window at his idle machine.

Mr. Fargo had always given me a friendly greeting if he was at home when I went to see Rosie, but now he didn't even seem to know anyone had come in. I gave him a swift look and hurried on through the sad, bare room. The piano was gone, I didn't know what else. There had been a rug on the floor, but now the bleached, splintery planks were uncovered. As I look back now, it seems to me there was nothing in the room but the old broken rocker and Mr. Fargo sitting there as wooden as the chair, wearing overalls Grandma would have put in the rags because they were too thin to hold a patch. I think I was a little afraid of him, as you might be of someone with an unfamiliar illness. He looked so strange—his high sloping forehead, usually shaded by his hat, seemed unnaturally white contrasting with the whiskery, deep-tanned jaws and chin. His set mouth was like a chalk mark drawn across a blackboard. I knew he wouldn't speak.

I went on in the kitchen. Mrs. Fargo and the girls were in there, not doing anything. Gladys, the oldest girl still at home, was standing at the back door looking out. Lucy May, the two-year-old, whose name Rosie had picked in my honor, was playing quietly at her feet with a threadbare rag doll. Mrs. Fargo was sitting at the big square table looking out the window. (The Fargos spent a lot of time looking out doors and windows, hoping perhaps to see deliverance coming.) She was rubbing Cloverine salve on the breaking-out she

13

had on her arms and neck, which I noticed had got worse during the summer. She was the one who had the strange disease, but we didn't know it then.

Rosie had been sitting there too—looking out the window, I suppose. She got up and came to greet me. "Mama's been sick at her stomach," she said. No one else spoke.

That wasn't a house to be in.

"I thought maybe you'd walk down to the bridge with me," I said to Rosie.

She didn't answer me, just said, "I'll be back after while, Mama."

We walked back along the way I had come, not saying much at first, just going along, looking down. Rosie was barefooted and red dust came up between her toes.

"Where's the boys?" I said.

"I don't know—off somewhere," she said. "O.B.'s lost his job."

O.B., the oldest boy, had been working on a wildcat oil well that had turned out to be a dry hole. The boss said they didn't have the money to drill anymore.

"We've been counting on all of us picking cotton," Rosie said, "but I guess there's not gonna be any to pick. Mr. Goodacre told Daddy he doubted that he could hire anybody this year, and if he can't I don't know who can."

"That's too bad," I said.

"Everything's too bad," Rosie said.

There was no use going on about it.

We came to the schoolhouse, and Rosie said, "I may not go to school this fall."

"You have to go to school," I said. There had to be high school and college and teaching in a big town.

"I'm tired of school," she said.

I knew that was a lie, but I didn't say anything.

Finally she went on, "Daddy thinks he can afford to send Wayne and Woodrow. Girls don't need schooling as much as boys do, anyhow."

That was so unlike what I knew she really believed that I didn't even answer it. I said, "Grandpa says we may not have much school

this year anyway, since they cut state aid and so many are not paying taxes."

Grandpa was a trustee, trying as hard as he could to keep a school
going at Perdue Springs. School buses had brought the trend toward
consolidation, and some people thought we would be better off going to Cottonwood Flats, five miles away, where they had an ac-
credited high school.

We passed the teacherage, pausing to greet Nancy Brock, who
was watering her jew on the front porch. We passed Mashburns'
and turned the corner at the crossroads. We looked in at Grandpa,
who was playing solitaire on a board laid across a cut-down oil
drum. The domino players hadn't come in yet.

"What are you gals up to?" he asked.

"We're fixing to go down to the bridge," I said.

"See that you stay on the bridge then," he said.

"Yes sir," I said.

We started on, and I said to Rosie, "I don't think I like that Dago
being down there, if we can't even go to the creek."

"I guess he'll leave," Rosie said. "Sounds like Mr. Goodacre don't
like him."

We stood on the bridge, against the iron truss that formed both
railing and support for it. Beneath us the creek lay still and green. I
thought of big old crawdads down deep in the shadows and wished
I could go home and get me a string with a piece of meat tied on
one end and take it down to a rock in the edge of the water. Like
Mr. Goodacre I hoped the Dago wouldn't stay long.

"I don't see anybody," Rosie said.

I hadn't looked, but when I did, I didn't see anybody either,
at first. The dog, free of its scarf, was lying asleep in a patch of
partial shade near the truck, as if expected to perform the duty
of a watchdog. Farther back, in deeper shade, next to the trunk of
a wide-spreading cottonwood tree, was somebody sitting in a
chair.

"That's not the Dago," Rosie said.

"Who is it then?" I was nearsighted and would have to get glasses
before long.

15

"It's a woman," she said. "She must have been in the house when he drove in."

I pressed the corner of my right eye with my middle finger. I don't know how I had learned that would help, but I could see a little better. "Does she have white hair?" I asked.

"Yes, and she's dark," Rosie said. "She's real old and real dark."

"You know what?" I said. "I bet you she's the one that tells fortunes. Raven could be a woman just as well as a man."

"She looks like a fortune-teller," Rosie said.

"We could go down there," I said. "I don't believe Grandpa would care if he knew there was a woman."

"And besides," Rosie said, "the Dago's gone."

"He might be in the house," I said.

The old woman, noticing us, got up from her chair and came to the edge of the creek bank below the willow thicket. She was a large woman—broad-hipped and full-bosomed. She wore a long, hot-looking black dress, and her cotton-white hair hung down her back in one long, thick plait. When she came into the bright sun, you could see how brown and smooth her face was, how placid her expression. There was nothing of youth in it—she was unquestionably old—but age had not put the kind of marks on her that I was used to seeing on the old women of Perdue Springs.

"Come down and talk to me, girls," she called. She had a clear, rich voice.

"We're not supposed to," I called back.

At that moment I had a vision of Hansel and Gretel nibbling at the house of bread and cake.

"Are you the fortune-teller?" Rosie called.

"I can read the cards," the old woman said. "Come down and I'll show you."

Rosie and I exchanged glances: we saw we did not want to go.

"I'll have to ask my grandma," I said. "We might come back."

"Tell your grandmother to come too," she said.

Rosie and I walked slowly back up the hill.

"Would you want to go back?" I asked.

16

"I might like to see her cards," Rosie said, "and find out what she does. I don't know whether I want to hear my future or not."

"Well, we know ours," I said.

Rosie didn't say anything.

I walked on with her to Mr. Goodacre's gate, but we didn't tarry there. She didn't seem to be in a very good mood.

At home, Grandma was making cornbread to eat with our beans for dinner. While I set the table and cut up some onion, I told her about the old woman.

"She may not be as old as you think," Grandma said. "Maybe she's the man's wife."

"She's older than you are, Grandma," I said. "I don't think she's his wife."

"Lots of people younger than me has got white hair," Grandma said. "My folks don't gray young."

"It's not just the hair," I said. In spite of the woman's smooth face, she might have looked out on the ages.

Grandpa, when he came in to eat, had already heard about the old woman. He even knew that Mrs. Gibson, who lived in the gin house, had been to have a reading.

"I reckon you already know what she found out, too," Grandma said.

"No," Grandpa said, "but they say she was looking right smug about it."

When Grandma and I had finished cleaning up the dinner things, she always wanted us to sit down with our handwork and rest a little while. She was making me hem cup towels and embroider daisies on them.

"Let's set in the living room," Grandma said, "where there's some breeze blowing in."

We had a nice living room for the time and place—fresh paper on the walls, a good linoleum rug on the floor, ruffled curtains at the windows, now blowing lightly, as a little breeze had indeed sprung up from the east. All the furniture was dusted daily (how well I knew) and polished with cedar oil once a week. There were three rocking chairs with spring seats, a cane settee, and a library table with an Aladdin lamp on it. We sat facing each other in chairs pulled out into the room where we could get the breeze through both the window and the front door.

"Oh Grandma," I said, as the Fargos' pitiful front room came into my mind, "I'm so glad we have a nice house."

She looked up from her darning, pushed her steel-rimmed glasses up on her nose and a stray lock of dark brown hair up into the bun on top of her head. It occurred to me that I liked her looks too: old-fashioned but right for a grandma.

She didn't respond to my comment but seemed to know what my thoughts were. "Tell me about the Fargos," she said.

I didn't know what she wanted me to tell her. "I don't know," I said. "Seems like they're just dwindling away."

"You mean they don't get enough to eat?"

"I don't know about that." I hadn't been there for a meal in a long time. "It's just—the house looks so bare. Everything's so quiet—even Lucy May. She keeps so still."

"What about Miz Fargo? Does she seem well?"

"That breaking-out's worse."

"I don't know when I've seen her," Grandma said. "She never did visit, but I used to see her at the store."

"I guess it's her clothes," I said. She had been wearing a stained, patched dress pinned across her breast with a safety pin.

"I think I'll walk down there after supper," Grandma said, "and take her the rest of that calamine lotion Grandpa used when he had that rash."

"You think it will help?" I asked.

"No," she said.

III

WE didn't hear much about the Dago for the next two or three days. Grandma kept me so busy around the house that I didn't get a chance to slip down to the creek, nor did I see anything of Rosie or George Earl.

Grandpa had a few bits of news though, collected from various sources by the domino players. The old woman was the Dago's mother. The Dago went off down the creek with his dog every day, while she stayed at the camp and minded a pot hung over a low-burning fire. Often she would talk in some strange tongue to a huge, long-haired black cat with eyes that burned in the dark like coals of green fire. When Mrs. Gibson's twins chased the cat because it was scaring their puppy, she waved a long stick at them and cursed them in witch-talk.

"I don't reckon them Gibson boys would know witch-talk from monkey jabber," Grandma said.

Grandpa's shaking shoulders betrayed secret laughter. I think he was pleased to find Grandma was at least a little bit sympathetic toward the Dago. It would have been just like her not to be: she liked for people to fit into well understood patterns. She was curious about these strangers, though, and seemed to take some interest in their welfare. I was satisfied she would go with Rosie and me to visit the old woman.

When she would I couldn't tell, but I hoped it might be soon. Rosie was coming to stay all night with us Saturday night and would spend the day Sunday. We could talk about the visit then.

She used to spend the night with us often, but this would not be an ordinary occasion. On Sunday, she was to sing a solo at the Perdue Springs Sunday school. She always liked to stay with us when she had to get dressed up for some unusual happening; she didn't have much privacy at home.

Every so often, probably not more than three or four times a year, Rosie would sing a solo at Sunday school. Gladys and Beatrice, her older sisters, used to sing with her sometimes, but when Beatrice left home the trio broke up. Beatrice getting married was a good excuse, but the real reason for the break-up was that Rosie's voice had grown so much lovelier as it matured that the sisters were jealous.

Grandpa said Perdue Springs was as worked up over Rosie's coming performance as it was about the campers. People felt that Rosie Fargo belonged to Perdue Springs—her songs and her smiles were for us. Everyone seemed to have some claim on her, some hope for her future. If we had lived in the age of beauty pageants, we would have expected to see her crowned Miss America.

I could hardly wait for her arrival Saturday afternoon. I kept going to look down the road for her, and then after all she was on the porch before I saw her so I didn't get to go meet her. Still I knew all Perdue Springs had seen her walking lightly along the dusty road, coming to our house, carrying her things in a bundle. Anyway I hoped they had.

As soon as Rosie had exchanged a few words with Grandma, we went into my room, which opened off the living room and looked out on the front porch. It wasn't very big, but it had a full-sized bed, a dresser, and a small wooden rocker with a ruffled pink cushion Grandma had made. Rosie sat down with a sigh, as she always did. She thought it would be heaven to have such a room, all her own.

I undid her bundle so I could hang up her dress. I had a cretonne curtain across one corner, concealing a rod that I hung my best things on. My Sunday dress that summer was a light blue piqué, made out of material ordered from the Sears and Roebuck catalog. I knew Rosie hadn't had anything new that year, and as I opened the bundle I was wondering what she had found to wear.

"This is beautiful, Rosie!" I exclaimed when I saw the voile dress in shades of rose, even though I knew that it belonged to Nancy Brock. She had bought it ready-made at the beginning of summer but hadn't worn it around Perdue Springs, so I thought maybe people wouldn't know it was borrowed.

"It's too little for Nancy now," Rosie said. "She said I could have it."

I didn't think it was too little. I thought Nancy just wanted Rosie to have a pretty dress to wear to sing in. And I was a little jealous, as I could be when anyone outside my family did anything for Rosie. But I said, "It'll look better on you than her anyhow."

Rosie took the dress and held it up against her. Certainly the color was right for her. And the flared skirt, which would be a little shorter on Rosie than the length most Perdue Springs women wore, had an air of something more exciting than a dress to wear to Sunday school. Probably, Nancy realized after she bought it that it wasn't a style she would have much use for at Perdue Springs.

"It is pretty, isn't it?" Rosie said. She held it close against her waist and took a few whirling waltz steps, making the skirt swing out.

Grandma walked into the room just then and I said, "Oh Grandma, just look at Rosie's pretty new dress. Nancy gave it to her."

I was trying to keep her from saying anything about Rosie dancing, and maybe I succeeded. She admired the dress, asked how Rosie's mama was, and then said, "I imagine you ought to take your bath right away, Rosie, so's your hair will have time to dry."

But I'm sure she had noticed the dance steps and would have said something if it had suited her to do so. Rosie and I had heard her condemnations of dancing more than once.

"She don't know I dance, does she?" Rosie said anxiously when she was gone.

"Well, I never did tell her," I said.

Everybody in or around Perdue Springs, except for some of the folks over in the Rough Creek country, considered dancing to be a sin. That was ranching territory, and, generally speaking, cowboys dance. Even so, the old people thought it prudent to pretend they didn't. So what they did, every once in a while, was to give a musicale (pronounced musical). People from Perdue Springs might even attend musicales. I had been taken once when I was a small child. We sat in chairs placed around the walls of the room and listened to a group of men playing tunes on fiddles, guitars, mandolins, and I think a banjo. Those who came only to listen were expected to leave early, but as I recall, the young folks couldn't wait and two or three couples were on the floor before we were ready to leave.

Grandma was furious and declared she would never go to that house again. But she kept up with who did go and who stayed late.

I would have been surprised to find out she didn't know Rosie, Gladys, and O.B. could often be seen among the Rough Creek dancers.

"She's right, I better take my bath," Rosie said. "On account of my hair."

Rosie's long hair was a trial to her, in a way, and a source of conflict at home. Her mother said it took too much time and too much soap to keep it clean, and at times Rosie grew impatient with it herself and threatened to cut it. I begged her not to, and got Grandma to agree that Rosie could wash her hair at our house. We always saved little pieces of Grandma's homemade lye soap for shampoo, and put them in a jar with a little water. This made a creamy liquid we could pour over our heads as we stood—in winter bending over a wash pan in the kitchen or in summer bathing in our back-yard shower bath.

No one in Perdue Springs had a bathroom, and for a long time we were the only ones with a shower, although after Grandpa showed the way a few others built them too. He had made a wooden framework covered with towsacks that afforded privacy and let the wind blow through. On top of the structure he placed an oil drum fitted with pipe and shower nozzle; we filled it daily with water pumped by the nearby windmill. As the summer sun grew stronger, the water grew warmer: we had to recalculate the best time for a bath with every change in the weather. On the hottest days it was best to bathe in the morning or after dark.

"The water may be too hot," I said to Rosie.

"Oh, not for me," she said. "I love a hot bath."

I knew she did. When we used to take baths together, I sometimes felt I was blistering my skin for her sake.

We did not take baths together anymore. Rosie was too much more developed than I was. That was the way Grandma had expressed her reason when she put an end to that practice the preceding summer.

I sat on a bench under a china tree. She was singing some sad song—"Mexicali Rose" was her favorite about then—and as I sat there listening, I could clearly picture Rosie in her bath. I saw how she was soaping herself, having run the water a little while and then turned it off, as we were instructed to do, so as not to use up the water in the barrel too fast. It was fun when we used to soap each other, discovering changes in each other's bodies. I don't think Grandma would have let us go on as long as we did, if she had realized how much Rosie was developing. But her breasts were always small, and Grandma might not have known how shapely and firm they were. I remember the feel of her breast, slippery with soap, and the surprise of her soft dark pubic hair showing through the suds. I am glad that loveliness eluded Grandma for a little while.

She turned off the water and I rose to go and meet her. She came out wearing my robe that Grandma had made out of old towels.

"Was the water hot?" I asked.

"Probably too hot for you," she said. "I loved it. When the wind blows in through the wet towsacks it feels so good."

"I might wait till after supper to take my bath," I said. "I'll comb out your hair for you."

I always did that. She ran in and put on a worn-out dress she had brought for that night, and then came back to sit on the bench so her hair could dry in the breeze while I worked with it. The only thing I liked better than combing her hair after a shampoo was brushing it at bedtime when she stayed all night with me. Long and heavy, but springy and alive, it gave me the feeling that a part of her being—a most secret, wild and unknowable part of her being—was moving through my body, flowing in from the ends of her hair through the tips of my fingers.

I was still playing with her hair, although it was almost dry, when Grandma called us to supper. We had fried chicken and gravy with mashed potatoes and English peas, a menu for an occasion a little out of the ordinary.

After supper Grandpa tried to get Rosie to practice her song. Everyone in town had heard she was to sing a new song, something Nancy Brock had found for her, but she wouldn't tell what it was. She knew Grandpa was teasing her, and only shook her head and smiled.

"Well, Luke," Grandma said. "Looks like you'll have to go to Sunday school with us, if you want to hear Rosie's new piece."

I didn't think he would, but he did. We all got dressed up—Grandma pressed Rosie's dress for her—and at ten minutes till ten left by the back door to walk to the tabernacle.

It has been many years since I have seen a tabernacle like ours, but they used to be everywhere, in villages and country towns. I suppose the plan of it developed from the style of the old brush arbors—it was hardly more than a large tent-shaped roof supported by posts. It had an earth floor and no walls, except perhaps on one side. Ours was closed in on the north, with a stage built across it and a little room on either side.

The tabernacle was always there, within my memory. Grandma said it had replaced a brush arbor built by the early settlers, who chose that site because it was close to the pool they used for baptizings. They took up a collection from everybody, of any denomination or none, in order to build the tabernacle; and although it was intended mainly for religious meetings, it was something like a town hall and might serve for any public gathering.

It was our summer place for Sunday school. All summer bird and insect sounds mingled with our hymns, providing background music for our golden texts and memory verses. Scents of grass and flowers drifted in, and as I remember it the sky was always blue around us. It was almost as though we had entered that "Land of Cloudless Day" we so often sang about.

Mr. Goodacre was superintendent, and when he stood at the lectern before us, with his angelic curls and his sweet expression, you knew that of all the roles he played, it was this he was created for.

"What a beautiful morning God has blessed us with!"

This was his invariable greeting as we sat in our first gathering. After some preliminary remarks, a prayer, and a song or two, we would scatter out in classes to different parts of the tabernacle. At last we would come together again for our class reports and a parting song. This was a fine August day, not yet uncomfortably hot. All the benches were full.

Mr. Goodacre was speaking his usual opening words—"It is a pleasure—" when he broke off, spluttering, and pleasure vanished from his face and voice. We looked where he was looking, below the stage and to his left, where someone was coming in under the roof.

It was the Dago's mother—Raven—the fortune-teller. She was wearing the black dress I had seen her in before, or one nearly like it, and had her long white braid in a crown.

"Lord help us," Grandma muttered. (She didn't use bywords.)

Then she made us all (Rosie, Grandpa, and me) scoot down along the bench, leaving room for the newcomer, and she beckoned to her.

"Let us pray," said Mr. Goodacre.

He prayed for the Lord to bless our Sunday school, to keep it pure as the fountain that flowed at the head of Perdue Creek. (He meant the springs, of course, but in religious meetings he always spoke of them as the fountain.) He asked for protection against influences from a world beyond the knowledge of our sheltered little band of Christians. He told the Lord how innocent we were, likened our condition to that of the original pair before the serpent entered the garden. We were not, like them, free from sin, but our sins were simple and would be forgiven by our Father in Heaven because we loved and forgave one another. "Let it be ever so," he continued, "and be with us as we pray."

We recited the Lord's Prayer, the stranger joining in freely, with a strong, carrying voice. After the amen, everybody stared curiously at her, as if trying to determine what kind of snake she was, and how dangerous. Then we sang "Dwelling in Beulah," and her voice came clear and recognizable, taking the alto part. I think we were bothered less by the woman's unusual appearance and uncertain origins than by her unselfconscious participation in our small rites.

Usually the congregation sang a second hymn, but today—as Mr. Goodacre stepped forward to remind us—we were to be favored at the end of our service by a special offering from one of our members. So we separated into classes then, Grandma guiding the visitor up onto the stage, where the adults had their meeting.

In our class, there were a good many whispers about the fortune-teller, until Mrs. Brock shushed us.

"She's probably here because she thinks this is a Christian gathering, open to everyone who is or wants to be a Christian."

"She don't look like a Christian," George Earl said.

Doubtless, that was the thought in all our minds.

When we had all gone back to our places, and had listened to attendance and collection reports from each class, Mr. Goodacre again stood before us. "As an added blessing from the Lord today," he said, "we are privileged to hear a special from Miss Rosanell Fargo." He said softly, "God bless you, Rosie," as he stepped down to take his seat.

As she faced the congregation, women all over the tabernacle sighed. A faint hum underlay the soughing of their breaths: it might have been a wind blowing lightly through tall grasses, or an ancient wordless prayer of pagan women to the goddess of all their desires. Men cleared their throats and shifted their feet, embarrassed by a beauty they could not quite comprehend and could never hope to possess.

I had helped her dress, and had sat with Grandma while she stood before us to see if we could find a flaw in her appearance. I had taken an almost personal pride in this confirmation and enhancement of her loveliness. But now that she stood apart, and I sat unremarked among the ranks of her admirers, I knew that for the moment my link with her was broken and she—no longer the sharer of my secrets—was separate, complete, perfect, like a flower that blooms alone among weeds and dead grasses or a marble statue suddenly revealed among rubbish and ruin on some desolate hillside. I had never seen a marble statue, except in pictures in my world history book. But I sensed their beauty. They were part of the glory that was Greece; and as I thought of those words, it came to me that all the glory of Perdue Springs reposed in Rosie Fargo.

She gave her audience a slow, sad smile; then her red lips parted, and we waited a long breathless moment before she began, without accompaniment, to sing. Usually, Nancy Brock played the piano for her, but Rosie did not like the sound of that instrument with this

26

song. She had told me that much: she said a guitar was right for it, but Mrs. Brock was afraid Perdue Springs would find a guitar out of place in church or Sunday school.

The song was "Wayfaring Stranger." None of us had ever heard it before, although it must have been a very old song even then. As I recall, it seemed timeless—a song of sorrow and of faintly glimmering hope, a song in a sad minor key, rising to a high, keening melody that in the end seemed to make of the hope our greatest sorrow. Rosie's pure, clear tones seemed neither to add to nor take from the meaning of the words and music. She seemed to sing as a bird sings the score nature hands it.

And yet I recognized that morning that the effect of Rosie's singing was in part a conscious one. She knew what she looked like, standing with understated grace, waiting with partly opened lips and lifted eyes while our moment of suspense expanded. And she knew that her singing was like music poured forth from the throat of a bird. I got an inkling then that art wasn't necessarily pine trees and mountains painted in dark, gloomy oils, and understood for the first time that line in one of my favorite poems about "profuse strains of unpremeditated art."

Rosie's singing was art, I dimly perceived, but it was, to some extent, premeditated. How fully she understood that I don't know, but I have wondered if the consciousness dawned that morning. If so, she might have realized, as well, how much she still had to learn.

As she returned to her seat, I was aware of the silence that now surrounded me. For a time—long or short, I'm not sure—no one moved or uttered a sound. Even the noises of nature—of wind, bird, animal, and insect—seemed shut off. At last Mr. Goodacre stood before us, but instead of saying his usual words of dismissal, he merely lifted a hand, as in admonishment or farewell.

Then came the push to gather round the singer. Women and girls wanted to put their hands on her. Their cheeks wet with tears, they would lean to her and say—in tones somehow both mournful and accusing—"Rosie, that was the prettiest *thang* I ever heard in my life." Men would say, more lightly, almost playfully, "Well, Rosie, you shore outdone yourself today." And Rosie smiled at them all.

Grandpa went on outside. Grandma and I stood apart from the crowd, waiting for Rosie. The Dago's mother came and joined us.

"That's the girl that spoke to me from the bridge one day," she said, resting her dark, veiled gaze on my face.

"Yes, ma'am," I said. "That's Rosie."

"And this must be your grandmother," she said, turning to Grandma.

"My name's Miz Stephens," Grandma said curtly. "We're glad to have you at Sunday school today. Come any time."

"Thank you," said the dark old woman, not apparently noticing any lack of cordiality in Grandma's tone. "I hope you will all three come to visit me."

No one else spoke to her. She turned and made her way back across the weedy lots that lay between the tabernacle and the gin. Rosie came to us then, ready to go home, and no one said anything about the fortune-teller.

IV

AFTER dinner, when we had finished with the dishes, Grandma said what did we think about paying a visit to the woman at the campground. "Oh yes, let's go," I said excitedly. Rosie said okay, but without much enthusiasm. She had seemed listless since Sunday school was over, but I wasn't concerned, because I had seen her like that before, after she had sung before an audience.

"Reckon you ought to put on your ever-day dress?" Grandma asked Rosie.

"I guess not," Rosie said.

"You're liable to get it messed up, down yonder," Grandma said.

"Maybe not," Rosie said, as though she didn't care, really, what happened to the dress.

Grandma gave her a searching look, but said only, "I'll put my smock and bonnet on."

28

We must have made a queer-looking trio that day. In her full-cut, starched smock and the bonnet like a horizontal length of stovepipe that she saw the world through, Grandma had a square, solid appearance, somewhat like one of our rocks. Her dress came almost to her ankles, so that she seemed scarcely more separate than they from the Perdue Springs earth. Rosie was probably six inches taller than Grandma, willowy and graceful in her swingy, rose-colored dress, like a flower blown free. And I—I was still a shapeless child, still waiting to be touched and claimed, whether by earth or by sky.

We left by the back door and skirted the rocks; then, taking the path that ran behind the blacksmith shop and past the gin yard, we moved on down the hill, deliberate as a delegation. We children often ran all the way down the road to the bridge and then slipped down the steep bank into the willows at water's edge, but this roundabout path was clearer and easier; it was the way Grandma would always go.

As we approached the campground, we could hear splashing and hollering in the baptizing hole. The boys were swimming, as usual on a Sunday afternoon. I thought George Earl was probably there. I wondered if they dared swim naked, as they customarily did, with the Dago's mother so close by.

"Listen," Rosie said.

"They're swimming," I said.

"No. Listen."

Then I caught, between the yells and the splashes, a sound out of place there—a low, throbbing hum, or more precisely, a strum.

"He's playing," she said. I didn't know what she meant. I have realized since then that she must have heard him before.

"What is it?" Grandma asked. By then we could see the Dago, sitting on the chair under the cottonwood tree, a guitar across his thighs. The dog lay on the ground beside him and as we approached, it stood up and began to bark, a deep woof-woof.

"Down, Bear," said the Dago, straightening to look at us and ceasing his music.

It pleased me to learn the dog was called Bear. I thought I'd tell Grandpa about that.

Grandma stood looking all around. When she got to the sign on the house, she turned to the man and said, "Good evening. Are you the fortune-teller?"

He was on his feet now, and smiling graciously, said, "No, ma'am, it is my mother who reads the future and she is resting just now, inside the house."

He talked funny. That was all we would ever be able to say about his speech. It was perhaps a little bookish, but in pronunciation not so different from ours. What we wondered at was the rhythm, the inflection, and to this day I can't say what language shaped it.

And of course, as we already knew, he looked funny. Now we discovered that even his body build seemed different: compact and muscular, long-waisted, short-legged. He was neither young nor old—about thirty-five, I think now. There was a glimmer of silver in his thick black hair and a glimmer of white when he smiled.

His mother came to the open door of the little striped house. "Does someone want me?" she asked, then saw who had come and beamed, greeting Grandma by name. "Please come in," she said.

"No, thank you," Grandma said, with a long look at the narrow ladder by which she would have to reach the truck bed. "We can't stay long, we just come to say howdy."

"Well, it's cooler out under the trees anyway," the fortune-teller said, and descended the ladder with more ease and grace than seemed possible, since she looked even heavier than Grandma. "John," she said, "will you bring the chair?"

The man leaned his guitar against the tree, then leapt to the truck bed, entered the little house, and reappeared with a folding chair that he set up under the cottonwood.

Grandma sat in the chair and told Rosie to sit on a low stool that stood nearby. "May can set on the ground—she hasn't got on a new dress."

I sat in the dry grass at Rosie's feet. The full skirt of her dress, flared out around her, brushed my thigh and touched my bare knee. Soft as rose petals, the light voile seemed to me.

"I failed to hear your name this morning at the tabernacle," Grandma said. "Is it Miz Raven I'm talking to?"

"Raven is my given name," the woman said. "Feel free to call me that."

"I have to know somebody pretty well to use their Christian name," Grandma said.

"My surname is Concolorcorvo," the woman said. (None of us understood the name then—we had occasion later to learn how it was spelled.)

"I'll call you Miz Raven," Grandma said.

"Very well," said Mrs. Raven with a shrug. (We were all going to call her Mrs. Raven; we almost forgot she had any other name.) "This is my son John Concolorcorvo—you had better call him John, even if you don't much like it."

John had sat down on the ground, back in the deep shade. He stood up and came forward now, and Grandma said, "Howdy, John." Rosie and I looked up at him but didn't speak. He went back to his place.

"Y'all have got a good situation here," Grandma said. "Are you aiming to stay long?"

"That's what the man asked me the first night," John said. "As I told him, we have no plans."

"Well—fancy free," said Grandma.

"So we are," said John. "Only I was hoping I'd find a spot to catch some fish now and then."

"There's not any in our creek, till it runs into the Clear Fork," Grandma said.

"There's crawdads," I said.

"Yes," John said, "I've been bringing in some crawfish."

"I don't know what you want with them things," Grandma said.

"They make a good stew," Mrs. Raven said.

Grandma couldn't think of anything to say to that. I don't believe she had ever heard before that you could eat crawfish. She couldn't imagine what kind of people would.

"Perdue Springs seems like a funny place to come to," she finally said. "Just by accident, I mean."

"Oh, we came here by direction," said Mrs. Raven. "I asked the tarots—the Hermit sent me."

"I don't know nothing about no hermit," Grandma said. "But I'd be surprised to learn he ever heard of Perdue Springs."

"I knew what he meant," Mrs. Raven said, smiling her placid little smile.

"Well, if he thought Perdue Springs was a place where you could make any money telling fortunes," Grandma said, "I have to say I think you're making a mistake to rely on him."

Mrs. Raven and her son laughed at that.

"We expect some gain from coming here," Mrs. Raven said, "but it may not be money. The Hermit does not say what it will be."

"In truth," said John, "it is not my mother's readings that provide the most of our income. Our main business is entertainment—putting on shows."

"What kind of shows?" asked Rosie. These were the first words she had spoken.

John said, "I'm a magician, that's our main act now. But sometimes we have other acts."

"You're surely not expecting to put on a show like that in Perdue Springs," Grandma said.

Mrs. Raven shook her head sadly. Her large dark eyes seemed made to express sadness.

"In ordinary times," she said, "I believe we could get an audience even here. But no, we do not expect it. We come to rest, only. Then we go on the road. There will be money when the cotton harvest begins."

"There may not be much," Grandma said. "Crops are bad, cotton's cheap."

"Perhaps I misunderstood the tarots," Mrs. Raven said.

"I still wonder how them tay-roes come to hear of Perdue Springs," Grandma said.

"I'm sure you can guess," said Mrs. Raven, "that the tarots never give names of people and places. They can only point the way."

"I still wouldn't know a tay-roe," Grandma said, "if I met one in the crossroads at high noon."

"The tarots are cards," Mrs. Raven said, "that bear secret signs going back to the beginning of time. Everything pertaining to the life of man or woman is contained in these signs, and we who have the sight to see into their depths can interpret messages coming from the time of timelessness."

"I wonder if you know what you're talking about," Grandma said. She was hurling no challenge; she was honestly perplexed.

"Yes, you would wonder," Mrs. Raven said. "But what if you knew that Moses learned these very signs in ancient Egypt and carried them with him to the Promised Land?"

"It don't say nothing about that in the Bible," Grandma said. "And Moses never got to the Promised Land."

"He taught everything he knew to the wise men of Israel," Mrs. Raven said.

"That may be," said Grandma. "But somewheres amongst the sayings of Moses it tells that fortune-telling is an abomination unto the Lord."

"Did you come to read me my sins?" asked Mrs. Raven.

"No ma'am," Grandma said. "A Christian woman's sins is between her and the Lord, and I reckon you're a Christian."

"Or I wouldn't have gone to Sunday school," said Mrs. Raven, and Grandma seemed to take that for an affirmative.

"Well," said Grandma, "I've enjoyed all our talk, but what I come for was to apologize for the way we done you this morning. I reckon we didn't act altogether like Christians, ourselves."

"Small country places are always this way," Mrs. Raven said. "I go to public gatherings when I please, but I don't expect the right hand of fellowship."

Grandma gave her a long look, then said, "I wonder if there's any place you're not a stranger."

"We're always on the road," Mrs. Raven said. She nodded as though to herself. "Wayfaring strangers." Then turning to face Rosie, who was looking at her wonderingly, she said, "Rosie, I've told John about your singing, how lovely it was."

"Thank you," said Rosie simply. She was never confused by praise.

33

"Would you sing it for him now?" Mrs. Raven asked.

"Yes, please do," John said.

I looked at Grandma. She had taken off her split bonnet and was fanning herself with it. I knew this meant she wasn't quite pleased about the way things were going. Rosie knew that, too, but she wasn't looking at Grandma. She was already on her feet, standing there waiting for something—some further word, I thought, although Rosie never made anybody beg for a song.

Finally she said, "Do you think you could play while I sing? It's D minor."

The Dago looked up at Rosie, his thick black eyebrows slightly lifted. I guessed he was trying to decide whether he thought she could sing well enough for him to take the trouble. At last he said, "You begin. I'll see if I can go along with you."

He took up the guitar, and I saw what a beautiful thing it was, made of softly glowing, deep dark wood. You almost thought it would be soft to the touch.

Rosie began to sing. The Dago strummed some chords. When she came to the long, high, sad notes, he touched the strings separately. She seemed to like that, and she leaned toward him a little as she sang those yearning bars.

We sat in silence, we hardly moved. Even the boys in the swimming hole were quiet. I suspected George Earl was listening and watching from the other side of the willows that screened the pool.

John laid down his guitar. "That," he said, "lacked very little being a professional performance."

I didn't know what he meant. It was the best she had ever sung in her life, I knew that.

I don't know whether Rosie understood or not. But she responded with a smiling thank you and what might have been the faint foreshadowing of a bow.

"We'd better go now," Grandma said.

We plodded back up the hill and were hot and tired when we got home. Grandma made lemonade and we sat to drink it in the white-painted rocking chairs on the front porch. I remember how restful it seemed there in the shade with our cool drinks and how we moved into one of those thoughtful little talks Rosie and I used to have sometimes with Grandma.

Rosie began it by asking, "Do you think some folks can really tell the future, Miz Stephens?"

"It may be so, I don't know," Grandma said.

"But what about the Bible?" I protested.

"It says it's an abomination," Grandma answered. "It don't say it ain't possible."

I too thought it might be possible, but I didn't like what that possibility implied. I said, "If what is to be will be, like you're always saying, then I guess there might be a way of finding out what that is. But if that's how it is, seems like we don't have any say about what we do in our lives."

"I think," Grandma said, "that we just have to do the best we can. Our striving is a part of what will be."

"So Rosie and I just have to try as hard as we can to be teachers, even though we may already be doomed to be something else."

Doom was the word that came to me, dark doom. But Rosie smiled thoughtfully and said, "There might be something else we'd like better, that we don't even know about yet."

"And somebody somewhere knows all about it, and is probably laughing at us because we're trying to be something we never can be."

"You're talking about God, May," Grandma said severely. "God don't think like people."

"I don't care," I said. "I don't believe even God can know what we're going to do before we do it. It hasn't happened—how can it be known?"

"A preacher explained that to me one time," Grandma said. "What is to be will be because it already is. Past, present, and future is all the same to God. He don't even need to know what time is."

We were out of our depth there, and the talk soon ended. Later on, when I was walking with Rosie to Goodacres' gate, she said, "I didn't understand all that talk of your grandma's too well."

"I didn't either," I admitted.

35

"But I understood this much," she said, and I saw her hunch her shoulders and shiver as with cold. "I understand enough to know it scares me."

V

THE Dago and his mother stayed about three weeks that time. No one found out much about them. Some thought they were gypsies, but Grandpa said gypsies traveled in tribes. Mr. Goodacre felt sure John was some kind of crook hiding out from the law. Grandma said she was willing to believe they were just what they said they were—poor folks trying to get along in hard times by doing the work they knew how to do.

I think Grandma meant to go and visit Mrs. Raven again, but she wasn't quite sure what a visit would lead to. And then she was taken up with other happenings in Perdue Springs.

George Earl's mother had a baby, and Grandma had to go and help with that. She was angry about the birth, and blamed Mr. Tadlock, who had been out of work much of the time for almost a year. He was a sort of substitute cowboy and had always made enough to support his family, but the ranchers weren't hiring extra hands very often in those days.

Then we found out what was wrong with Mrs. Fargo. Mr. Goodacre had the doctor out to look at Mrs. Goodacre's leg, and Mr. Fargo hailed him at the crossroads and got him to go and see what he thought about Mrs. Fargo. Word quickly spread about that; it was Nancy Brock who came to tell Grandma.

Mrs. Fargo had pellagra. That was the thing that caused her breaking out and her stomach trouble, and would in time kill her if something wasn't done. Whether anything could be done Nancy wasn't sure. The disease was caused by not eating right: too much cornmeal, not enough meat, eggs, milk and butter, fruits and vegetables.

"How come they don't all have pellagra?" Grandma asked.

I remembered when I used to eat supper with the Fargos sometimes. All they ever had was mush. There would be some milk, a little butter, and molasses, never enough to go around. And Mrs.

Fargo always said cheerfully that she liked her mush best without anything on it. "She does without," I said.

"And I imagine," Grandma said, "that having all them childern kept her pretty well pulled down."

Whatever it was, and whether anything could help, we must do all we could. Grandma baked a pound cake that day—with a pound of eggs and a pound of butter in it—and next morning she and I set out early to take it to Mrs. Fargo.

At the crossroads we met John the Dago, coming up the road from the creek. "Good morning, John," Grandma called brightly.

Slowing his pace, he said good morning and called us by name.

"How's your mama?" Grandma said to him, just as she might to anyone in Perdue Springs, where nearly everybody had an old or ailing mother.

"Not too well, I'm afraid, Mrs. Stephens," John said. "She feels dizzy when she wakes up in the morning, and rarely leaves the house till afternoon."

"Well, I'm sorry to hear that," Grandma said. "I hope she's able to do her work."

"Her work" to me meant cleaning and cooking, washing and ironing, but John took it another way.

"She hasn't had many clients," he said, "but she has been able to help all who came."

"That's good," Grandma said.

"Therefore," John said as, walking down the middle of the road, we came even with Mashburns', "I am able to buy some groceries again."

He flashed a smile of goodbye to us, and Grandma wished him good luck.

"You sound like you really wish them well," I said to Grandma as we walked on down the road.

"Of course I wish them well," said Grandma. "There's not many folks in the world I don't wish well, and if there's any a-tall I pray the Lord will forgive me."

At Fargos' you couldn't tell anything new had happened. Mr. Fargo sat in the front room, looking out the window. "How are you, Mr. Fargo?" Grandma said, and he answered, "To'bly well, Miz Stephens," just as he always had done.

O.B. and the boys were gone—there is never any place for boys and young men in a house of sickness. I had thought we would find Mrs. Fargo in bed, but she sat in her same place at the kitchen table. Ointment was smeared over the broken skin of her face, arms, and hands. Lucy May played on the floor and the big girls stood as if aimlessly waiting.

Grandma set her offering on the table, and said what she thought fitting. I backed away toward the outside door. Rosie turned to me and perhaps made some gesture. We moved out of the house without conscious thought or communication; we found ourselves, presently, standing on the hard, clean-swept red earth under a skimpy china tree.

"Whatchy been doing?" I asked.

"Nothing," she said.

We stood looking down. Up close to the trunk of the tree, the dirt was powdery and there were doodlebug holes that she stirred with her toes.

"Does your mama need you all the time?" I asked.

"No," she said, "there's not much to do for her."

"Stay all night Saturday night," I said, "and we'll go to Sunday school."

"I don't think I can," she said. "I might."

Grandma came to the door and called me. I don't know whether Rosie made any response or not.

Walking home, I told Grandma I had asked Rosie to spend the night. "But I don't think she will," I said.

"Her mama's pretty bad," Grandma said.

"What did you really think about her?" I asked.

We went on several steps before Grandma spoke. "I didn't hardly think she knowed who I was," she said at last.

The weather was cooler Saturday morning, on account of a fresh little breeze that Grandma called the first norther. I was eager to be out of the house, and Grandma let me go before all my usual chores were done because Grandpa was going to shoe Mr. Tadlock's horse that morning and he wanted me to watch. He said the way the world was going, that might be the last horse he would ever shoe.

There were several spectators at the shop, including George Earl, who stood with his daddy next to the big bay horse and pretended he was helping. I sat on the ground just outside the door. I knew, because Grandpa had told me, that the horse didn't feel pain when the fire-hot metal was held against his hoof or the nails driven in; all the same, I didn't feel quite easy. The procedure seemed a very long one.

When it was done, Mr. Tadlock rode off toward the bridge, on his way to the Rough Creek country, where he was going to work for a few days while he visited his folks there.

"Do you ever go to the creek?" I asked George Earl.

"Sure," he said.

"I haven't been in a long time," I said.

"I tell you somebody that goes," he said.

I said "Who?" even though I knew what his answer would be.

"Rosie," he said.

"I bet she don't," I said, not really doubting him.

"I seen her down there oncet," he said. "That Dago was setting on a rock by the baptizing hole, and she was back in the shade of a cottonwood, just listening. Still as a mouse, hid from him by some plum bushes, and you could actually see her listening."

I could picture very well how she yearned toward that music.

"We could go down there," George Earl said. "She might be there now."

"I better stay close to home," I said. "She may come to stay all night."

He walked off down the creek road without saying anything more. I prayed he wouldn't see Rosie.

I wasn't expecting her, really. Grandma told me I'd just as well not. But late in the afternoon she came walking up the hill from the creek, carrying her bundle. Grandma saw her from the kitchen window, and I went to meet her.

"Where've you been?" I asked.

"Nowhere," she said. "I just decided to walk along the creek."

I thought about telling her what George Earl said, but I didn't.

Grandma fixed a good supper, and we played dominoes afterward. Grandpa would never play with us, he had enough of dominoes at the shop, but he popped us some corn. It was a pleasant visit, but somehow Rosie wasn't quite like herself. Her mind seemed to stray—she kept making wrong plays. Grandma shook her head at me when I started to say something; I knew she thought Rosie was worried about her mother. I thought so too, but I also thought she had something else on her mind.

She let me brush her hair when we were getting ready for bed. I knew that ritual both soothed and excited her. If she was tempted to tell me a secret, it was often while I was brushing her hair that she let it out.

At last she did. "May," she said, "will you promise not to tell anybody in the world, not even to hint, if I tell you something wonderful?"

"Yes, Rosie," I said. "I promise."

She didn't speak at once, but finally said, "I've been slipping off down to the baptizing hole." She paused, I waited for more. "To hear John play the guitar," she said.

I didn't say anything about George Earl. I didn't say anything.

"Oh May," she breathed, half whispering, "you never heard such music."

"Like he was playing the day we went to see Mrs. Raven?" I asked.

"Like it," she said. "But so much stronger—or wilder, I don't know. And then not wild but sad as a cooing dove. Oh it's everything—sometimes I think it will kill me, but I can't stay away."

It wasn't like Rosie to exaggerate that way. I couldn't think what to say to her. It occurred to me that I sometimes had almost the same feelings about some of my favorite poems, but I would never have spoken aloud such words as she was using.

"Does he play every day?" I asked.

"No," she said, "and I can't tell when he will. But I go in hope of it."

"Does he know?"

"I don't think so. I try to keep out of sight. Yesterday he looked toward me and smiled, but I don't really think he was seeing me. He was just happy. I think it makes him happy to play like he does."

"You went today?" I asked.

"I waited a long time," she said, "but he never came."

"You ought to let him know how much you like his music. I bet he'd tell you when he was going to play and let you come every time."

"I wouldn't dare," she said.

"Do you think he's a nice person?" I asked, more interested in the man than his music.

"Oh I don't know," she said, impatient with me. "Does it matter?"

We didn't talk after we went to bed, but I knew she was a long time falling asleep. I imagined she was lying there letting John's music echo through the chambers of her mind.

And then next morning at breakfast Grandma told us he was gone. "Before it was hardly daylight," she said. "I heard that truck chugging up the hill, and I couldn't think at first what it was. Then I seen that blue and yeller flag a-flying. They left just the same way they come."

"I didn't think they'd go this soon," I said.

"They're ginning cotton in some of the counties round about," Grandpa said. "I reckon John thought it was time."

"Him or the Hermit," Grandma said.

I don't think Rosie said anything. She ate a few bites of breakfast and then told us she thought she wouldn't go to Sunday school. She felt like she needed to go on home and see about her mama.

VI

ONE warm fall day Rosie and Grandma and I were sitting on the porch sewing, and Grandma told us some news. The trustees had decided school would start the first Monday in November, which was less than three weeks off.

"It don't make any difference to me," said Rosie. "I won't be going to school."

I had told Grandma what Rosie said about not going to school, but I hadn't thought much more about it, because I didn't believe it.

"Who decided that?" Grandma said drily.

"Nobody decided," Rosie said. "Nobody says anything about it. It takes more money to go to school than it does to stay at home."

"But what will you do?" I protested.

"Help take care of Mama," she said.

"I mean—when you're old. What will you do when you're thirty?"

"What is to be will be," Rosie said.

Grandma laughed. "So it will, Rosie," she said. "And what is to be this fall is you're going to school."

Then she explained a plan that she had already presented to Grandpa and the Fargos, gaining approval from all three. "You will stay with us," she said to Rosie. "You can help May with her chores, to pay for what little extry it costs to keep you. You can go home any time they need you, but you can move your stuff up here and sleep with us."

Rosie seemed dazed. "I don't know," she said.

"You may need clothes," Grandma went on. "May does, too. I aim to remodel some old dresses and cut down one of my coats for her. I may be able to find some things for you too. Of course we'll have to buy shoes. I'll order you both a pair of shoes, and we may not have to buy another thing."

At last Rosie smiled. "Yes, Mrs. Stephens," she said, "I'll go to school."

I jumped up and hugged them both. "Oh Grandma," I cried, and "Oh Rosie."

We stood on the outline of a foot in the catalog and took measurements for our new shoes. And of course Grandma bought more than just shoes. She ordered some bloomers, and she let us pick out percale prints to make us each a new dress. Mine was a brown and yellow plaid, and Rosie's was Copenhagen blue with little red and white figures.

We wore our new dresses on the first day of school. George Earl had made us promise to wait for him so the whole ninth grade (we three) could walk together. The ninth was the highest grade taught at Perdue Springs and at that time was the second year of high school in the state of Texas. If we went on to Cottonwood Flats the next year, we would be juniors.

I always used to be excited about starting back to school in the fall. This year I felt jubilant. But that feeling didn't last. Living with Rosie—eating and sleeping with Rosie, walking to school and back with Rosie—wasn't, somehow, as wonderful as I had thought it would be. Because Rosie had changed. Everyone knew it, but no one knew quite how or why.

"What's the matter with Rosie?" girls at school asked.

"She's worried about her mother," I told them.

And in truth I know she was. She would often run across the road to see her at recess. We weren't supposed to leave the school-ground then, but Mr. Brock told Rosie she could run home when she needed to.

"But that's not it," the girls insisted. They suspected she was in love.

"Who's she going with, May?" was a persistent question.

Rosie was not going with anybody. I knew she could be if she wanted to. George Earl would have given anything to ask her for a date, but I didn't think he ever would dare. There were some half a dozen boys about O.B.'s age, though, that did ask her. Grandma wouldn't have liked it; she didn't think a girl should be allowed to go with a boy before she was sixteen. But Rosie would have gone if she had wanted to.

She didn't even want to go to the Rough Creek musicales. "I don't think I could stand it anymore," she told me, "after hearing real music."

Another change was that she wasn't interested in our school sub-jects the way she had been. She did her work all right and kept up her grades, but she never wanted to talk with me about what we read for English or to sit with me at the dining table after supper while we worked out algebra problems together. She seemed to get her lessons done in the free time we had at school.

The fall was warm and dry. People talked a lot about the need for rain and said if we didn't get some moisture during the fall and winter we would have another crop failure next year. But the November sunshine was golden and gentle. Sometimes there wasn't anything we had to do right after school, and then (at Rosie's suggestion) we would walk along the creek, going as far as the bridge and then up the hill home.

I loved our creek in autumn. The water was low that year, but it still flowed from the springs. The grass along the banks was skimpy, but it turned as always to a soft, faded gold. Leaves and berries changed to shades of red, yellow, purple, and russet brown. Rosie and I rediscovered these fall wonders every year and showed them to each other. Or we always had before.

One thing we especially watched for was the display of wild chinaberries. There was a china grove just below the bridge, where after the leaves began to fall we would see the berries glowing like jewels. Rosie used to strip them greedily from the branches, to carry home and string like beads for necklaces and bracelets.

One day as we came round a little bend in the creek I lifted my eyes and saw them, translucent amber against a sky of Copenhagen blue. I caught my breath. "Oh look!" I said. "There they are." (The first glorious glimpse of them in the perfect sunlit setting— that was what I meant. For of course we had known the berries were turning.)

Rosie, who had been walking a little ahead of me, watching a stick she was trailing in the water, dropped the stick and straightened to look up the creek, toward the yellow crowns of cottonwoods that shone above the campground.

"Where?" she cried. "I don't see them."

"In the grove, silly, where they always are," I said.

"Oh," she said, and didn't even glance that way.

It was probably less than a week later that Grandma met Rosie and me at the door as we came home. We had not gone by the creek that day, having planned to work on some history questions before supper so we could play dominoes with Grandma that night.

"Well, there's news in Perdue Springs," she said.

"What is it?" I asked excitedly.

"They're back," she said. "Mrs. Raven and the Dago."

Rosie dropped into the porch swing, the color draining from her face. Grandma stood inside the door and I went on in, nudging her into the room. I didn't quite know why, but I didn't want her to notice Rosie.

"Where are they?" I was urging. "When did they come? What are they doing?"

"Well, come on in the kitchen," Grandma said. "I've got to cut up some onion for the soup pot."

Rosie, looking a little better, came with us.

"Are you all right?" Grandma said. "You looked right faintified."

"I didn't feel too good today," Rosie said. "But I'm all right now."

"Time of the month," Grandma said.

Rosie nodded, but I knew it wasn't, and I think Grandma did too.

In the kitchen, Grandma told us to get us a glass of milk and a raisin muffin, and we sat at the cook table with our snack while we heard how the Dago's truck had rolled down the hill just a little past noon, stopped in front of the blacksmith shop, and then gone on down toward the campground.

"Well, I couldn't wait till your grandpa come home," Grandma went on. "I put on my bonnet and went right straight out there. He was by hisself," she said, "so I just outright asked him what was happening. He said John come in and asked him about him and his mama camping here for the winter. He said they didn't feel like they had enough money to start down south this year, and besides Miz Raven is not too well." She turned to the stove, to rake her cut-up onion into the soup pot.

"So what did Grandpa tell him?" I demanded.

"What could he tell him?" Grandma said. "It's not his place to give anybody permission to camp down there. Or anybody else's, for that matter."

45

"So will they stay?" I asked.

"I reckon so," Grandma said.

"Well, I never thought of such a thing," I said.

"I thought of it," Grandma said, looking at Rosie. But Rosie didn't say what she had thought.

"I guess we'll hear more about it from Grandpa," I said.

And we did, at the supper table. "Cornelius come to see me this evening," Grandpa said.

"I figgered he would," Grandma said.

"He seemed to think I ought to have sent John to him, to ask about camping."

"Of course he would," Grandma said.

"He claims that as justice of the peace he's supposed to enforce the law. I don't reckon that's quite the way of it, but I didn't say so. I just told him I didn't know of any law about who could camp or how long. He had to admit he didn't either, but he said that didn't mean the citizens of Perdue Springs couldn't have some say about the kind of folks that stayed there. He said we had to look after our own welfare."

"Does he think John and his mama's dangerous?" Grandma asked.

"I asked him that. He said he figgers the Dago equals the unknown quantity. He says if he don't operate outside the law he's pretty close to the edge. And he talked about Miz Raven telling fortunes and scaring the kids."

"There's times anybody would like to scare them Gibson twins," Grandma said.

"He knows that," Grandpa said. "We talked a good while, and the upshot was that he told me to give John a warning. Said tell him he'll be keeping his eye on him, and if he sees the least excuse he'll have the sheriff down here in less than two hours. He'll hunt out some law against fortune-telling if he can."

"Well, I aim to do my duty this time," Grandma said. "That woman's my neighbor and she may need help. I'll give 'em a day or two to get to feeling settled, and then I'm fixing to pay a visit."

46

When we were in bed, Rosie asked me if I thought Grandma would let us go with her to the campground. I thought she probably would, and she did.

VII

MRS. Raven was sitting in the skeleton shade cast by the almost leafless cottonwood tree, the black cat at her feet. We didn't see John and Bear.

Greeting us all by our names, she rose laboriously to her feet. She said she had let herself get too heavy, and was troubled with pain in her knees.

"Now set back down," Grandma said. "You don't need to stir around none for us."

Mrs. Raven let herself back down into the chair. "If you find it warm enough here in the sunshine," she said, "maybe one of the girls will go into the house and bring a chair for you. I haven't lit a fire inside today—it's warmer out here than it is in there."

Rosie and I both started toward the truck. "Yes, both go," said Mrs. Raven. "You may like to see what my house is like."

As we were climbing the ladder, she called out, "The chair is against the wall by the door." The cat flashed past and was inside as soon as I had the screen door open. The wood door, which was painted blue like the blue stripes of the house, had been left open.

The tiny room was like a house in a fairy tale, I thought, and again the gingerbread witch's house came to my mind. We stood still, almost forgetting what we were there for.

It was dim, as a fortune-teller's house ought to be, but light came in through the door and a lace-curtained window at the rear.

There were two beds, one above another, built across the rear wall. The lower one was spread with something dark and heavy, like a tapestry curtain. There were silky cushions scattered over it—the cat had leapt immediately to one and started washing herself. The upper bunk just had an army blanket over it.

47

Cabinets and shelves and chests were built in on both sides, and a table let down from the wall. Bright-colored pottery and odd pieces of china filled the shelves.

In the middle of the room stood what we used to call a bachelor heater, good for both heating and cooking, but the stove was cold. A blue granite teakettle stood on it.

"Oh, I wish I had a house like this," said Rosie.

"Where's the chair?" I said. "We can't stay here."

"By the door," Rosie said, "but I don't see it."

"Behind the door, maybe," I said. I pushed the door nearly to, and there was the chair, folded against the wall.

"Oh look!" Rosie exclaimed.

She was looking at a large printed poster, tacked to the door. It showed a full-length photograph of a dark, slender young woman in a costume something like those we saw in pictures of old movie stars. I think of Theda Bara and Pola Negri—maybe because there were beads and fringe and a headband. And a shocking expanse of leg and bosom showed. Beneath the picture in tall, leaning capitals ran the words SHEBA DANCES.

"Who can she be?" Rosie whispered.

"I don't know," I said, "but we better go."

"It just barely covers her nipples," Rosie said, still studying the picture.

I picked up the chair and started out. "Come on!" I said.

"I wonder what color it was," she said.

When we finally got out with the chair, Grandma said, "Well, you girls took your time. Did you look over everything Mrs. Raven owns?"

"It's so cute," I said. "The house is. We couldn't help looking a minute."

Grandma sat down. The two old women were facing each other in the bright sunlight.

"We saw the picture," Rosie said.

"Do you like it?" Mrs. Raven asked.

"Oh—yes!" Rosie said.

48

"She was my son's wife," Mrs. Raven said. "Her name was Lillie Ann."

"Is she dead?" Grandma asked.

"Yes," Mrs. Raven said. "She died five years ago, having their baby. It died too."

"Well, I'm sure sorry to hear that," Grandma said.

"But who is Sheba?" Rosie asked.

"That was her stage name," Mrs. Raven said. "She was a dancer. She was part of our show. We had a big show in those days."

Rosie had sat down on the ground near Mrs. Raven's chair. I sat, too, on the little stool that stood by the site of their campfire.

"What color was the dress?" Rosie asked.

"It is red," Mrs. Raven said. "I still have it."

"Ooooh," said Rosie, a long drawn-out questioning syllable, as if she might be trying to believe the dress could still be.

Then she asked, "Did she dance by herself? Tell me how Sheba danced."

"I will tell you sometime," Mrs. Raven said. "I doubt that Mrs. Stephens is very much interested."

"Well, I am," said Grandma. "But maybe I ought to say what I come for."

Mrs. Raven waited patiently, the hint of a smile on her face.

"I think you know," Grandma said, "that not everybody in Perdue Springs is tickled to have you back here."

"Maybe we made some enemies," Mrs. Raven said. "I had hoped not, although I had to be harsh with those twins that were torturing my cat. Their mother seemed interested in me at first, but she turned against me."

"Nobody pays much attention to Maudie Gibson," Grandma said, "especially when them twins is concerned. And that's not the kind of thing I mean." She frowned. "I don't hardly know how to explain it."

Mrs. Raven placidly waited.

"What it is, I think," Grandma went on, "is that we just ain't used to strangers."

"Especially dark strangers," Mrs. Raven said.

"Well, I reckon," Grandma said. "Or just anybody we don't understand. And there's a lot we don't, because we live kind of cut off from the world, in a way. There was a schoolteacher here one time that called Perdue Springs the town that time forgot, and in some ways that's about right. I don't reckon we've changed much since the first settlers come. And I've heard tell they run some folks out of the country because they didn't like their looks."

"Dark, perhaps?" asked Mrs. Raven.

"Well, maybe," Grandma allowed. "I ain't so sure I know the straight of it. It had something to do with a old sheepherder named Perdue or something like that."

"The one the place is named for," said Mrs. Raven.

"I reckon," Grandma said. "Although some says his name was Pardue, or Pardee. I don't know. I guess the true name is lost."

"Yes," said Mrs. Raven.

"Anyway," Grandma continued, "that's how they was, and how we are. Good Christian people, but that's how we are."

"'Thou shalt neither vex a stranger nor oppress him,'" muttered Mrs. Raven.

"'Be not forgetful to entertain strangers; for thereby some have entertained angels unawares.' Are you a angel, Mrs. Raven?"

"No, nor even a devil," said Mrs. Raven, "although I can turn the Scriptures inside out if I choose."

"What do you mean?" asked Grandma suspiciously.

"Did you ever suspect," asked Mrs. Raven, "that you might have among you a stranger unawares?"

Grandma looked keenly at Mrs. Raven, who sat smiling her rather mysterious smile. "I don't hardly know why I said all that," she said at last, rising from her chair. "All I really come for was to say beware of Cornelius Goodacre."

"The Sunday school man?"

Grandma nodded. "I think he might be able to use your fortune-telling against you," she said, "if he can find a law. I believe you might be wise to take your sign down."

"Yes," said Mrs. Raven, "I believe it is time to do that."

VIII

W̶E grew accustomed to our neighbors at the campground, although (as Grandma foretold) we could not quite forget that they were strangers in our midst. Mrs. Gibson kept up her feud with them and always referred to Mrs. Raven as that old witch, but she never made any specific accusations against her. The old woman had not returned to Sunday school, probably because at this season it was held in the vacant room at the schoolhouse and the distance was too great for her to walk.

One Saturday afternoon Mr. Goodacre caught John shooting craps with some young men on the flat rocks by the baptizing hole and threatened to bring charges against him. But the crapshooters were as much a part of Perdue Springs as the domino players, and one of the regulars was Mr. Goodacre's nephew. Grandpa said Mr. Goodacre tried to figure out some way of getting John in trouble without involving the Perdue Springs boys, but he couldn't find anything to go to the sheriff with.

The weather continued pleasant, but the season was a strange one, nonetheless. Fall was the time for cotton-picking, money in pockets, talk about what Santa Claus might bring; but this year wasn't like that.

Children began to realize that Mr. Brock hadn't said anything about drawing names for our Christmas tree.

"Ain't we gonna have a tree this year, Mr. Brock?" one of the little Tadlocks finally asked.

Mr. Brock said we might put up a tree if we wanted to, but he thought it would be better if we didn't draw names, because we all knew how hard times were and he thought it would be a nice gift for our parents if we didn't ask for money for school presents. There was some groaning, but not much. After all, we did know about hard times.

Two or three days later, Mr. Brock told us he had a surprise for us. He told us the man we knew as John—and he had to admit he himself didn't know John's last name—had offered to entertain us with a Christmas program. He said he didn't know exactly what

51

John would do, but he was accustomed to giving shows and assured Mr. Brock that he knew how to provide entertainment suitable for children. John had asked only that he be allowed to have one pupil to help him, and Mr. Brock said he was sure we would understand why he wanted Rosie Fargo.

Rosie wouldn't tell what she was going to do on the program, but now she openly went down to the campground after school every day. I knew, but I never found out whether Rosie did or not, that Grandma went to talk to Mrs. Raven about the program and Rosie's visits. She must have been satisfied that everything was all right, because if she hadn't she would have been taking steps to put a stop to the whole plan. She told me she could see now why Rosie and I were so charmed with Mrs. Raven's little house, that she wouldn't mind living in it herself. But she never seemed to give her whole-hearted approval to the program or Rosie's part in it, and I thought I knew why. Unless Mrs. Raven had removed it from its place on the door, she had to have seen the picture of Sheba dancing.

But Rosie never seemed to notice any coolness on Grandma's part. Or maybe she didn't care. She was so full of her new experiences that she couldn't keep from talking to me about them—in bed at night or walking to school in the morning.

"Oh May," she said to me once, "I have actually seen the dress." Later she said she had tried it on, and Mrs. Raven said it fit her just the way it fit Lillie Ann. "You couldn't keep from dancing in that dress," she said.

One day when I saw her coming up from the creek and went to meet her, she began to run toward me as soon as she saw me. "May," she cried breathlessly, "I have found out the most wonderful thing. Raven used to be a singer and dancer, and when she was young she performed in a theater in a big city."

"Raven?" I said.

"Well, of course," she said. "Her name is Raven. That's not her surname."

At first she told me many things, but she never would say what she was going to do on the Christmas program, and after a while seemed too busy and tired to talk at all. She would fall asleep at night as soon as she lay down.

Two days before the program, though, John had told her not to come to the campground. She needed to rest, he said.

It was one of those bright warm days that we always seemed to have just before Christmas, and after changing clothes and finding ourselves apples to eat, we drifted out to the rocks. And there, as we sat on the big flat one near the corner that had always been our special place, Rosie told me one more secret.

"May," she said, "I have had a reading."

"Oh Rosie!" I cried in awe.

"Promise me you'll never tell your grandma," she said, and I promised.

I thought she was going to tell me what the cards predicted for her future, and I believe she did too at first. But she didn't say anything else. She found a sharp, broken piece of stone and began scratching at the specks of glitter in the rock we sat on.

"What did the reading say?" I asked. "Did you believe it?"

"Oh, I can't tell about it," she said. "And maybe I believe it, I'm not sure. I'm not even sure if Raven does." She began scratching a sort of picture on the rock—a tarot sign, I thought it might be. "But listen, May," she went on, "and you mustn't tell this, you don't dare. Raven's teaching me what the cards mean. And don't ever ask me what—they're mysterious and secret."

"Will you learn to give readings then?" I asked.

"Maybe," she said. "Raven can't tell yet if I have the sight."

Everybody was invited to the Christmas show, which took place in our big room, and almost everybody came.

The big room, which had housed the higher classes when Perdue Springs was a two-teacher school, had become the fall and winter place for Sunday school. All the benches had been moved to the schoolhouse from the tabernacle, and people crowded onto those benches that afternoon as they seldom did on Sunday mornings. Mr. Goodacre was there, in his Sunday place, wearing his Sunday suit.

Already on the stage, which we had hung with greenery and berries from the creek, sat a big black shiny metal suitcase, brought in from John's truck by some of the big boys. John, wearing a shiny red jacket and a long silk scarf, sat at the end of a front bench, waiting for the crowd to gather.

After the children had filed in, Mr. Brock gave the welcome; and then Rosie, wearing her blue dress that made her eyes shine darkly, stepped forward and climbed to the stage, where she stood easily looking out over the audience. "We are all going to sing 'Silent Night,'" she announced, "but first we are going to hear the melody played for us on the guitar by Mr. John Concolorcorvo." The thing that surprised me most was that she had learned to say his name.

John came forward, his guitar slung over his shoulder, and played the one Christmas song we all knew. I almost understood then what Rosie had tried to say about his music. Sometimes it was like church bells ringing across a snowy meadow (so I imagined), and then it was like the singing of a flock of golden birds, and at the same time there was a depth and a strength that I had thought only an organ could produce.

After John had brought us back to earth with a few simple chords, Rosie led the audience in singing the carol, and with her voice to guide us we did make a joyful noise.

Then John gave Rosie the guitar and she sat on the edge of the stage with it. (And that was one thing she had been doing—learning to play the guitar.) To her own accompaniment she sang a Christmas song that few of us had heard then. It was only an ordinary carol, one we hear over and over every Christmas now, but in those pre-electronic days no song ever became tiresome to us. It was an ordinary carol, but having been descended from Christians for whom Christmas in church was Papist and abhorrent, we scarcely knew any Christmas music. I had never heard "Oh Little Town of Bethlehem" before, and I have never heard it sung so beautifully since.

When the song was finished, Rosie stood and bowed (someone had taught her that), while applause filled the room. And while

Rosie stood before us, flushed and smiling, John came onstage and
picked up his tin case. He took out a small folding table, over which
he placed a floor-length white cloth. He called for his assistant.
Rosie gave one more bow and went to stand at his side. He began
to talk about strange things he would show the audience, and at his
direction Rosie took out of the case an array of drinking glasses,
ribbons, cords, and colored handkerchiefs.

With his shiny red jacket, his long silk scarf, his mysterious man-
ner, his dark piercing eyes, John had his audience following every
word. Then almost before we had prepared ourselves, he began his
magic: producing eggs, paper flowers, and more handkerchiefs,
pulling them out of his sleeves by the yard, or finding them under
tall metal cones that he used in several tricks.

Gradually he built up to the feat he said would be most difficult
of all. He would mix water and wine and then separate them again.
"Now I must admit," he said, as he poured out a dark liquid into
a glass, "that this is not actually wine. Somehow it sounds better
to say wine, as they do in the Bible, you know—but this is grape
juice, which any of you could drink with no harm done, and may
presently do."

Finally he poured the liquid from both glasses together into a
decanter, then set it on the table. The decanter and the two glasses,
one at each side, sat upon little stands and each then was covered
with one of the metal cones. John explained that at his command
the mixture would separate and pass into the empty glasses. "Now
it's your choice," he said, leaning intimately toward the audience.
"Which glass do you want the wine to go into?"

"That one!" all the children cried, pointing to one glass or the
other.

"Well, it seems you can't agree," John said. "I'll have to ask one
child to come up here and choose."

Most were too shy to volunteer, but several did. John finally
chose Gordy Gibson, older brother of the twins.

Gordy came to the stage and was allowed to pick one of
the glasses. Then John fastened a yellow ribbon to the middle
cone and let it reach to the ones at each side. We were asked to

believe the wine would travel down one way and the water the other.

"Now we must count to ten, very slowly," John said, and the children shouted the numbers.

Then with a flourish John removed the covers and revealed the liquids in the chosen glasses, just as he had promised. And he gave Gordy the grape juice to drink.

"Is it good?" John asked.

Gordy nodded, unable to speak. His eyes were wide and dark in his pale face.

"Who else would like a drink?" John asked.

"Me, me!" cried all the boys and some of the girls.

John picked George Earl.

But then, looking all around him in bottles and other containers, he had to say with great disappointment that he could find no more grape juice.

George Earl started back to his seat.

"But wait!" John cried dramatically. "We can take back the juice this young gentleman has just drunk, if I can find my magic funnel."

Then Rosie came forward with what appeared to be an ordinary tin funnel. John demonstrated that it was empty, then told Gordy to bend his elbow and hold it over the mouth of the funnel. "And you, young man," he said, addressing George Earl, will have to take the other arm and work it up and down. Gordy here has turned into a pump."

George Earl obliged, with a comic flair that surprised us all. The children shrieked with laughter as the glass John was holding under the funnel filled with the purple juice.

John presented the glass with a bow, and George Earl drank it down.

That was his last trick, John announced, but he was going to produce more wine—though not by magic. He then gave instructions to Gordy and George Earl, who went out to the truck and returned with two large urns and a box that turned out to have paper cups in it. The liquid was grape juice sweetened and heavily diluted with water, just the way we always drank it at home, but we accepted it as a miracle. And it was good.

IX

PERDUE Springs would not easily forget our Christmas miracle. Many said they appreciated what John had done for the school children. Those who missed the program were sorry not to have gone. Grandpa said the domino players all agreed they'd be willing to pay admission if they had another chance to see the show.

We were talking around the fire in the living room one night after supper. The weather had turned bitter cold, though still without rain or snow, and we drew our chairs close to the stove.

"Why couldn't you-all put on a show for the whole community, and charge admission?" I said to Rosie.

"Well, that's the man's business," Grandpa said, as though he didn't think my idea such a bad one.

But Grandma said, "There's some would be against it. Cornelius, for one. He didn't like that joking way John talked to the kids about drinking wine, and I can't say I blame him. It would be pretty easy for him to get folks to thinking John could be a bad influence on their children."

Rosie didn't say anything. It was just about then that I began to realize how seldom she did.

I learned not to argue with her about getting our lessons at night. Or I learned I couldn't argue with her. If I said, "Let's get our history questions for tomorrow," she would say, "You go ahead, I'm not ready to do mine." If I asked when she would be ready, she would say, "Oh, I don't know, I may not do that." When I began reading *The House of the Seven Gables,* the novel in our literature book that year, I was eager to talk about it with Rosie. But she never even started it. "It looks dull," she said.

I told Grandma she wasn't doing anything in school, and she said she knew it.

57

"I ought to send her home," she said. "But I promised her folks I'd keep her this school year, and they need help just as much as they ever did."

There was still no work for Mr. Fargo, and there wouldn't be unless it rained and made road work necessary. O.B. went off to look for work right after Christmas; they didn't know where he was.

The bank in the county seat failed, and the school district lost its money. The trustees decided not to try to have school at Perdue Springs anymore. Mr. Hodges, who had his money there too, was wiped out. He sold his stock to Mashburns' and closed his store, and then went to town to live in a little two-room house back of his daughter.

Grandpa said if it wasn't for providing a place for the domino players, he'd close the blacksmith shop too.

It was a sad, gloomy winter, followed by a spring that made no promises. Warm weather came early, and our lilacs bloomed in mid-March, struggling against the dust-laden wind. When I think of that spring, I remember the odor of dusty lilac, a fragrance without freshness, a loveliness veiled and dead.

And my first heartbreak. Rosie and I had always had our little spats, but I knew at once this was different.

I think I knew I shouldn't wait for her. Mr. Brock asked her to stay after school and talk to him a few minutes, and I shouldn't have waited. It was none of my business what they talked about. But I knew he was going to talk to her about her schoolwork, and I had to know what he said. There was only one more month of our six-months term, and there wouldn't have been money for that if Weldon Brock hadn't told the trustees he would teach the last two months without pay. There wasn't much time left, and Rosie was failing every subject.

I went and sat in the farthest swing, where I couldn't be seen from the schoolhouse windows. I was sure Mr. Brock was going to give Rosie a chance to make up her work, but at the same time I knew he wasn't going to give her a grade she didn't earn. He didn't like to fail anybody, he seldom did, but with Mr. Brock you didn't pass unless you did the work he assigned. I thought Rosie could still pass to the tenth grade if she would halfway try. But I no longer had any idea what Rosie would do.

I didn't have to wait long, maybe not more than fifteen minutes, maybe less. When Rosie came out the door, I went to meet her.

She wasn't pleased to see me. "What are you doing here, May?" she asked.

"Waiting to walk home with you," I said.

She didn't say anything but walked on, rather fast, toward the road. I stayed in step with her.

"Didn't you need to bring home any books?" I asked.

"No," she said.

"I thought Mr. Brock might give you some make-up work," I said.

"Did you?" she said.

The way she said it let me know he had, and she had said she guessed she didn't care to do that. Or something to that effect.

"Oh Rosie," I said, "why won't you do it? I know you could still pass, and go on to Cottonwood Flats next year and be a junior."

"I'm sixteen now," she said. "I won't have to go to school anymore."

"But you do have to!" I insisted. "We have to graduate, and go to college, and teach together and everything."

"Oh May, grow up!" she said.

I should have known there wasn't anything to say after that.

But I kept on. "I don't know what you mean," I said, "but I know it's not childish to plan on getting an education and being a teacher."

"All that silly stuff about crows and statues and purple curtains," she said contemptuously.

There was no way she could have made her meaning any clearer. There was no way she could have hurt me more. And so, although in all the years of childhood I had never thought of hitting Rosie, I had to hurt her back. Words weren't good enough.

I dropped my books on the ground and shoved her backward with both hands. She almost lost her footing, but recovered it and slapped me across the side of my face with such force that I lost my balance and sat down hard on the ground.

That incident happened right out in the middle of the crossroads, and I didn't even care. I don't know how many must have seen us, but only one person ever mentioned the fight to me. Grandma had to have seen the broad red mark on my face and the streaks of tears. Even without them, she could probably have guessed what happened. But she never said anything about it to me.

The only person I ever talked to about it was George Earl. Early Saturday morning Woodrow came to tell Rosie their mama had the trots real bad and Gladys wanted her to come and help. So she went, and although we hadn't spoken to each other and I supposed never would again, I felt lost and aimless without her. As always when gloomy or depressed, I felt myself drawn toward the rocks. I wandered among them as if trying to find my way through a maze.

And, as often happened, George Earl came along and found me there. We sat down together on the big corner rock where we had so often sat with Rosie.

"I seen y'all in the crossroads yesterday," he said.

"I'm so mad at her," I said.

"What was it about?" George Earl asked.

"School," I said. "She won't even try to pass, and Mr. Brock is doing his best to help her."

"Do you think she's struck on that Dago?" he asked. "Is that why?"

I shook my head. I thought it was music and dancing that lured her, and I thought she was fascinated more by Mrs. Raven than her son. But I knew that might just be what I wanted to think.

"Folks are talking about 'em," George Earl said.

I knew that. Going to the creek to meet a man meant only one thing at Perdue Springs.

"All I'm sure of," I said, "is that Rosie will never go to school again."

"And she'll just stay at home?" George Earl said.

"I guess so," I said. "Her mama's getting sicker. I guess they'll need her."

"It'll be the end of us," he said. "Us three, I mean. Together."

I didn't think it had ever been quite like that—the three of us together. I wanted Rosie, and George Earl wanted Rosie. To have her, we had to put up with each other.

"I don't know how it will be," I said.

School was nearly out. I didn't count the days, as I had always done before—Rosie and I, together, counting, planning, walking along the creek to watch the greening and flowering. And George Earl with us sometimes, though never admitted to the intimacy of our dreams.

I tried to hold the days back. Even now, I can't remember an unhappier time of my life. Rosie still slept in my bed, but never a word did we whisper to each other. She often went to her house when school was out—to help, as she said. I suppose she did go home, and I suppose she helped, but often, when I was at the kitchen window doing some suppertime task, I would see her coming up from the creek.

Though this wasn't a happy time, I didn't want it to end. For when it was over all the dreams of my childhood would be gone and Rosie lost to me forever.

Once I went crying to Grandma and said something like that to her.

She scolded me. "You're trying to build up something like one of them red-backed novels," she said, "when all that's happening is just a natural part of growing up."

I couldn't slow the passing of the days. Mid-April came, and school was out. Forever. Men came from Cottonwood Flats the next day and started tearing down our schoolhouse, to use the lumber for some new building there.

Rosie took her things and moved home.

Weldon and Nancy Brock went to stay with her folks in Denton, so he could go to summer school.

My vast, empty summer began.

X

Every morning I went to Mashburns' to see if we had any mail. There was always a little gathering at mailtime, where you could learn what people were thinking about in Perdue Springs. The Fargos didn't come very often, as I don't think they ever expected mail, but one morning Rosie was there.

When I went in, Old Man Gibson (grandfather of the twins) was saying, "He's a funny feller," and I knew he was talking about the Dago.

"He put on a good show at the schoolhouse though," somebody said.

There was speculation as to whether he might put on another show, now that the nights were warmer.

When Rosie left, I walked out with her. It was hard for me to speak to her, but harder not to. "Don't you wish he'd give a show?" I said. "Wouldn't you like to help him like you did Christmas—one more time before he leaves?"

"Oh, is he leaving?" she said.

I walked with her to Mr. Goodacre's gate, but she didn't seem disposed to linger. "I've got to take this medicine to Mama," she said.

"I've got to help Grandma in the garden," I said.

So far, we were planting only in the fenced garden close to the windmill, where we could irrigate with water from the well. We couldn't plant anything in the big patch until it rained.

"No mail," I said to Grandma. I had taken Grandpa's *Star-Telegram* by the shop.

"Did you see anybody?" she asked.

"Nobody much," I said. "Folks got to talking about John, saying they wished he'd give a show."

She went on dropping seeds into the shallow trench she had made with the hoe.

"Rosie was there," I said. "I believe she thinks he'll give a show."

"Why? Take that hoe and cover up them okry seed. Did she say so?"

"No," I said, obeying her order. "I just got the idea from something she said that he's not gonna leave right away. Why would he stay, if not to give a show?"

"You may be right," Grandma said. "They'll have to have some money if they're fixing to start out on the road again." After a minute or two she straightened up, pushed back her bonnet, and wiped her brow with the back of her hand. "But oh, I do *wish* he wouldn't do it," she said.

The next time I went to the store, there was a sign posted by the front door. It had been commercially printed, except for the date and place, which had been filled in by hand: "MAGIC SHOW by Concolorcorvo the Magician. Perdue Springs Tabernacle, May 14, 7 P.M. Admission 10¢ and 20¢." The last line, in italic type, was SHEBA DANCES.

"Sheba dances?" said George Earl, stepping up beside me.

"I guess that's just an old poster," I said, "that he had before his wife died."

"Rosie wouldn't dance," he said.

"No," I said.

He walked to my gate with me. We didn't go on talking. But as we paused there, he said, "She would though."

"She'd have to practice," I said. "People would know."

"There's just one place they might go," he said, "where nobody would see what they were up to."

"I don't know where," I said.

"I heard a guitar when I went down there one day," he said. "It was just as hot and still—you couldn't hear nothing but the locusts in the gin trees. Only there was something: it kinda blended in with the locusts but it was something else. Finally I figgered out it was the Dago strumming that guitar, but I never did see him."

"Where was he, then?" I asked.

"In the gin," he said.

Of course. The gin floor—a wide, smooth place. And nobody coming around the gin, or likely to, till late summer. Maybe not even then, if it never did rain. Grandpa said Mr. Gibson was worrying a lot about whether he would have his usual job for the ginning season.

"He would play the music for her," I said. "If she danced."

"Sure," he said.

"They'll probably be practicing every day now," I said.

"Bound to," he said.

"I imagine about four o'clock," I said. "Don't you?"

I went by the tabernacle path; he went along the road. We planned to go all the way to the creek and then slip back up to the gin. That way neither Mrs. Raven in her chair nor Mrs. Gibson at the gin house would be likely to notice either one of us. And we would not come together until we reached the willow thicket.

He was waiting for me in among the willows. It was damp and cool in there, and the light was green.

"I heard him," George Earl said. "He's in the gin."

We climbed up out of the willows, quiet as lizards in the grass. Then we ran across the open space and in under the shed where the cotton wagons drove. No one could see us there, unless they came looking for us among the shadows. We were moving toward the music, which came out the open door to meet us, so fast it was like a whirr, yet with each separate note ringing clear.

There under the shed the door and one window opened into the gin room. "Won't they see our heads against the light," I whispered, "if we look in the window?"

"It's pretty dark under here," George Earl answered. "I don't believe they will if we keep low."

I moved forward, he kept close by my side. We dropped to our knees, so that just the tops of our heads showed above the windowsill. It was dark inside, darker even than under the shed. My eyes sought the source of the music, and I could see the Dago's figure, crouched at the foot of the stairs leading up to the platform that held the baling machinery.

"Look up," George Earl whispered in my ear.

Light from a high west window streamed in and lit the platform where Rosie was whirling in a climactic movement of her dance.

She was wearing something diaphanous and wine-red. I pressed the corner of my eye, trying to see the dress more clearly.

"They won't see us," George Earl whispered. "They can't see anything."

I nodded. We stood up then, our faces pressed against the window glass. The music slowed and changed. *Sinuous,* I guessed, might be the right word to describe it. Rosie swayed and bent to it, turning ever more slowly, until at last she sank to the platform, her skirt spread out around her.

I could tell what she was wearing then. I knew it was the costume in the picture. There was a glitter as of diamonds across the gauzy bodice of the dress. "It barely covers her nipples," Rosie had said once. Now it served less well.

From a shadowed corner of the platform Mrs. Raven appeared, and I knew she had been sitting there watching all the time. She stood talking to Rosie, and Rosie looked up at her earnestly, even perhaps reverently.

"She's teaching her," I said.

"We'd better go," George Earl said.

But the music began again, the whirring, circling melody that we had first heard, and Rosie began the whirling dance she had done before. The music and the dance grew faster, and Mrs. Raven stood nodding in approval.

"We'd better go," George Earl said again. He took my hand and drew me away from the window.

Unspeaking, hand in hand, we went back to the willows, and there—in a little open, grassy space at the heart of the thicket—we clung to each other and cried.

That night after supper, when Grandma and I were sitting in the porch swing, Mr. Goodacre came walking by, pausing at our gate.

"Howdy, Cornelius," Grandma called.

He came into the yard and along the plank walk, which was bordered by pink and white periwinkles.

"You must really have to pour the water to these, Hattie," he said.

"That's a fact, Cornelius," she said. "If it don't rain pretty soon, I guess I'll have to give up on 'em."

He spoke to me, and asked if Grandpa was at home.

"I'm right here, Cornelius," Grandpa said, stepping out the front door. "Set and talk awhile."

The two men sat in the white rocking chairs.

"What's on your mind, Cornelius?" Grandpa said. "Dry weather and hard times?"

"That's about it," Mr. Goodacre said. "In fact, I was wondering how you-all would feel about a meeting at the tabernacle to pray for rain."

I knew Grandpa and Grandma didn't much believe in praying for rain.

"What is to be will be," Grandma said.

"That may be so and it may not," Grandpa said. "But I do recollect it says in the Bible that the Lord knows what we need before we know it ourselves."

"'Ask and ye shall receive,'" said Mr. Goodacre. "But to some extent I do agree with you. I would say we ought to pray for forgiveness of our sins. And then the Lord may bless us."

"I'm not much for public prayer," Grandma said. "I always think my sins is between me and the Lord."

"Maybe we've got public sins to be forgiven," Mr. Goodacre said.

"Like the way some folks has treated John and Mrs. Raven?" Grandma said.

"I was thinking," Mr. Goodacre said, "more about those among us who have tolerated and even encouraged a dark and alien force in our midst."

"Judge not, Cornelius," said Grandma.

"It's one thing to condemn, Hattie," Mr. Goodacre said, "and another to condone. And that's something else I want us to talk about: have you-all seen the signs about that show?"

"What d'ye think's wrong with a show, Cornelius?" Grandpa asked.

"God knows," said Mr. Goodacre. "And I can tell you one thing for sure: He won't look with pleasure on us if we allow magic and dancing in His tabernacle."

"Whether that building belongs to the Lord is a question in my mind," Grandpa said. "We've used it for box suppers and elections and, if you'll think back a little, you might even remember a medicine show."

"Well, there's a difference between those gatherings and that Dago's show," the Squire said, "but I don't aim to argue with you about it. I'm fixing to go talk to this feller and tell him our constitution and bylaws prohibit any kind of entertainment in the tabernacle. And I want you to go with me."

"That's the first I've heard of any constitution and bylaws," Grandpa said.

"Well, we ought to have 'em. We ought to've had 'em a long time ago, and we're fixing to have 'em."

"I might as well tell you," Grandpa said. "I've already talked to John. He come to me, and I told him there wasn't nothing I could think of to keep him from going ahead with his show. The tabernacle's a public place, and I don't believe you could come up with a legal way to keep him from using it any decent way he wants to."

"I'm disappointed in you, Luke," said Mr. Goodacre sadly, as when he mourned over the heathen sometimes in Sunday school. "I'll go and talk to him myself, and try to make him see this won't do. And if I can't stop him, there's one thing I can do. I'll be there myself to see that the show stays decent. If it don't, that'll be another story."

"I think you had better tell John what he said about the show being decent," Grandma said, after we had watched Mr. Goodacre to the crossroads.

"Oh good Lord, Hattie," Grandpa said. "What d'ye think the man's gonna do—put on a strip-tease?"

"I haven't got the least i-dy what you're talking about," Grandma said, and got up and went in the house.

XI

Gᴇᴏʀɢᴇ Earl got a chance to work with his daddy on the McCormick ranch a few days, and I didn't see him again until the morning of the show. He was at the store when I went after the mail, and he walked back with me to the rocks. We didn't sit on the big flat one near the corner. There was room for the two of us on a smaller one farther back from the road.

"Are you still going to the show?" he asked.

"I guess so," I said. "Grandma said at first we wouldn't go, but now she says it's some kind of duty."

"She'd never do that in the tabernacle," he said. He didn't seem to want to speak Rosie's name.

"No," I said, "I don't think she would. Unless she forgets where she is."

"She did that, didn't she?" he said.

We sat silently awhile, thinking about Rosie.

Finally he said, "I could take you. I've got some money."

"I'll have to ask Grandma," I said.

He waited on the rocks while I did. She said I could go with George Earl and sit with him, but I would have to pay my own way and we would have to walk back with her and Grandpa. After I started back to George Earl, she called me to say she didn't want to see us holding hands or sitting too close together.

I felt lost—disoriented—that night, getting ready to go to a show with Rosie in it and not even knowing where Rosie was. She ought to be with me, I kept thinking. I ought to be combing her hair.

George Earl came early, just as I was finishing supper, and Grandma said I could go on if I wanted to. She had plenty of time to wash the dishes and wasn't interested in getting a front seat.

"You look nice," George Earl said as we started down the front walk. I was wearing my last year's blue piqué, but I had been letting my hair grow a little, and I had it combed back from my face and tied with a blue ribbon.

"You do too," I said. For him, he did. The haircut he had got right after school was out had grown out about right, and he had on a starched white shirt.

A few cars from the farms around Perdue Springs were already parked by the tabernacle. George Earl's kinfolks from beyond Rough Creek had all come in a wagon, and the horses stood lifting their heads to the light, cooling breeze. Just under the tent-like roof, at the back of the tabernacle, Mrs. Raven sat in her folding chair, a cigar box on a wooden crate that stood upended at her side, and accepted the dimes and quarters for admission.

"Good evening, May and George Earl," she said to us happily. "John and Rosie brought me and set me up an hour ago, and John has his things here already. Go on in and get yourselves a front seat."

Inside, the low sun struck the pine benches with gold but left the stage in shadow, waiting for the magic that would bring it alight. Little knots of people sat apart from each other, and nobody talked. We followed Mrs. Raven's suggestion and found places on a front bench. Up close we could see on the stage the draped table and the big suitcase John had used at the school program, plus two big wooden boxes like caskets.

Having sat down, not too close together, we turned around to watch the crowd arriving. Mrs. Gibson with her children and some others about their ages took the rest of the front seats. (Whatever she might have said in her rage at Mrs. Raven, she wouldn't have missed a show.) Grandpa and Grandma sat on a bench in the second row, where I could see them by turning my head pretty far to the left. Farther back, where I could see him out of the corner of my eye, sat Squire Goodacre. The Fargo children sat near the back. I had no idea what they thought of Rosie in a show. They probably weren't sure themselves.

Finally John came in from the campground path and mounted to the stage, where he slowly and ceremoniously lit the four kerosene torches set up there. At the schoolhouse, wearing his red jacket and scarf, he had looked tricky and gay; but now he wore black—tight-fitting trousers, with a satin stripe down the side, a long-tailed black coat, and a stiffly starched white shirt with a flowing black tie. Absolute silence prevailed. Even a bawling baby near the back shut up suddenly.

I didn't see Rosie come in; when I looked, she stood on the ground at the foot of the steps, waiting. She wore a scarlet robe that fell almost to her ankles. It could have been a choir robe, I suppose, but in the flickering light, reflected in the long gold chain around her neck, the effect was magical.

When John finished lighting the torches, he and Rosie went to where Mrs. Raven sat. Everybody turned to watch while John helped the old woman up and supported her to the front, with Rosie following, carrying the folding chair. They placed her at the end of the bench I sat on, and the old woman smiled at me with great contentment.

Then John and Rosie ascended to the stage, her hand in the crook of his arm. He stepped to the draped table at the front; she kept a little behind him.

And out of the shadow, into the flickering torchlight, came a show, came illusion, striking down reality—the most anyone had hoped for. The patter John kept up was like nothing any of us had ever heard; it might have come out of a book; it probably did. He performed all the tricks we had seen at the schoolhouse, and more. Rosie moved at his instructions like a mechanical doll. In the last trick, she sat like a statue in the folding chair, her robe spread out around her, while the magician drew roses out of her mouth.

The audience cheered and clapped. Many rose to their feet. Children were standing up on the benches. If this had been the whole show, everybody would have said they had their money's worth. But there was more.

John took his guitar from the back of the stage and sat on the steps (just as he had done in the gin) strumming softly, calming us down. It was only then that I realized the tabernacle had grown dim; darkness had come up around us. Now all the light was on the stage, and as we began to listen to the music we knew we were waiting for someone to appear and fill the space. And there she came—out of the little anteroom at the side of the stage, and yet she might almost have materialized out of shadow. She wore a white shawl over her shoulders, fastened in front with a red velvet rose, like those that had seemed to come from between her lips. Her dark red skirt hung in soft folds almost to the floor.

Mrs. Raven (I suppose) had showed her how to use a little rouge and lipstick, but I doubt that many guessed she was made up. Her hair fell like a dark cloud over the white silk shawl.

We watched her, and waited.

She began to sing, as John switched to soft accompanying chords on his guitar. She sang songs we had known a long time, and then she sang "Wayfaring Stranger." Then the rhythm of the guitar changed and the one new song she had learned ("La Golondrina," though none of us then knew the name) came piercing our hearts.

Then Rosie stopped singing. She bowed. At first it seemed no one would applaud; we sat as if stunned. Then someone behind me and to my left—it was Grandpa, I felt sure—began clapping heavily, and soon everyone joined in.

And all the time John was still playing softly, still playing "La Golondrina." When at last the applause died down, he began to play louder and faster, although it still seemed to be the same song. Then the tone itself changed, and I recognized the dizzying, metallic music George Earl and I had heard in the gin.

And Rosie dropped her shawl. Letting it lie on the floor, she whirled away into the heart of that music.

George Earl and I looked at each other in relief. She was wearing the Sheba dress, all right, but her bosom and shoulders were covered with a bertha made of red lace. It hung free, and as she danced it fell to one side, revealing a bare shoulder and the swell of her breast. But the effect was demure, compared with what we had seen.

The music slowed, and Rosie moved into what I recognized as a waltz step, holding out her arms as though beckoning a lover. Then it was fast again, faster and faster, and as she whirled, her skirt stood out till you could see to her knees and even a little above them.

I heard a rustling behind me, as of heavily starched percale. I turned my head only slightly; I knew what I would see. Grandma

71

had risen and was walking away. I refused to look back, but others were leaving as well, and I had no doubt Squire Goodacre was among them.

John glanced at his mother; she raised a warning hand. The music slowed, but not to the sinuous strains I had expected. It was almost a march, and when it quickened it became something like a peasant folk song that called for clapping hands and stamping feet.

The audience (what was left of it) began to clap in time. With a shout from John and a leap from Rosie, the number ended and the two came bowing to the front of the stage. Again the applause was enthusiastic. The audience would have liked more. But John thanked them and sent them home.

George Earl and I were among those who crowded to the stage to compliment Rosie, and she thanked us with a sweet smile. But there were too many wanting to talk to her; we didn't stay.

"We'll see her tomorrow," I said.

"Sure," George Earl said.

Outside, I looked for Grandma and Grandpa. "I guess they went on home," I said.

The moon wasn't bright, but the road was clear. We walked slowly along. At the corner, the rocks looked like sleeping monsters.

"You know," George Earl said, "I don't believe she ever knew we spoke to her."

XII

THE rhythm of John's music throbbed through me as I lay in bed by my open window. I thought I'd never sleep. I heard a car go by—late; how late I couldn't imagine. A dog barked down by the creek. I thought it was Bear. Whoever it was set up a chain of barking all through the village. But I was falling asleep by then. The music of the show was dying down.

I was awakened by shouts, loud and hoarse, and a heavy hammering at the front door. I reached the door just ahead of Grandpa, and in the pale moonlight could see Mrs. Raven standing there—looming dark and enormous out of the night, calling down strange curses upon the town of Perdue Springs.

"Come in, Miz Raven," Grandpa said calmly, "and tell us what the matter is."

Grandma came then, with a lamp in her hand, a white nightgown on, her hair down her back.

"It's your fault," cried Mrs. Raven. "You're the one. I ought to have heeded the Hanged Man."

Grandma set the lamp down and drew Mrs. Raven into the room. "Please do set down," she said, "and tell us the trouble."

Mrs. Raven sank into a rocking chair. She was breathing heavily, and trembling.

"They took John to jail," she said.

"Now I didn't have a thing to do with that," Grandma said, "but I want you to tell us what happened, because I've got a i-dy about it and we'll help you if we can."

She moved a chair to face Mrs. Raven and sat down. "May, bring her a drink," she said.

I went to the kitchen and dipped water into a glass from our white enamel bucket. From where it stood, just inside the back door, I could see Grandma fanning Mrs. Raven with a flimsy *Farm and Ranch* magazine. It was a scene I'll always remember—Grandma in her long white gown, Mrs. Raven in black, each with her long plait of hair down her back, contrasting with the color of her clothes. They were a Kodak picture and its negative; but was Mrs. Raven a negative of Grandma, or was it the other way around?

Grandma waited till Mrs. Raven had drunk the water and then said, "Who brought the charges, Miz Raven?"

"Mr. Goodacre, so I understand," Mrs. Raven said, calmer now, although her voice shook as she added, "but the sheriff mentioned your name."

"And just exactly what was the charge?" Grandma asked.

"Contributing to the delinquency of a minor."

"I never said anything like that in my life," Grandma declared.

"You walked out," Mrs. Raven said.

"That was the dress in the picture," Grandma said.

"I altered it," said Mrs. Raven.

"I kept seeing it the same," Grandma said. "And that sign said Sheba dancing."

"Now here's what we'll do," Grandpa said. "First thing in the morning, I'll take Rosie and Mrs. Stephens and we'll go to town and tell the sheriff how things really was. I don't believe they can keep John up there on such a charge."

"And I'll fix you a bed here," Grandma said. "You mustn't go back down there by yourself tonight."

"No, I can't stay here," Mrs. Raven said.

"Have you got that dress she was wearing—or has she?" Grandma asked.

"I have it," Mrs. Raven said.

"Well, you bring it back with you, Luke," Grandma said. "We might want to show it to the sheriff."

I went with Grandpa to Fargos' to get Rosie the next morning. She showed no reluctance to go with us, once she understood what had happened, but she didn't have much to say. We stopped by the house to get Grandma and were on the way to town by seven o'clock.

"Everything will be all right, Rosie," Grandma said.

"Yes ma'am," Rosie said.

Rosie and I were in the back seat. The way the Model A rattled over those rough, rocky roads, she had to lean forward and raise her voice to be heard in the front.

"Are you worried about John?" I asked as she sat back.

She didn't answer. She might not have heard me. It was hard to talk in the car.

Nobody said much. I heard Grandma say something to Grandpa about how bad the bare fields looked, how gray the pasture grass.

Rosie never said another word, until about halfway to town. Then she sat on the edge of the seat and began to speak in a strained, loud voice. "I've decided to tell you-all," she said, "what I'm fixing to do."

Grandma looked back.

"I haven't told my folks yet, but I will when I get back. And I

74

want you-all to know, because you've always been good to me, and May has been my dearest friend."

Has been—was once. Few friendships can have had an ending so sharply defined as that was.

She was looking at Grandma, right into her face, as though after all she was the one that had to be told. "Just as soon as John gets things ready, him and his mama will be leaving Perdue Springs. I guess this business might set him back, but I reckon not much. And when they leave, I'll be going with them."

She stopped, as if waiting for some response, but no one said anything.

"I'm gonna help with the shows," she said, "like John's wife used to do. Only, as I won't be his wife, he aims to pay me."

"How much?" Grandma asked.

"I don't know, what he can," Rosie said. "But however much it is, I aim to send it home for Mama."

"Well, I know you wouldn't forget your mama, Rosie," Grandma said. "And maybe you can help more this way than you could staying here, I don't know about that. But there's more than that to think about. The kind of life you'll be getting into. Where it may lead. I don't know much about all that, and neither do you."

"You think Raven is all right, don't you?" Rosie said.

"As all right," Grandma said, "as a woman with a name like that could be. I guess she'll look after you, in whatever way she thinks is right. But if you start to dancing in that red dress without the bertha, you don't know where you'll end up."

"I guess I don't know for sure," Rosie said. "But I know I'm going with them—it's just the way my life has to be."

Grandpa finally spoke. "Well, it may be all right," he said. "It may even be what's needed the most. But will your daddy let you go? You're not of age, you know."

"I guess he will let me," Rosie said. "I know he can't stop me."

It took a while to find the sheriff. Finally Grandpa tracked him to a cheap cafe that he said womenfolks had better stay out of. He went in and brought the sheriff out to the car.

"Ma'am," the sheriff said to Grandma, bending down to the window she sat by (for he was a tall, lanky man), "are you the lady that walked out when the girl started dancing?"

"I did," Grandma said. "But it was a matter of personal preference. I don't think you'd find anybody in that audience to say she wasn't decent."

"Except your justice of the peace," the sheriff said.

"I've got my doubts about that," Grandpa muttered.

"Show him the dress you wore, Rosie," Grandma said. "Get out and hold it up to you."

The red dress, with bertha attached, looked dowdy, held up against Rosie's faded brown print.

"You're the one that danced?" the sheriff asked.

"Yes, sir," Rosie said.

"And that's what you wore?"

"Yes, sir."

"And you danced of your own free will?"

"I reckon you would say that," Rosie answered. "Didn't nobody make me."

"Well," the sheriff said, "I can't do nothing today. What I wish you'd do is get Mr. Goodacre to come to my office tomorrow and withdraw his charges. I'm heading out of town to pick up a prisoner, but I'll be in my office in the morning."

"I believe we can get him to come," Grandma said.

"Well, if you can't," the sheriff said, "there's other ways you can go. But it's liable to cost you money for a lawyer."

Grandpa thanked him. We drove to the jail, and he went in to see John. When he came out, he said John was all right and appreciated what was being done for him. He sent word to Rosie to go and see about his mother.

Back in Perdue Springs, we took her by the campground before going home. She started toward the Dago's truck, then turned to us briefly and waved goodbye.

"We really have lost her this time, Grandma," I said.

Grandma nodded. "Nobody made her go," she said, "and yet it's not of her own free will."

76

Grandpa left early the next morning, to present John's case to Mr. Goodacre. Grandma and I were still sitting at the breakfast table.

Then, almost at once, he was back, calling Grandma from the back door.

"Hattie," he said, rather as if he were scolding. "I wish you'd come out here a minute."

Just so had he spoken years before, when he found our calf run over in the road.

I followed them. We went the way Grandpa must have gone as he started to Mr. Goodacre's—out our side gate, across the gravelly drive space, to the path that led alongside the rocks. Coming to our house or leaving it was about the only reason for anyone to take that path.

We had to get nearly to the rocks before we could see what Grandpa was leading us to—Mrs. Raven, lying back among them, her head caught between two rough stones in an unnatural position you couldn't bear to look at.

Grandma turned to Grandpa.

"Yes," he said, "she's dead."

"But why here in the rocks?" I said.

"She got confused, I guess," Grandpa said. "Lost her way."

"It was a stroke," Grandma said. "It must have been a stroke."

The shock of sudden death in a place like Perdue Springs is quickly felt by everyone. Mr. Mashburn, unlocking his front door, saw us and came to find out what had happened. I don't remember who came next. I don't know when George Earl came along, or how Squire Goodacre heard about Mrs. Raven, although I suppose Grandpa sent for him.

Grandma made the men carry Mrs. Raven in and lay her on the bed in our spare room, with Mr. Goodacre protesting all the time that the corpse should be left where it lay until a doctor pronounced on the cause of death.

And Grandma stood up facing him, as tall as he and fierce. "Cornelius," she said, "if you think I'm fixing to leave that poor woman's body in the hot sun for two hours, while we wait for a doctor, you're crazier than you was when you went and got the sheriff to put her son in jail—which I don't doubt is what killed her."

"Ah, Hattie, you're upset," said the Squire, but he protested no longer.

Grandpa brought him into the kitchen and asked me to get them some coffee. Then he quietly told the Squire what he had done to get John out of jail and what he thought had better be done next.

"Under the circumstances, Luke," Mr. Goodacre said, "I will submit to your argument. I still believe it was a bad thing to let that man and woman stay in Perdue Springs, and what harm has been done to this community I still don't know. But what's done is done, and I am not a heartless man. You and me may discuss the law another time."

He said he would go immediately and get John, and while he was in town would send a doctor.

The doctor pronounced that Mrs. Raven had suffered a stroke. He said it was possible death had occurred when she hit her head on the corner of a large stone, but he could in good conscience give a certificate of death from natural causes.

When John came to talk to Grandpa and Grandma about burying his mother, he brought a note she had left for him, written in a shaky, spidery hand. "Dear Son," it said, "I have gone to Mrs. Stephens as I am not feeling quite well."

He said he kept thinking she was somewhere waiting for him. He couldn't imagine how life would be without her—he had never thought she might die.

She herself had thought of death though. John said she had an insurance policy to pay for her burial.

"Where do you aim to put her, John?" Grandma asked.

John said he didn't know. "We never belonged anywhere," he said.

"She'll be buried right here in Perdue Springs," Grandma said. "She belongs here. I don't doubt but what she come here to die."

"You were her friend, Mrs. Stephens," John said. "I'll be thankful to leave her here with you."

The men helped John put his mother's body in her bed in the little striped house, and several offered to go with him to the undertaker's. He told them he had already asked Mr. Fargo to go with him.

"I guess that's fitting," Grandma said when she heard.

They had the funeral service the next day in the tabernacle. As was customary with us, Mrs. Raven lay in her open casket and everyone filed by to give her one last look. Mrs. Gibson, holding a twin by each hand, stood over her a long time.

At the cemetery, when the burying was done, I told Grandma I'd find Rosie and see if she wanted to come home with us.

"No," said Grandma. "We'll wait a little while, and if she wants to, she'll come."

I knew she wouldn't.

Driving home, I said, "Maybe things will be like they used to be again. After a little while."

"No," Grandma said, "not ever the same again."

"But she'll get over John, won't she?" I said. "Even if she's in love with him."

"Rosie's not in love with anybody," Grandma said. "Love ain't what it's about."

"What will she do?" I wondered.

"She'll have to stay in Perdue Springs, that's all," Grandma said. "A girl can't go off with a man."

I awoke next morning to a heavy stillness filled with the false promise of rain and the oversweet odor of honeysuckle. Sounds carried all over the village.

There came a loud bang like a gunshot. I recognized it as the sound the Dago's truck made sometimes when he was cranking it, and I was surprised to think he was leaving already. I sprang out of bed, slipped out of my pajamas and into a dress, and ran barefoot out the front gate and into the road. George Earl was coming down the hill from his house.

It was right that we should watch together as the Dago left town, but I wished Rosie was there with us.

George Earl and I walked slowly down the hill and paused by the rock on the corner. By then we could see the blue and yellow flag gently waving.

"It'll seem kind of funny without him," George Earl said.

"I wish he'd never come here," I said.

The truck was nearly to the crossroads. We didn't know whether John would go south, the way he had come, or turn west, the way we went to town. We waited by the rock.

"There's somebody with him," George Earl said.

"It's Bear," I said.

"No, look," George Earl said.

"Yes, it's somebody," I said. I couldn't tell who it was. I didn't want to know who it was.

But the truck came on through the crossroads, slowly past the rock where we waited, and I couldn't help knowing.

She sat on the outside next to us, her blowing hair held back by a red bandanna. Bear, in the middle, wore his blue scarf, and the Dago had on his headband. They might have belonged to a band of gypsies. They looked happy. Laughing and talking, Rosie never turned her head.

George Earl and I had moved close together without thinking, and he had taken my hand.

We walked slowly back toward our house that way, and in the driveway met Grandpa and Grandma coming from the side gate. I don't believe Grandma even noticed we were holding hands. I didn't think about it then, myself.

"Did you see them, Grandma?" I asked.

"If I can believe my eyes, I did," Grandma said.

As we stood in the driveway, stricken and wondering, Squire Goodacre drove up. We gathered close to hear his view of the latest happening, for we knew that, coming from the south, he must have met the truck.

"Well, Hattie," he said. "I hope you're satisfied. And Luke. That devil you defended has carried off the finest thing Perdue Springs ever had."

"Can't you send the sheriff after 'em, Mr. Goodacre?" George Earl asked.

Mr. Goodacre shook his head sadly. "No, son, I can't," he said.

"Why not, Cornelius?" Grandma asked.

"Because they come to me yesterday evening with a marriage license. And Walter Fargo with 'em, declaring his consent."

"And you married them two?" said Grandpa.

"I married them, Luke. What else could I do?"

"Nothing," Grandma said. "There never was anything any of us could do, not from the very first."

Hardship

Margot Fraser

My thanks to Hallie Stillwell and other friends in the Big Bend and Davis Mountain areas for supplying anecdotes and a wealth of historical detail.

Margot Fraser

THE DAY Uncle Sam crooked his finger at Son that left only three of us to run the ranch—me, my husband and our fifteen-year-old boy, Jared. We were mighty surprised that he did it, Uncle Sam, I mean, because it seemed to us that Son was a whole lot more useful where he was. It takes a lot of muscle power to run a two-hundred-section spread in some of the worst country that God ever shoved out of sight as a bad investment. Well, Son could have kept right on doing that, he sure did know how. That boy was a fine hand, even Hunter thought so, though of course he never said it. Hunter rarely said anything, but I saw it in his eyes, the way he watched that boy, easy in the saddle as if he had been born in it (which he practically was) and a roping arm smooth and accurate as any arrow. Kind of a quiet pride Hunter had. But big. And growing every day. Yessir, Son could have kept us going fine during those hard years but Uncle Sam seemed to think otherwise. He wanted our boy in uniform, out serving his country somewhere else. So there wasn't anything we could do except shake our heads and put in a longer day. We were used to that anyway, and it wasn't the first time we'd had some cause to wonder at the wisdom of the government.

So Son went off wearing his Levi's and returned on leave a few months later in pants with razor blade creases and shoes shined fit to shame the sun. It was the first time in his life he had ever been out of his boots. He looked and smelled like a stranger. Even his horse didn't know him.

Jared said, "How in hell you gonna die with your boots on?"

(I noticed that Son didn't appear to have as much suntan on his cheeks as he used to, or maybe it faded a shade about then.)

"I ain't exactly fixin' to *die*," he said. "Besides, I ain't a outlaw, what do you think?"

Jared spat, something he had only recently learned to do with authority. The two of them were standing in the middle of the corral, Son's pony snorting off to one side. Jared spat to explain what he thought. "You ain't the same no more. Different somehow. Somebody else."

Son shook his head. "No, I ain't. Just different clothes, that's all. That don't make *me* any different."

"The hell it don't."

"Lissen here, little brother. Cussin' don't make a man any more than his getup does."

And they fought, Son holding Jared off with one hand and the little shaver swinging for all he was worth, tears streaming down his face. Jared screaming, "You ain't comin' back!" And Son, "The hell I ain't" And he pitched his little brother in the hayrack.

Hunter wanted to put a stop to it but I said no. "They're scared, both of 'em," I said. "Let them work it out."

So our son went off to war with a black eye and a cut lip.

Nearly a month later we got a letter from someplace in North Carolina:

Dear Mom and Dad and Salty Red,

Believe it or not, it didn't matter after all how I looked when I got back to the Base. All beat-up, I mean. The other guys had been on leave, too, and raising hell, so they looked the same or worse. They slapped me on the back—all that old boy stuff, you know. Guess they figured I'd been up to something pretty interesting. Anyway, they have got the idea that I am some kind of hot stuff. Guess I got you to thank for that, Red. You sure got your licks in.

No idea where we are headed yet but the scuttlebutt (Now ain't *that* some name? Might be a good handle for one of them spring colts!), it says we are aiming for England. Guess we will have to wait and see. That's mostly what we do anyway—

wait. That's the Army slogan: Hurry Up And Wait. The only other guy in my outfit from Texas is named Herman Lopez. He is from down around Brownsville but that's about as far as we got in our conversation. These sergeants are so dumb they pronounce his name Lo-*pez*. Well, I don't know how to write it like they say it, but they put all the steam on the back end.

Otherwise everything is okay. I'll write when I can.

Love,
Your Son

(Pfc. Forrest Collingsworth, AcDiv. 177326–85)

P.S. It's real lonesome here. Not like lonesome there, but *lonesome*.

I know what he means. About lonesome here, anyway. Where he is leaves an empty feeling. But out here—well, a person gets used to being alone. We learn to get along with ourselves pretty early and we're comfortable that way. But yonder where Son is—in a barracks overflowing with other folks, some of them yelling orders, and no place to go and just be quiet—well, I know he must be miserable a good deal of the time. Me now, I haven't been anywhere but here for fifty years, made my first and last trip down from New Mexico in the back of a wagon when I was only six years old. So I guess I shouldn't talk. I really don't know how it is to be someplace else a long way from home. All I know is how to be here. Up on a hill in a sweet breeze, not another sound for twenty miles, only the wind combing its fingers through the grass—now that's lonesome. But the good kind. Peaceful. The feel of a good pony under you, nothing but blue sky up above and nobody to talk to for the next few days— I guess some folks would call that lonesome. And they would be right in their own way—but we wouldn't be talking about the same thing. Being alone is no hardship in this country, it's our way of life. Maybe that's why we are such silent people. Also why we cut loose sometimes—or the young ones do.

I like to ride up that canyon with the big overhang, the one with all the Indian paintings on the walls. Some of them are half wiped out by smoke but others are as clear as if they had been put there yesterday. It gives you an eerie feeling, a story spelled out in figures, mostly red from the cinnabar, but black and yellow, too. I've looked at them for years, never could figure out what those Indians were trying to say. Just the same, I like to go up there. In a funny way it's like being among old friends.

The boys and I used to ride up there all the time, take a picnic lunch. I'd put Jared down on a blanket and Son would wander off on his lonesome. So I know that he knows what it means; he knew then. It was so quiet in that canyon . . . a deep, gentle kind of quiet that goes on, like it's been there always and will stay that way no matter what we do. I remember Jared lying on the blanket staring at the clouds or the dragonflies—whatever it was he saw, whatever a baby looks at all the time—and me just hugging my knees with happiness and listening to the call of that little wren. Sometimes I'd make up stories to go with the Indian writing. A few I'd keep to myself but others I'd tell Jared. He'd lie there staring at me, listening as if he believed I could teach him about the world. Or maybe make up a better one based on those Indian scribbles.

Pretty soon we'd hear some peculiar noises—sounds of an animal thrashing in the brush—and Son would reappear, his face tomato red and his boots peeled down to the lining. It was a constant battle to make him cool off before he ate. Soon as he was done, he was gone again, usually wading in the creek. Then I'd lie back and watch the clouds awhile, maybe have a little nap, Jared curled beside me breathing like a daisy. But as time went on and those boys grew, I used to dread waking up. Son got pretty good at catching things— first tadpoles, which weren't so bad, but I confess to getting jumpy when water snakes slid out of my thermos. I have never been squeamish but I'll tell you, in a country fairly crawling with rattlers and two young'uns to look after, well I wasn't exactly thrilled to pour out a snake along with my tea or water or whatever it was. Damn things. Naturally Jared took an interest in them, too, and all through those boys' childhood there was at least one bull snake curled up under somebody's bed and a collection of rattles drying on top of the dresser.

But lonesome we all knew. I reckon we cherish it down here, this country so big and so far from anywhere else. The men have it in their eyes—a kind of washed-out fading blue, like distance. Hunter had it more than most. Even looking at him over a bowl of mashed potatoes at Mrs. Foley's Boarding House in town, I perceived he had some special kind of wisdom. And I have never been proven wrong: him sitting on top of the corral fence having one last smoke of the day, just a silhouette against the sunset—you'd go up to him then and his eyes would be filled with gold and purple light. He would smile, maybe pat the rail beside him so that I would climb up, too. Slip his arm around my waist, say something like, "Mighty hot in that old kitchen, ain't it?" But it was his silence, big as a sunrise from the rim . . . and up there they say you can see for a hundred miles. I don't think he meant to keep everyone else out, it is just the nature of solitude.

But lonesome? Yes. High lonesome. We all have our share of that. And when I think of freedom it isn't flags that come to mind, it's hawks—hawks circling on the evening breeze.

Dear Son,

It is hard not knowing where you are, but wherever it is I hope you know that you are missed. Not to mention appreciated. None of us realized how much you did around here until we started trying to take up the slack. I guess you earned your keep all right. Jared and your daddy have been working so hard and this ranch is so big that I took pity on them. I shortened the stirrups on your saddle and went out to help. I was all set to take my own saddle but Hunter got that squint he gets and said, "Hell, that thing ain't no good for ropin' and ridin' the brush, you better take Son's." So I did. Not the fancy number you won in the rodeo, of course, the other one. I contend that it is not a saddle at all, but an instrument of torture—more about that when you get home. Snaking heifers out of the brush is nothing new for me, I went right at it. But cows are perverse. Lately they have taken to hiding in the most inaccessible canyons and act like they've never seen a horse and rider before in their lives. Salty as some of them are, maybe they haven't. Still, it's nice to be riding for a living once again. I used to do a lot of it before you and Jared came along. After that I was too busy trying to break and gentle you two. That buckskin of yours sure is feeling his oats—or his grass, I should say, since we finally had a good rain. I rode him only the other day and he sashayed sideways more often than he went straight. Jared was dying to ride him but I knew you wouldn't want that. Jared does have hard hands and I know you broke this colt special. He is a good pony. I get so tired I like to fall off but he is still rarin' to go. Mescalero is a good name for him.

Wherever you are, maybe you don't want to hear about horses and cows. But I've been sitting here for ten minutes trying to think of something else to say and I guess that's all I know to talk about. Hunter wants to know if they're feeding you enough. I told him nobody to date has ever fed you enough, you were born hungry and always got up from the table that way no matter what.

I'm sitting here at the kitchen table by the old kerosene lamp and wondering what you do with yourself? It's awfully quiet around here. I keep listening for your boots on the stairs, waiting to hear you scrape your chair back. I miss hearing you whistle up those ponies. Well, no need going on like this. Pretty soon I'll be making us all blue. The only way to say we miss you is to say it.

Write whenever you can.

Love from us all,
Mama

Yesterday we drove all the way into town just to see if there might be a letter and mail this one. No letter. Just bad news, papers full of it. Sometimes I can't help myself, I worry about that boy. Only twenty last December—seems like his life is just barely getting started. He and that frisky colt of his—both of them young and full of the devil.

But no letter. Seventy-six miles each way, twelve of that washboard and washout, with us on gas and tire rationing. We get some allowance, being in "agriculture," but it's not enough. That old pickup drinks gas like water. I had to laugh, though, Hunter standing there on the sidewalk scowling furiously at the coupons. "What the hell are these things for?" I tried to explain but it was the principle of the thing that he couldn't accept. He and the other cattlemen all gathered in the hotel coffee shop and I could tell they were busy cussing the government the whole time I was trying to exchange those coupons for the things we couldn't grow or make ourselves. It infuriates the men to accept anything like that. They think it smells of government meddling. I said, "Hon, look at it this way. It isn't folks like us who started this war or anything to do with it. The government did that. And there's bound to be shortages. I guess this is the only way they know to deal with it. Maybe they are tryin' to make it fair . . ."

Hunter frowned as only he can. He said (loud enough for everybody to hear), "The only thing for sure about the blankety-blank government is they got their head up their ass." After a minute, he added, "I hope they enjoy the view." And grumbled off in the direction of the feed store. "They know where they can put them goddamn coupons, too."

Later, on the drive home, I thought he had cooled down but I was wrong. He was fuming. He said, "You know what those lamebrains in Washington are trying to tell us to do? *Us,* mind you?" He waved a letter in the air. "Those S.O.B.'s think they can tell us how many cows we ought to run per acre. Per *acre!* Godalmighty! You'd think we was runnin' a dairy farm down here. Boy, what I'd give to get me one of them dudes out yonder in the catclaw for a day or two. Give him buttercups to eat . . . Shoot."

When we got back to the house and I had a chance to look at the letter I saw what he meant. The government wants meat for the War Effort and the boys overseas. Well, they could have had a lot more if they'd let us keep our own boy home. As it is, he is probably eating Spam and powdered eggs. When I had a chance to read the newspapers and magazines in that stack of mail, I commenced to get riled myself. Everywhere I looked—*Rosie the Riveter!* Women tearing down the factory doors to get at that steel plate and join the War Effort. Big articles on how noble it all is. In a pig's eye . . . Pictures of hefty females brandishing welding torches, ex-waitresses throwing wrenches around, Rosie herself (tits nearly busting her overalls) leading the parade. And down on the farm—healthy young heifers (human variety), holding little buckets of milk and baby lambs, heaving a few stems of wheat on the end of a pitchfork. Not one word about women out on the range, not a single syllable. I guess we aren't photogenic. We get dirty. And sweaty. Dust is somehow harder to sympathize with. Little spots of grease strategically placed get more attention. Makes me hoppin' mad, so I can see how Hunter feels. Here we are, two men, one of them only half-grown, one woman, and a thousand head of ornery cows to chase across two hundred of the roughest *sections* on earth. I suppose the picture of me doing my part for the War Effort would show a clean, pretty, cheerful woman shelling peas at her kitchen table while a cool breeze ruffles the curtains.

Not likely.

I spend very little time at the kitchen table. I'm too busy. At least once a day, the only thing between some wild-eyed steer and the dropping-off place is me. Just me, my rope, and a trusty pony. While all those girls are carrying their lambs around, I am over my head in mesquite, my rope wrapped around a tree, a bawling heifer on the far end and the cinch coming loose on my saddle.

Come to that, I've lost track of the pipe I've welded. Or how many times I've tied the pickup together with baling wire. While those waitresses are trading their coffee cups for screwdrivers, I'm out splitting stove wood so I can fix dinner. After dinner, Hunter and I've got to work on the windmill pump. In the morning we have the blacksmithing to take care of—horses wear out shoes faster than kids do. If I get a breather, I might do the laundry—which means cutting some more stove wood if I want hot water.

I guess I'm not very patriotic.

Only three of us down here now. Takes one-hundred-percent effort just to keep going.

Dear Mama and Daddy and Jay-Red,

Well, my guess about where we were going turned out to be right. I can't say where exactly but boy howdy it sure is *green!* Just like a big lawn all over. And the *sheep!* They look like they just this minute stepped out of a bathtub. I reckon they are the lawn mowers for all this here pretty grass. As for the people, I haven't seen many so far. The Army keeps us locked up like a bunch of wild animals. The few folks I've got a glimpse of seem a little skittish and they don't understand a single word I say even though we're both speaking the same language. At least, I *think* we are! I don't understand them too good, either. Course we just now got here so I reckon things are bound to improve. Thing is, this country is so *small!* The whole of it would fit inside Texas at least three times, I figure, and never even crowd the edges. I can't see how come they have made such a fuss over it all these years. Cause they do—make a fuss, I mean—a tremendous one. They take it all very serious what with the castles and kings and queens and even the policemen on horseback, good lord. "Pomp and circumstance" said the guy who sleeps in the bunk to my right. He's been to college so I guess he knows. But it is real pretty and I think I will like it here okay. Mighty damp, though.

And speaking of damp, the trip over here on that boat was *miserable,* let me tell you. Two weeks of unadulterated heaving, first the ocean and then us. I never thought I'd be willing to see so much food go to waste. Even now my innards feel like they've been wrung out and left to dry and the sight of a puddle makes me downright queasy. One of the jokers on the boat was from New England and I gather he has his own sailboat. Anyway he stood around very much at ease, superior you know, making remarks about all us sissies (that ain't exactly the word he used) getting seasick. When I could hold my head up, I invited him to come on down to the ranch and ride one of our bulls soon as the war is over. He looked kinda puzzled.

I don't know how long we will be here. The outfit keeps getting split up and rearranged like they can't make up their minds what to do with us. (Just between you and me I don't think these here generals and whatnot always know what they're doing.) Some of the guys have pulled out already. But they never let you know a damn thing, just stomp in here at all hours of the day and night, holler everybody up and us stampeding around in our underwear . . . war is a wonderful thing. Right now there are two guys from Oklahoma in my outfit and an Indian from Arizona who to my knowledge has never said one single word. There are lots of guys from the South, one fella with a tail. No kidding! Long, furry thing just like a pack rat. Come to think of it, he looks like one, too. Well, he wouldn't let them cut it off—caused a terrible ruckus from what I heard—so they make him wrap the darn thing around his waist. Damndest thing you ever saw. (You can add that one to your Ripley's Believe It Or Not collection, Jared. I saw it and it's true.)

The food here is beyond description—on the minus side so I won't even try. Boy, I sure could use some chile macho— some enchiladas, tacos . . . my mouth ends a ten day drouth just thinking about it. Me and you got a date, Jared, for when I get back. Some Saturday night we'll get slicked up and drive in to La Cocina and make fat, hairy hogs of ourselves, flat-out disgusting gluttons. How about it? As for the other things you (Jared) might be interested in—them things in skirts, you know? I'm sorry to report that I have seen damn few. They keep them all locked up in the castles—safe from us wild animals.

Well, I'm running out of things to say. Sure do miss y'all. Oh yeah, one other thing. These folks over here all drive on the wrong side of the road. It's no wonder they're confused.

Love,
Son

I am relieved to see that Son's spelling is not as bad as I thought it might be. He never was much of a one for school. Neither of my boys was. They are smart enough, they just didn't take to it. Probably if I'd had a daughter she would have followed in my footsteps more. For some reason girls always do better in school than boys. As for me, I loved school from the very beginning. When I was a youngster the world looked flat—empty and wide and arid all at the same time. I guess that is a funny thing for a child to think but somehow I didn't see any peaks or high places in my life. Education changed all that. I learned that there was a lot more to life than I had ever dreamed. In fact, school taught me to dream, opened all kinds of windows in my imagination. So I went as often and for as long as I could, even put myself through State Normal. Then one day my student days were over, and it was my turn to teach. There was a little ceremony—all of us girls proud, high-colored and giggly and two or three pale young men with limp hair and white hands. Somebody shoved a certificate in my hand and ordered me to go forth. I felt like Moses in the wilderness. And believe me, in those days, it was a wilderness. Children were scarcer than cows by a longshot and a whole lot farther apart. The only position I could locate was down on the River alongside the Mexican Border. My family had a fit! You'd have thought I was going off to do missionary work among the headhunters. Well, I told them I was a big girl (I was all of eighteen) and when Papa finally ran down, I packed a six-gun in my purse and set out full of hope and glory. I was assigned a room in the abandoned jail (not an auspicious start, I'm afraid), equipped with several benches, a bucket and dipper for drinking water, a box of chalk, and instructions to teach anybody who wandered in. I scrounged up a battered old desk, settled my six-gun in a drawer, and declared myself open for business. I have never to this day regretted it.

My first customer was a cowboy whose brain had been pickled by tequila long before he reached the age of twenty-five. I don't mind admitting I became a bit nervous when he appeared. He hadn't had a shave or a bath in weeks and one of his front teeth was missing—kicked out by a mule, he said. I figured he was a troublemaker. But as it turned out he was dead serious: he wanted to learn to read. Well, I was stumped. Normal school had never prepared me for anything like this. But since I didn't have any pupils anyway, I told him, "You get yourself cleaned up and sober. Then you come on back. If you can bring five children with you I'll teach you how to read."

Bleary-eyed and swaying, that boy looked like he might hit the floor any minute. I cracked open the drawer on my six-gun and busied myself about my desk. Presently he staggered out. I called after him, "And while you're at it, get ahold of two flags, one American and one Texas." But I figured I'd seen the last of him. And during the next few days I had a lot to think about, anyway. I began to wonder what in the world I was doing down there. It was even wilder than I had imagined—Pancho Villa whooping and hollering, setting off fireworks. The walls of the former jail were pitted with bullet holes and at least once a day I had to hit the floor to keep from being ventilated. "How am I ever to teach children in this situation?" I asked myself. "No wonder they won't come to school, they're afraid to come out of the house."

I had no idea what to do. But the problem was solved by the least likely candidate. One morning I arrived at my classroom to find the cowboy (polished, clean-shaven, and sober) plus five little Mexican children waiting for me at the door. We all looked at each other for a minute. The cowboy took off his hat. "I'll get them flags tomorrow, ma'am," he said. And he did.

What a maverick classroom that turned out to be! First of all, the cowboy—who called himself Clete Rising Star and whose only absences were as a result of disagreements with the law—and finally, by twos and threes, a total of twenty children of various ages. Fourteen of them couldn't speak a word of English and nine of these waded over to this side of the River every morning and back *al otro lado* every night. Just as clean and neat as they could be. And smart! One of the boys, a goatherd by the name of Pedro Nachez—I guess he must have been around twelve years old, none of them knew their ages and it tickled them that I thought it was so important—anyway, Pedro learned his letters in one week. By the end of the month he had read the entire primer and was pestering me for something else to read. Well, there wasn't anything. I didn't exactly have a library down there. So I had him translate the primer into Spanish. His writing was better than mine anyhow, so I had him print the whole thing out so the other children could learn it in both languages. We must have been the first bilingual school in Texas.

The other six children were Anglos. Two of them belonged to the owner of the mercantile store—rawboned, redheaded boys, boneheaded as well, I am sorry to say—and the other four to a Baptist preacher who lived downstream—three girls and a boy. Those Christian children—the Baptists, I mean—I used to feel sorrier for them than anybody. Pale, puny little things, short on energy and wits, as if maybe their daddy had used up all his strength for the Lord before he got around to making them. I guess that isn't a very charitable thing to say . . .

Those little Mexican shavers though, they did keep me busy! Smartest kids I ever taught. And draw? Those kids could make a picture out of anything. Loved to do it. And I never had to ask what it was, either. What they drew was not only recognizable but alive with feeling as well—roosters chasing hens, horses (naturally *vaqueros* and bandits were their heroes), goats standing on their hind legs and nibbling the last leaves off a tree, even their mothers grinding corn. I still have a picture drawn by a little girl named Annunciación. It portrays a burro with a load of firewood and every detail is perfect. By comparison, the pictures the little Baptist children made were careful pastel houses with a wisp of smoke creeping out of the chimney, flowers lining the front walk, and somebody peeking out the window. I asked one of the little girls who it was in the window. "Who is that lady?" I said.

"Jesus," she quavered, and began to cry.

I made a vow never to ask again.

Those kids and I had a high old time. And Clete, when he could make it. I loved living down there. The evenings were so soft. Warm and sweet-smelling, they eased slowly into night. And the old Rio Grande, lazy and tranquil, pretty with the sunset colors spread over it. I used to take a book and go sit under the carizzo cane by the water, though I did more dreaming than reading. Before long I got to where I even liked the smell of mud and to this day I can't eat a catfish without getting a little twinge of longing for the River and those long, glorious evenings. Rivers are like time—all the poets say so and it's true. I learned a lot about time from that River and from the Mexicans. There is a certain time meant only for human beings and it's got nothing to do with clocks.

But like I said, there was often a sort of international Fourth of July going on. Every Saturday night there was a shoot-out. Either the Mexicans on that side or the Mexicans on this side mixed up with a bunch of wild-eyed hellions with that Gone-To-Texas look. I had taken a room up over the mercantile store and many's the time I had to lie flat on the floor in order to read. I can still see the pattern of that linoleum. And in my mind certain of Emerson's *Essays* are forever punctuated by gunfire.

There wasn't much to that town in those days. (There still isn't, for that matter.) Just Rosa's Cantina, the Mercantile and Post Office combined, and the new jail and the old jail that had been converted into my school. After about a year my folks insisted that I return to civilization and take up teaching in a community which could lay claim to the name—someplace where I didn't have to keep a loaded gun in my skirt pocket or in the desk drawer. So I came up to town and took a room at Mrs. Foley's Boarding House—which is where and how I met Hunter. Both my boys went to the same school where I had taught. Which is why I am glad to see that Son's spelling is no worse than it is. Of course, I didn't teach him. I had gotten married and moved down to the ranch long before that.

We were greatly relieved to get Son's letter. Jared packed it off up to the boys' room and I guess he must have read it to death because the next time I saw it it resembled something that had been through my wringer. I said, "Jared, you be careful you don't lose that letter. I want to get the address off it."

His chin stuck out. "I done wrote it down already."

My younger son's English isn't all it should be. I don't know why unless he takes after his father. I don't mean that unkindly. Hunter never had any schooling beyond the fifth grade and he always "spoke plain" as he calls it. And since it gets the job done (often more effectively than my schoolmarm grammar), I never let it bother me. Hunter used to claim I would contaminate his language, talking the way I did. But now I see it is the other way around. Jared is the living proof.

Something is eating him, Jared I mean. He used to tease and whistle all the time, now mostly he is silent. Fidgety. Stares off into space and then explodes at the slightest thing. I suppose it has to do with Son being gone. Jared worships that boy and I don't know that Son always deserves it. He does have a way with him though—Son. Always been the kind of person others look up to and admire. And I know Jared misses him terribly. Lost without him. He was always so proud to be seen with Son—and Son so tolerant and magnanimous, using Jared to enhance himself. There were times I wanted to hit him for it. I never did, of course, never said a word, but not because it didn't cross my mind. I dreaded confronting those hurt and puzzled eyes: "Who me? What did I do?" And Jared muscling up behind, fierce and ready to die in his brother's defense. Both of them turning on me, bonded together even more. The contrast always worked for Son, him being the tall one—dark, with hazel eyes like mine and those lazy good looks he got from God-knows-where. Not me, certainly. Nor Hunter, either. Jared, on the other hand, has always been small. Wiry. Sandy. Light eyes, light hair, freckly skin. Son used to call him the runt of the litter and I did whip him for that. Now I think he calls him something worse, but not within my hearing. Still, I worry. Jared is way behind for somebody fifteen years old. Son had his growth and even a downy beard by then. Jared looks to be a long way from either. Judging by the size of his feet, however, I have hopes. Maybe he is a late developer. I wish he'd get on with it—soon. I know it hurts him. He sure is a scrapper, though. The last person who called him "shrimp" is still looking down a bent nose. Actually it might be best to have Son gone for a while but right now it is hard. Jared seems to have some far-fetched notion that his brother is never coming back. I don't know where he got such a silly idea but he is stuck on it. Maybe it's his way of saying things will never be the same.

Children . . . I don't know. I never really planned on them. But here they are—two people I wouldn't have met otherwise. And sometimes they are strangers, total mysteries. Other times I'd just as soon *not* have met them. Funny when you think about it, how folks end up with each other. No rhyme or reason that I can see. I thank God at least once a day that there are only the two of them. Those poor Mexican women—nine, ten, thirteen. I shudder to think. And I am equally grateful there are no girls. Girls would be the death of me. I know that's a terrible thing for a woman to say but I mean it just the same. I wouldn't know the first thing about rearing girls— all that reproductive business, periods and trappings, then dating— no thank you. Sons I think I can deal with. Cows, horses, chickens even—but not girls. Come to think of it, that's probably Jared's trouble right there. Girls and grieving for Son. Maybe Hunter will have a talk with him. I suspect that Jared smokes anyway, so they might just as well sit down and have a cigarette together, just the two of them. Yes. I'll speak to Hunter, maybe Hunter will have a talk with him.

Dear Son,

You remember that place alongside the highway where all your life you've begged to stop because you said the view was so pretty? Up yonder just as the road tops out onto the high-lands, that meadow where you always said the hills run away blue? Well, it sure is pretty now. Green as it can be with all the rain we've been having. Maybe not as green as where you are but mighty plush for around here. Grass high and wavy and a million wild flowers—paintbrush, evening primrose, lots of those little cone flowers. And of course a goodly crop of weeds. I have always held that cattle prefer the weeds. You can offer them good hay and if there are any weeds within a mile those cows will eat the weeds. So just now they have a complete menu. They are happy and it shows—sleek and fat, calves kicking up their heels and full of mischief, looking at you with those innocent and soulful eyes. I figure we'll have our hands full in the fall. The colts, too. Wild as the wind. Some good little horses from what I can see, sassy, flipping their tails. They can say what they want about Texas being the jumping-off place. Sometimes I couldn't agree more, but right now it is a pretty place.

I am surprised that you are still in "greenland" and I thank my stars that you're not farther to the east. Hell's a-poppin' over there from what I hear. Folks ask me how you're doing and I am almost afraid to answer. Superstitious, I guess. By the way, watch out for those girls in the castles. According to history, some of them were pretty wild.

Son, do you think you could find time to write Jared a letter? I'll even relinquish one of mine, much as I hate to. But he misses you a lot and I think it would mean a great deal to him if he could hear from you himself. He read your last letter over so many times it looked like a rag.

Two wetbacks came to the house the other night. Actually the dogs set up such a ruckus it scared them and they climbed up in one of the trees. Your daddy went out to see, calmed the dogs down, and here came two men creeping out of the dark. I dished up all I had left over from supper, which was a fair amount for a change, and they squatted down on their heels with your daddy out there for quite a spell, smoking and talking. Hunter asked them how things were in Mexico and they shook their heads. *Malo. Muy malo,* they said. Seems the chief honcho, the *jefe,* forces the people to turn all their livestock over to the government. Then the government (with Señor Jefe getting his cut, no doubt) turns around and sells the animals to the highest bidder, usually Germany. As you know, Mexican beef never has been worth a darn. But isn't that just like Mexico? Those people down there are starving, you and I know how it is with them. Hunter offered these men work but they were set on going to Los Angeles. They think they can find jobs out there in the factories. Mexicans have always imagined that Los Angeles is heaven on earth. And they've got relatives out there! I expect there's work to be had, but I don't know how good their chances are of getting there. Guards on all the trains now, and nobody gives a hitchhiker a ride unless he is in uniform. Nobody is going to give a Mexican a ride anyway. As for us, I guess we can expect to lose a few extra dogies. Since they have a tendency to wander across the River even in the best of times, I guess a few more won't matter.

Well, they say there'll always be an _____. (Where you are.) I hope they are right, since you're in it. *Adios*.

Love from us all,
Mama

I suggested to Jared that he write to his brother but he flared up like a kitchen match and stomped off to the barn. These days that boy is a mixture of dynamite and powder. Later I had to go up to their room to see how many dirty clothes I could gather and I noticed that Jared's wastebasket was clear to the top with balled-up sheets of notebook paper. Well, I knew he hadn't been studying. Those pages were dozens of false starts, letters he had begun to Son and never been able to finish.

This morning, as I was enjoying a few moments of that rare commodity, tranquillity, Hunter clomped up on the porch and into the kitchen banging the screen door behind him. I had been watching him through the window and I was tickled, although I didn't dare let him see it. He and one of his prize bulls had been doing the two-step all around the corral. Now, my husband doesn't normally

dance with the livestock, so even without the music to go along
with it, this was high entertainment. Of course I knew the reason—
the bull had a wire cut on his rump and Hunter wanted to get a
look at it. Trouble was, they didn't see eye to eye. Or rather, they *did*
see eye to eye but that was the problem. Every time Hunter would
maneuver down the flank and get in position for viewing, the bull's
natural modesty took over and he'd sashay right back around one
hundred and eighty degrees and there they'd be again. The bull
wasn't ornery—in fact, we had even named him Ferdinand after the
one who sat around all day eating daisies—so I wasn't worried about
my husband. What I did worry about was my own peace and quiet
the minute I heard his boot heels hit the porch.

"What do you want me to do?" I asked.

Hunter looked surprised, or pretended to. (Men never come inside the house during the daytime except to eat, or unless something
is terribly wrong, or unless they want you to do something for
them.) In less than a minute, I was standing in front of old Ferdinand and I'll never forget the innocent look behind those long white
eyelashes.

I was there to provide a distraction and I did. Just as Hunter
tiptoed toward the tail, that "gentle" bull commenced an all-out
charge at me. I will never know whether Hunter touched a sore
spot or what (theory wasn't foremost in my mind just then), but all
of a sudden that bull had his head low, bearing down full tilt, and
I was hightailing it for the fence barely out of reach of his horns. I
don't know what transpired next except that one minute I was going mighty fast and the next I was flat out in the dirt. I remember
the *sound* of that bull coming—like a freight train on the downhill
slope with all the cars loaded. Lucky for me, Hunter's rope snaked
out about then and pulled the bull up short. That critter piled dust,
then turned and took after Hunter in a red-eyed rage. Lord, I
never saw my husband move so fast! He shinnied up that gate like
greased lightning. Meanwhile, I picked myself up out of the dirt
and crawled up the corral fence. For a while all you could hear was
the sound of breathing—mine, Hunter's, and the bull's. Presently
Hunter climbed down and came around the outside to where I was

perched, shaking off bits of straw and dried manure. They say that cowboys and ranchers are men of few words and those not always the most chivalrous. I can testify to that. My husband looked at me, covered with dirt like I was, and said, "Why the Sam Hill did you fall down?"

Dear Jared,

Hey, old pal, how ya doin? You wouldn't believe where I am now. Don't ask me how I got here or why because I haven't got the faintest idea. Don't ask the Army either. Neither one of us knows. But in any case I seem to be moving in the opposite direction from the real rodeo—which is okay by me—but at this rate I'll be bivwhacked at the North Pole before long and doing battle with the penguins or maybe hunting polar bears. Could be I'll get an audience with Santa Claus. Is there anything you'd like? Meantime I am lucky to be here according to local legend put out by those folks who haven't perished in the godawful climate. The only reason I can figure for them sending me here is on account of I know so much about horses. There is some kind of cavalry regiment up here, and I guess they must have sent all the officers over to be cannon fodder or something because they forgot to leave anybody at home to train these guys to ride. That's where I come in. Which I would rather not as they are the worst bunch of greenhorns I ever laid eyes on—the kind who climb on a horse backwards and say giddy-up to the tail. I can't see it myself, a cavalry detachment, I mean. Much as I love horses. What are they going to do against tanks and airplanes? It doesn't make sense but I've learned you don't ask stupid questions in the Army.

I keep myself awake nights laughing, though. Picturing these guys riding a fast trot in those skirts they wear. It could be *uncomfortable,* if you know what I mean. Not to mention chilly. They all wear these little short skirts—just like in all the pictures—and all kinds of other stuff besides. Long socks and spats and drum major hats that would throw a herd of cactus into a panic. Believe me, they get a lot of mileage out of them skirts, swishing them along like they do. But—and I tell you the truth, little brother—there ain't nothin' ladylike about these guys. No sir. Couple of smart asses in my outfit made some remarks to that effect (called them pansies) and barely lived to regret it. These here *ladies* eat a lot of oatmeal.

And the *racket* they make! Godawfullest noise you ever heard in your life. Wish I could send you some of it—but I wouldn't do that to my worst enemy. They puff up and blow on some kind of pipe thing stuck in a sheep's bladder or some such and it wheezes and wails something awful. They love it of course, stirs them up. I think it sounds more like a train whistle mating with a coyote.

We spend most of our time marching behind this apparition—them swishing and wheezing and howling all over the damn countryside. Armies seem to take marching very seriously, a logic which escapes me. Then the rest of the time we are frantic with the spit and polish—belt buckles, buttons, boots, any damn thing that will catch the light, which there ain't much of up here anyhow. I hate the marching business. It's nice to get out in the fresh air, but the minute we start it commences to drizzle. Never an outright honest rain. Description of the weather—nine months of rain and three months of damn bad weather. Besides that, I am not used to spending so much time on my *feet!* It is downright degrading.

Meanwhile, back at the cavalry, I am still trying to work out this little patch of a thing they call a saddle. (See enclosed snapshot.) Now ain't that a sight? Don't show it to my horse, he'd die laughing. Did you ever think you'd see your own brother sitting on a thing like that? Not even *blushing?* Believe me, Red, I *was* blushing when they took that picture. There I sit before God and everybody, both me and the horse feeling silly as all get out. I don't know what war is all about but somehow I don't think this is it.

Tell Daddy that I get plenty to eat, it's just that they boil the pee out of it. Tastes and looks like wet cardboard. Have you got that little black pony broke yet? I sure would hate to miss out on *your* rodeo! Wait till I get home and he'll be that much bigger and meaner. Pitch you sky-high! Now that's a sight I wouldn't want to miss. Not on your life. Ha! Ha!

Well, I got to go now. Love to Mama and Daddy. You, too.

Your Blushing Big Brother

Looks like summer is upon us. The mornings are as fresh and cool as spring water and the evenings soft and thick as blue talcum. In between, the days stretch long and hot. The green is beginning to fade out, grass burning up—but at least we got a good crop of it this year, lots of crowfoot which is the best. If only we could get a little more rain it would be perfect. I love this time of year, hot as it is, and can usually find some excuse to ride out early of a morning to make the most of it. And it is fine then—meadowlarks singing, a mockingbird not far off, and the sky so big and blue. Most people would be surprised to learn that Texas is beautiful, but it is. You just have to know where to look. Take the Spanish Daggers, for instance; this spring they were spectacular. Mile after mile of tall creamy blooms—no wonder the Mexicans call them the "candles of God." Hunter and I rode out one night when the moon was full . . . All those flowers . . . it was a sight I'll never forget. And the perfume . . . the air was as heavy as satin.

These long afternoons I like to find me a cool spot and shade up just like the animals do. Sometimes you have to set all the work and worry aside and make time for something else. Clouds, for instance. I love to lie out there steeping myself in the heat and watch the clouds. Summer thunderheads . . . I guess they're my favorite things of all. Slow, majestic, and the purest white, I see them sailing across the sky like Spanish galleons. Some afternoons they build to towering heights, the hulls turn purple with promised rain, and the sails boil and spark with lightning. By evening, those same clouds have changed into huge scoops of ice cream—peach, raspberry, lemon, vanilla, and grape.

I guess I picked the wrong line of work for a daydreamer. And I do wish I had more time to read. When I was a girl I read everything I could get my hands on. I remember the early ones best: *Ramona,* that was a favorite. And *Black Beauty. Girl of the Limberlost*—that was a strange one. I liked Zane Grey, too, but I had to sneak around with his books. They weren't "fittin'" for a young lady. I remember how perplexed and thrilled I was by his tantalizing hints of sex.

Now though, when I try to read, it seems like my mind has gone flat. Empty of everything but wind and sun. It bothers me some, I'll admit that. I used to have such wide horizons. I still do—but I live on them and my thoughts get dry and stretched. The realities of rock and pain and dust have overcome my dreams. This world can be so big and at the same time so small. All I read now are the newspapers, magazines, livestock reports. Books are sly with me anymore. The page is there with all the words on it but my mind just slips off as if the page were made of glass. I might as well try to read the sky.

These days, however, the sky is not always empty. Often we see airplane formations, silver wedges like geese migrating west, but so high and cold. Living way out here, we hear them long before we see them. At night they wake us up, big engines throbbing through the darkness. There is something unsettling, even sinister about them, some mindless force going on about the business of war.

One time some planes came over just as I had topped out. I had ridden up Aquila Peak by myself as I had some thinking to do. I had saddled up while it was still dark so it was very early. Those planes came right out of the sun. At first I couldn't see them, then there they were all pink and gold and shining. I hooked one leg over the saddle horn and watched until they were out of sight. When they were gone they left no mark behind, no message, nothing to say they had been there. Yet somehow the sky was changed. I sat there for a long time. After a while I noticed something else moving in that clear, early light. One of my hawks. It circled, looked me and the horse over, then sailed slowly off. One small living thing in all that space—fierce, beautiful and belonging, never stirring a feather, letting the wind do all the work.

But life isn't easy for any of us, not hawks or other wild things or people either. Last week for instance, Jared was off riding fence way up in the Oven Mountains when he happened to spook a bunch of yearlings we had somehow missed last fall. They were as naked as the day they were born, not a single mark on any of them. Hunter decided we better bring them on in and tend to them before they got any bigger. So we all three saddled up long before sunrise and set out to catch the varmints. Naturally they were hiding out in the wildest possible country. Saltiest bunch I ever saw. We chased those calves around all morning, scrambling up one side of a canyon and sliding down the other. That day I wished I'd had chaps to wear all over. By the time that brush was through with me, my shirt was in shreds and underneath I looked like raw hamburger. And hot! Not one breath of wind back in there, heat bouncing off every available surface. Oven mountains, all right.

About two o'clock we finally bunched those rascals up and headed home. Naturally that wasn't simple, either. Every few minutes one of them would hightail it for the boondocks. Whoever was riding that side got to go along, too, getting tireder and thirstier by the minute until pure brutality or natural intervention in the form of cliffs or drop-offs enabled us to turn the little critters. Normally I don't take offense at animals, but this was the orneriest swarm of hellers I ever tried to corral.

Finally, along about sundown, we rode into headquarters and, after a few false starts during which they bulged at the gate and all but exploded over the sides, we got the lot of them into the big pen. Once they were in, they spent a quiet night, too pooped out to do anything else. We scraped the dirt off ourselves, ate a silent supper, and fell into bed.

First thing next morning we were out considering the situation, leaning our arms on the top rail of the fence while the sun made long, spindly black shadows out of everything, including us. As it climbed higher, that sun sucked up the shadows like water through a straw.

Hunter sighed. "I reckon maybe we ought to take these devils only one at a time."

The calves milled around and looked at him out of the whites of their eyes.

Jared agreed, "I don't much think we could keep more'n one of 'em down."

I nodded, but without enthusiasm. From the looks of those wild, rangy animals I doubted that we could even *get* any of them down, much less keep them there.

We started in, Hunter doing the heeling from his big gray roan, Raton, and Jared and I throwing and tying. One of us would grab the calf's tail while the other worked one hand down the rope, then we both gave a mighty heave and with any luck got the calf down. It took perfect timing and sometimes, despite all our years of practice, things went wrong.

I guess we had done about a dozen calves that morning when I got careless or absent-minded. I let my hand get in the way and that sucker let me have it with the full force of his hind foot. Jared and I both heard the bone go *crack!* and before my son could even get the S.O.B. tied down, my hand was the size of a July melon. The pain almost made me faint but I avoided the anxious look in Jared's eyes and focused instead on a spot near the toe of my boot. We both knew I had to keep going; there wasn't going to be anybody else volunteering for the job.

The next calf was a heifer the size of two hogs. I could tell she was going to be a tough one so I let Jared tail her over. Soon as I got a good grip on the rope, she suddenly slacked off, sending me head over heels, and I ended up flat on my fanny under Raton's belly. The sight of a sweaty roping cinch was all I was going to get of Heaven, apparently, because with any other horse I would have been stomped into the ground. Raton, thank goodness, calm and savvy as he was, just eased himself on around so he could get a better look at what was going on in his noontime shade. Then he put his nose down, blew, and waited for instructions from the boss up top.

By this time, I had had enough. I got up and headed for the gate. Halfway there, I thought of Son. There he was, overseas and maybe eating bullets, and here I was safe at home whining about a broken hand and a bruised backside. I looked back at Hunter and Jared standing there so quiet, just the two of them, covered with dust and sweat, and when the next calf stretched back at the end of the rope, I was right there sitting on top while Jared did the tying. Pretty soon I forgot all about my hand: my jaw ached too much from gritting my teeth.

While we had them down, we gave those critters the works: Jared wielded the branding iron, Hunter took care of ear-marking and castrating, and I vaccinated against blackleg. It took a combined effort and naturally the calves were not happy, especially the young steers who had just been deprived of their manhood, so to speak. At that point they would charge anything and, more often than not, we had to light out for the fence. Up and down like that all day— hot, bloody, endless hours in the dust. By the time it was over, we were all about done for, the calves too, dejected as they usually are after being cut.

Dear Son,

That snapshot of you surely is a pinup. Which is exactly what we have done with it—pinned it up over the mirror by the back door. Now every time we comb our hair or put on our hats to go out we have to look at you. Your daddy's face when he saw you perched on that pancake saddle was another picture worth having.

Are they treating you all right, Son? I hope so. Down here we hardly know there's a war on. Seems like most of it is happening to somebody else and going on far away. Nothing changes much out here, we go on like we always have. But we do think about you a lot—kinda like a hole in a tooth. At least you know you're on our minds.

We try to keep in touch with the rest of the world but it isn't easy. Last week, for instance, we drove into town. It was a real extravagance because it is harder to get rubber than it is to get gas. And you know how the tires on that old pickup are. I said to Hunter, "Why don't we take the car?" But he was in one of his stubborn moods (you know them, too) so we went all crammed together in the cab. Our purpose for going was to see the newsreel at the theater. We went early so we could have some supper and visit with the folks in town. As it turned out, we learned more from them than we did from the newsreel anyway.

Everybody is suffering some. There are shortages of almost everything, but the hardest one for us to fathom is *beef*. Can you believe it? I can see how they might have trouble in New York or Detroit—but in *Texas?* There must be more cows than there are people in this state! And of course we have been ordered not to slaughter our own. You know we won't . . .

Around home the only one in pain is your daddy. All his favorite things are either nonexistent or in short supply: coffee, sugar, and cigarettes. Whiskey I understand is also hard to come by. Over in the oil fields they are raising sand about that—but you can imagine who they are hiring what with the draft and all. Those boys don't know a derrick from a drill bit. Every Saturday night they have a regular brawl. Any whiskey to be had, they fight over it. If there isn't any, they fight over the loss.

One other item you might be interested in. The telephone company has invented an air raid siren which can be heard for ten square miles. It is so loud it shatters the eardrums of anybody fool enough to be standing within a hundred feet of the thing. Since nobody wants one (the cities and towns don't want a thing to do with it; they insist they would suffer more damage from the noise than from enemy aircraft) the Army is considering employing it as a combat weapon. Between your mounted police and lethal weapons such as this one we ought to be able to win the war in no time. All you have to do is mount up your greenhorns and we'll turn on the siren.

I guess that is enough of my drivel for now.

Love from us all,
Mama

Dear Son,

More thrilling news from the Home Front. This darned V-Mail stationery doesn't give a person room to say much. I felt short-changed on that last letter so decided to send another one. Besides, we are having a good old summer thunderstorm and I have a legitimate excuse to stay in the house and sit. Looks to be a good, long rain, all the draws are running full already.

Now for some of my observations:

I believe this war is going to go down in history, all right, but sometimes I wonder for what reasons. For instance:

Just the other day Winston Churchill conferred with our President while wearing only his birthday suit . . . insisted he had nothing to conceal from the President of the United States. I guess protocol or a desire to show similar candor demanded that FDR comply, so there they were, pink as two scrubbed whales, Roosevelt with that long cigarette holder and Winnie holding out his cigar. This is how the policies of state are made. I do hope they were careful with those hot ashes.

Meanwhile everybody else is hysterical about war bonds and victory gardens. Frankly, I can't see either one. Everybody knows how the government manages money. And then there are these blurry photos of folks in places like Portland, Oregon, planting potatoes in the spaces between the sidewalk and the street, poking around in the mud, their faces as long as their underwear. The accompanying article goes on to explain that citizens are forbidden to grow corn because enemy agents might be able to hide in it. Try telling that to these Mexicans down here on the River! They'd look at you like you were *loco*.

As for victory gardens, I have had mine for darn near forty years and have yet to win a battle. The weeds have always won my war—as you know since you had to do a good deal of hoeing and complained every inch of the way. The watering defeats me, too. Until this rain, anyway. Those onions are going to be hot as Hades.

There's another drive on for scrap metal. Apparently anything will do. I have seen pictures of children sacrificing their tricycles . . . which I believe is going too far. But then children love to be martyrs . . . for about five minutes. Next thing you know, old folks will be tossing in their wheelchairs and spectacles. All we can contribute is some old barb wire, that broken windmill, and a pile of worn-out horseshoes. And speaking of horseshoes, I hear they auctioned off a set belonging to Man o' War the other day. Along with a pair of Betty Grable's stockings. I defy you to think about that.

Anyway, I guess that is enough of my inspiring news. I'm sure it will give you great confidence in your country. The real reason I carry on this way is to make light of that which is heavy to bear. Also to put off for a while what I can't any longer—the bad news. Your high school friend, Jack Hazlip, has been reported killed in action. The first one for our area. He was in the Marines, serving in the Japanese theater. We are all so saddened to learn of his death. I didn't want to tell you but felt I had to. I know Jack was a special friend. Thank the Lord everyone else seems to be all right, including and most importantly you.

Love from us all,
Mama

Dear Jared,

You are out of your cotton picking mind. I don't care what the posters say, there ain't *no* glamor to Army life and that is straight from the horse's mouth. So don't you give another thought to any wild idea of lying about your age and enlisting.

Besides, you know very well that Mama and Daddy need you right there. They couldn't get along without you. You will do all of us a favor (including yourself) by just staying put and doing what you know how to do best. Seriously.

I haven't said much about Army life but I can tell you it's nothing I would *recommend* to anybody, certainly not my own brother and most certainly not on a volunteer basis. Anybody who *joined* the Army would be a pitiful case and the best thing would be to put him out of his misery. So don't you go believing in them slogans. They tell you it is exciting and challenging, the opportunity for travel and all that—like hell. Tiresome and tedious is what it is. Most of your traveling is done to the latrine trying to digest the nails and old socks your buddies in the kitchen have mixed in with the mashed potatoes. Besides cooking, the two things the Army is best at are confusion and humiliation. They deserve a medal for either one. This ain't no glory machine, Jared, it's just plain mechanical failure, a broke down tank maybe or a truck convoy mired in the mud. There is plenty of flag waving but it is all done at the top, at the head of the column. Guys like me and you are more likely to be stuck in the tire treads licking up mud.

I respect your sense of duty. But the Army does something to a man. I know I sure wasn't ready for all this and I doubt you are, either. You better think on it awhile, little brother. Like I say, you're doing more good where you're at.

The country around here is real pretty, rolling hills and streams and lakes everywhere. They call the lakes *locks*—with a gargle on the end. Beats me. Colors are kind of misted over—green, lavender, gray and blue. Not like at home where it's either a blind-dazzle or all washed-out and no in-between. Well, this here's the in-between. Real soft. I go out in the country whenever I can. The other guys go into one of the little towns around here and drink themselves senseless. (It is no wonder we have a bad reputation.) I went along a couple of times and all I saw was the less desirable side of human nature, something I figure the Army has taught me enough about already. So I just go for long walks on my days off. (*Walks?* I can hear you sputtering from here. Yep, that's right. They won't let me take any of the horses off the base so it's either my own two feet or a bicycle. I figure my feet are more reliable. Did you ever hear of any self-respecting cowboy riding a *bicycle?*) At first I felt pretty silly. But over here everybody walks, so I am getting used to it and I really enjoy it. It is very peaceful and quiet out in the countryside—the only peace and quiet I ever hear, if that makes sense. Some days I just go and sit under a tree or lie back in some field and watch the daisies waving against the sky.

The people here are friendly and like to stop and talk just the same as country folks everywhere. They have a sweet way of talking but sometimes we have trouble understanding each other. They have a good sense of humor, too, I'll say that for them! And as for hospitality, well I know it is some kind of blasphemy, but I can no longer say for certain that Texas invented it. These people here have been mighty nice to me. They are forever begging me to come in and have a cup of tea. (*I hate tea.* But good manners work both ways, as I believe your mama and mine is fond of saying.) Last week I went farther than I ordinarily do and ended up having supper with a sheep farmer up in the hills. He spied me walking along and hollered at me to come on in and have the everlasting cup of tea. I went, mainly because I didn't know how not to. He was an elderly guy, white hair and all, but with them rosy cheeks they all have, a sturdy, happy kind of man. Just him and his wife—they said their barns was all growed up and gone. I didn't know what the hell they were talking about. I looked around fully expecting the worst. I mean, who needs barns up and charging around the countryside? Turned out they meant their kids. "Bairns," they call them. Lord. Coulda fooled me. How they did laugh! She had to wipe her eyes on her apron before we was done. I had a good laugh myself, once I understood the situation.

From the barns we went on to the cow, which they pronounce so that it rhymes with "moo." I said I guessed there was something to be said for naming things by how they sound but I'd hate to have to refer to a pig or a burro working on that assumption. We laughed some more, then they had me sit down by the hearth and we all had "tea." I reckon they must have figured out that I didn't care much for the national brew because they gave me about a quart of the coldest, sweetest milk you ever tasted in your life. Then we had eggs—yes, *eggs*. Real ones. Boiled. And some kind of bread filled with jelly and running over with fresh butter. Jared, I made a hog of myself. I could barely move by the time I finished and they kept pressing me to have more, but it was getting late by then (they have the longest evenings up here—the daylight lasts much later than at home) so I told them I better be going. Before I left, I asked them if that was "tea," what on earth were they going to do about supper? They didn't quite understand but their eyes twinkled so I reckon they took it as a compliment. As for me, I waddled back to the base.

I've been out to see them several times since. I can get some things here at the base which they would otherwise have to go without, so I guess I pay for my "tea." We, the old man, whose name is Angus McGregor (his wife is called Mary), and I, talk about all sorts of things but mostly livestock and farming. He raises sheep, maybe a hundred head, but he doesn't own his land, rents it from some lord or other. I said we had gotten rid of that kind of thing a long time ago. Old Angus, he sucked his pipe for a spell. "Aye, maybe," he finally conceded. But I don't think he was convinced. He flat refuses to believe me when I tell him the size of our ranch. "Och, Sonny!" he says. "Then you're no a bonnet laird!" I don't know what the heck he means, but I think it has something to do with the size of the hats they wear. Later he took me over to a neighbor's place and showed me the cows they raise there. Angus, they call them. Black Angus. I asked him if they were named after him and he had a good chuckle over that. Prettiest cows I ever laid eyes on, heavy and low to the ground—plumb loaded with prime rib.

And they even seem to have a little sense. I asked Angus how he felt about sheep in that respect—being so *stupid,* you know. I said I thought sheep were the dumbest things under the sun. Well, old Angus, you don't get ahead of him. He lit up his pipe, taking a good long time at it, then he peered up at me from under those bushy eyebrows (they are built that way to keep out the mist). I can't translate exactly, but what he said went something like this: "Well noo, Sonny. If a creature's head is all made of wool" (he gave me a sly little look) "and for the very purpose of wool gatherin' . . . why then, what would he be needin' with brains?"

I had to admit he had a point.

But the more I see of them cows I wish I could find a way to bring some home. I'll bet they would mix real good with the Herefords. Maybe we could start a little herd of our own, huh Jared? Sure might be worth a try.

Well, my thumb is wore out with all this writing and if I don't quit right now I won't have the strength to priss around on those ponies in the morning. Remember what I said, though.

Love to y'all,
Son

One morning Hunter reported the pickup missing. On further inspection, Jared turned up absent as well. After giving the matter a little thought, we both came to the same conclusion and went on about our business, figuring he would be home by dark. He was. There was no mistaking his arrival. He sheared off a gate post and parked sideways, nose snubbed to the barn. He must have gotten hold of some rot-gut and he was a mess. But at least he was home. Hunter carried him upstairs and put him to bed.

I can understand boys raising hell now and again, in fact I would worry if they didn't. But something about Jared worries me. It isn't the usual kind of busting out, there is something uneasy in his eyes. I know he feels Son's absence—we all do—but Jared is fixing to

117

explode. I look at him and I see one of those firecracker wheels rolling out of control.

Dear Mama,

Business is picking up around here, they are keeping me as busy as a skunk in the henhouse. Fortunately I am not having to try and teach these dudes how to ride a horse—they have found a dry-cleaned officer with a paste-on mustache to do that—although I am keeping in mind your suggestion about the siren. For the present, all I do is pose as flank rider, pick up the fallen bodies and round up the strays. But it keeps a person right busy all the same. I don't know where they get these guys. They handle the reins like they were driving a truck. Maybe they figure that's all there is to hang on to. To sum it up, I don't think this outfit will lead the charge that wins the war, siren or no siren. They are far more likely to bring up the rear and stampede.

I wrote to Jared like you said. I hope it did some good. I am afraid he is considering enlisting so maybe you better tie him up for a few days. I did what I could to discourage it.

Tell Daddy they got some real nice cows over here. I am sending him some magazines on the subject. I think he might be interested. We might be able to crossbreed something real good if there is a way to get it going.

Wish I could send you-all some of this rain. We have had a steady drizzle for two weeks now. They call it mist. I have another name for it which begins with a "p" and rhymes with mist—more or less. You never knew I'd turn out to be a poet did you? Thanks for all the letters. Keep them coming if you can. Got to go now.

Love to y'all,
Son

It has been over a month now since that last letter. We are all worried and trying not to show it. We can't imagine what might have happened. It is no use to contact the War Department; we tried and they have no time to fool with anxious parents. The waiting is terrible. Waiting and not knowing . . . that is the worst part. Hunter is taking it hardest. I guess men are never long on hope or optimism and lord knows ranchers have never had much reason to have confidence in either. Hunter though . . . worry is eating at his face like erosion. And Jared. I think that boy would go crazy if anything happened to Son. There is still that air of violence around Jared, he fairly hovers with it. Me . . . well, I guess I could hang on. I guess I would have to. I think Hunter could stand it but it would be like watching a mirror break, all his dreams falling down around his feet. He hardly says a word anymore so I don't know what's going on inside. But Jared is so young and untried. I am almost more afraid of what might happen to him than I am of the other possibility, the one I won't admit to but which frets along the edges of my mind. We have to keep going. They say no news is good news. I hope they are right.

Dear Mama and Daddy and Jay-reddy,

I guess you're wondering why I haven't written in so long. Maybe the return address of this hospital will help explain it. I been here the whole time, about a month I calculate, trying to get myself stuck back together. I reckon it must be going pretty good because at least I can write now which is a lot more than most of the guys in here can do. Nothing wrong with my *arm* at any rate.

I sure wish I could tell you that I charged to the front, saved the whole U.S. Army and maybe even won the war—but that would be a lie. I'm afraid it isn't as glamorous or heroic as all that. (Hurts just as much, though. Seems like I ought to have more to show for that part.) Anyway, not to keep you in suspense any longer, the plain truth is that I got squashed, flattened out like a run-over snake. It happened this way: some of the guys got to rodeoing around (they still don't know one end of a horse from the other) and these horses are high-spirited so nature took her course. To make a long story short, one of the ponies got wild and took off with the guy on top of him flapping like loose leather. Hero that I am, I rode alongside and tried to grab hold of the bridle. Just as I leaned forward, my own horse shied, slipped in the mud, and fell—with me under him. I couldn't get shed of those pesky iron stirrups. The last thing I remember is a vision of mud and flying hooves. They scraped up what was left, brought it here, and for the past month they have been trying to mend and reassemble the parts. I figure they have succeeded because here I am, most of me anyway.

I know this worries you-all and I sure hate that. But the medics insist that I will be okay. *How* okay, or when, they aren't willing to say just yet. The only good thing to come out of it is that at least I will never be sent into the fighting, not now. I never said much about that but it was something I wasn't looking forward to. I never have made up my mind whether or not I'd be able to kill another guy. As it is, I am spared that decision. So in a way, I am better off here. I'll let you know what the Army has in mind for me to do just as soon as I'm allowed in on the secret myself. As to the other casualties in the affair, both horses are fine and the other guy suffered a sprained ankle.

Love to y'all,
Son

P.S. Don't worry.

Separately and together we have read Son's letter over and over. For a whole day nobody said anything. Except Jared. Jared said, "I'll be a son-of-a-bitch." And showed no signs of sharing his brother's reluctance to kill. The irony of the situation mocks us: to have that boy go thousands of miles only to have a horse fall on him. I suppose there will come a time when we will laugh about it, but not now. Right now, I see despair and defeat in my husband's face. And my younger son has an anger in him that won't quit. All I know to do is fold the fear and sadness inside.

Dear Son,

Now that you have so much time to rest, I think you ought to brush up on your Spanish. With that in mind (I guess I will forever be a schoolteacher!) I am enclosing a verse or two from one of the old *corridos* of this country. You probably remember it—many was the night I sang you to sleep by it. Well, you can sing it to yourself now. Maybe it will cheer you and those other boys up. Here it is:

> Tengan señores presente
> Lo que pasó el treinta y uno
> En esa corrida afamada
> En el Rancho de Ciento Uno.
>
> El día trece de julio
> Me acquerdo bien de ese día
> Tumbó un caballo Chonito
> So lo quitó con t'uy silla.

Here it is in English (in case you've forgotten):

> Remember, you men present,
> What happened in 'thirty-one
> At that famous roundup
> On the Ranch called One-O-One.
>
> The thirteenth day of July,
> I remember the day well,
> A horse pitched off Chonito
> Threw him saddle and all.

Maybe you would like to add some verses of your own. (Jared has some suggestions and choice names for the greenhorn you so gallantly attempted to save.) The name of the bronc is El Moro or El Ingrato, either of which seems suitable. By the time you get home, old Salomón will have your own *corrido* put together and we will have us one big *baile* and invite the whole county.

We were shocked, of course, to learn what had happened to

you, but mainly relieved you are alive and on the mend. The Collingsworth men are tough so you have a good tradition to fall back on. Tell those folks to take good care of you. Needless to say, I wish you were home with us.

> Love from us all,
> Mama

Dear Sonny,

How are you? Good I hope. I am okay but I can't make sense out of things anymore. I mean, ain't that the damndest thing? You going all the hell over yonder just to get mashed underneath a horse? You could just as well of done it here. Shit. It don't make sense to me. What good is the Army anyway? I got me a personal grudge against that S.O.B. you tried to rescue and I aim to settle it one day.

Everything is all right here, I guess. Mama and Daddy took it pretty hard, you getting busted up. Grass is all brown now. Clouds pile up like ice cream but can we squeeze a drop of rain out of them? Hell no. Water holes starting to stink. Weeds stick to your pants and no matter how hard I look there is always a burr under the saddle blanket. Every morning I go sailing, barely missed a bath in the water trough yesterday. Mama makes me so damn mad—she comes out on the back porch and sings that song about the guy who flies through the air with the greatest of ease. Me, I come up cussing. Don't do no good. You know her.

Wish I was over there. Or you here. There's nobody here to talk to. Remember how we used to lie awake nights staring at the stars? Guess I got to start school next week. At least it's for the last time. I'll be a senior. Yea! Maybe me and you can get in a few days fishing down on the River when you get home?

> Adiós Pardner,
> Jared

Dear Mama and Daddy and Big J.,

I am still in the band-aid factory and I have about as much get-up-and-go as a plate of fresh liver. I reckon it takes time for a mess like this to get the starch back in it. Well, I am waiting.

Meanwhile, I just lie and look out the window at the leaves. I have been watching them for some time now and they have gone from a bright, fleshy green to pure gold. I checked on them every day and I never saw how it happened, but it did just the same. Ever so slightly at first, like the light wearing them thin. Then bit by bit, they began to bleach out, kinda like the grass does at home only more so. Then one morning there they were—like a Spanish treasure hanging in the window. Not like any leaves we got back home—bigger. Big as plates. They look real cheery against the sky since it is mostly gray these days. I wish we could see more sunshine—but that is like wishing for the moon. At least so the nurses tell me. Over here, it's like it's fixing to rain all the time. Which I guess it is because it does. Rain, I mean. Pretty near every day. These yellow leaves are my sunshine.

I think about you-all and home a lot, picture it in my head. Sometimes I close my eyes and go over every detail of some particular thing in my mind—like the tooling on my saddle or the way the wood is worn on that post from all the horses scratching and rubbing over the years, and that hole Daddy shot in the weather-vane where the sun pricks through. I try to remember faces, too, but they have a way of dissolving, like they were under water. I have to pester the nurses to get me my billfold so I can see what you folks really look like. You seem so small and pale compared to the way I remember. Snapshots don't do you justice. And Mama—! Your face is *always* swallowed up in the shade of your gardening hat! I try to remember how the days go there so as to line them up with mine. I think, well now Mama is laying the fire in the stove (and I listen for the kindling to pop) and now she is putting on the coffee (I hear the rattle of that old chipped lid), and then the screen door slams, Daddy coming in, his boot heels ringing and his spurs going chink, chink, chink. And now the skillet (bang) and then the heavenly smell of that bacon! Makes my mouth water just to think of it! Right about then, just as I'm fixing to swing my legs over the edge of the bed and brace my toes against the shock of a cold floor and convincing them (my toes) that it's worth it for that coffee and bacon—why, long about then they show up here with a tray of gray oatmeal and tea, and I've got to eat the stuff or perish. The contrast is enough to confuse anybody. And later, when I try to get back to the cold linoleum and the smell of bacon, it is impossible. The oatmeal kinda puts a damper on things.

It feels like years since I've been there. On the ranch, I mean. I shut my eyes and try to smell the sweet wind coming off the grass and the warm fuzzy smell of dust laid down by a little rain. I listen for the windmill creaking and the calves bawling. I'll tell you, I sure can't wait to get back to that country. They can keep the travel. I've never been much for religion but I find myself praying (I guess that's what it is, anyway) for this cuss-word war to end so that I can come home. So I can come back to God's country. And I put in a word for some of these other guys, too. Lot of them are in worse shape than me. This war has done some terrible things to people. I reckon we'll be awhile getting over it.

I guess you-all are getting set for the fall round-up. I think about that a lot. Helluva job—but what a good feeling when it's over! Boy, would I love to be there! Not that I would be much use at the moment. Still, I wish I could be there. Gathering cattle is no small job. I can smell the dust and horse sweat from here and wish like hell I could add my yell to yours. And that old move-'em-out whistle . . . well, wishing don't make it so. I hope you've had a good summer. Y'all never say much about your troubles but I reckon you've had a few.

Well, not much news from here except for a change in the bedpan schedule and I'll spare you that.

Love to y'all,
Son

We are into the swing of round-up all right and from the looks of things it is going to be a big one. Calves are big and sassy and there are a lot of them. We've got our work cut out for us, but thank God for friends and neighbors. We were just fixing to start out the other morning when here came Worth and Matt Childress, Joy riding in the back and the truck all rigged for chuck wagon. They said they had just finished gathering their cattle and saw no reason to quit so they came over to see if maybe we needed a hand. They were a mighty welcome sight. We collected extra horses, threw in our own gear, and took off. Camped at a water hole until we could bring the herd together and drive them on in toward the loading pens. Along about the third night a little dust storm kicked up. I thought I'd be real clever and sleep in the back of our pickup and that way keep the dirt from blowing in my face. So I shoved some stuff over, tossed in my bedroll, and lay down. Well, the bed of a pickup is no place to sleep. It has all those metal ridges to drain out water or protect the surface or something. Whatever their purpose, it escaped me that night, and they got higher with every passing hour. To make matters worse, a calf had kicked me in the jaw and I had burned the skin off my right hand when a rope seared right through my old gloves. So I wasn't feeling real good to begin with. Next thing I knew, that little wind turned chilly and I lay there shivering on that cold metal. I was a sorry thing—miserable, lonesome, and filled with self-pity. Over by the fire I could hear the others snoring away. Finally, toward daybreak, I gave up trying to sleep and crept out, my jaw feeling like it had been wired shut. I stoked up the fire, put on a pot of coffee, and sat there trying to thaw myself out. By the time I'd swallowed three cups of hot coffee, my jaw consented to move, but it wasn't much use since there wasn't anybody to talk to; they were all fast asleep. Pretty soon the stars began to fade and first light showed in the east. It was so still . . . not a sound. I seemed to be the only living thing in creation. The sky washed over with pale light and the stars began draining into it. Then, kind of flustered, a bird started up. It woke up another bird and before long there were several chirping and peeping, still half-asleep. Presently groans and movements began to emerge from under the saddle blankets and bedrolls heaped around the fire. Another work day had begun. I'll never forget that sunrise. But I had no way of knowing then what kind of a day it was going to bring.

We had barely got the last tail twisted up against the rear door of the cattle truck when here came this telegram. Our other neighbor, Fritz Newsome, brought it. Hunter took one look and turned chalk white underneath his tan. He took the envelope between his thumb and forefinger, held it out and then handed it to me. Well, I took it and ripped it open. No sense in prolonging the agony. If it was bad news (which is what we all thought) then we might as well get it over with.

The telegram read:

GUESS WHAT! ARRIVING HOME NOV. 10, 2:45 P.M. TRAIN. RECKON Y'ALL CAN MEET ME? YIPPEE! LOVE, SON

Well, we were *floored!* We didn't know whether to laugh or sing or dance or what, so we compromised and just stood around looking at each other. Then Jared threw his hat in the air and let out a war whoop. After that we all cut loose and hugged and hollered all around. Hunter and Jared did a jig, then they each gave me a whirl. When we got back to the house, we all looked at the date again and got busy.

I turned out the downstairs bedroom for Son, not knowing how strong he might be just yet and figuring it was time he had a room to himself. Jared soaped and oiled his brother's saddle until it shone, saying, "Mama, you'll have to find you another saddle. I done let the stirrups back down on this one." Then both Hunter and Jared rode out and brought in that pony of Son's and started trying to gentle him down a little. I said, "I don't know if he'll feel too much like riding for a while yet."

Hunter said, "Well, it won't hurt to smooth out some of the kinks 'fore he gets here."

And Jared (glaring at me), "Heck! It ain't gonna take *him* long to mend. Not once he gets home."

So I washed my hands of the horse business and went on back inside. I could see that Son was lined up to be a hero whether he wanted to be or not.

After a month of Sundays the big day finally came. We got ourselves all gussied up and arrived at the station a full four hours before the train was scheduled to pull in. (I held out that an extra hour's sleep might do us more good, as well as a substantial breakfast, but Hunter looked mulish and Jared said, "Heck, we might have a flat on the way. We might have *two* flats!") So there we were in the morning light prancing around the station and staring down the empty tracks. Pretty soon we all began to feel a little silly, so we went over to the hotel and drank coffee with everybody who would put up with us. Then back across the street to the station, this time with only an hour to spare.

Since our boy wasn't exactly a war hero, not in the usual sense anyway, there wasn't a brass band in formation or the Legionnaires in uniform or anything like that. But a lot of folks came just the same. Close to fifty, I guess. Maybe more. It brought tears to my eyes: there is nothing in the world to compare with the loyalty and friendship of the people in this ranch country, and that is a fact. A couple of Jared's high school buddies brought their horns and there was a girl with a drum, so I guess you could say we had a band of sorts.

When that train whistle blew, my heart took off like a bird. Then my eyes commenced to mist over and I saw everything from then on through a blur. The train was packed with soldiers, most of them hanging out the windows. I remember wondering if they were coming home, too. And I smiled at them—rather foolishly, I'm afraid. But as best I could make out through my blur, they all grinned back and some of them waved. Then down the line a door popped open and a couple of soldiers jumped out and put down some steps. Then they began helping somebody off, somebody who moved very slowly and looked to be on crutches. But where was Son? We all craned our necks up and around but we couldn't see him anywhere. I grabbed hold of Hunter's arm. "Surely we didn't get the wrong day, did we, hon?" Just then the two soldiers who were helping that other poor fella stepped aside.

The first thing that came to mind was a scarecrow—an especially rickety one. Lord, my heart went out to that poor boy. I thought, "Now what in the world can have happened to him?" And I was moved to pity for his mother.

Then I realized I was looking at Son.

You could have heard a pin drop. He stood there swaying on those crutches, hardly anyone we knew. A wreck of the boy we remembered, white, thin and wobbly, spraddle-legged as a newborn calf. Leaning on the crutches, he looked at us, watching to see how we would take it, trying to read the looks on our faces. A shy half-grin lit his own, then went away again, snuffed out by what he saw. The shock, dismay, and horror on our faces reflected on his. I think he had some remnant of hope until then, but what he saw caused him to give it up. It was an awful moment for us all. But the worst part, the part I can never forget no matter how much I try, is the anger. My own anger rising hot in me, my own outrage and betrayal. And shame. Yes, shame. Thinking: "He didn't tell us he would be on crutches. He could have warned us . . . he never told us he would be on crutches, that he would look like that . . ."

Even after all that has happened since, that memory is still the worst part.

The two soldiers who were holding Son up looked at us. At each other. Then back at us. Anger in them, too. *He is one of us,* their faces said. *If you don't want him, won't deal with him as he is, we'll take him with us. You don't deserve him, anyway. And, what is more, you will never understand—never, never.* They meant it, too. Contempt and anguish fought in their faces. There was a moment, a split second, when it almost happened. I had a vision of the same thing occurring all over the country: the hoped-for—and rejected—sons . . . longed after, worried over, wept on . . . welcomed and denied in the same breath, their wounds repulsive and their weakness unforgiven. Coming home—but never to the places they had left—heroes taken in like poor relations. Oh, the silence of that day. It has destroyed forever the quiet I once knew. Always at the base of things we are so selfish.

It was Jared who saved that day. He stared at us—his parents, his elders—all the people he had been told to look up to. His jaw clenched and his face went white beneath the freckles. He balled his fists and would have spat except that his mouth was probably too dry. His eyes darkened, narrowed, took us in. He threw us away that day: he had seen us for what we were. Alone, he stepped forward. Walked up to that ghost—the hero of his life—and stuck out his hand.

"Howdy!" said Jared, in a voice that was rough and newly deep. "What kept you? We been waitin' the whole damn mornin'." On the last two words, the big, new voice quavered and broke and I saw his shoulders start to shake. Son looked at his little brother and the tears glistened on his own thin cheeks. There they stood, our two boys, before God and everybody, bawling their hearts out and holding hands.

My little mist turned into a downpour and I heard Hunter clearing his throat. Just then Jared's friends let out a blast on their horns, the girl hammered on her drum, and for some reason everybody cheered. Hunter gripped my arm in the most painful hold I have felt since my wedding day and we marched forward to greet our son. But that other boy stood between us. Small and tough, miles away in years and fury, he stood guard over his brother. Wedged fiercely in front, violently protective, Jared dared us to come any closer. So that we had to walk around him finally, and embrace our older son as best we could from around crutches and behind the young soldiers.

Son turned his face at last and kissed me. There was such a sadness in his eyes—not just his own grief but ours as well—the dismissal and destruction of his body, the flagging of our courage, the failure of our souls. So that in that small West Texas station, surrounded by friends and family, under the unblinking eye of God, we stood utterly exposed, all of us, unprotected.

Hunter raised his arm with abnormal stiffness and gave his boy a fatherly slap on the back. More of a pat, actually, but he managed to make it look like a slap. "Well now!" he beamed, and looked around with a defiance so proud and so precarious that no one would have dreamed of challenging it. I could not bear to look into his eyes. In fact, from that moment on, we never looked into each other's eyes. Not in the way we had. We became polite and kind and careful. That was the thing—we learned to show mercy toward each other. And mercy is a close relative of fear and pity. I guess it is all right for saints and judges but it was all wrong for us. We didn't know how to act. We ceased to live together, lost our old rambunctious bunkhouse manners. That day, I don't know, something went out of our lives. Our eyes took to the ground and we lost sight of the hawks.

But Hunter. Too loud, "Well now! I'll bet you could eat a buffalo! How about it?" Beaming off to the side of Son's sloping shoulder. "Let's us mosey on over to the *ho*-tel and put away some steaks."

Son smiled and nodded, but I thought he looked pretty wan. Maybe Hunter saw it, too, or maybe he was hoping to make up for the previous few minutes because suddenly he turned to the other two soldiers. "Y'all too! Y'all come on! You boys look like you could use a little beef and we got enough over yonder to feed half of Texas! Come on now!"

The two GI's smiled politely and shook their heads. Thanks a lot, they said, but we've got to be going now.

"Hell," said Hunter. "In that case we'll feed the whole damn train!"

There was an embarrassing silence. Hunter plunged on. "Well then, lissen. If y'all are ever down this way, you stop in, ya hear? We always got the pot on and you boys are more than welcome. Come see us. I mean it now!"

But no matter how desperately he tried, they left him in charge of his son. Gracefully they backed away, gently. Kind, those boys were. Kind to us all. Sure, they said, nodding and smiling politely. Right. We'll take you up on that one of these days. Then they shook Son's hand. Take it easy, buddy. Be seein' ya. Good luck. And climbed back on the train with the whole town watching. One tossed the steps up to his partner, then swung himself aboard just as the train started to move. He hung there for a minute or two, smiling and waving from the door. It was the only hint I ever had of how transient and fleeting—and therefore how precious—the friendships forged in wartime got to be.

Son stood and watched until the train was out of sight. Then he gave a little sigh, as if bracing himself, and turned to us. Smiling.

"Hi there, George! How ya doin'? Bill Bob? Curtis? Hey, good to see ya! Oh nothing much . . . I fell off a horse. Sarahbeth? My, now *you are lookin' good!* Oh no, I'm fine. Minnie . . . Sure sweet of you to come. Caleb Pulliam—who is this boy? He can't be Sam . . . No! He's growed three feet . . . No, thank you. I got my old buddy here, old Jay Reddy. I know for a fact I can count on him. I'll just lean on him a little . . . Daddy? You too, if you don't mind. Boy howdy! I ain't tasted steak since I left home. You know what they feed you over there? Oatmeal. Sickening. Tastes just like putty. It's no wonder I'm a little on the puny side."

I think all he wanted to do just then was lie down and close his eyes. It was enough for him just to be home. But he couldn't let them down. I watched as they made their way—*inched* across the street, him in the middle thin and pale as a windowpane—then somebody shoved a Kleenex in my hand, ordered me to blow and marched me along, too. After that I was pretty much all right.

Hunter had slaughtered one of our own steers (we made jokes about the fatted calf) so the hotel could offer us all meat. The Mexican cooks came out grinning and served us themselves, the thickest, juiciest steaks any of us had seen in many a day. But I noticed that Son barely touched his food. Jared, who had put away his own weight several times over not counting the biscuits and gravy and pie, noticed it, too. He kept watching his brother trying to figure him out, to recognize him—this stranger who looked and smelled so different but was the same, was surely the same? If Hunter paid any attention to Son's plate, I don't know. Men have their own defenses. His was to become loud and jovial. Hearty and shouting, he became the life of the party. Lots of backslapping, jokes and stories. The life of the party all right, and a good thing, because otherwise it would have fallen flat.

But Hunter. A man of few words.

We drove home about dusk, Son in the front seat next to his daddy and Jared and I in back. Son was very quiet, looking all around. He seemed to be soaking up everything, filling his eyes with sunset colors. Once he turned around to me and smiled and I noticed how much older he looked. Off to the west, the clouds caught fire. It was like watching the mountains of Hades going up in flames. We rode home in a blaze of glory.

When we pulled up at the house, Son climbed out very slowly and then took a deep breath. His smile was as wide as the evening.

"Boy," he said. "It sure is good to be home again."

But he no sooner got inside than he put on a pair of his old pajamas and went to bed. He didn't even bother to unpack. He apologized and of course we all assured him that it was all right. But we were disappointed. Jared's face fell and his spirits settled somewhere down around his boot heels. None of us knew quite what to do with ourselves so I went out to the kitchen and made a pot of coffee. We sat around the table, the three of us, not saying much, just sipping coffee until it was dark enough that we could decently go to bed.

We never did say anything. We were so accustomed to going on no matter what, that we went about our business as if everything was still all right, sidestepping the real issue, avoiding each other. I guess each of us hoped things would improve despite the odds. We had done it so many times before—when sickness swept the herd or rain refused to fall, when coyotes took the new calves—but those times, hard as they were, pulled us together, made us close. This time it was different. The distance increased—as if we radiated outward from each other. And Son at the center, helpless, pushing us apart. Maybe if we had stopped one day, said, "Wait a minute!" and looked each other in the eye. Or if we'd cried or even yelled. Then it might have been different. Maybe we could have dealt with it better. Maybe there was no way *to* deal with it. Only something to be gotten through. Which is what we were used to and what we did.

From one day to the next.

If you can think of a family as a fist, then you might say we lost our grip, Son slipping away from us, loosening our hold. When he first returned and installed himself in that bedroom, for a few weeks he seemed to be home again. We fell all over each other spoiling him and he grinned and let us. Jared and Hunter colliding in the bedroom doorway, one with a glass of milk and the other with a plate of cookies, both of them embarrassed and about half mad. Son laughing, singing out, "Why, thank you, boys! I never had me such sweet and pretty nurses overseas! Y'all come right in here and set on my bed." And me of course, fixing all those goodies to tempt him.

In those first days he told us so many stories—most of them funny. His face took on a little color and his eyes had life. He ate better but still only a pitiful amount. Jared, on the other hand, commenced to eat hugely. As if to compensate in some way or give extra strength to his brother. Son watched him do that. He knew what Jared was doing. He teased him a little but not enough to make him stop. Son had such a gentle smile in those days and he smiled often.

One day, with Jared helping, practically carrying him, he struggled down to the corral. He leaned across the fence and held out a handful of oats to that horse of his. Mescalero snorted, edged up, stamped his feet and blew the oats away. Son laughed and so did Jared. But I think they both realized then that he would never ride again. He would never talk about it, about what had happened to him. But more and more we saw how bad it was, not only so many bones broken but his insides crushed as well so that they no longer worked. He was in pain all the time.

I said to him, "Son? Why can't they do something more for you than this?" We were alone in the kitchen, as we often were in those days. "I mean, what do they expect? It seems to me that you're just the same as anybody who was wounded in battle or shot down. Is this all they're going to do? Just stick you back together with tape and baling wire and send you home?"

He looked at me then. I'll never forget that look. I'd seen him size up a rope that way, or a horse, studying its worth, measuring how much he thought it could take. I guess he decided I'd do because he said, "Mama, you know as well as I do that the only thing left to do with me is take me out and shoot me. I reckon we have to give the Army credit for having the sense to see it, too."

I had no reply to that. He asked a lot of me, that boy. I only hope I lived up to his standards. He expected as much of me as he did of himself, but he neglected to figure on a few things. One, it is different for each of us. Two, he was going while I was staying. And three, I had Hunter and Jared to think of.

He withdrew from our lives as gracefully and as kindly as possible. There was a period when he tried to stay, made a real effort (for our sakes, I believe) all the while knowing otherwise and only prolonging his own agony. And ours. Once he understood that—that it was our pain as well—he quit. Let go. From that day on he seemed to be walking backwards, moving steadily away. Or maybe we moved on while he stayed. He spent more and more time in his room and said less and less. What he *was* saying was: I'm not going to be around much longer and I want you-all to get used to the idea.

And Jared? Well, I guess something good comes out of most everything. Jared started growing like a weed. He grew four inches in that one year and put on thirty pounds. I could claim it was my cooking (I was taking special pains) and all that extra food, those meals of Son's he put away. But I think it was more than that. Jared had someplace to go, too. Those boys were like a juniper tree that's been hit by lightning—one side all charred and split and the other branch growing extra to make up for it. That's how they were in those days . . . and both of them knowing it some way.

Hunter. I still can't talk about that. All I know is, women are stronger than men when it comes to some things. Women are born knowing grief but it comes as a terrible surprise to men. Incomprehensible, frustrating, and cowardly. I think they believe that fate should come out and fight. Death makes them mad, they have no use for it. Women, meanwhile, have seen it coming all along.

That was a strange time for me, watching two of my men shrink before my eyes and the third grow hand over hand. By then there was nothing I could do so I stepped back and let it go. I set up my fortress in the kitchen and cooked and baked and scrubbed and was so busy that nobody dared bother me. Nobody except Son. He would come to the table and sit. Sometimes smoke and drink coffee, but mostly just sit. Watching me, memorizing the room, storing up memories, I guess. I never knew. We were at ease with each other and had no need for speech, were way past it. Hunter and Jared came and went, not looking at us or only glancing sideways. Locked in their own separate sorrows, they walked backwards also, sometimes accusing us, Son and me, but also heading toward some destination of their own. That is what I mean when I say we began moving apart, radiating outward from each other.

After he came home, Son stayed with us only five months.

That same year Jared got to running with a wild crowd. I guess with all that growing, life began to move too fast for him. The night of his high school graduation—about a month after Son died—he and some of his friends were driving down to the Border, heading for God knows what sin and celebration. The car went out of control on a curve, flipped over four times, and bounced into a canyon. From what we were able to learn later, Jared was driving. They had all been drinking. He must have been doing at least ninety. Well, I guess that's how he wanted it.

As for Hunter, he died of a broken heart. Call it what you will—and the doctors had all kinds of names—I saw it happen and I know. He simply cracked at the center and gave in.

I buried all three of them out there on that ranch—on a quiet hilltop where the wind moves freely and there is nothing between them and the sky. When I sold out, I asked the new owners to give me an easement so I could go in and visit whenever I wanted to. They offered to put a little rock wall around the spot but I said no. The fence has yet to be built that would hold those three. So they are up there in the open where they belong, or where what I knew of them belongs.

IT is a long time now since all that happened. These days I have a little place in town with a cow pat garden in the back and a white picket fence all around. I still can't get used to the idea of fencing things *out*. It's contrary to everything I know. And I can't say I'll ever learn to like it.

I don't claim not to miss them, the days go more like years. But I busy myself. That has always been a woman's salvation. If Hunter could have had some of it he might have made it, something concrete and ordinary to hold onto. But his world was so different. Consequently his ways were different, eyes fixed always on the far horizons. And everything he dreamed of gone—his sons, the purpose of his life, and finally that life itself.

Naturally I miss them. The extra dimension they gave me is no longer there. But for all my loss and loneliness I did once know the fullness of love. For that I am thankful. And to tell the truth, what I long for most is that ranch. It was my life—all our lives—for so many years. Our time and our place. We would never have fitted anywhere else, it was only there that we existed.

Sometimes of an evening I park off the road in a clump of live oak trees and walk out in the pasture a little ways. It is good to feel the land under my feet. But I've had my eyes on the ground for so long that I've almost forgotten how to look up. When I do though, they're still there. The hawks, I mean. Circling, sliding down the wind, as wild and free as ever.

The Sun Gone Down,
Darkness Be Over Me

David L. Fleming

BACK IN THE pines, it was shady in the day and dark at night. Everything in that world had a shadow on it, like the black sleeve of an old wool coat sliding down a man's arm. The ground where the grass grew and the ground where pine needles were so thick nothing grew both had the shadow on them. The side of a barn had that shadow, and the bluejay, who is like a thief who does not care, had that shadow on its blue and black and white wings when it flew from something that was his to something that was not his.

Back in the woods, down that road that bloomed dust and the smell of dust behind automobiles in a hurry to find another road, lived a man by himself named Willie Temple. He had lived down that road all of his life, in that shade and shadow, except for those years when he rode around East Texas from Beaumont up across the Neches River to Jacksonville in long-snouted International trucks, working in the oil fields, but that wasn't living then. That was just staying where the work was, like visiting. He never did any living except down that road where his family lived too, and died, or moved away, and tragedy and sickness took him from that giant that he was, giant enough for any storybook for children to read and shudder about, to what he was now: old and beat up and waiting to die. He did not care about anybody now. He had tried that once, and his heart had been hurt worse than his body was that time the chain snapped off the drill.

Used to, a long time ago, he would drink to forget the things that drove knives into his heart, but the knives would stab until he would raise his arms above his head, his fingers outstretched and his palms upwards like he was Solomon holding the disputed infant to the sword, and he would throw back his lined, black face to the night or to the ceiling of a colored honky-tonk on the edge of town that was made of stud two-by-four and old sheet iron from some haybarn, and he would cry, "MY SOUL!" like the sound of wind and thunder in the tops of the trees that thrashed and shook and howled enough to make a man down on the ground, in the gloom, tremble and stare and pray to Jesus. Then all the men would stand back away from him in terror and wonder and know somebody was going to die that night, but Willie Temple was not a killing man, except almost, that time he pushed a smartmouth backward so hard that that smartmouth hit the sheet iron wall and broke through it the way air pops out of bubblegum in a child's mouth.

When he was eighteen and ragtime music flowed out of night-clubs on streets dark and paved with red brick from Corsicana, he was tall, and broad too. His father, sick on his inside from something the doctors did not have a name for, something his father claimed he could feel crawling inside him at night, would watch William, as he was called then, play with his baby sister Dorothy May in the yard of the house where Willie lived alone now, and his father would say, "He broad as a smile on a lawyer face."

His mother, pushing blackeyed peas out of withered pods, would say, "No. Not a lawyer. He broad as the smile on the face of Mister Teddy Rosefelt."

And his father would say, "Why not the lawyer, woman?"

"'Cause when *he* be smilin', somebody over yonder be payin' for it, that's why. William just smile 'cause he happy."

His father would nod his head, satisfied, but something on the wind soon enough caught that broad giant that Willie Temple used to be and took away his smile the way a cloud moves across the face of the sun. He turned his broadness on his family and moved his feet in the dust of that road that nobody went down now unless they were on their way to Four Mile Road where it twisted around and Y-ed into the state highway to New Waverly. Perhaps his bigness had given him something special, some special sight or even poetry. He was too big for the sawmill in the little town nearby, and he was too fierce for the homes being built in the shade in New Waverly or Huntsville. But in the oil fields, his size and the grip he danced around the chain that wrapped the drill were just right, and the money was good for a while. The other men called him "Weeper" because of the look in his eyes, like someone in mourning for his own soul.

It was typhoid that took his father, not the crawling thing inside him, and it took his mother also. He had come back home then and paid for the funeral with money he unrolled from his trousers pocket, and he had put them in the unfenced cemetery beside brothers and sisters that he had never known, who had come into the world and gone out again without leaving so much as a footprint in the soft sand. He had mixed the concrete for the headstones himself, and scratched his father's and mother's names in them with a sixteen penny nail while his sister Dorothy May cried and shook her head with the rhythm of a woodpecker, which is the rhythm of grief.

He reluctantly stayed two winters doing odd jobs for small money until the Depression put all the money away from the reach of men who lived in the shadows beside dusty roads in the pine trees, and he put leaving from his mind altogether. It suited him to stay where the shadows were deep. He felt marked, somehow, in the sunlight, singled out and glared upon. As time went by, he even felt a certain joy in staying. There had been women in his life, low-waisted girls whose names all sounded the same, but there had never been a woman, and all the unused love in his inarticulate heart he gave in innocence to his sister, the last of his family.

But Dorothy May grew from girl to womanhood and put lipstick on her lips and was gone from the house when William came out of the woods with something he had hunted along the creek in the shadows and crooks of hickory or sweetgum trees, small rips in the legs of his overalls where thorny vines bit the material and surrendered their spiked seeds. When she came home again, they would circle each other and blame and shout and curse, and William would raise his face to the rafters, the lantern on the table throwing his huge shadow across the room and over his sister. He could hear her later, crying in her bed in the next room, and he

143

understood her misery. He was miserable too, huge and unloved and lonely.

Then one night, Dorothy May did not come home, and she did not come home the next day either. She never came home again. Men told William whom she had married and where she had gone, but he only stared at them, his heart in a sealed, dark place, and said, "Don't have no sister. Man don't need no sister."

He went away again, and the clinging sections of stovepipe rusted and collapsed on themselves. Raccoons crawled through the hole and lived in the corners of his house, sleeping amid their litter during the day, and crawling out at night to wander the sandy banks of the creek. Hunters broke down the fence in the back, and possums lived under the porch, hissing at sudden noises in their secret, petty way. The trees down that road grew and took for themselves that much more of the sunlight.

When William came back, he was broken and hunched over from something that had happened in the oil fields. He moved back into the house where he had been a child, and the animals, afraid of his shadowy shufflings, moved out and left it to him. He lived like a ghost, secret and alone in that house in the shadows down that road.

The Second World War came and was over, and he never thought about it. Men built a gin for cotton down the road, and wagons went by his house all through August and September, little children rocking on top of the picked cotton, the lint in their hair and clothes, but cotton played out, and the gin shut down. No one went there anymore until a few years ago when a government man looking into Klan activities was found stabbed to death in the empty office with the broken windows. During the investigation, Willie Temple was too secret to say whether he had seen anything or not, so the sheriff, Arthur Rose, who had known and liked Willie all his life, quit stopping by or sending his deputy, and the shadows fell across his house and porch, and the murderer was never found.

Now Eisenhower was president and Chevrolets roared through the little East Texas town nearby, driven by boys with baseball caps on their heads and time on their hands. The Rural Electrification

144

Act had given Willie electricity, but all he wanted was a plug for an icebox, and that was all he had. He lived far away from the rest of the world, broken now and hunched over, worn out, and waiting to die. People didn't call him William anymore, but the diminutive, and that seemed appropriate, for he was not a giant anymore, and instead of pulling things to him, which is the natural way with men, he had begun to count the things that he no longer needed.

He did very little except sit in the pine rocker on the front porch and mumble the words of some song he had learned a long time ago in the Mt. Zion Church that had mysteriously burned to the ground during the war. Morning after morning, he sat and watched the sun break weakly through the tops of the pines and heard the woods come to life with birds and insects. Evenings would find Willie sitting on the porch again, watching the shadows stretch across the barren yard and waiting for the nighthawks that came sweeping in with the twilight. He had a crooked cane which hung over the arm of the rocker while he sat there. The curve of it was a dark and oily brown, but the rest was nicked, white oak. Willie was proud of the cane because it was one thing that he had never lost. He would often rub the handle with his pale palm, all the while humming something that went high and low like a spiritual, and, in its time, something else would appear on the list of things he no longer needed. His mumble would be the judgment: "Man don't need no . . . *pretty yard!*"

Seasons came and went, and Willie waited to die. It was a hard thing to do, but Willie had had enough of life. He had lived the best of it, and it had been bad. For a while, he had thought of killing himself, but then he decided it would be better to die a little bit each day. So the waiting was all that was left to him. He sat among the shadows and did nothing, living on monthly checks he had no interest in spending, eating what he had or what people who felt sorry for him brought him.

After a time, he began going into town on Saturdays, if the weather was good. He walked in early and was there on the bench in front of the grocery store when the town began to come to life. He seldom left the bench for anything other than a bottle of soda water or a bag of Bull Durham. It was a pain to him to walk and carry anything, but it was right that he join the few old men, who were also waiting to die, in that public place. It was there that he was most diminished, and that was right too, because his size had been his curse. It was better to be called "Willie" and to be diminished because that meant he was closer to being what he wanted to be, which was nothing.

Mr. Reynolds, the postmaster, helped him in this. He had never been driven by goodness or ideals, or the loss of them, and he misunderstood what it was in Willie that brought him to the shadows of the bench where men sat without family or occupation while the rest of the world got in pickup trucks and made noise in the sunshine.

One Saturday, Willie was given a plastic thing by Mr. Reynolds, who then called Isaac Hansen out of the grocery store. Isaac Hansen was a tall man with blond and gray hair, and his eyes were like slits in his face.

"What's goin' on now?" he asked, exchanging looks with Mr. Reynolds. "What you got there, Willie?"

"Tell him, Willie," Mr. Reynolds said.

"This here one of them *heckabobs,* Mr. Hansen. Mr. Reynolds say I be able to judge for myself whether the earth be turning left or right."

"Well, say Willie," Isaac Hansen said then. "How does this thing here, this *heckabob,* work?"

"Mr. Reynolds say I put it on the fence at night, and if it be there in the mornin', the old earth turnin' to the right. If it fall off, the old earth be turnin' to the left."

Then Isaac Hansen and Mr. Reynolds laughed and pushed each other. The other black men, who remembered Willie when he was young, did not laugh or say anything, but sat looking down as if they were deaf. It was a familiar game, and Willie did not mind being laughed at by Mr. Reynolds and Isaac Hansen. It was part of a dark agreement between the three men that nobody else knew anything about.

In the evenings, before sundown, he was gone suddenly with only the stab-holes his cane made and his shuffling footprints in the sand beside the road to show that he had come into town at all. It was lonely and quiet out on the gin road, and Willie never walked it at night. He was home by dark, sitting by the woodheater in cool weather, burning oak limbs and cooking a squirrel or rabbit that someone had brought by. Sometimes Willie whistled quietly to himself while the pot bubbled, and the sound he made was like gusts of wind through a window screen in a house where no one lived anymore.

Summer passed, but the days were still hot through September. Then, mornings became misty with fog and dew, and October came. On the second day of October in the twilight of 1957, the sun went down with a difference, and in the darkness that followed, Willie heard footsteps on his porch, and he stood, reaching for his cane, facing the door and waiting. It was two people on his porch. He could tell that much, but he had no idea who they could be. He thought of the man found murdered in the office of the old gin, and fear gripped him with cruel fingers, but that had been on an August night, a long time ago.

"Willie!" a man called loudly, too loudly for the quiet. "You in there, Willie?"

Willie felt the grip release. The front door was already opening, and George Jackson from the bus station came in leading a thin, pretty girl whose expression was a mixture of curiosity, fear, and wonder.

"Evenin' Willie," George Jackson said. "This here is Esther Ruth Freeman. She come in on the seven-fifteen. She say she your blood relative niece from Tyler, only child of your late sister, Dorothy May. I brought her over soon as I got off work."

All the time George Jackson was talking, Willie looked suspiciously at the thin, big-eyed girl who was standing in front of him. She was wearing a blue cotton dress and was tall enough to be seventeen. There was something of the child still in the curves of her face, and in the innocence of her eyes, but the rest of her was at the edge of womanhood. Her eyes were dark and intense and filled with expectation, and when Willie looked into them, he looked away again, confused.

"Girl, this your uncle, Mr. Willie Temple," said George. He waited a minute, looking at the two of them, neither of whom said a word or made a movement, then, uncomfortable and already late, he backed out the door and hurried to his pickup truck.

Willie stood with his back to the woodheater, waiting for the girl to say something or go away. The lamplight played on the pretty mystery of her expectant face and on her lips which trembled, but she did not move or say anything. Willie looked around the room, as if she had already hidden something in his house which he had to find and get rid of. He got tired of standing, so he moved to his chair and sat down, turning his back on her.

After several minutes, the girl put down her cardboard suitcase where she stood, pulled out one of the ladderback chairs from the table, and sat down too. She watched him with her intense eyes. She had a blue clip in her tight hair that matched her dress, but neither the clip nor the dress seemed to suit her.

"Dorothy May gone three years," Willie said, not looking at the girl. He remembered the letter he had gotten three years ago, but he could not remember his sister. He had locked her memory out of his mind the way he had locked it out of his heart.

"Yes sir." The quiet, high voice of a girl was in his house, like a bird that had flown through the open door.

After a while, Willie glanced at her. A piece of wood burned in two and fell among the ashes in the woodheater with the soft sound of resignation.

"And your papa?"

The girl burned him with her eyes. "He ran off. He ran off a month ago. If I ever see that son of a bitch again, I'll kill him with a butcher knife."

Willie looked around quickly, and his cane slid off the arm of his chair and clacked to the floor. He could tell by the girl's eyes that she could never do such a thing, but it was bad luck to speak a murder out loud.

"Don't say that, girl," he said, lowly, picking up his cane and looking behind him at the place where the lamplight ended and the shadows began.

"I'll say it if I want to. He left me all alone in the house and run off with a baby-talk woman who served drinks at the saloon. When the man came to collect the rent, I had to move out with nothing but what I got in my suitcase."

The girl raised her voice, and Willie lifted his cane and put it back on the arm of his chair. He looked at her through yellowed eyes.

"Why you come here?" he said.

"There wasn't no other place to go. Dorothy May told me stories about you. She said you were tall as a tree and people were afraid of you. She said you could take care of anything."

"Me?"

"That's right, but you don't look like the William Temple she talked about."

"Folks call me Willie."

"This place smells terrible. Don't you ever clean it, ever at all?"

Willie felt like someone had put a light on him. "Man don't need all that clean," he said, not looking at her anymore.

"What happened to you?"

"You watch your mouth, girl."

"This is worse than anything I ever thought of," the girl said, then she added in a quiet voice, "I ought to get back on the bus in the morning."

Willie heard the girl and felt again like a light had been put on him. Man don't need no nieces, he thought slowly, but he knew he was bound by blood to keep her as long as she had no other place to go.

"Man don't need it," he said and looked sideways at the girl.

The girl eventually ate some of the soup Willie had made for his own supper, but it was coarse and saltless, and she did not like the taste of it. He watched her secretly as she moved about, passing from shadow into light and back into shadow again, and he tried to remember his sister and what she had looked like, but all he could think was that she had been a girl like this one.

"She been dead three years?" he said aloud without meaning to, deliberately keeping his sister's name in shadow.

"You said that already," the girl said, looking around at the bare, dark walls of the house and the exposed rafters under the roof. If he had been the man she had heard about and expected, she would not have used the tone with which, now, she let him know how disappointed she was.

"Bad car wreck," Willie said, remembering.

"Yeah," the girl said, grimacing at each thing of Willie's that caught her eye.

"Man don't need no car," Willie said.

"You don't have a car?"

"Man don't need no car."

Willie tried to remember what his sister had looked like, but he could not recall her face, and trying to made him feel as if he were going to choke, so he gave it up, humming instead until he felt the girl's intense eyes on him. Then he only sat and let the woodheater warm him, looking sideways at the girl whenever she moved as if he were afraid she was going to sneak up on him. Several times he went off into some other year, trying to remember that place, that small-headed man he had fought with, some figures he had suddenly begun to wonder about. The girl seemed to have inspired in him a flood of memories and thoughts that he had dammed up long ago.

Finally, she said she was tired, so Willie led her into a small, square room at the back of the four-room house, and he told her she could sleep in it and make it her own if she decided to stay. The girl stood in the edge of it, looking at the bare wooden walls and floor, and at the low rafters of the ceiling. Directly before her was an iron single bed under a dirty mattress piled with boxes filled with empty coffee cans, fruit jars, and wire, all covered with a layer of dust. The room had one small window, but it was closed, and after heating all day, the air in the room was thick with the smell of pine and dust.

"It's like a coffin in here," the girl said.

Willie was standing behind her, near the door. He had been looking at her in the lantern light, wondering about her. He was drawn to the girl, but he knew it was a false and dangerous attraction, like the attraction of the lantern light for the bugs that came through the holes in his window screens. "Don't use it much," he said.

She took the lamp from him, and he watched her walk around the tight cell of a room. When she started moving things off the bed, he tapped his cane on the floor like a blind man. She appeared not to notice him and went on piling in the far corner all the boxes of things Willie did not need, but would never throw away.

She put the lamp on the floor and turned the mattress over after she had cleared it off. She stood looking down at it for a moment, the bow in her hair crooked now and the soft lines of her face wrinkled with determination. Then she looked around at the walls again. Something about her softened the way dry leaves do in the rain.

She said, "At home, I had flowers and pictures on the wall, and they made things bright and pretty."

Willie turned to leave the room, then looked back over his shoulder. "Flowers belong in the ground. Man don't need no flowers in the house, nor pictures on the wall."

Later, when the house was dark and settling, Willie lay on his side listening to the girl in the next room turning over and over on the squeaking bed as if she had a fever. She had not blown out the lantern, for the shadows frightened her, and on the closed lid of her suitcase was a road map folded back so that the highways that webbed East Texas could be studied. Willie heard the girl crying and talking to herself in angry, muffled words. It made him cold to hear it.

He remembered how his sister would cry in the night sometimes when she was a little girl. He remembered very clearly cradling her small head in his large hands so that she would know he loved her and that it was all right to close her eyes. Then she had grown up and cursed at him and run away. Man don't need it, he thought, and the shadows moved around his bed in the dark room like the ghosts of children who had forgotten how to play.

In the morning, before the sun was up, Willie got out of bed and pulled on his pants and fastened his suspenders over the shoulders of the collarless shirt he slept in. He slipped on his brown wool coat, lifted his cane, and walked outside in that peculiar, painful shuffle that his injury had forced on him. He stood at the edge of the porch to urinate before he remembered the girl. He stepped off the porch and walked to the corner of the yard where a twisted cedar grew. He shuffled back to the porch, adjusting his pants, and he went to the rocker and sat down.

It was one of those days that had long ago been named Indian summer, when the woods and earth rested in the final warmth before the cold, wet days of winter. Willie heard a mourning dove in the woods. He heard a dog picking up a scent, and he heard the busy sparrows. Old morning, she comin' in now, he thought, and he rocked and hummed softly, but he was not happy. His back hurt him, and he was stiff, and in the night, an emptiness had come back to his heart that he thought he had pushed away forever.

The door opened while he was watching a mockingbird hop from the fence to the yard, then back again, pursuing and torment-ing a grasshopper. The girl came out on the porch. She was wearing blue jeans and a light cotton shirt whose open collar revealed her smooth throat and the curve of her shoulders. Willie, absorbed by the morning, had forgotten about her again.

"What you doin' dressed like a man?" he said.

"I dress the way I want to dress."

"Hmm," Willie said. "Girls 'round here wear dresses."

"What are you doing?" she asked, ignoring his caution, her sharpness coming and going, like sunlight under a tree when the wind blows.

"Sittin'. That's all."

Willie watched the girl step down one step, then sit back on the floor of the porch. Her hair was brushed back into two pigtails that were held tightly by rubber bands.

"How long you lived out here by yourself?" she asked.

"Long time," Willie said.

"Since Dorothy May left?"

"Long time," Willie said again.

"Don't you get lonely?"

Willie was surprised by the question. Loneliness was something he had made up his mind about a long time ago. "Man don't need to get lonely," he said.

"I been lonely lots of times in Tyler, and that's a city," the girl said.

Willie rocked and looked into the shadows of the sunrise. "Young boys around all the time," he said.

"Not around me. I had too much to do taking care of my grandpa to mess with boys."

"Be comin' 'round," Willie persisted.

The girl looked up and down the empty road, feeling the quiet.

"You know what they grow in Tyler?" the girl asked.

"What?"

"Roses. The prettiest red and yellow and white roses you ever saw. They grow all them pretty roses."

"That so."

"It's still the lonesomest town I ever been in," the girl said. She was staring at nothing, at a memory, perhaps, her eyes open and blank, then they narrowed and a shadow crossed her face. She turned abruptly and looked at the bent man in the rocking chair, the shadow still across her face, but when he looked back at her, the shadow went away, and she smiled.

Willie felt vaguely uncomfortable, as if he had been awakened from a deep sleep by a sound he wasn't sure he had heard.

A truck came down the road in the sand with its front lights still on, although the sun had come up. It turned in at Willie's broken gate and stopped. Two old hounds rose up in the bed and sniffed and whined, their paws on the side of the truck. Mr. Reynolds and his oldest boy got out of the truck and walked up to the porch. The girl stood up and went to the door, but did not go in.

"Mornin', Willie old boy," shouted Mr. Reynolds. "Which way is the world turnin' this mornin'?"

"To the right, sir."

"Well, I'll be. Now that's just what I told Mark here as soon as I got up this mornin'. Now Mark, I said, I bet the old world's a turnin' to the right today, but suppose we drive down and ask old Willie just to make sure. And while we're here, I thought we might run a few squirrels, if it's all right with you."

"Yes sir. Go right ahead."

"Well, we'll sure do it. Say, who's the girl belong to?"

"I don't belong to nobody," the girl said from the door, fixing her intense eyes on Mr. Reynolds. Mark glanced at his father's face.

"You be still, girl," Willie hissed, looking at her. Their eyes met in an even match. Willie turned back to Mr. Reynolds. He said, "She my niece. Come last night on the bus from Tyler."

"I didn't know you had any nieces," Mr. Reynolds said. He looked hard at the girl by the door. "Don't look much like you, does she?" he said.

"I'm his niece, not his daughter," the girl said.

"You're an insolent missy, I'm thinkin'," Mr. Reynolds cut her off with his loud voice.

"Let's go, Dad," Mark said.

Mr. Reynolds nodded. "Sure," he said. "Get in the truck." To Willie he said, "I guess they do stuff different up in Tyler, but I know you'll talk to the girl."

"Yes sir," Willie nodded.

Mr. Reynolds got back in the truck and drove down the lane beside the house that led down into the hickory bottom along the creek. The hounds rose up and sniffed as the truck went by. The girl went to the edge of the porch and watched the truck until it went into the woods. When it was out of sight, she turned back to Willie.

"Who's that?" she asked.

"That my friend, Mr. Reynolds."

"What's he got on you?"

"What you talkin' about?"

"I know his type. He's a mean, white-trash man that gets along by having something on people."

"You behave," Willie said suddenly, but he knew that he had waited too long, and that the fire was too hot.

"What do you call behaving? Saying 'Yes suh?'"

"Stop now!" Willie said and tapped his cane on the floor of the porch. It was his warning sound, but she was past being warned.

"How much you charge them for hunting down there?"

"A friend don't charge a friend."

"He's not your friend," the girl said, looking at him with her dark eyes. "You just think he is, which shows how much you know."

Willie swung his cane out in front of him, but she was feet away.

"Look at you, like a snake blinded by the sun! What is going on around here? You're not old. You don't have to act like this."

Something rose in Willie that he had been keeping locked down for twenty years. It was all the words he had wanted to shout at Dorothy May when he first heard she had married and disappeared. He had buried them to prove to himself he never cared, but they rose now, not as a vocabulary, but as a pressure, and he had to draw deep breaths to push them down again.

The girl crossed her arms and stood at the edge of the porch watching him. Curiosity and pity were in her eyes, but the pity was the cold kind that is closer to contempt.

"I been hurt," Willie said, finally.

"We all been hurt," the girl said, watching him. When he began to breathe normally, she asked, "What is that nonsense about which way the earth is turning?"

Willie wouldn't answer her at first, but she kept on until he told her about the *heckabob* and pointed to where it was still balanced on the torn fence. The girl went out into the yard and snatched the thing off the wire where it was held on by a small piece of string because Willie knew it was better for the world to turn to the right. The devil was on the left. She brought it back to the porch, swinging it against her thigh.

"This isn't anything but an old red plastic coathanger from the cleaners without the hook in it!" the girl said. "How can you let those white men play with you like that? All the time they laughing at you like you were a crazy old uncle. All I ever heard was stories about what a giant you were, but you ain't nothin'. You ain't even small."

She threw the coathanger out into the yard and went back in the house. For a time, Willie heard her banging and knocking around, then the house grew quiet. He thought several times that he would get up to see what the girl was doing, but he was comfortable in the rocker, so he only sat, listening first to the noise, then to the quiet and the sounds of the woods. He had begun to hum when the door opened again.

"Come in here and eat your breakfast," the girl said.

"I ain't, because I ain't hungry, thank you."

"You got to eat to stay alive."

"Man don't need to eat no breakfast."

"Now listen," she said, walking up to him where he sat. "I already cooked it."

Willie raised his cane slightly in her direction and frowned, but she only fixed her intense eyes on him, so he finally got to his feet.

"You know when the bus leave?" he asked.

"I don't care when the bus leaves," she said. "The bus can leave all day for all I care about it."

Willie went slowly behind her into the house and sat down at the bare, scarred table. Beside a chipped china plate was a cup filled with dark coffee. Willie looked at the plate which was a Victorian blue, with a picture of a large house and fields and people riding horses. It had been one of his mother's plates. He pushed it away from him.

"Where you find this?"

"On the top shelf. What's wrong with it?"

"I eat on the plain ones. If I wanted to eat on a picture, I'd eat on the calendar."

"That's a perfectly good plate."

"Man don't need to eat on no calendar."

Willie reached across the table and got the plain white plate the girl had set for herself. The girl sighed and put two wide pieces of fried pork on it and gave him two large, floury biscuits. She had been unable to find any baking powder on his shelves.

Willie began to eat. He was not used to eating a breakfast, and he ate slowly. The girl sat across from him, and they looked at each other.

"I'm sorry I got mad and sassed you," she said, after a while. "You remind me a lot of my grandpa. I had to treat him just like a baby up until he died."

"I ain't your grandpa," Willie said, but the girl only looked at him with a tint of sadness on her round face.

"Are you going to let me stay?"

Willie ate. "Don't know," he said, chewing a biscuit.

She watched him eat without saying anything. Then she said, "Why don't you have a bathroom in here?"

"Privy's out back."

"I mean a bathtub."

"Man don't need no bathtub. Wash in the sink. Ain't decent sitting buck-naked in no trough."

Willie looked down and ate. Occasionally crumbs dropped back onto his plate from his mouth. The girl watched him.

"I can clean and cook for you, if you let me stay," she said, and it sounded formal to Willie, as if she were not his blood relative at all, but just someone seeking employment.

"Suppose so," Willie said. "Cain't eat no breakfast like this every morning. Man don't need it."

"You don't have any money, do you?"

Willie looked up. He was confused by all her questions. The sound of her voice was insistent and demanded an answer or comment from him. He said, "Don't need no money to get by."

"You could get by better if you'd charge them white folks for hunting," the girl said, hearing a rifle shot from the dark woods behind the house, where it was said that sometimes ghosts walked carrying things in their hands.

"Man don't need no money in this life."

"Things would be easier. That man isn't your friend anyway."

"Don't want to hear no more talk like that," Willie said, wiping his mouth.

The girl got up and lifted the coffeepot from the stove. She poured more in her own cup, but Willie had not touched his. He looked at the steam rising from the cup in smoke-like swirls, and he wondered what it would taste like.

"I think I'll finish mine on the porch," the girl said, leaving him alone.

She sat on the porch for almost an hour before she heard the truck. When she heard it coming up the lane, she stepped off the porch and into the road and waited. She had made up her mind to do something that was against all the rules that she had been taught.

Mr. Reynolds drove right up to her before he stopped. She walked around to his side of the truck.

"What do you want?" Mr. Reynolds asked. He looked at her with one arm across the top of the steering wheel and the other hanging down the outside of the door. There was dried blood on the fingers of his hand. "Who are you really?" he asked.

"You heard Mr. Temple. I'm his niece."

"Like hell. What do you want anyway?"

"Mr. Temple has decided to start charging for hunting."

"What?"

"You heard me."

"Girl, I hear you sayin' words, but it's all crazy talk."

"One hunt cost you five dollars," the girl said. She raised her chin, and her dark eyes were intense and secret.

"Five dollars! Listen, you're new around here, so I'll take it easy on you. Me and that old man got an agreement, and five dollars ain't part of it."

"Why don't you pay her, Dad?" his son said.

"You stay out of this," Mr. Reynolds said. He looked back at the girl and spit. She had to jump back. He laughed and pulled out his wallet. He took out a five-dollar bill and shook it in her face.

"This is for Willie, see? This ain't for you. I'm goin' to find out about you. Niece, my ass. Willie ain't got no family. He ain't got nothin'. He's just a dead old nigger and likes it that way."

When the girl stepped forward to take the bill, Mr. Reynolds twisted his hand beneath her reach and caught the front of her shirt. He pulled her toward him, looked at her, then flipped the bill inside her shirt.

"There," he said. "I got my money's worth."

Mr. Reynolds let the clutch out and moved on, out the broken gate and onto the old gin road. The dogs in the back rose up and yowled, still on the hunt.

Willie came out on the porch at the sound of the dogs, and he met the girl as she climbed the rough oak steps and picked up her coffee cup. She was breathing fast, and her eyes had tears in them, but Willie did not notice.

"What Mr. Reynolds say?"

"Listen," the girl said angrily. "What do you want me to call you, anyway?"

"Ever'body call me Willie," he said, sitting slowly in his rocker.

"Willie is a child's name. I'll call you Uncle William."

"Folk used to call me William. Long time ago. Just call me Willie now."

Willie began to hum. The girl went into the house. In the shadows, she remembered the man in the truck, and she shivered as if someone had stepped on her grave.

The beautiful Indian summer lingered through that first week in October. The breeze built during the day from the southeast. Grasshoppers crackled on dry stalks of grass, and crows called their hollow, echoing caw from high in the treetops of the deep woods. The temperature was warm, and the air was narcotic in the afternoons. The sun went down behind the trees in a red haze of dust at the end of the day.

The girl began cleaning Willie's house from the front to the back. She swept the dust and spiderwebs from the corners and rafters, moving a chair with her across the floor to stand on. Then she swept the whole house, including the front porch. She washed the windows and threw away the yellowed, stiff newspapers that Willie chinked the sills with from winter to winter. Finally, since Willie had no mop, she scrubbed the floor with rags she found under the sink.

Willie sat on the front porch, rocking with stubborn disregard while the girl worked. What she wanted to do was her business as long as it required no effort or interest on his part, and he paid little attention to her as she went in and out, dirty, cobwebs in the front part of her hair that was not covered by the knotted scarf she wore.

At the end of the second day, Willie was surprised at how much light was in his house. The girl had even washed the chimneys of the lanterns, and they burned so brightly that he could not look straight at them without the confusing after-spots clouding his vision. The girl asked him once how he liked the house now, but Willie only said, "Man don't need all that bright."

Undaunted, she said, "Your clothes are next."

She also got down on her hands and knees in the garden patch behind the house that was still roughly fenced from when his mother used to grow peas there, and she pulled the weeds out of it. Willie sat in the shade, poking at the ground with his cane, and watched her, asking her from time to time what she intended to do with all that turned-up ground. She told him about the garden she had had at home and her plans to plant greens and spinach for the winter months.

Once, for a while, after he was tired of watching her, he stood up and shuffled along beside her, knocking the weeds out of her way after she had pulled them up. But this made him remember that he didn't want a garden, and he stopped following the girl and went and sat on the porch in his rocker. He didn't watch her after that or ask her about what she was going to plant. Rocking slowly, he thought, man don't need no garden.

That night, Willie told the girl to warm up the leftover meat from the night before, but she told him she had thrown it out. Willie felt like he should have known this would start to happen. He was angry at himself for not seeing it, and he sat in his chair by the woodheater tapping his cane on the floor as if he wanted to hit her with it.

"You think a man got to eat somethin' different every time he come to the table? He don't. If you gon' stay here, you gon' have to learn that. You eat it till it gone, then you scrape the pot clean. If you gon' stay, you gon' learn that one."

Willie tapped his cane. "Good Lord provide till He see you throwin' the providin' out the back door. Then He cut you off."

The girl fixed her intense eyes on him. Nothing had been said about her staying or going for over a week, but now Willie seemed to have going in his mind again.

"Without no drop," he went on. "Cut you right off."

"I can cook something else," the girl said.

"Can throw good food out."

"Now you can just stop about that, or you can cook supper yourself," the girl said, raising her voice.

"Some things you better learn," Willie cut back.

"You just keep on and on. I don't want to hear any more about it. I'm sorry, okay?"

Willie raised his cane and narrowed his eyes. "You can cook whatever you find. Just don't throw it out before I have a chance at it."

Willie knew he had gained an advantage over the girl, and he decided to keep it by not saying anything else while she cooked or while they ate. She asked him once at the table how he liked it, but he never answered her, and he knew he really had the advantage then because she could not know what he was thinking. He knew, too, that if he ever was to keep her from hurting him, he had to have the advantage.

After they had eaten, Willie went back to his chair by the wood-heater. He opened the little rusty door on the front of it and slid in two oak limbs that he kept with the rest of his stovewood in a dynamite crate he had had ever since he worked the oil fields in the thirties. He pushed the door shut again with his cane and leaned back in his chair, feeling the heater warm him. For years now, his blood had felt yellow, and it had not been enough to keep him warm. The heater and the sun helped. In the winter, he was never warm.

Willie listened to the sound of the girl doing the dishes. After all the years of silence, the sound was strange to him, so that he could not ignore it any more than he could ignore the other sounds the girl made around his house. As he listened to the china bump in the sink, he pulled a pouch of Bull Durham from his coat pocket and a folder of cigarette papers from his shirt pocket. Very carefully, listening, he rolled a cigarette, spilling some of the tobacco on the floor between his shoes as he always did.

When the girl was through, she sat down in the other chair by the woodheater, and Willie became aware that she was watching him with her intense dark eyes. Willie went on smoking and did not look at her.

"You spilt ashes on your shirt," she said, after a while.

"*My* shirt."

"You're going to set fire to yourself if you're not careful."

"Never have yet."

"There's holes all in your shirt."

Willie smoked. He knew he had the advantage.

"I wish you had a radio," the girl said.

"What for."

"To listen to. It's so quiet out here, like a graveyard or something."

"Any time I want music, I just hum me a little song. Man don't need no radio."

"The ashes are falling on your shirt again."

"Now don't worry me, girl," Willie said.

"You've burned holes all over your shirt."

Willie shook his cigarette in her direction. "Dadblame it, girl, why cain't you shut up and let an old man smoke."

The girl looked at the floor, and Willie went on smoking and spilling ashes on his shirt. After a while, the girl looked at him again and asked, "What's that song you're always humming, anyhow?"

Willie tried to think, but he knew he had forgotten the words a long time ago. He couldn't remember the name of it either, only that it went high and low and had darkness in it. He had forgotten everything else but the tune.

"It sounds like *Nearer My God to Thee,*" the girl said, and she began to sing, and Willie knew she was singing the right song. Her high voice was sad and whispery in the quiet room.

"Though like the wanderer," the girl sang, "the sun gone down, darkness be over me, my rest a stone, yet in my dreams I'd be nearer my God to Thee . . . "

"That's it," Willie said, throwing his cigarette in the woodheater.
The girl looked at him, and he wrinkled his forehead. "Say," he
said. "How that one part go again?"

"Which part?"

"The part about darkness."

The girl sang it again, and Willie listened to it and was happy.
Then, before she was through, Willie felt that something was not
right, that something was changing that was not supposed to
change ever. Before she was through, he began to shut it out.
He was thinking that he still had the advantage, but he was not
sure about it. It seemed to him that the girl had managed to slip
like a ghost into a secret place that he kept locked tight. If he
was going to protect himself from her, he would have to keep his
mind on it.

Saturday dawned clear and cool and was the first true day of fall. A
soft norther had swept through the tops of the trees the night before
and had driven out the humidity and clouds. The northerly breeze
tugged at hickory and sweetgum leaves, setting them free, and
teased the withering ends of honeysuckle vines as if the tendrils were
strands of a girl's hair.

Willie was ready to go into town as soon as he got up. After he
had gone outside, he shuffled into the dark back room to awaken
the girl. He said her name, but she did not stir. He moved closer
to the bed and noticed that the girl had brought a new smell into
the room, a woman-scent that was at once pleasant and disturbing
in the memories it evoked. He looked down at her sleeping. How
small her bones were and how young her face looked when he did
not see her eyes. Looking at the girl, he saw his sister clearly for a
moment. He remembered how light she was when he used to carry
her around the yard on his shoulders, and a hurting that was part
anger, part longing, and part regret filled his chest. That had been
a long time ago, he reminded himself. His sister was dead now.

Willie poked the girl with his cane. Her dark eyes opened and
fixed on him.

"What is it?" she asked.

"Time to go to town."

"All right, Uncle William."

He turned to leave.

"Uncle William?"

"Huh?" he said. He watched her.

"Nothing."

Willie went slowly through the house and out the front door onto the porch, where he sat down. He looked at his cane for a moment, then hung it over the arm of the rocker. He looked out across the empty yard to the empty road and across the road to the woods where the sun turned the daylight to shadows. He heard the same familiar sounds, even the bell of the same hound, far away, running a deer most likely, his nose sandy and wet with dew. He rocked and felt the day warming. The morning was coming in like it always did, he thought, but a sound from inside the house made him aware that it wasn't coming in like it always did, that the girl made a difference.

She came out on the porch wearing the same blue dress she had worn the night she came to his house. She carried a pocketbook in her hands. The plastic had split at the edges and revealed a part of the cardboard underneath. Willie stood up and moved to the edge of the porch and went down the steps into the yard.

They walked slowly in the sand beside the road. Willie always went the same way, and there was a path there now with holes poked in it like rabbit tracks. Willie walked bent over, and he looked around him as they went. The girl asked him about things she noticed along the way: the knocking sound of a woodpecker, a late-blooming flower, an old house. He had seen and heard all the things she asked about many times in his walks alone, but he had never thought much about them. In the past, he had only walked and looked and noticed, but now there was somebody to tell it all to.

"That?" he asked when the girl wondered about a collapsed and rotting shack in a weedy clearing. "That just an old house used to belong to an old colored man. Some folk think he was crazy, but I never knowed him any. He stuck to hisself. When he died, nobody knew it for two weeks."

It was the same with everything she asked about. He was careful not to tell her everything he knew, but he told her enough to make it clear there were many things he knew something about.

After walking a mile and a half, they were close enough to town to see the high false fronts on the stores. The trees opened out into the fall sunshine as they passed the Phillips 66 filling station and the Short Change Cafe. At the corner, they crossed the empty street to the other side which was lined with stores and offices. They went up the sidewalk to the bench in front of the grocery store where two old black men were already sitting. They were older than Willie by a decade, but because of Willie's trouble, they accepted him into their static, waiting lives, and in some ways they thought of him as being even older than they since he seemed so much closer to and reconciled with his own death.

The two old men looked up with their old yellow eyes, and Willie introduced each one of them to the girl, each time saying her complete name and pointing to her with his cane.

"Praise the Lord," one said. "He done sent you an angel to take care of you in your old age."

Willie thought about it. "You reckon that's so?" he said.

"Uncle William doesn't need anybody to take care of him," the girl said. "He takes care of me."

Willie straightened a little, and the other two stared at the strange sound of Willie's old name.

Willie sat down and held his cane between his legs with his large hands resting on top of it. His head was swimming, and his back hurt him, but he felt a kind of pride in being that he had not felt for a long time.

"I'll sit here awhile," he said then. "You go on and have a look 'round."

"I'll be back," the girl said.

She went up the sidewalk looking in store windows, and Willie watched her for a minute. He was glad she had not argued with him in front of the other men, and he was glad, too, to see them nodding their heads in approval as she walked away.

The girl stopped in front of the window of a dress store she knew she could not enter. In a display littered with construction paper leaves were two mannequins wearing fall outfits. One wore a brown wool dress with a white collar and a soft, short wool jacket. The other wore a dark plaid print skirt and a thick sweater with orange snowflakes across the bosom. The mannequin with the suit wore a small hat, but the other wore a silk scarf tied over her blond fake hair.

Two girls a bit older than she came out of the store carrying flat boxes. She looked sideways at the girls, but not at their faces. She looked at their clothes and how pretty they were. Her own dress was second-hand and too small. The girls turned the other way. One of them, blond like the mannequin with the sweater, was teasing the other one and bumping her with her shoulder the way some people use their elbows to get laughter when they tell a joke that isn't funny.

The girl looked back at the store window, the mannequins blurring until she saw her own reflection. Her hair would never be loose and blow in the wind. Then, in her imagination, a man stood behind her. He wore a sleeveless undershirt, and his face was clenched in anger. He was holding her empty pocketbook and shaking his fist at her.

The ghost was silent, but the girl could hear what he was saying. She turned away from the window and went up the sidewalk. She passed the open doors of a drugstore and could smell pies that had been freshly made and set out at the soda counter, and she could smell the coffee from the big urn behind the counter where the thick white cups were stacked upside down. Beyond the drugstore was a shoe store and a washateria and a barbershop with a plastic barber's pole spinning irregularly in a tube of glass. At the end of the block was a five and dime. On the next corner was a feedstore, and opposite it was the bus station.

Back up the block, and across the street, Mr. Reynolds raised the blinds on the front windows of the post office. He saw the girl hesitate on the corner before crossing the street to the feedstore. He stared at her back, then pushed the taut string sideways to lock the blinds.

After they had eaten supper, Willie sat at the table listening to the girl tell him what she had seen in town, his jaw held loosely in a deprecating attitude that foiled the excitement of her discoveries. She cleared off the table, putting the empty dishes in the sink, but she was too preoccupied to wash them that night. As she wiped off the table, Willie pushed away from it and moved to his chair by the woodheater to sit and think.

The girl joined him, holding a compact mirror and a thick-bristled brush. The lamp was still on the table, and it threw their shadows against the empty back wall where the woods looked in at them through the single curtainless window. Willie pulled out his bag of Bull Durham and his cigarette papers, but before he could begin to make a cigarette, the girl stood, put her mirror and brush on the chair seat, then knelt beside him.

"Can I do that?" she asked.

"What for?" Willie asked, holding the things away from her.

"I've been watching you, and I want to know if I can do it."

"Girl cain't roll no cigarette."

"Let me try," she said, reaching for the pouch across his arm.

Willie felt the touch of the girl for the first time, and her hair was under his nose so that he could smell her. He was so stopped by her presence that she easily pulled the tobacco and papers from his hand. He stared at her. She opened the flaps on the package of rolling papers and pulled one out, sitting back on her heels on the floor beside him.

"Here," she said, putting the rolling papers back in his hand. She pulled open the drawstring of the cloth pouch. "How much do I put?"

"Not much," Willie said, watching her.

She balanced the paper on the fingers of her left hand while she tipped the pouch.

"That's enough," Willie said.

"Whoops," the girl said, pouring too much.

"You be makin' a cigar with that," Willie said.

The girl laughed, and Willie smiled, so absorbed in what she was doing that he forgot to shut her out. Her laugh was the quick laugh of a little girl, still mostly giggle. She poured some of the tobacco back in the pouch and gave the pouch to Willie.

"Now pinch it smooth," Willie said, squinting in the shadowy light.

The girl smoothed the tobacco along the length of the paper. "Now roll it?" she asked.

"That's right."

She rolled it. "Now I lick it?"

"Just a little bit."

She licked the edge of the paper and folded it over, then twisted the ends slightly so that the dry tobacco would not spill out. She held the cigarette between her thumb and index finger, with the other fingers spread like she was making the okay signal. She smiled.

"Ta da!" she said.

Willie took the cigarette and looked at it. He nodded and put it in his mouth to smoke it.

"I always wanted to do that," the girl said, returning to her chair. She picked up the mirror and brush and began brushing her hair. Willie heard the sound of the brush in her hair, but he did not watch her.

After several minutes, the girl made a disgusted sound like a gnat had flown up her nose, and Willie looked at her. "What," he said.

"All the really pretty girls are white."

Willie smoked. "*They* say."

"They are. They can do so much with their hair and make themselves look so different."

The girl looked at herself in the compact mirror trying to catch the weak light of the lantern. Willie smoked, and the smoke drifted toward the stovepipe, then up along it toward the shadows of the roof.

"Sometimes I feel so stuck. I want to be somebody else."

Willie shook his head gently, as if at a memory. "No you don't," he said. "Colored girl more beautiful than any other."

The girl put the mirror down and looked at him, doubt on her face. Willie went on softly, "Colored girl got the brown skin and eyes that match, the way things supposed to match. And the colored girl more mysterious because man cain't see the blush if she don't want him to. Her eye be pure and secret at the same time. Her hair bend or lie smooth by the way she feel about a man or whoever touch it, and when she wash it, her hair wear shining drops of water like it some kind of crown."

Willie sat forward and dropped his cigarette on the damper below the door of the woodheater. "Yes sir," he added. "Colored girl proud thing to be."

The girl held the mirror and brush in her lap and stared at him, the lantern light reflecting in her liquid eyes.

One afternoon in the second week, Willie showed the girl where he used to pen hogs back in the days when he had raised them for money. He walked slowly around the house, past the small garden, down to where the pens stood rotting in the weeds, and he told her stories of raising hogs. He talked slowly, and his head hurt him sometimes, but the day was warm, and it felt good to talk and remember the hogs.

"This here," he said, shaking his cane at the rotting outline of a pen, "where I used to keep the sows. Kept the boars over there. Some folk keep them together all the time, but not me. Don't want just any boar mating with my sows. You know about mating?"

"I know about it."

"You got to have good stock. I trapped some good wild hogs down in the bottom. They the best stock there is. I mixed them up with some fat old tame hogs, and I have a tough strain that got fat too."

"Why did you stop?"

Willie paused beside the fence and rested against one of the posts that had not fallen. It had been a long time, and he couldn't remember when he had begun to stop doing all the things that once he had enjoyed.

"I get a check now, once a month. Man don't need no hogs."

"How long ago?" the girl persisted.

Willie was quiet, thinking. A bluejay flew across a clearing at the edge of the woods. "Long time," Willie said.

"And all this time you just been doing nothing?"

Willie looked at the girl with a sharp glance. "I get by."

"But just doing nothing?"

"I get by, doing nothing."

"You might just as well be in your grave."

"What do you know about it? What do you know about the grave? You think the grave just in the ground? That what you think?"

The girl stared at him, and he turned away. A wind came up from the shadow of the woods and blew across him. Without thinking about it, he straightened his bent back and knees and raised his face to the sky. The girl's eyes widened at the height of the man. Then Willie folded again and turned back toward the house, his face a shadow.

Saturday came, and the two of them walked into town in the early morning, the smell of sand and dead leaves and pine trees intensified by the dew and the stillness of the early morning air. Willie looked forward to having the other men see the girl with him again, but he did not admit it to himself or let the girl know it.

As they approached the town, the girl reached in her pocketbook and produced a piece of paper she said was a list.

"List of what?" Willie asked.

"Of things to buy. Here's what I wrote down."

She read off the list to him, and he tried to picture the things in their succession.

"Setting hens!" he said suddenly.

"They'll give us eggs and eat bugs too. I saw some at the feed-store last week."

"I don't want no chickens scratchin' 'round my house and climbin' 'round my porch."

"I'm buying them with my own money, and I'll take care of them myself."

"Where'd you get any money, girl?"

"I got some."

"Well you best save it. You bring chickens 'round my house, and you'll be needing it for the bus."

"Don't pout, Uncle William," the girl said.

Willie stopped. "I won't have you talk to me that way, uncle or not," he said, shaking his cane at her. "You forget who you be. Keep a civil tongue or get back on that bus. Hear me?"

The girl looked at him, her eyes wide, as if he had just dropped from the sky. She nodded.

When they got to the bench, Willie sat down and waved her on. "You go on, girl. Buy whatever you want, long as it your own money. 'Cept for chickens."

The other men nodded.

About eleven o'clock, Mr. Reynolds walked over from the post office for a soda water. Willie saw him coming and watched him cross the street. The other black men saw too, and each of them looked down at their feet, their faces closed.

"Mornin' Mr. Reynolds," Willie said as the man stepped up on the sidewalk. He didn't look at Willie, but went right on in the store without saying a word. Willie felt a tingle of strangeness, as if there were a sudden change in the weather, and looked down, wrinkling his forehead. After a few minutes, both Mr. Reynolds and Isaac Hansen came out of the store. They leaned against the wall. Mr. Reynolds was holding a bottle of soda water.

"Well, Willie," Mr. Reynolds said. "I'm surprised to see you here this mornin'."

"Always come in on Saturday," Willie said.

One of the old men got up abruptly and moved off down the sidewalk. His going was like the breezeless calm that precedes a blowing summer thunderstorm. Mr. Reynolds took a long drink and looked at Willie. Isaac Hansen looked at him too, but didn't say anything.

"Yeah, that's right," Mr. Reynolds said. "That's right. I just didn't think you were our friend anymore."

"We been friends a long time," Willie said.

"Yeah. That's right. At least, that's what I was thinkin'." He took another drink. "But I wasn't too sure. I didn't think friends charged money for huntin' a few squirrels."

Willie thought. "I never did that."

"You must have forgotten. Or maybe your niece didn't tell you." Mr. Reynolds said *niece* as if it were the name of a stinging insect that had crawled under his collar.

"Tell me what?" Willie said, his face solemn and serious.

"She charged me five dollars the other mornin'. That's what."

"I didn't know that, sir. I owe it to you."

"Don't worry about it. What's done is done, right?"

"Yes sir."

"That's always been our agreement, hasn't it?"

"Yes sir."

Mr. Reynolds tilted the bottle and finished it off. He wiped his mouth with the back of his hand and looked at Willie.

"There's somethin' else too, which ain't none of my business, but I thought you would like to know it."

"What's that?"

"That girl ain't your niece."

"What?" Willie felt pushed back.

"I checked it out," Mr. Reynolds said. "That gal's first name is Louella. She come from Tyler, all right. She lived next door to your sister with her grandfather. She had plenty of chance to hear all about you before your sister was killed. When her old grandfather died, she just come out here tryin' to fool you, lookin' for a handout."

Willie tried to see past the shadow of the porch, but he couldn't. He had let down his guard, and it was all happening again. He should have died a long time ago. The chain that snapped and broke him should have killed him, but it had not, and now the betrayal and the hurt were happening all over again.

"She ain't your niece at all."

"How you find all this out, sir?" Willie asked, his voice barely a whisper in his dry mouth.

"Went to Tyler myself on business, and while I was there, I

checked. I was only thinkin' about you. There's no tellin' what this gal has on her mind."

"No sir," Willie said.

"I think you ought to get rid of her," Mr. Reynolds said.

"Think so?"

"Hell yes. I wouldn't keep no girl like that around. Nobody would blame you, either, once they found she wasn't even your kin. Besides, she don't understand our ways. There may be a lot of things changin' in other places, but things don't change here, do they?"

"No sir," Willie said automatically, responding more to the tone than to the words, the way animals do when they try to sense human language. Then he said, "I don't know what to do."

"I'll tell you what to do," Mr. Reynolds said. "You send her back to the bus station, and I will personally make sure she never bothers you again. You just leave that up to me."

The old man sitting next to Willie got to his feet and walked away as if he had suddenly remembered something he had to do, and his going was like the first echoing sounds of thunder from a coming storm. Mr. Reynolds gave the bottle to Isaac Hansen and the two smiled.

"You do that for me?" Willie asked.

"Sure," Mr. Reynolds said. "We're friends, ain't we?"

Willie thought, and his eyes narrowed. "I don't want her 'round no more," he said. "Man don't need it."

"I'm glad you still know what's best for you," Mr. Reynolds said.

He was resting in the shadow of a golden sweetgum tree when he heard someone call a name he had stopped using a long time ago. He turned, leaning on his cane, and he looked at the girl. She was a stranger now, and ugly and hurtful to look at. She walked toward him, carrying a brown paper bag in one arm and a wire cage with two young hens in it in the other hand. Her dark eyes were fixed on him from a long way off, and when she came closer, he saw that she was frowning. The locked-up feelings began to flow from their hiding place.

"Why didn't you wait for me?" she asked.

173

Willie turned without saying anything and walked away. He had stopped thinking about advantage again, and she had taken it from him. She was there to hurt him, the way he had been hurt so badly before, and he knew he had to get rid of her.

He looked back over his shoulder. "Girl," he said. "I told you not to buy no goddamned chickens. I told you that, didn't I?"

"We need them," the girl said.

Willie stopped and looked at her, his eyes narrow and hard. He was gaining the advantage.

"I also told you I don't charge friends for hunting on my land. I told you that too, didn't I?"

"Uncle William," the girl said sharply, but he was too quick for her.

"I ain't your uncle," he said. "Louella!"

The girl was taken aback. Willie thought of something. If he could get home before the girl, he could lock her out. He had the advantage now. He whirled on the girl suddenly, still bent over, all the words he had never had the chance to say to his sister unlocked and loose in his mind.

"All I ever done to take care of you, to give you what you wanted, and you just cut around behind me and stomp on my heart."

He lashed out with his cane and knocked the wire cage from the girl's hand. The chickens squawked and flapped their wings, throwing feathers out between the wire mesh. The girl stepped back and looked at him, her eyes wide and unbelieving.

"But William," she started.

"Ain't no William," Willie said. "Not no more."

He went down the side of the road, making sharp jabs with his cane in the bare sand of the path. The girl watched him, then snatched up the squawking cage and ran after him. From time to time, Willie turned and swung at her with his cane, but each time he did, the girl dropped back and followed him at a distance.

When he reached the porch, he lifted himself into his rocker and held his cane ready in case the girl tried to go into the house. She started to once, and he swung out at her, forcing her back onto the steps.

"You ain't goin' in my house no more," he said. "Not no more."

The girl put the cage down on the porch, still holding the brown bag in her left arm.

"Now listen," she said. "I got milk in this sack, and I'm going to put it in the icebox before it spoils."

"No you ain't."

"William Temple!" she said.

It was like a stranger's name in his ears, but he unconsciously squared his shoulders at the sound of it.

"I'm going in that house."

"Stay away." Willie raised his cane at her.

The girl's eyes widened, the way eyes do before a fight, and she stepped up on the porch. "What are you going to do? Hit me with that cane?"

"Damn right!"

"Well go ahead then. You think I haven't been hit before? Go ahead. Hit me as hard as you can because that's what it's going to take. Hit me! Go ahead. Isn't that what you did to Dorothy May?"

"Ahhhh!" Willie cried. His hand opened, and his cane dropped to the porch floor as he got to his feet. He turned his face upward and raised his hands high above him. He felt all the pain and hurt and misery that he had tried to bury years ago rise up sharp as knives in his heart. He froze for a moment, like a dark statue of eternal beseeching. Then, as the girl stared, he collapsed and folded limply back into the rocking chair.

William Temple was a young giant, walking in new shoes down the middle of the sandy road where grass grew and there was less dust. He had a gold chain clipped to a new pocket watch, and his touring cap was back on his head so that he could feel the breeze on his forehead as he walked. Ahead of him, by the gate, stood a young girl, with large round eyes in a round and pretty face. She was waiting for him, too shy to run out into the road to meet him, afraid he wouldn't want her to touch his fine clothes or stare at the bright gold of his watch chain. William Temple smiled at her and pirouetted in the road so that the girl could see what a sight he was. He felt light as a cardinal feather drifting down from where the startled bird had taken flight.

"William," the girl said, shaking his shoulder. She was holding a glass with an inch of smoky liquid in it and trying to put it in his hand. He pushed it away and looked out at the dark shadows in the yard. He could feel the chill of late afternoon.

"Take it, William," the girl said. "It will make you feel better."

She put the glass in his hand. He closed his fingers slowly around it.

"What is it?" he asked, sniffing it.

"I found your whiskey."

Willie sat back and raised the glass to his lips. He felt the whiskey bringing him back to life, and in a clear instant he realized that the whiskey was a part of all the other things the girl was trying to do to him. With a sudden movement, he threw the glass out into the barren yard.

The girl started and looked at him. "Now look what you've done," she said.

Willie sat back and did not look at her. He had found his cane on the arm of the chair where she had put it and was nervously tapping the hard wood of the porch.

"Too late," he said. "Too late to turn it."

"What?"

Willie looked at her, then looked away. He said, "The sun gone down. Darkness be over me."

"You got too excited. You don't know what you're saying," the girl said. There was a desperate look in her eyes that Willie had not seen before.

"It was better before you came," Willie said. "Folks knew how to let an old man live. They know to let him be and die, if that's what he want."

"That isn't what you want."

"What do you know about it? All my life I been alone and pushed by somethin' I never could determine. Now what? Now *nothin'!* Let it be over."

"Listen to you," the girl said, the desperate look in her eyes. "You've given up." She knelt in front of him. "I know I came here with a lie, but I didn't know what else to do. I always heard what a giant you were. You should have heard the stories Dorothy would tell about you, about what an important and wonderful man you were, and big enough to lift a house if you felt like it. To me, hearing those stories, you were like a black Superman who could do anything, help anybody. I been looking for that man ever since I got here, because I needed him. I couldn't go with my father when my grandfather died. All my father ever did was drink and take my money and hit me. Dorothy May was the only person ever understood me, even if she wasn't my mother. That's why I came here. It's like she sent me here."

"Get away from me," Willie said, turning from her. "Who you to say things like that? You just a stranger, that's who. Mean-mouth, lyin' stranger girl all you is. Man don't need that kind of trash 'round his house."

"Listen to me!"

"No."

"Listen to me, William!"

"Man don't need it!" Willie's voice rose to meet hers. "Man don't need it."

The girl put her hands on his knees, but Willie kicked her away. She had tears in her eyes and was sobbing when she looked up at him from the porch floor.

"Man don't need it," he said again. "By God, all he need is a porch and a rockin' chair and peace to die. Get along fine without all that other, without no nieces."

He was quiet, taking deep breaths, listening to the girl sob. He looked at her and remembered what Mr. Reynolds told him.

"Why don't you go find out when that bus gon' leave?"

She looked back at him, her eyes intense through the tears. Twice she started to say something, but couldn't. She rolled onto her knees.

"You're already dead," she said in her ugliest, most torn voice. "I don't need you!"

177

She got to her feet and went in the house to collect her belongings. She did not look at Willie when she came back out with her suitcase. She stepped off the porch and crossed the yard to the broken gate.

Willie watched her go and rocked, his chin raised and his jaws set tight.

The girl walked back to town in the clear October afternoon. Cars and pickup trucks went by on the road without paying her any mind. Leaves scuffed and crackled under her shoes. When she looked down, she saw the footprints she and Willie had left. Each one was like an angry word.

Before she was halfway to town, she left the path and entered the dark, unfenced woods. She sat on her suitcase under a pine tree for a long time and cried and thought about what she would do. In that way young people have, she had put all of her hopes on the man she pretended was her uncle, but he had let her down, and now she wanted to hate him. The disappointment closed her heart so tightly that the new feeling did not even make her sad. There was only emptiness where there had once been hope.

She had enough money to ride the bus back to Tyler, but there was nothing there for her, not even a sweetheart whose parents she could appeal to for a place to stay while she looked for some kind of work. She never knew her mother, and her father was gone, but she wouldn't live with him anyway. She was old enough not to, if she didn't want to.

When she got to town, most of the stores were beginning to close. A woman came out of the grocery store carrying a bag of groceries. The girl stepped around the woman on the sidewalk and stopped to look again in the window of the clothes store. The same mannequins were beautifully poised behind the glass, their empty, painted eyes like the eyes of people in the town she passed.

The bus station sat at the end of the street by itself. Without a bus in front of it, it looked as deserted and empty as the other buildings with offices that had already closed. She looked up and down the street, then angled across to the bus station, still with no clear destination in her mind. The nearer she got to it, the more she felt like crying until, when she stood under the Greyhound sign, tears filled her eyes and blurred the front door.

From the window of the post office, Mr. Reynolds had watched the girl cross the street. He moved closer to the glass and stared at her back as she hesitated, then went inside the bus station. He smiled to himself.

When the shadows had covered the day, Willie still sat in the rocker. He gazed out into the yard, moving his eyes from the over-turned glass to the broken gate, and out toward the old gin road. Then his eyes came back inside the yard and focused on the thing Mr. Reynolds had called a *heckabob*. Now, as he sat in the old pine rocking chair, he thought about what the girl had said about the thing, and he knew she had been right. She had been right about that.

He rocked gently until the chill crept inside his coat, waiting to see the nighthawks that came out in the twilight to chase bugs. They ate plenty of bugs, and they were no trouble, not like chickens scratching around and making noise. He looked around, wondering what the girl had done with the chickens. If he found them, he would kill them and eat them.

He could just see the nighthawks out over the gin road, but they did not come flying over his yard as they usually did. He got up and went in the house.

He built a fire slowly and warmed a stew from the icebox. When the stew was bubbling, he opened the cabinet above the sink and reached for the first plate he felt, filled it, and sat down at the table to eat. The house was deep and quiet outside the lantern light. Willie had turned down the wick as low as it would go and still burn to keep it from being so bright. The room was filled with shadows, but he was used to that, and it was familiar to him. Man don't need to get lonesome, he thought. He looked around like he wanted to say it out loud, but then he went on eating.

He sat by the woodheater for a while, smoking, letting the sparks fall on his shirt, and he thought about his sister. He wondered at the stories she had told of him out of pride or guilt. He tried to remember her and what she looked like.

"Let's see now," he said to himself. "She just a young girl when she run off. 'Bout so tall. Seem like it was fall. Yeah. She leave one evenin', wearing a blue dress. A young girl."

He went on thinking, trying to imagine what her life had been like in Tyler, a city he had ridden through in rough-springed trucks in the middle of a dozen nights, and trying to hate her, but he did not feel like hating her. He did not, in fact, even realize that it was not his sister he was thinking about.

Abruptly he got up and moved to the back of the house, carrying the kerosene lamp shoulder-high and squinting to keep the light out of his eyes. He went into the room he had given to the girl, and he looked slowly around the bed, searching for something she might have dropped or forgotten. Then he raised his eyes to the bare, dull walls.

"Man don't need no bright pictures," he said.

He looked at the mattress, bare now, sunk in the middle where the girl had curled herself up and slept.

"I guess she gone now," he said aloud. He didn't like the way his voice sounded and turned away from the room.

He went back to the woodheater, but he didn't sit down. He looked at the chair where the girl had sat watching him smoke and fretting about the way she looked. He could almost hear the high, whispery voice of the girl when she sang, but he couldn't remember all of the words. Willie remembered the first night the girl had come, and he remembered the sound of her crying. He thought about that and wondered why she had come at all.

"Man don't need—" he started to say, but he knew before he finished the sentence that blocking things out would not work anymore. There were too many things a man needed in his life. He thought of Mr. Reynolds, who said he was his friend, but who had always made him feel small. Mr. Reynolds would make sure the girl never came back, but all the girl had done was to try to give back something to Willie that he had thrown away a long time ago. When he thought of the girl and Mr. Reynolds at the same time, guilt and remorse cut his heart like the slash of a knife. He drew back his left arm defensively, so intense was the feeling, and the lamp slipped from his hand, dropping to the floor at his feet. The chimney broke, and the flame went out. Shadows rushed out of the corners at him.

"The Lord done cut me off," he said, his voice shuddery with emotion. "Darkness be over me."

From outside came the roar of a truck engine, the squealing of thin brakes, and the sudden, urgent honking of a horn.

By eight o'clock, the girl had eaten two Butterfingers, drunk an RC Cola from the drink machine, and looked over the map of Texas a dozen times. She sat at the end of a single row of straight-back oak chairs, her suitcase on the floor beside her.

George Jackson had finished carrying out the trash and cleaning the restrooms. It was time for him to go, but he sat down by the girl instead. The only other person there was Joe, the night clerk. He was a small, nervous man with red hair.

"You all right?" George asked.

"Just dandy," the girl said.

George shook his head. "Willie is a strange one. I remember when he could terrorize the whole county on a single night if he wanted to, but something happened to him. Folks kind of leave him alone. Y'all have a fight?"

The girl shrugged. "I don't care about him."

George shook his head at the strangeness of it. "Goin' back home?"

"I don't have a home."

"Well, you can always come back again." George said, ignoring the bitterness of her last remark. "Wait awhile. Let him get used to the idea."

"I don't care what he does," the girl said.

"You'll change your mind," George said. The girl did not look at him. "Well, I be headin' out now. Take care of yourself."

The girl made a sound like a laugh torn in two.

George patted her knee, then stood up. He had daughters of his own, and he recognized her look. If she didn't leave during the night, he would see Willie in the morning and have a talk with him.

George went around behind the counter and got his coat and lunch sack. He folded the sack and slipped it in his coat pocket. As he put on his coat, the front door opened and Mr. Reynolds walked in, looking around as if he had never seen the bus station before. George shook his sleeves down inside the arms of his coat and felt the coldness of fear in his stomach.

Mr. Reynolds walked past the girl without looking at her, and stopped at the counter. "Take a break, Joe," he told the man at the desk.

Joe looked up from a magazine. "What's going on?"

"Nothin', as far as you're concerned. Take a break."

Joe looked over the top of the counter at the girl, then got to his feet and started for the door, grabbing his coat as he went.

Mr. Reynolds watched him go, then looked at George. "What are you doin', boy?" he asked.

"I was just leavin', sir."

"Then leave."

George nodded and hurried out the door. He knew why Mr. Reynolds was there, and he knew that the only chance the girl had was if he could get help. Outside, he saw Isaac Hansen standing by Mr. Reynolds's truck, his arms folded across his chest.

"Where you goin'?" Isaac Hansen said with an edge on his voice.

"Home, Mr. Hansen," George said. "So long."

George went to his own pickup, got in, and slowly drove away. At the corner by the grocery store, he turned left and headed out of town, letting the truck pick up as much speed as it could. When he got to the gin road, he veered off, sliding a little in the deep sand. He turned in at Willie's gate, his hand slapping the horn.

Willie came out on the porch. "Who's that?" he called, the coldness of dread inside him.

"Willie, come on. You got to hurry. Mr. Reynolds and Mr. Hansen at the bus station with your niece, and they look like plenty of trouble."

"She not gone," Willie said in wonder and relief.

"Willie, don't fool around, goddammit. That girl's in big trouble."

Pulled by George's voice, Willie moved down the steps, steadying himself with his cane, while George bounced on the truck seat to make him hurry.

It had been a long time since Willie had ridden in a truck, and the speed as George raced through the tunnel of his headlights brought back memories of the oil field and the wild times the roughnecks had on their days off. He sat up straighter to see over the high dashboard. Neither of them said anything, although George had had enough time to wonder how Willie could help the girl. He had acted on the memory of stories he had heard about Willie when he had been a giant.

George slid to a stop at the bus station, relieved to see Mr. Reynolds's truck still parked at the side. Willie fumbled for the door handle, while George looked around for Isaac Hansen. When Willie got the door open, he said, "Get the sheriff." He climbed out, one hand still on the door.

"But Willie—"

"Get him now."

Willie slammed the door, and George spun his bald tires toward the other side of town. Without watching him leave, Willie turned toward the bus station. He shuffled to the front door and pulled it open with his free hand.

There was a light in the ceiling just inside the door that threw Willie's short shadow ahead of him, but the rest of the waiting room was dark except for the lamp on Joe's desk. The girl's suitcase stood alone. He had to step forward before he saw that the two men were behind the counter with the girl. Willie tapped his cane on the floor.

"Hey," Willie said.

Both of the men were holding the girl, bending her back over the desk while she struggled and kicked to get away. At the sound of Willie's voice, Isaac Hansen jerked the girl up, pushed her toward

Mr. Reynolds, and let go of her. He came around the counter, wiping his hands on his hips, his mouth twisted in a sneering kind of smile and his eyes slits in his face.

Willie could not remember what Mr. Reynolds had told him the girl's name was. He said, "Let my niece go."

"Now, Willie, you just go on home," Mr. Reynolds said, breathing hard. "We'll take care of this girl."

Willie looked past Isaac Hansen at him. "Let her go," he said.

"She ain't nothin' to you," Mr. Reynolds went on, holding the girl tightly. "Hell, she was tryin' to rob you. She might have cut your throat in the dark, if I hadn't found out about her."

From the other side of the counter, the girl fixed her intense and desperate eyes on Willie. Isaac Hansen looked from one man to the other, waiting.

"Let her go, Mr. Reynolds," Willie said quietly, tapping the end of his cane on the floor.

"Get out of here!" Mr. Reynolds shouted.

"I'm tired of messin' with you, Willie," Isaac Hansen said. "Now go on. Who the hell do you think you are, anyway?"

From behind the counter, the girl cried, "He's William Temple!"

At the sound of his name, Willie straightened himself to his full height, and the light behind him threw his shadow across the floor, over the counter, and onto the surprised face of Mr. Reynolds. For the first time in almost twenty years, William Temple was the giant he had once been.

"William Temple!" the girl cried again.

Isaac Hansen ran at him, and William Temple raised his cane with all his force and brought it down across the other man's face. The shank of the cane broke with a sound like a rifle shot, and Isaac Hansen, blinded, staggered back into the row of chairs and fell.

"Let her go," William Temple said, harshly, turning his face to Mr. Reynolds. He could feel the stretch and tear of his muscles.

Mr. Reynolds pushed the girl forward. She caught herself against the counter and ran around the end of it toward William Temple. She put her arms around him like he was a tree, and she pressed her face into his shoulder, but William kept his eyes on Mr. Reynolds.

"What you gon' do now?" he said. "Whatever it be, go ahead."

Mr. Reynolds stared back at him but didn't move. He seemed small, standing behind the counter, and William Temple wondered that he had never noticed what a little man he was.

There was a crunch of gravel, the sound of car doors slamming, and the sheriff pushed into the waiting room of the bus station, his pistol in his hand.

"What's goin' on?" he shouted.

"I can tell you—" Mr. Reynolds started, but William Temple cut him a look and said in a loud voice, "No suh!"

"Mr. Rose," William Temple said. "On August 12, 1952, this man and that man stabbed a government man to death in the office of the cotton gin. I saw them take him in there and come out without him. It nothin' to me, so I don't say nothin', but this business with my niece be different. Man don't need it."

"They were going to hurt her, Mr. Rose," George Jackson said from the doorway, his voice too loud in the quiet room.

"You believe that—?" Mr. Reynolds pointed his finger.

"Shut up, Sam," the sheriff said. "Put your hands on that counter where I can see them and don't say another word. I believe what I know."

From the floor, Isaac Hansen groaned and held his hands to his face. The sheriff made certain Mr. Reynolds obeyed him, then he turned to William Temple. "Thank you, sir," he said. "You have helped out a lot of people tonight."

William Temple nodded. "I remember your father."

As the sheriff went around them, William Temple fell against the girl, feeling the strain of standing erect. The girl caught him under his arm and held on to him. She was crying, but her intense eyes were proud.

"You came to get me," she said. "You didn't have to, but you did. Nobody ever did that for me in my life."

"Broke my good cane," William Temple said.

"You don't need it," the girl said. "I'll be your cane."

William Temple dropped the broken end of his cane on the floor and looked at the girl. His head was spinning, and the torn muscles felt like fire, but there was something inside of him again that had not been there for a long time, something made of love and pride and forgiveness and peace, something that had the face of his sister when she was young and happy.

"You didn't go no place," William Temple said as they moved toward the door, unaware of the sheriff, who was handcuffing the two men, or George Jackson, who had retrieved the girl's suitcase.

"I didn't have no place to go to," the girl sobbed, holding on to him.

"Uh-huh," William Temple said, and slowly, the way the sun comes up, he smiled as if he knew a secret.

Already in his mind, there was a list of things he needed. There was a garden to plant, wires for electric lights to be put into the house, a bathroom with a bathtub, a radio. There would be boys coming around, he knew, but this time he would not be abandoned. It seemed to him that Dorothy May had somehow left him something after all, and as they passed under the light in the ceiling above the door, the darkness and gloom that had lain over him for so many years were dispelled forever by the sobbing embrace of the strange, lost girl from Tyler, Texas, who had claimed to be his niece and whose real name he had completely forgotten.

Summer Seeds

Clay Reynolds

I

THIS IS IT!" Rusty whispered breathlessly to his three companions as they scurried across the banked sand road and slid into the ditch alongside. They had crossed the field opposite the road quickly, jumping and hopping because of the ugly sandburrs that attached themselves to their socks and bootlaces and stuck to their skin and drew blood. Once across the field, they fought their way through a stickery plum thicket on the road's western side, gingerly avoiding the thorns and vines that snatched at clothes and threatened to put out eyes.

The four of them lay sore and sweaty, panting in the bottom of the deep ditch that was choked with tumbleweeds and other debris caught by the Johnson grass along the top, listening to the cicadas and grasshoppers singing their mindless songs of July heat. Sweat ran down their faces, streaking the red, sandy dirt that covered them, and their throats were choked with dust and grit from their exertions in the summer sun.

"Take a break now," Rusty ordered, looking into the three faces that focused on nothing in particular in their fatigue. Their legs ached from the half-mile journey over plowed ground from the railroad tracks where they left the handcar. "Save your water," Rusty said. "Just sip. Don't drink. You'll get cramps if you gulp it down."

He removed a dented canteen from his web utility belt and unscrewed the cap. The water was warm and gritty and tasted metallic, but it soothed his throat. His companions were following his example, but the youngest, Kevin, was gulping his, spilling the water down his dusty T-shirt and onto the ground.

"You'd better save some for later," Rusty screwed the cap onto his canteen. "You won't get any of mine if you run out."

Kevin started to invoke a little brother's privilege and protest, but he thought better of it, replaced the cap on his own canteen, and began trying to fasten it back onto his own civilian-style belt.

Rusty, Kevin's older brother, was the acknowledged leader of the group even though Gary was older by ten months and Tommy was taller by six inches. At Rusty's reprimand of the youngest boy, the others also took smaller sips, and then refastened their canteens to web belts resembling Rusty's. Tommy produced a crumpled cigarette pack from his fatigue jacket, and they passed around a bent Winston, inhaling the smoke, feeling as if they had just accomplished something tremendous.

It was a long way from their campsite on Rusty's dad's farm five miles west of the ditch in which they now hid along the perimeter of Kyle Cooper's watermelon field, but the trip was going to be worth it. They were sure of that. Rusty had made a solo scouting trip overland two weeks before. He laid out the plan then, and he briefed each man on his part in the operation. The only unexpected development had been Kevin.

For five years Rusty, Tommy, and Gary had been coming out to Rusty's dad's farm to camp and hunt. They had become a team, learning to respond to each other's quirks and kidding around, and they had become best friends in the process. The weekend outings began in early spring—"as soon as there's green on the mesquite," Rusty's dad always said—and continued until the first really icy mornings of the fall.

For each excursion, the planning began early in the week as the boys gathered provisions and gear for the two-night stay on the two hundred acres bordering Blind Man's Creek. Excitement would build to a fever pitch by Friday noon when Rusty's dad or one of the other parents would drive them out from town and leave them on their own until Sunday night when, exhausted, satisfied, and filled with plans for the next time, they would be picked up and hauled back.

They didn't go every weekend, of course, and each time they tried to do something different. When they were younger, they fished in the creek and cooked perch and catfish on open fires. They supplemented their meals with peaches from the farm's orchard, plums from the ubiquitous thickets, and corn from the small plot Rusty's dad kept as a part of a vegetable garden surrounding an ancient, deserted farmhouse.

As they grew older, guns appeared as a part of their gear. At first their parents, Tommy's especially, were apprehensive about three youngsters being "turned loose" with firearms. But wheedling, crying, and begging prevailed, and ever since they were eleven, they had brought guns with them, mostly .410 shotguns and .22 rifles that replaced the BB guns they had toted on their earlier adventures.

In the course of these armed campouts, they added to their store-bought provisions with freshly killed rabbit and various game birds. Once they bagged a small white-tailed doe out of season. That was a major secret. They had crudely dressed and butchered the deer and had eaten all they could stand of the stringy, half-cooked venison before dumping the carcass into a limestone cave.

Although none of the boys was officially trained in woodcraft or outdoor life, they had all gradually acquired the skills and knowledge necessary for safety and comfort. The fact that Rusty's father owned the land had automatically elected the red-haired boy as the group's commander, a role he took seriously. He was adamant about firearm safety, demanding that guns always be carried pointing toward ground or sky, that they be unloaded when crossing fences or the creek, and that none of them ever clown around with a weapon. He would become enraged if anyone idly or indiscriminately fired his gun. In all their years of bringing weapons to the farm outings, no one had been hurt or even frightened because of monkey business with the guns or, for that matter, anything else.

Their care and attention to method and safety, however, had backfired a bit when Rusty's mother inserted Kevin into their group.

The smallish, younger boy was an interloper, a legendary tattletale who was likely to report the minor transgressions of the campers: illicit cigarettes, bad language, and the occasional flask of whiskey Tommy could smuggle out of his father's liquor cabinet for passing around late at night when the storytelling and newly discovered sexual fantasizing became intense.

As a result of Kevin's unexpected intrusion into their group when the plan for stealing watermelons came up, the boys were forced to postpone that action for two weeks. They brought Kevin along on a trial basis first and limited their activities to minor sins to see just how much, if anything, he would report to Rusty's mother.

He proved himself a real trooper, so badly did he want to be a part of the excursions. The thought of tattling about Gary's stories about Eddy Carlysle's mother undressing in front of an open window or what Tommy had really done with Janey Riley in the balcony of the Palace Theatre during a John Wayne double feature never crossed his mind. He was soon pronounced trustworthy by the group, even though they not-so-secretly wished he had gotten sick and missed this particular weekend.

But when Wednesday rolled around, Kevin was more excited about the trip than any of them, and they realized his presence was inevitable. So the operation was scheduled to go ahead as planned. Like it or not, they were a foursome.

Rusty stood up in the ditch. So deep was the trench between the road and the watermelon field that the boy's copper-colored hair, revealed in its disheveled damp mat as he removed his OD hat to wipe sweat from his forehead, didn't show over the top of either side. Digging his toes into the sandy walls of the ditch, he scrambled up the field side and peered over the top. He grabbed a large clump of Johnson grass to keep from sinking in the red sand and tumbling to the culvert's bottom.

The other boys tried to follow his example, but their combined weight and digging toes began to erode the sides of the ditch, and Rusty snapped at them. "Get down, dammit. Get down! Check your weapons or somethin'. *I'm* on reconnoiter right now!"

They half slid, half fell back into the ditch and began inspecting their guns. Tommy and Gary carried .410's, pump action. Kevin had a small, single-shot, bolt action .22 rifle that had been Rusty's. The three began opening and closing the breeches of their guns, dry firing one time to make sure nothing was jammed or clogged with sand. No one spoke. Rusty demanded a strict military discipline when they were on an operation.

From the time they had started bringing BB guns out to the farm, Rusty had taken on the role of a military leader. They had discarded their Boy Scout style camping clothes and equipment, preferring instead a mishmash of paramilitary gear from the army surplus store in town—field jackets and blouses, fatigue pants with jungle camouflage, OD hats and web belts, combat boots, and even military haversacks and backpacks. Only Kevin was still in "civvies," since he had not yet had time to mow enough lawns or to run enough errands to outfit himself like the bigger boys.

They set up shelter halves for pup tents, slept on "rubber ladies," and ate from GI mess kits. One summer, two years before they decided to try to steal watermelons, they did odd jobs around town to make enough money to purchase by mail five cases of surplus K rations, which they figured would give them greater mobility from their campsite than the store-bought provisions they usually brought. But they were sorely disappointed to learn how tasteless and nearly inedible the military fare was, and they wound up burying what they didn't throw into Blind Man's Creek on their first attempt to survive in the field like soldiers. It was the worst weekend they ever spent on the farm. They couldn't even find a rabbit to shoot, and that summer's drought had dried all the corn on the stalks before it ripened.

Things military fascinated them, even so. Had they thought about it, they would have claimed that the military equipment was cheaper than the BSA camping gear at Sears or Montgomery Wards, and it was less expensive than civilian products. The surplus stuff was more comfortable and more expendable as well. They also relished being separate from what Rusty called the "pussy Boy Scouts," since he had been thrown out of a troop for bringing cigarettes on a campout. The Boy Scouts dressed in short britches and spent all their time trying to sharpen tent stakes or to build a fire rubbing sticks together. Rusty found the whole organization rife with "fairies an' mama's boys."

The truth of the matter was, however, that the military dress and equipment made them feel more manly. The guns complemented this masculine image, as did the cigarettes and the whiskey, although neither of the latter ever amounted to more than a parson's share for each, and as they strolled over the bluffs and arroyos of the farm's pastures, they each secretly enjoyed the fantasy they discovered in their shadows that seemed to silhouette soldiers of fortune—guns at the ready, smokes dangling from tough expressions—stalking slant-eyed Communists or yellow peril, square-headed Nazis or devious Italians who lurked behind every clump of scrub cedar. They called each other "men," and somehow they always felt taller when they were out on the farm. It was a vision, they secretly thought, of what they would become.

Satisfied with his observations, Rusty slid down the bank and inspected his own weapon, a brand-new Browning 16-gauge automatic shotgun. It had been a birthday present from his dad, and it was a beauty—fully-choked, gold-plated trigger, heavily carved designs in the bright hickory stock. He had lusted after the gun in Greely's Hardware Store for over a year, and when his father had presented it to him a week before, he had been speechless with gratitude and love. He wiped off the shiny blue steel barrel with a camouflage towel he found in his haversack, frowning over the pitting the sandy terrain might cause. He hoped they could get back to camp before dark. So far, he had only fired it at targets, and he was dying to shoot at a rabbit or some other living thing just to see what the weapon could do.

"Time check," Tommy said, glancing down at his wristwatch. He also was proud of a birthday present, an electronic watch, one of the first of its kind, his uncle had given him earlier in the summer. He and Gary had almost had a fistfight over whether the astronauts would soon be trading in their Omegas for the kind Tommy now wore on his freckled arm.

"Mark, 1930," Rusty said, checking his Timex. The others looked at their timepieces and nodded in confirmation. "Okay," he went on, stowing the towel safely away. "The plan is for us to enter the perimeter at 2000 hours. Let's sit back and get what shut-eye we can."

He didn't feel foolish saying what he said in such tones or in such a play-like atmosphere. All four of the boys had become caught up in the make-believe reality of the "operation." They tacitly agreed that every outing required planning and precision, even if it only involved stalking a rabbit. They weren't just waiting in a ditch to steal watermelons. They were raiding a Chinese Communist ammo dump, a secret Nazi rocket base, a Jap prisoner-of-war camp, a Russian headquarters. Raised on war stories told by their veteran dads and uncles, well read in Sergeant Rock's adventures, and enthusiastic fans of movies and television programs about battle and the courage of combatants, they easily fell into the adult game of combat and the parlance of warriors.

What they were planning may have been nothing more than a time-honored prank—stealing two watermelons—but they invested it with greater significance. Indeed, the watermelons themselves, fruity and delicious as they would be, were of secondary importance. What mattered was the operation, the success of the mission, the quality of the adventure.

After five minutes of silence broken only by the din of cicadas who sensed sundown coming, Rusty looked intently at each of his comrades and hooked a thumb toward Gary. "If you're not goin' to sleep, then go up an' take a look," he ordered. "We need to keep watch just to make sure we ain't been observed."

Gary rose and leaned his shotgun carefully against the bank of the ditch. He moved down the trench-like dugout away from where their previous climbing had eroded the high wall and climbed up to scan the field and the road alongside. After a few minutes, he returned.

"All clear," he whispered. "Ain't nobody in sight."

The military pretense stopped short of assigning rank. While Rusty was the leader, he refused to participate in the wrangle that always took place when Tommy and Gary argued over who would be second in command. When Kevin had joined them, there had been some talk of calling him "private," but the argument immediately resumed over who would be sergeant and who would be corporal, so they dropped it. Kevin went along with their pretenses anyway and seemed to accept his unnamed inferior rank easily, without protest, unless he found himself too often assigned to menial chores around the campsite while the others did nothing.

"Let's go over it one more time," Rusty suggested. He took a handmade map from his jacket pocket and pressed it flat on the floor of the ditch.

Stealing the melons in the first place had been Gary's idea. The boys frequently stopped with one or more of their parents and bought watermelons and cantaloupes and cucumbers from Kyle Cooper—"Ol' Man Cooper," everyone called him—but there was no challenge in that. Anyone could buy food. Instead, the watermelons wound up being the final touch in a master plan developed and nurtured around the campfire since early April, a plan Rusty dubbed "Seeds of Survival." It was designed to see just how much they could get away with. Their mission, Rusty explained to them, was to survive one weekend totally on stolen food; each of them was to provide a significant item of "rations" to feed all of them, with the catch that everything had to be acquired in some illicit way. The whole idea frightened them, and as much as they talked about it, none of them, especially Rusty, believed it would ever happen.

Then Tommy came up with a canned ham, stolen from his home pantry, much to the confusion of his mother, who discovered it missing just before she began cooking Sunday dinner for his grandparents. It was almost more than he could do to keep quiet as she called Mr. Colby, the proprietor of Colby's Grocery, and argued with him for half an hour about whether or not she had paid for the ham and whether or not the box boy had packed it with the rest of her purchases.

Tommy wrapped the purloined ham in oilcloth and hid it in a hole he dug behind their garage. He held his breath when his father mowed there and stopped to puzzle over the freshly turned earth. Finally, though, his father apparently forgot about it, and Tommy smuggled the ham out to the farm on their next outing and presented it to his comrades as the first step in implementing Rusty's original idea. They hid it in what Kevin called a "hidey-hole," actually an old tack box they had found in the ramshackle barn near the farmhouse, and eagerly made suggestions about other food items they would need.

The following week, Gary brought some canned vegetables he had shoplifted from the hapless Colby's stock, and he topped Tommy's generous contribution with a six-pack of Falstaff beer, stolen from his eldest brother's car while he was packing for a fishing trip. These rations joined the ham in the hidey-hole.

That was nearly a month ago, and now, while the boys sweated in the lingering heat of the summer day, slapping the biting flies that seemed always to swarm from a plum thicket for a mile around, the beer cooled in the creek. A fire would cook the ham and vegetables as well as some roasting ears Kevin would be dispatched to "steal" from his father's garden. The plan was nearly a success. All that remained to complete their evening "mess" was Rusty's contribution; and that's what had brought them to Kyle Cooper's watermelon patch.

From the time he first suggested the whole scheme, Rusty had been unable to come up with an idea of how to add to their provisions. A loaf of bread or, perhaps, some tomatoes or something might have been easy enough to lift from his mother's kitchen, but those seemed paltry contributions; and he knew that even had she caught him in the act, she would have been pleased to let him have them. He needed to figure out a way to outstrip his friends' efforts, a way to establish once and for all his superior ability to plan and lead such expeditions as the campouts had become. He needed an idea that was both difficult and daring. If possible, it needed to be dangerous as well. Finally, Gary came up with the idea of stealing the watermelons.

The idea instantly appealed to Rusty, since it involved more than a simple theft of something from one's parent. Such an operation would require leadership, strategy, tactics. He quickly began working on an elaborate plan to involve the whole group. He spent two afternoons in the library poring over county maps, and during the next week's campout, on foot and alone, he made the trip from his dad's farm over to Cooper's watermelon patch, scouting the terrain. He planned every detail of the operation, even drawing an intricate and accurate map to scale.

Rusty's dad's farm was a marvelous place for boys to camp out and hunt. The two hundred acres consisted mostly of worthless pasture on which his dad ran a few scrawny head of cattle and grew some vegetables that were perpetually overrun with weeds and insects and ravaged by indigenous critters like skunks and rabbits. There were some pecan trees, a peach orchard, and a hay field. His father occasionally put out crops that required little maintenance other than planting and harvesting.

Rusty's dad was an attorney, and he had plenty of income from his small office over the drugstore on Main Street, more than enough business, in fact, to occupy him without worrying about a farm he had bought as a tax write-off in the first place.

Originally the farm had been a part of a larger operation with the two hundred acres now owned by Rusty's dad as the center and headquarters for five tenant farms. The depression ruined the owner, and it was split up and variously owned and leased by ranchers and farmers who lived elsewhere in the county. Rusty's dad bought it two weeks after his red-haired son was born. It was a hedge against rising costs of higher education, he said to anyone who asked why he held onto it.

It was also a place well designed for boys' adventures. Cut through with bluffs, arroyos, and rills from the creek that found its deepest and widest proportions just north of the farm's boundary, the place offered an endless variety of topographical features ranging from the grassy pastures and squat mesquite trees to the sandy loam of the western border.

Years before, a railroad spur had been cut through it to connect the gyp mill in the western portion of the county with the siding in town south and west of the farm. Modern trucking made the track obsolete; it was abandoned sometime during World War II. But the steel rails and bed, choked with weeds and mesquite, remained; and it was along that track that the boys discovered an overturned and forgotten, rusty and broken handcar one summer morning.

After Rusty's dad inspected the vehicle and gave his permission for the boys to try to get it running—something he privately doubted they ever would do—they spent the better part of a month working on it. With books checked out of the county library, a variety of borrowed tools, and the assistance of a retired railroad brakeman who came out to look over the antique handcar and helped them raid the abandoned roundhouse in town for spare parts and a bucket of axle grease, they managed to make it operational.

By hanging their combined weight on the handles of the old car, they could start it. Then only one on each side was required to keep it rolling. They moved it up and down the length of track—which they had to clear with machetes and axes—within the barbed wire perimeter of the farm, and no campout since the car had been repaired was complete without a round trip. Two of them would take turns pumping the car while the third sat in the middle, rifle at the ready to fend off attacking Indians, German panzers, Japanese sappers, or any small game that came into view.

The handcar played a central part in Rusty's plan to steal the watermelons. On his solo scouting expedition, he found that traveling ten miles from their campsite on Blind Man's Creek to the melon patch and back was strenuous enough, but to do so carting the melons would be next to impossible. But by removing the barbed wire at the farm's western end and continuing down the track, they could ride to within a half mile of the melon patch, leave the car, steal the melons, and pump themselves back before dark, pausing only to restore the rusty barbed wire.

The only major difficulty Rusty foresaw was transporting the melons from the field to the handcar over rough fields filled with burrs and stickers. There were, in addition, two plum thickets and two shelter breaks that had to be negotiated, and all were overgrown and possibly infested with rattlesnakes and other unpleasant surprises. By rigging up shelter halves between two of them, he figured, they could make it easily enough, provided they took turns carrying the heavy melons.

There was more to the operation than that, though. There had to be. They had prepared tactics carefully—not firing their weapons after they left the campsite, loading their pockets with extra "ammo" in case they ran into trouble, and staying well off the roads, lying low whenever they were in sight of a farmer's truck or tractor passing by. On his first scouting trip, Rusty also discovered that the afternoon sun reflected directly off the back windows of Old Man Cooper's house for almost exactly fifteen minutes. This glare, he reasoned, would be very bright, painfully bright, to anyone looking directly into the west, especially just before sunset, and it would provide them with a natural cover for their raid. By consulting an almanac and calculating the differences in times of sundowns between his scouting trip and the evening of the operation, he figured that the full glare of the sun would strike the house's windows at exactly 7:58. If they waited until 8:00, they would still have plenty of time to scramble into the field, select the melons, and make their getaway through the plum thicket on the other side of the road.

They had gone over their plan a dozen times that week and had three briefings since they arrived at the campsite that afternoon. The idea was to choose four medium-sized melons, bring them back to the ditch as quickly as they could, and then decide which ones to haul back. Each would be studied for size and shape, and only the two most easily carried would be chosen. They would sling them on the shelter half and take turns, but the two men whose melons were picked would get the extra two beers from the six-pack—that was agreed.

No talking was to take place after "M-Hour," the moment they went "over the top." They felt confident that none would be necessary. Old Man Cooper probably wouldn't care, they each secretly believed, even if he saw them. And even if he did, he had more melons than he could ever sell, so they each rationalized as they contemplated the more serious aspect of their raid.

"Time check," Rusty whispered as he finished going over the plan once more. He had just reviewed their route back to the tracks, taking into consideration that something might go wrong and suggesting landmarks along the tracks for a rendezvous in case they were separated. "We'll wait five minutes, no longer," he cautioned all of them with an especially hard glance at Kevin, who winced slightly.

"It's 1955," Tommy said, grinning in anticipation of the coming action. It was hot in the ditch, although the shade now came from the western side as the sun sank behind the plum thicket. They all licked the grit from their lips and squirmed, feeling the sandy soil uncomfortably close to their skin beneath their clothing.

Rusty looked over his men. Tommy's blond hair stuck out from under his OD cap. He always needed a haircut, but his parents never seemed to make him get one. Gary wore a crewcut so short his hair looked more like wire bristles than anything else. Kevin looked around to Rusty, and his big brother frowned. He really hated it that Kevin was here. It wasn't that he didn't like his brother or anything. It was only that he didn't want him to be a part of everything he did. But there he was, and Rusty felt a tinge of resentment against his mother as he recalled her smile when she forced the boy on them and refused to hear any arguments against it.

"If you want to go out to the farm, then Kevin goes with you." She held up her hand to stay any protest. "And if you don't want to," she went on, "then you can just stay home and clean out the garage." There was no choice: Kevin was with them.

"Take your positions, and—good hunting," Rusty said in a serious tone. He glanced once more at Kevin to make sure he was okay. He seemed to be, and the four boys aligned themselves up and down the ditch and waited for Rusty's order to go "over the top."

Rusty climbed to the crest of the ditch and peered at Old Man Cooper's farmhouse. The sun lit the windows with a blinding flash, and there was no one coming on the road from either direction. The old Dodge pickup he had seen parked there so many times before was near the chicken coop, but the old man was nowhere in sight.

"Okay," he yelled. "This is it. Let's go."

Moving together, the quartet scrambled out of the ditch and felt themselves immediately sinking into the sandy soil on the field's edge. Old Man Cooper had terraced the sides of the field to catch as much as he could of the infrequent rain.

The four youngsters moved more or less abreast about fifty yards into the midst of the watermelon vines, tripping quietly through the gourds, looking for likely candidates to pull up and haul back. It had to be a careful selection, they knew, for a too-heavy melon would be rejected, as would one that was too round and difficult to carry. But it had to be large enough to feed them all. Each was anxious to have his selection chosen as much out of pride as out of a desire for the second beer in their cache.

Kevin settled on a bright green melon, slinging his rifle on his shoulder as he leaned over to pick it up and tried to pull it free of its vine. Tommy was using a Swiss Army knife to slice his free, and Gary was reaching to his web belt for his machete to chop free his choice. Their faces were wide in grins of anticipation and success. For a moment, all thoughts of their paramilitary make-believe were forgotten.

Rusty was frowning, though. At his feet were two candidates, but he couldn't make up his mind. One was larger than the other, but something about the smaller one looked more inviting, juicier, or just fresher in the way only a watermelon-lover could understand. He squatted down and thumped first the larger one and then the other, and then he stood up, shouldered his gun on its swivel strap, and rubbed his chin. The other boys were already moving back toward the ditch.

Suddenly, Rusty decided on the smaller one. He could argue for its quality based on his vast experience with watermelons, he reasoned. If that failed, he would pull rank by pointing out that it was his dad's farm and this was his operation. He reached down to his boot and pulled a large hunting knife from its sheath and began to cut it free. It exploded in his face.

For a second all four boys froze and looked at the pieces of green gourd and red meat and black seeds that flung themselves into the air. Rusty scowled at them, reckoning that one of them had played some trick on him. Then the sound of the rifle's report—a loud *carack!*— caught up to its bullet that had struck the melon, and the boys' heads snapped in unison toward the glaring reflection from the windows of Old Man Cooper's house.

"Hit the dirt!" Rusty screamed, flinging himself down directly onto the smashed gourd at his feet. "Get down! The son-of-a-bitch is *shooting* at us!"

After a half-second's hesitation, the four boys dropped their melons and fell prone onto the sandy soil, burying their faces into the bitter-smelling vines that covered the field. No sooner had they fallen than another melon off to their right exploded exactly as the first had, and the rifle's "carack" sounded right behind it.

"Don't move, for the love of Mike! Don't move!!" Rusty yelled at his comrades, but his order was unnecessary. An earthquake couldn't have lifted one of the boys from the marginal safety of the vines and melons surrounding him.

"Oh shit," Rusty said to himself through gritted teeth. "What am I goin' to tell Dad?"

II

Kyle Cooper's watermelons were a local legend. For over three decades, the man who had become "Ol' Man Cooper" to just about everyone in the county had raised watermelons, cantaloupes, and cucumbers for sale in town. It was his only livelihood, and folks from three counties around and even from Oklahoma would drive down the hot, dusty, sandy roads to his remote farm to haggle over the prices of his prized produce.

Watermelons grown on Kyle Cooper's farm had been consistently sweet, large, and delicious since his father had planted them a century before. When Kyle's parents died and his sister ran off to marry a soldier she met when she worked at the USO hospitality room next to the train station in town during the war, Kyle carried on.

203

No one was certain just how old he was. He claimed to be seventy-two, but county records failed to record his birth, and the family Bible that Kyle read every night until full dark confused his birth with that of a brother who died young, so there was no telling.

Tall and skinny as a post, Kyle Cooper was the picture of old age. His balding head with only a wisp or two of white hair covering his pink pate and his toothless mouth lined with deep wrinkles that were frequently covered with white stubble and food crumbs topped a body that limped through life with arthritic knees and liver-spotted hands. He sucked continuously on a battered old Dr. Graybo pipe filled with his one concession to luxury—Sir Walter Raleigh tobacco, which he bought by the pound can. His mouth was usually filled with blackened spittle which he was fond of splattering onto the shoes or boots of whomever he was arguing with. And he was always arguing with someone, that is, if he was speaking at all.

He was deliberately mean, what the old folks called "crotchety," foul mouthed and vile tempered, but he grew wonderful watermelons, and he was a sharp businessman. No one ever got the better of Kyle Cooper.

With the exception of those years when a hailstorm or a heat wave would wipe out a crop, Kyle enjoyed a good profit on his produce. He trucked the best of his crop into town to Colby's Grocery, but he always kept enough for people to come out and pick themselves for a lower price. He figured long ago there was more to be made having customers pick their own and pay him directly, and it meant less work for Kyle Cooper, too. For a while he tried putting in blackeyed peas and okra as well, and he even planted corn one year, but the yields were low, and he found the bugs, the weeds, and the general risks involved weren't worth it. So he planted the whole farm in the three crops that had always worked for his father and him alike.

He worked out a special deal with his hired help. They would work the fields in exchange for the produce at half-price, which they could then sell at roadside stands for whatever they could get. They did his planting for him, thinned the crop according to his personal methods, set up the irrigation pipe when it was needed, and then harvested what the customers left, leaving him only the plowing and preparation for the next season. It was just as well, he knew, since he had for many years been too old to do the whole job by himself. Two families of blacks came out once or twice a week to help him in the early months, and they would gather up about twenty or thirty people for the final watermelon roundup in August.

Since his sister ran off—for such was how he thought of her elopement—Kyle Cooper lived on his place alone. There were no other brothers or sisters, save one boy who had departed in anger after a fight with their father before Kyle was old enough to know what it was all about. The house was a vintage, turn-of-the-century farm abode, devoid of the normal creature comforts one would expect to find in a successful farmer's home. Electricity was represented by a single bulb in the center ceiling of the main room of the house and one crude wall outlet in the kitchen from which a frayed extension cord had been strung out to the chicken coop where it hooked into a homemade combination incubator-heater. There was running water in the bathroom, which had been added after World War I, but the kitchen depended on a handpump and cistern system, supplemented by a shallow well that doubled as a source of irrigation water. Light for the rest of the house came from oil lamps, heat from kerosene and mesquite wood. The latter also served as the chief fuel for cooking in an antique cast-iron stove that probably would have brought more from a dealer in Dallas or Houston than Kyle Cooper's whole farm was worth, watermelons and all.

He lived without telephone, gas, or television. He did own an old radio, but he only used it during severe storms, and then static drowned out his reception. His only vehicle was a pre-War Dodge pickup that perpetually had low, balding tires, didn't run three days out of four, and was so covered with reddish, sandy loam that its original color couldn't be discerned. He also owned a small Ford tractor—the newest implement on the place. He kept a few chickens for eggs and an occasional fryer and shot rabbits and other small game for meat, but the rest of his food came from Colby's Grocery, which he visited on monthly buying trips.

Kyle's needs, in brief, were simple. He hunted a bit, rabbits and deer when they were in season, although there were almost no deer left anymore anywhere in the county, and he fished occasionally in Blind Man's Creek, which crossed a corner of his property on the southwest end. He dressed in heavy workboots perpetually crusted with the red, sandy mud of his farm, and blue overalls faded as white as the bleached-out long underwear he wore beneath them winter and summer, adding a starched and faded blue workshirt for Sundays. In the coldest winters he wore plaid jumpers and hats with ear flaps.

Kyle found his entertainment the same way his father had—in his fields and in his Bible. Although he was foul mouthed and not a "loving neighbor," Kyle was an extremely religious man. Taken by his parents from a time before he could remember to the Hoolian Pentecostal Church, he had grown up in a fundamentalist environment that devoted itself to mystical interpretations of scripture and the literal meaning of God's Revealed Word. After his parents died, Kyle continued to be a loyal and regular member of the congregation, even serving as a lay reader in the small clapboard church perched on the banks of Blind Man's Creek. Every Sunday morning, Sunday night, and Wednesday evening found him in attendance in stiff, fresh overalls and his starched workshirt, cleaned if not shined workboots, and a wide hand-painted tie his sister had presented to their father before he died. Kyle prayed and sang with the best of the worshipers, often waving his hands in rhythm to the accompanying accordion music to encourage more enthusiasm from his fellow singers.

Although the decline of residential farms in the county had diminished the congregation by more than eighty percent in recent years, Kyle continued to be faithful. The church had no regular preacher any longer, but the chore was tended to by various remaining members of the congregation who would dig back into their memories for biblical interpretations to share with the brothers and sisters of the group.

Kyle never thought much about his faith or about his church. It was simply a part of his life, something he did just as he went out to check his fields every morning, ate his meals, or smoked his pipe and read his Bible—a natural routine that never needed to be questioned and never could be broken.

Every night, weather permitting, he smoked and read his Bible out on the porch of his farmhouse until full dark. Although the words he read had long ago failed to have any real meaning to him, if they ever did, he found great pleasure in the activity, and to retire without his reading was unthinkable.

In his younger days, he had amazed the congregation by speaking in tongues and being able to interpret others' divine messages when they gibbered unintelligibly, showering those around them with spittle, and astonishing everyone with their sacred ability to act as a conduit for God's Holy Words. But the gift of prophecy had left him years ago, and no one had broken out in a spontaneous tongue in the Hoolian Pentecostal Church for a long, long time.

It was, however, his talent for mystical interpretation and ability to speak gibberish that led him to marry five years after his sister ran off and he had been alone for so long. After falling into a trance one Sunday morning and spewing out a long sequence of babble, Kyle "came to," amazed to learn that his message from God had been interpreted by one Bertha Hynes, an overlarge member of the church who was barely on the near side of forty and whose chief talent had been previously found in baking apple and pecan pies for church socials. No one could have been more shocked at Bertha's pronouncements than was Kyle, for no one could have been less willing to marry than Kyle. But that, according to Bertha's interpretation of Kyle's spit-washed gibberish, had been God's very message. They were meant for each other, her deep voice had proclaimed, and God's Will was that they become man and wife. Everyone in the church had heard it, and all agreed there was nothing else to be done about it. They were married the following Sunday.

Kyle gave in without a word of protest. He donned a new pair of overalls for the wedding, oblivious to the enormous and lace-fringed white wedding gown covering Bertha's corpulent body. He refused to kiss her, however, when Brother Wilson pronounced them man and wife, and he had little to say to anyone at the reception, which was enlivened by a banquet feast and Malverna Sampson's accordion music, accompanied by her son Alvord's new trap-drum set and Willa Pearson's tenor guitar. No dancing, of course, was permitted.

There was no honeymoon. Kyle drove Bertha to his farm in the Dodge pickup, which was considerably newer if not cleaner then, and delivered her to his house where she would be his wife. For two weeks she cooked sumptuous meals on his ancient wood-burning stove, cleaned the house until the well-worn floors shined, and organized his pantry and household until he couldn't find his pipe tobacco or pocket knife without asking for them. Through the whole two weeks, however, Kyle spoke to this strange, fat lady who had invaded his privacy only when he had to. And the marriage remained unconsummated.

At night, Bertha would shuffle into the small bedroom, put on one of her new nightgowns, and slip between the rough flannel sheets. Kyle would come in after the sun went down and reading his Bible was no longer possible, quietly take care of his business in the bathroom, and lie down beside her—but on top of the counterpane—wearing the long underwear he seemed never to remove. Eventually he would begin to snore, and Bertha would fall into a confused, angry slumber.

Daytime was little better. Kyle went to the fields before dawn, never even mumbling a thank you for the delicious breakfast she cooked and placed before him. He returned at noon, washed briefly in the cold water at the kitchen pump, and then silently ate whatever wonderful concoctions she served for dinner. At night, he ate his four-course supper with the same silence, and answered in muttering monosyllables any questions Bertha might pose, never once starting a conversation on his own. Then he would light his pipe, go out on the back porch, and read his Bible until the dimming light of the sun's rays signaled time for him to retire.

In the third week of their marriage, Bertha was finally overcome with frustration and self-pity. "Kyle Cooper!" she railed at him as he forked potatoes and gravy from his plate into his mouth, unmindful of the drippings on her sparkling clean oilcloth. "It was

God's Will that we marry, an' I s'pose you mean to thwart His intentions!"

Kyle looked up slowly, as if realizing for the first time that she was even in the same world with him, and wrinkled his forehead in puzzlement. "What you think we done?" he asked as gravy dribbled down his chin.

"I don't know," she whined, "but it surely ain't His Will for you an' me to be man an' wife in name only. The Bible says 'Be fruitful an' multiply.'"

Kyle stared at her, his fork suspended in midair, still laden with potatoes and gravy. "What in hell're you talkin' 'bout?"

"The Bible says it's better to marry'n burn," she went on, pounding her pudgy fist on the table to make her point. "But we ain't married, not in no real sense of the word. You treat me like a fiel' nigger! Ain't you goin' to be no *real* husban' to me?" She ran her fat hands through her blond curls, pulling great strands away from her red face with her fingers. She was more embarrassed than she had ever thought she could be, and Kyle simply continued to stare at her.

Finally, he lowered his fork and rubbed his chin. He was now growing angry. "What do you mean by that?" he growled. "What in hell're you tryin' to say?"

"You take any meanin' you want out of it, Kyle Cooper," she cried, noting the edge in his voice but also aware that she had gone too far to back down. "All I know is, I'm burnin' for you, an' all you do is snore like a sawmill an' eat like a starvin' Mescan."

"Woman!" Kyle started, his anger brimming up, almost overwhelming him. Before he could continue, she burst into sobbings that shook her enormous breasts and belly so vigorously that Kyle thought she would surely explode. Then she ran from the kitchen into the bedroom and slammed the door.

Confused and angry, Kyle lit his pipe and went out to his rocker on the porch. He automatically grabbed his Bible from the table by the rocker, but for the first time in years, he found no pleasure in reading it.

Bertha finally got up from the bed where she had flung herself to weep and undressed. She put on her nightgown and was just lying down again when the door burst open and Kyle appeared like a wild man.

Pushing her down and jumping on top of her, he turned her roughly over onto her back and began massaging the flab of her breasts and stomach. He took no care of hurting her, and she almost cried out, but bit her lip to stop herself. She found herself truly afraid of him.

After a few minutes of kneading and punching, he reared up in the middle of the bed, unbuckled his overalls, and forced them down as far as his knees. He pulled open the underwear buttons down the fly, and with a wild expression of contempt and rage on his face, he fell forward on top of her, prying her legs open with one hand as he wriggled down into her.

In a few minutes, it was all over. Kyle stumbled out of the bed, pulled his underwear closed, and dropped the overalls on the floor. He went into the bathroom where she heard him washing. She didn't move. Eventually, he returned to the bed, and without giving her so much as a look, he jerked the counterpane and sheet back and got in beside her. After a long period of silence, his snoring told her he was asleep.

A week went by before anything was said between them, and that was only an inquiry as to what she might need when he went into town for his monthly shopping. Another week passed, and silence was a wall between them. They attended church and sat quietly through the services, but otherwise, Kyle never came near her again, and their previous routine was restored.

Her period came and went. Kyle said nothing to her still, and she found herself afraid to ask him anything at all. Finally, after a month had passed, he stopped eating supper in the middle of a chicken leg and stared at her long and hard.

"You pregnant?" he asked her quietly. His gaze fell on her breasts and belly so intently that she felt he was trying to see right inside her.

"No," she answered, amazed at the question. It was the last thing on her mind.

"You sure?" he asked again, now putting down the chicken leg and fishing his pipe out of his pocket and starting to light it, never letting his eyes leave her as they stared over the match's flame.

"I'm sure," she said as softly as she could. She wondered what he was getting at.

"Then get the hell off my farm," he said, drawing in a great volume of smoke and letting it out through his nose, snuffing out the match.

"What?" She felt a strong blow to her chest, as if he had struck her. Her breath was gone.

"I said, 'Get the hell off my farm,'" he repeated in the same calm but even tone, "an' don't give me any more bullshit 'bout bein' fruitful an' multiplyin'! *I* was fruitful, an' I planted the seed. If you can't multiply it, then it ain't my goddamn fault. An' it ain't God's Will, neither."

"Kyle!" she exclaimed, finding her voice but unable to think of what to say to him. "One time! One time—one time don't prove nothin'! 'Sides—"

"Bull*shit!*" he yelled back at her as he stood and moved toward the door. "I been farmin' over forty goddamn years, an' I know when you plant seeds an' plant 'em right an' they don't grow, it means somethin's wrong in the ground."

"But *Kyle!*"

"Listen to me, woman. If I didn't know you to be a Christian, I'd think you tricked me. Fact of the goddamn matter is, I ain't for sure you didn't anyhow. It ain't no more *God's* Will than it's *Bertha's* will, an' that's for damn sure! So, you get the hell off my farm, tomorrow, an' don't come back." He slapped the oilcloth so hard his glass overturned, spilling buttermilk all over the floor. "God*damn* it, woman! Who the hell do you think you are?" He stomped outside and picked up his Bible and read until the sun's rays disappeared behind the plum thicket across the road west of the house.

The next morning when he came back from the fields for his noon meal, she was gone. She had left him a big pot of beans cooking on the stove, a fresh peach cobbler for dessert, and a note, but he ate the food without so much as a thought of her. He wiped his mouth on the note to save a paper napkin and scraped it into the slops pot to be carried out and burned with the rest of the garbage. He never heard from her again. He never knew where she went, and he never asked anyone. When people in the church asked about her, he froze them with an icy stare and they quickly scurried away from any mention of Bertha or her famous pies. She was gone, and that was enough for Kyle Cooper or, so far as he was concerned, for anyone else.

After a while, Kyle forgot a woman had ever been a part of his life. He went back to the simple meals of bachelorhood: fried meats and boiled vegetables. And he ate in blissful silence, following his supper as always by smoking his pipe and reading his Bible until sunset on his back porch.

Kyle's second pleasure in life was, of course, his watermelons. He cared for his cantaloupes and cucumbers as well, but the melons were a source of such pride that he often wondered if they might not also be the source of some sin or other. He entered them in county and state fairs when he was younger, and he had won hundreds of blue ribbons, but even such formal recognition was nothing compared to how happy it made him to see people drive up the sandy road to his house to pay for the pleasure of picking out their own red-meated gourds.

Every day he walked his melon patch, and before they had reached anywhere near maturity, he could recognize each one by sight, or at least he believed he could. He would play a secret game with the customers, allowing them to make their selection while he looked elsewhere, and then he tried to guess where, exactly, the melon had come from. After they left, he walked out to where he thought they had found it and searched briefly for footprints in the sand or a sticky, freshly cut vine, to see if he was right. More often than not, he was.

From time to time, years before, he wagered the price of the melon against an additional one if he was wrong. His intimate knowledge of his fields usually paid off, though the modest prices he charged people who came out to pick their own melons made the wagers harmless. Still, he lost so rarely that few veteran customers would take him up on the deal.

Now, when the Negro families worked his fields for him, he took delight in spending hours every day walking around the watermelon field inspecting his crops, noting where the acreage was too dry, where melons were ripening too fast, and where they seemed stunted in development. He measured their color, their plumpness, and, of course, their size. He liked to brag when he went into Colby's Grocery or to church that he could spot a Cooper melon a mile away. He would exult in catching a fellow congregation member cutting into an "imported" melon at a church supper and would enjoy the embarrassment he caused when he cackled triumphantly that *this* sure wasn't a Cooper watermelon.

He checked his other crops for quality and progress, but the cucumbers and cantaloupes never held the fascination for him that the watermelons always did. His father had been first in the county, some said in the state, to grow watermelon as a cash crop. The cultivation techniques handed down from father to son—ways of thinning, hoeing, and irrigating the melon patch, the type of fertilizer, the depth of planting—had made Cooper melons the best in the area. It was a life's work, a sense of accomplishment that was renewed every season, and while he dimly realized that he would be the last of the Cooper line to carry on the tradition, he also acknowledged the importance of so small an indulgence in a world so troubled by sin. His work, he felt, was God's work, not some silliness about wives and marriage.

Thoughts of specific troubles seldom bothered Kyle Cooper when he strolled his melon patch. The fields extended from the dooryard in back of his farmhouse to a road one-eighth of a mile to the west, and considerably farther in the other directions. A road cut directly through the field to the house, but it was little more than a bed of sand built up by infrequent visits from a bulldozer man. Occasionally, Kyle would cover it with caliche, and during heavy rains, it was sliced through with ruts that plagued but did not discourage prospective customers.

One morning two days before Rusty and his band of melon

thieves descended on Kyle's watermelon patch, the old man made a disturbing discovery. He noticed a new fruit stand on the highway between town and the cutoff to the road that led to his farm. As he returned from Colby's Grocery with his monthly supply of food and tobacco, curiosity overcame him, and he pulled the old Dodge pickup over and got out. A grinning Mexican-American who apparently spoke no English happily displayed for him a large pile of freshly picked watermelons alongside equally fresh and abundant cantaloupes, cucumbers, and other vegetables.

Kyle's curiosity vanished as he stared at the pile of melons, one of which was sliced open to show the succulent meat inside. He scratched his unshaven chin and shook his head as he stared. He was sure these were Cooper melons, and he was equally certain they had come from the western end of his patch. But he was also absolutely certain that these Mexicans hadn't *bought* a single melon from him.

He returned to his battered old Dodge and raced home, got out without unloading his groceries, and hurried out to the suspected area. Sure enough, footprints and crushed vines told the story. A good forty or fifty melons were missing, a number he confirmed easily by counting the freshly cut vines. When he tallied the forty-second, he was furious.

Kyle knew that from time to time passing farmers or field laborers would help themselves to a watermelon or two. He tolerated this pilfering within limits. If he spotted the theft going on, he would yell and run or drive out toward the culprits, but it was more of a show than any serious attempt to catch them. He had long ago accepted the inevitable irresistibility of a watermelon patch in hot summertime. The only time he actually became angry was when he discovered several dozen melons smashed along the road about a mile away. That was wanton waste and vandalism, and he would have none of that!

He hired Carl Fischer to come out with his backhoe and dig deep ditches all around the fields, the cantaloupe and cucumber as well as the watermelon, to prevent easy access from the road. He could have put up a fence, he knew, but the ground was loose, loamy, and that meant fence posts would have had to be sunk deep in concrete;

fences also required maintenance. The ditches were over six feet deep in places, and although he had to have them cleared every couple of years, he discovered that they were not only an effective barrier, they also served as an excellent source of extra water after a rain. He terraced the fields, building up the sides, turning them into large plates that would retain the initial rainfall. Then he installed powerful pumps at key points along the ditches to draw water standing in them and pour it onto the fields after the rains had passed. The natural irrigation source added to his well water and made his melons especially fat and juicy even in the driest of summers when other farmers lost their crops because they pumped their wells too often early in the season.

But the big advantage was an end to stealing. Few people would risk running into snakes or other varmints in the thorny tumbleweeds and other trash that clogged the ditches' bottoms during dry weather. And after a good rain, the trenches were simply too muddy to cross, even for the most determined thief.

But this was different. Kyle walked around the edge of his fields until he found what he was looking for. Two large wooden planks were poorly concealed on the other side of the road in the plum thicket. Indentations in the sandy rims of the ditch revealed the Mexicans' method of entrance and exit to the field: They just pulled their truck up, laid the planks down, and simply walked the stolen melons across. So sure were they of their safety, the thieves hadn't even taken the boards away with them, which meant they would be back after they sold their first haul.

Kyle was angrier than he could recall being—ever. He leaped awkwardly into the ditch and scrambled over the other side, wincing with pain from his arthritic knees. He walked over to the planks, intending to destroy them, but suddenly he stopped.

If he broke or took away the boards, they would simply be replaced. No. He had to stop the stealing before it got worse. They also had a load of vegetables, he recalled, and chances were the greasers were stealing from every field and truck farm in the north part of the county. Kyle was incensed at the thought that he would have happily let them have the melons wholesale, or even on consignment, since this year's crop had been especially good and he would likely have to plow under some good produce if Colby didn't want it.

He recrossed the ditch, leaving the boards where they were, and strode across the field to his house. Hastily unpacking his groceries, he took his old .30-30 from the corner, opened the bolt, and selected a shiny new cartridge from a greasy box in his cupboard. Settling the shell in place, he rammed the bolt home, picked up the box from the shelf, and went out to his back porch and took a seat in his rocker.

From his chair he could command a view of the whole western end of his patch, the part that ran along the road where the boards were hidden. There would be no Bible reading this night, he thought grimly, sighting down the long barrel of the rifle toward the plum thicket opposite the road. But he was sure he would soon put an end to the stealing.

Like most farmers in north central Texas, Kyle Cooper kept a fair-sized arsenal in his house—several shotguns, a couple of rusty pistols, a .22 rifle, and two high-powered deer rifles, one of which now lay across his lap. Many of the guns his father had kept around had been sold or thrown away after rust had completely claimed them, but Kyle kept the .30-30 in good shape. It had been a present from his father, and in his youth, he had taken pleasure in hunting deer in the Red River's bottom and sloughs. He could recall going out after bear one time, although no such animal turned up, and the rifle kept coyotes and bobcat away from his chicken house. In recent years, he used the rifle to kill skunks and other varmints he discovered raiding his chickens or fields. He was a crack shot in spite of his age and weakening eyesight, and he liked to use the big .30-30 because of its deadly accuracy and good range.

He sat on the porch all night, not even lighting his pipe for fear of giving away his watch, rocking and waiting for the thieves to return. But when dawn broke and they hadn't come, Kyle realized that they probably had enough to get them by for another day or so.

He left the porch, fired up the Dodge, and drove deliberately up the road to the Hoolian townsite, which consisted of little more than a garage and gas station, a barbershop and feedstore, and a bait shop and general store. From the barbershop he phoned the sheriff's office and demanded that someone come out to protect his melons or he would "shoot to kill."

"Now Kyle," the sheriff's voice soothed from the other end of the phone line, "are you sure those are your melons they got out there?"

"Goddammit!" Kyle screeched back at him. "I *know* damn well somebody's been messin' in my fields. I got the by-God proof! Now you get your lazy ass out there an' check it out, or I'm goin' to take matters into my own hands!"

"I'll drive by there tomorrow or the next day—"

"Tomorrow!?!" Kyle screamed. He was uncomfortable under the glare of the barbershop's patrons who ceased their gossip and chatter to stare at the crazy old man dancing around the telephone in the back of the shop. "Goddammit! *Tomorrow* they'll have me stole blind. Get your ass out there today!"

"Tell you what," the sheriff compromised quickly, "I'll go by the fruit stand this afternoon, but we got a city council meeting in the morning, and I can't get out to your place until tomorrow night at the earliest, so—"

"I won't be responsible for what happens!" Kyle yelled loudly into the receiver. "I'll not be goddamn stole blind while you sit 'round in town an' jerk off that fat-assed mayor!" Several people in the shop laughed out loud when they heard that, but Kyle was too angry to notice. "If you're goin' to put this off till you get goddamn good an' ready to sashay on out here, then you best bring a hearse with you when you come!"

He slammed the phone down with a loud curse directed toward county and city officials and stalked out of the shop without leaving the customary nickel for using the telephone in the ceramic dish by the door. The old Dodge spewed gravel as he swung out of Hoolian and drove home at breakneck speed, nearly ruining his driveshaft on the ruptured road leading up to his house.

For two days he sat on the back porch cursing the sheriff and leaving his rocker only to tend to the most demanding chores or to wait on the infrequent customer who might venture out on such hot days. He knew he was highly visible on the porch rocker, and anyone passing down the road could see him if he looked hard enough. But only an occasional farmer drove by, often as not lifting a hand in automatic greeting, and Kyle was disappointed. Nothing resembling the large truck he had seen parked by the vendor's stand appeared, and the sheriff failed to show up as well.

He really didn't expect the Mexicans to come in broad daylight, so he kept his vigil through the night again, wrapping himself in an old quilt and dozing between long stares into the blackness west of his house for the telltale beams of lanterns or flashlights. But the second night passed without anyone stealing his precious melons.

On the evening of the second whole day of watching, Kyle felt the effects both of fatigue and of hunger. He had only eaten cheese and crackers during his guard duty, afraid to leave his post long enough even to put on a pot of coffee, and what little sleep he had managed in the rocker was far from restful. About seven fifteen, he rose and fed the chickens, gathered some eggs, and climbed the porch with an eye on the setting sun, remembering how uncomfortable it was to stare into the western sky at that time of day. He decided to take a real break and fix something to eat.

Leaning the rifle against the doorjamb, he went inside, put on some coffee, and began frying some eggs. After working the wood stove for a while, he soon had an evening breakfast sizzling on the griddle. He pulled his kitchen chair around so he could see the field through the crusty, fly-blown window, sat down, and dug into the first real meal he had eaten since Wednesday noon.

All of a sudden a series of movements caught his eye. It was hard to make out what exactly he was seeing since the sun seemed to be directly behind the field, just atop the plum thicket, and the dust and grime on the windowpanes reflected the light brilliantly, making the glass a mirror with its layers of dirt and flyspecks. He squinted hard and was then almost positive he saw the shape of men in the watermelon field. For a long moment he stared through the kitchen window, frozen in concentration. Egg yolk ran down his unshaven chin, and his palms were moist with increasing nervousness. He squinted harder and harder, and then he spotted them for sure.

He was absolutely certain. Three or four shapes were outlined in the field, silhouetted against the sun's rays, and they were unmistakably moving through the field in the attitude of men making selections from the melons. Kyle rose from the table so rapidly he banged his sore knees against its edge and the chair tipped over backwards onto the floor. A glass of buttermilk overturned and dripped off the oilcloth. He moved as quickly as he could while rubbing his sore legs, flung open the screen door to the back porch, and took up his rifle.

The figures were still there, closer than before; he could make them out clearly as black shapes moving through the vines, stooping to inspect the melons. He didn't spot their truck, but he was sure they were the same men, and his anger combined with his fatigue to wear him down and exasperate him. They must not be able to make him out, he reasoned, otherwise they would run.

He lifted the rifle to sight on them, but his legs were shaking, so he sat down in the rocker and raised the weapon again. He had no thought of actually hitting any of them, but he did want to put a scare into them they would not soon forget. He squinted into the sun's blinding light and took aim at a large melon at the feet of one of the figures. Slowly and methodically he calculated elevation and windage, then he pulled the trigger.

For one brief, horrible moment, Kyle Cooper thought he had killed a man. After his recovery from the rifle's recoil, which rocked him back in the chair, he squinted into the fierce sunlight and was surprised to see no figures at all. He had expected to spot them running away and to put a shot or two over their heads for good measure as they scrambled to the ditch. But they had been too far from the culvert to make it in the short time since he fired, and they apparently had disappeared into the very ground they stood on.

He stared hard at the end of the field and tried to figure where they had gone. He raised the rifle from his lap again, opened the bolt, and ejected the empty casing. Replacing it with a fresh shell, he took aim at a dark hump he recognized as a large melon off to the left of where he fired before, and he squeezed off another shot. That brought a renewal of movement, and he realized that the men had simply fallen down where they were when he fired the first time. If he *had* hit one of them, he figured, that one might have fallen, but he was now certain they had just dropped down out of his clear vision, and their actions confused and disturbed him.

This was not what he expected, and he didn't know what to do. If he just went inside and didn't try to scare them away, they might do anything, even come for him in the house. If he stayed here and continued to fire, they wouldn't move at all. It would become a stand-off, them not knowing what to do and just lying there, him having to continue to stand guard until one of them gave up.

He thought for a moment, reloaded the rifle, and fired once more, this time aiming high over the prone figures, which he could just barely make out in the sunlight's glare as dark lumps in the midst of the raised forms of the larger melons. He decided to keep up a steady fire in their direction but not *at* them. He reasoned that if he could keep them nervous and penned down, they would soon become scared enough either to give up or to jump and run away. Then he would be shed of them for good. And if they didn't give up or run away, he thought, then the worthless sheriff would be along someday and could take them off to jail. Either way, they wouldn't be likely to come back.

He fired again, and then counted to four and fired another round, then he counted and fired, and began a rhythm, each time rocking back in the chair with the kick of the big rifle, automatically working the bolt to eject the empty, placing a new shell in the breech, closing the bolt, raising the rifle, sighting, and aiming high before he squeezed the trigger. It was a pleasing activity after so many hours of just sitting and waiting, and he began to hum "The Old Rugged Cross," counting off the measures with the rifle's "carack" as a downbeat for each, grinning and wondering what those damned Mexicans must be thinking and how long it would be before they just purely shit themselves empty out of fear.

III

Faces buried in the sand, noses full of grit and the bitter smell of crushed vines, the four boys ceased all movement, even breathing it seemed. Their hearts pounded in their ears; their mouths were powder-dry. Their eyes were wide with terror and disbelief, and their fingers dug into the loamy soil, holding on to the earth as if it were some great spinning ball trying to fling them upwards into the path of the screaming lead.

The rifle shots came at more or less regular intervals, but there was never time to risk jumping up and retreating to the ditch some fifty yards behind them. The banking along the ditches' edges made crawling impossible as well, for as soon as they reached the lip of the culvert, they would be completely exposed to the maniac who was sniping at them from the porch of the old farmhouse.

By lifting his head between the regularly spaced "caracks," Rusty spotted Old Man Cooper rocking back and forth and firing at them. He thanked God the old fool was such a bad shot, for they were hardly covered at all down on the ground among the vines and melons. A wetness in his crotch told him he had pissed all over himself when he fell down, but his embarrassment was overwhelmed by his self-reproach for being caught so unawares in the first place. How could he have been so stupid, he asked himself, to assume there wasn't at least a chance that the old man would spot them? He flushed with shame. He was supposed to be a leader, but all he had led them to was one hell of a fix.

"Is everybody okay?" he yelled at his youthful comrades who lay roughly abreast of him to either side.

One by one, they responded, "Okay," and he breathed easier. At least nobody had been hit, he thought, but he didn't know what to do now. He was more badly frightened than he had ever been in his life. His palms were sweating horribly, gathering huge matted clumps of sand every time they touched the ground. His mouth was ashy, and sweat ran in great rivers from under his OD hat, burning his eyes when he lifted his forehead and tried to squint toward the house.

"What're we goin' to do, Rusty?" Tommy's voice reached him in muffled tones. Although he was physically the largest of the group, he was also thin and wiry. He could run faster than any of them, and Rusty toyed with several plans that had Tommy running for help to get them out of this mess, but every plan involved exposing

221

his friend to the deadly fire from the porch, and he rejected each as hopeless.

Gary was scrambling around, and Rusty turned his head to see what he was doing. He had apparently dropped his shotgun when he fell, and he was slowly fishing it up to him with his toe. He finally grabbed it and pulled it up next to his body.

"Gary! *Gary!*" Rusty ordered. "For Chrissake, don't shoot back!" Rusty's mouth was so dry the words were difficult to form. His tongue felt swollen to three times its normal size and he could hear his voice cracking when he yelled for all three boys to hear. "Don't anybody even *show* a goddamn gun!"

"He's shooting at *us,* goddammit!" Gary yelled back at him, and Rusty was horrified to see that Tommy also had pulled his gun up and was checking the breech to make sure a live shell was in the chamber. "What're we supposed to do? Just lay here an' get killed?"

"Just hold on an' let me think," Rusty ordered. He was relieved to see both boys relax their grips on their shotguns. He realized that even if they tried to shoot back, the small gauge weapons wouldn't come close to reaching the porch, and even if they could cover the range, their effect would only be to make Old Man Cooper madder than he was. His new 16-gauge wouldn't make the length of the field with any kind of result. Another "carack" flew by him as he pondered the problem.

"Rusty! Rusty! *Rusty!* I'm scared! I want Mama!" It was Kevin. Holy shit, Rusty thought, swiveling his head to try to glimpse his brother behind him. He'd forgotten Kevin was part of the group. The awesome weight of fraternal responsibility added to the burden of guilt he already felt for getting his friends into such a predicament. He rolled over and spotted Kevin's huddled form. The younger boy was bunched up into a kind of ball with his buttocks sticking straight up, exposed completely to the line of fire.

"Get down, Kevin! *Get down!*" Rusty yelled at his brother. Kevin refused to move. "Get your ass *down!*" Rusty felt anger and frustration welling up in his throat. *"Kevin!* Get your ass down, or it's goin' to get shot off!" He was screaming now, but Kevin ignored him.

"I'm scared, Rusty!" Kevin's voice was muffled. He was crying. "Make him stop shooting at us! *Please!*" Kevin still hadn't moved, and his face was covered by his hands as he seemed to be trying to bury his head in the sand. He refused to make any move to flatten out his body. "Go get Dad! Do *something!* Make him stop! *Please!*" Another "carack" ricocheted into the plum thicket behind them.

Rusty closed his eyes and turned over on his belly and tried to think. This couldn't be happening. It was too much like a nightmare, and he bit his lip harder and harder trying to make himself wake up. But when he opened his eyes, all he could see was a ladybug walking lazily across a vine inches from his nose, and all he could hear between the echoes of the rifle's "carack" and his heart's pounding was his brother's whimpering. What would he tell his mother if something happened to Kevin? He didn't want to face that. He decided he would be better off with one of Old Man Cooper's bullets in him.

He closed his eyes again and tried to force his mind to work. He needed a plan. He knew that, and he glanced at Tommy and Gary for ideas, but both were staring at him, waiting for him to tell them what to do. He was their leader, he reminded himself, and the responsibility for this whole series of events rested with him. But he didn't have a clue as to a way out.

"I can't stand it any more, Rusty!" Kevin's voice pleaded. "I want Mama! Make him stop! *Puleease make him stop!!*" Kevin's voice was getting shrill, and Rusty knew he had to do something fast. His little brother was cracking. The youngest of the foursome did not have the years of make-believe discipline and training for fantasy battles that the others had. He was just a scared little boy who relied on his big brother to save him from this totally unexpected, unimaginable horror. *"Rusty! Do some—"* Another "carack" cut off his words.

"Hold on, Kevin! He'll stop soon. He'll run out of ammo," Rusty yelled. He looked for confirmation from his two companions, but they said nothing. They were busily wriggling down into the sand, effectively creating slit trenches with the force of their bodies' weight in the soft soil. Kevin's rear end was still sticking up in the air, and his head had become invisible in the sand and vines beneath it.

"God*damn* it, Kevin!" Rusty yelled in as deep a voice as he could muster. "Get *flat! Now!!*" But his brother made no movement except to shake from the sobs that racked his small body.

IV

O<small>N</small> his porch, Kyle Cooper was in no danger of running short of ammunition, but his hearing was bothering him a mite since the echo of his rifle's muzzle blast had started his ears to ringing. In addition to the cartridges remaining in the greasy box he had brought from the cupboard, there were two more boxes stored in the kitchen and another box-and-a-half of shells in the pickup. He reached down and lifted the cardboard container up and set it atop the Bible on the table next to the rocker. Then he reloaded once more and continued his rhythmic pattern of fire.

He found himself more and more perplexed by the behavior of the trespassers in his field. Rather than running away or giving up, they apparently had burrowed down into the field. He couldn't even make out their humped figures among the melons and vines any longer, except one of them who seemed to be crouched in an odd sort of way.

Kyle still had no intention of shooting to hit any of them, even if they stood up and ran. He deliberately placed his shots over their heads, four or five feet above where they lay, or where he estimated them to be, aiming directly at a line of derelict telephone poles that stuck out at slanted angles from the plum thicket across the road opposite the field. He had used those poles for target practice since before they were abandoned years ago, and he concentrated on hitting one or the other of them with each shot. Bursts of dust from the weathered gray poles told him that his success rate was running high, and he found that in spite of a simmering level of anger he was enjoying himself for the first time since he was a boy.

The sun was now sitting atop the plum thicket, almost completely blinding him, but he forced his eyes to squint at the poles and to avoid looking directly into the yellow fireball just above them. In a few more minutes, the sun would dip past the thicket's

224

branches, and he would have a clear view of the field. He considered that he might just call out to the men at that point, tell them to get the hell out. His shoulder was aching from the rifle's kick, and the ringing in his ears was growing painful. He cleared his throat and spat, then rose and went into the house for another box of cartridges.

V

THE sun's rays now blasted back toward the boys in the field from the house's windows, creating a flashing mirror that obstructed their view of the figure on the porch. Kevin continued to whimper and cry and refused all commands to lie prone, and Rusty was growing more and more worried. Any minute now, he thought, that crazy old man's going to hit Kevin, and that would be all she wrote for sure.

Anger began to coalesce inside him as his fear gave way to a growing concern for his brother. He was still wary enough of the regularly paced flying bullets overhead to keep down on his face in the bitter sand where his body had now wriggled a trench. Why had his mother made him bring Kevin along? he kept demanding of the bugs and vines that crowded around his face. He wanted to yell the question. This was a bad enough turn of events without that burden. Why had she saddled him with this extra problem? Why?

Sweat ran down into his face, causing the sand to stick to his freckled cheeks in gritty clumps. He wanted to yell and cry at the same time, but all he could do was remain hidden in the sand and vines and pray that Kevin would eventually faint or something and lie down out of the line of fire.

"Rusty?" the muffled voice from his left came from Tommy who had barely raised his face from the sand. "Rusty? What're we goin' to do? We got to do *something*. That crazy ol' fart's goin' to kill us!"

"Yeah! Let's shoot back or somethin'!" Gary agreed from Rusty's right, and Rusty swiveled his face over toward his friend who was taking aim through the sun's glare at where he was sure the man was on the porch.

"Look!" Rusty said loud enough for both to hear. "You can't reach him with those pop guns, for Chrissake! You shoot back, an' he's goin' to just get madder and madder. He's likely to come out here. He's got a *rifle,* an' he can hit us a mile away if he can see that far. Just thank God he's a piss-poor shot an' keep your ass down an hope he can't find us 'fore it gets dark." He took breath, thinking and hoping they understood him.

"What if he comes out here anyway?" Tommy asked.

"Yeah, what about that?" Gary agreed.

"If he starts out here," Rusty responded in a flat tone, "I guess we'll have to shoot back."

"You *guess!*" Tommy said. "Well, you can guess all you want. But if he gets close enough, I ain't goin' to just stand up an' wave my dick at him."

"I doubt he could see it," Gary snickered loudly, and all three gave way to the relief of nervous laughter. It broke the tension and they all began breathing more easily.

"Just keep watch," Rusty ordered. He turned his head to look at Kevin who was now squirming around. "Kevin," he pleaded, "get the hell down. Please."

The rifle's "carack" had been regular up until that moment, but suddenly the expected report didn't come. Rusty raised his head and chanced a look at the porch, but all he could see was the blinding reflection of the sun's rays. He pulled his 16-gauge Browning up next to him and thought of trying to rush up a couple of dozen yards. He might be able to reach the porch from closer in, he knew, but he also knew he probably wouldn't be able to get close enough to do much more than pepper the old man with harmless birdshot. That would make him mad. Besides, Rusty reasoned, the old man might just be waiting for one of them to stand up so he could take a clear shot. A sudden noise behind him made Rusty turn to look at Kevin again.

The younger boy, tears streaming down his face, seemed to take cue from Rusty's thoughts and leaped to his feet. His baseball cap fell off to reveal a white, clean forehead above the line of dirt where sweat had muddied the sand into which he had pressed his face. He raised his arms and waved the .22 over his head.

"Don't shoot!" Kevin screamed. "Don't shoot, Mister! We didn't mean nothin'. Just stop shootin'."

VI

K YLE Cooper emerged from the screen door to his porch with a fresh box of bullets under his arm and a new shell bolted into the chamber of the .30-30. He had been inside less than a minute and had taken only a few seconds to pick up his cold coffee and drink a swallow. As he opened the door, he saw one of the figures jump up and wave at him. He was dancing around like a crazy man! They were taunting him! he thought. They were daring him to hit them. He looked at the insane dancing figure silhouetted in the sun's flashing light, and he suddenly realized that the jumping and laughing figure was waving a rifle at him!

"Thievin' sons-of-bitches!" Kyle bellowed. He set the fresh box of cartridges down roughly on the Bible, spilling it open and scattering most of the contents on the porch's wooden floor. "Laugh at me, will you! Point a gun at me from my own goddamn field, will you! By *God!* You ain't seen the day, you ain't. God*damn* it! You son-of-a-pepper-bellied-Mescan-bitch!"

Fury swept over him like a fever. He steadied his aching legs, raised the powerful rifle, and aimed directly over the head of the dancing figure. He squeezed off a perfect shot designed to "part the hair" of the taunting, threatening trespasser in his watermelon field. But just as the trigger pulled and the rifle's "carack" deafened him, another figure caught the dancing man in a perfect tackle and knocked him down into the vines and out of sight.

"Greasy, bean-eatin' son-of-a-bitch!" Kyle swore and worked the bolt feverishly and resumed his seat in the rocker. "Think I'm funny, do you? I guess that'll put some starch in your britches!" His legs were shaking so hard that his knees were actually knocking together. His whole body trembled with rage and pain. Taking a breath to calm himself as he sat down in the rocker, Kyle jammed another cartridge into the breech and resumed his firing routine.

VII

JESUS Christ!" Rusty yelled just as his shoulders met Kevin's midsection and knocked the boy back into the melons and vines behind him. When he saw his brother come to his feet and start waving and yelling, he had not hesitated. Jerking himself to his knees, he launched his body through the air across the space between them and aimed his head directly at Kevin's stomach. He brought his arms up and wrapped them around his brother's waist, knocking him backwards just as the rifle's "carack" sounded overhead.

His oath was from both relief and anger. He was sure he had reached Kevin in time, but he was also mad at either Tommy or Gary—he wasn't sure which—for chunking a large piece of melon at his younger brother just as he made contact. He had been showered with red meat and hot, sticky juice which now ran into his eyes and burned and blinded them. He rolled off Kevin to one side to try to wipe his vision clear.

"You okay?" Gary yelled back at him.

Rusty cleared his eyes with his shirt tail and opened his mouth to answer, but words failed him. Kevin's forehead was covered with the piece of melon. A hunk of white rind stuck obscenely from his nose and mouth, and he was apparently cold-cocked to boot. He wasn't moving.

"That was a goddamn stupid thing to do!" Rusty yelled at Gary, figuring it was he who had thrown the melon, but then he noticed that Kevin *was* moving. He was heaving in large spasmodic gasps; his mouth was open, working frantically as if he were trying to drink in the atmosphere in desperate swallows. Rusty looked again at his brother's face and saw that his eyes were open, staring at nothing, wildly gaping as he struggled for air. He examined the hunks of melon all over Kevin's head and suddenly, horribly, realized it wasn't melon at all but chunks of Kevin's head, brain and bone, blasted apart by the terrible force of Kyle Cooper's bullet.

"The son-of-a-bitch shot Kevin!!" Rusty screamed as he scrambled through the vines and gourds over to his brother's body and grabbed his shoulders. He raised himself dangerously high over the younger boy's heaving chest. Idly, he noticed Kevin's .22, its stock broken nearly in two, sticking up in the sand a few feet from where they lay. His brother had been hit by a ricochet off his own rifle, Rusty dimly realized as he helplessly massaged his brother's chest and arms. The powerful rifle's bullet had hit the other's bolt and driven itself down through the stock and right into Kevin's brain.

Tommy had seen the whole thing, realized what had happened, and lay still and terrified. Gary stared disbelievingly at the two brothers. After a few moments, he belly-crawled over to them.

"He's all right," Gary said over and over. "He just got hit on the head. You knocked the breath out of him. That's all."

Tommy finally came to himself and crawled over to join them. "I can't believe it," he said in a soft voice. "His head just flew apart. Just as you tackled him. Goddammit! I can't believe it!" A warning look from Gary shut him up.

Tommy pulled a camouflage towel from his haversack, but he could see it was too late. Rusty lifted his face to his friends. Tears streaked down his cheeks making tracks in the blood and gore that covered his face.

"The old bastard!" Rusty cried hoarsely. "The old son-of-a-bitchin' goddamn bastard! He shot Kevin! Help me. Tommy, Gary! For Chrissake! Help me!"

Tommy said nothing but only ducked as the distant rifle's "carack" echoed overhead. He pulled what was left of Kevin's mouth open and tried to free his tongue, but the boy was no longer gasping for breath or even breathing at all.

"He's hurt real bad, Tommy!" Rusty said, grabbing the towel away from his friend and trying to stanch the blood flowing from Kevin's forehead. Tommy shook his head. "No!" Rusty protested. His eyes raced between Tommy and Gary's faces. He sensed what they were thinking. "No! He's hurt real bad. We got to stop the bleedin'. That's all!"

Tommy looked at Gary, who turned his face away and was loudly sick. His retching forced him into a half-kneeling position before he emptied his stomach and then lay back heaving for a moment. Finally, he rolled over, rested for a moment, and started crawling back to his former position.

"Listen," Tommy said, trying to keep his voice from shaking and his eyes off Kevin. He gagged slightly and shut his mouth tightly against his stomach's revolt. The rifle's report sounded once more. "You remember when I was in that bus wreck last year? All those people got killed. Remember?" Tommy's experience in a car-bus wreck had been a topic of many tales around the campfire. He was the only one of their group who had ever actually seen a dead person. "You remember?" he repeated. He grabbed Rusty's fatigue jacket and forced him to look into his eyes. "Well, I seen guys like this." Their eyes met and locked. "I'm sorry, Rusty. He's gone. Kevin's dead."

He released his friend's jacket, and Rusty turned his head to look at his brother's blasted face. For a moment nothing was said. Only the rifle's continuous, steady "carack" broke the silence in the field. Even the insects had fallen silent.

"What am I goin' to tell my mom?" Rusty whispered hoarsely. He buried his head in his brother's chest.

"Rusty?" Tommy said quietly. He gently shook his friend's shoulders. "Rusty? What're we goin' to do, man? He's killed one of us. He's got to kill all of us now. He can't just let us walk away. We're witnesses, man."

Rusty lifted his head and stared at Tommy. A profound change was apparent in his face. The frightened and grieving and confused boy visibly hardened. His blue eyes almost turned gray with determination and resolution.

"Walk away?" he asked Tommy. "The bastard just killed my brother over a goddamn watermelon. What makes you think I'm goin' to just walk away?"

Tommy glanced quickly at Gary who was watching them from his position.

"He's right, man," Gary said flatly. "We can't just walk away. Not now. Not even if he'd let us."

"Okay," the thin boy said with a brief glance toward the farm-house. "Let's get him."

"Damn right," Gary agreed after only a moment's hesitation.

"Get back to your position," Rusty ordered. He looked once more at Kevin's blasted face. "Get back and let me think."

Overhead, the rifle's "carack" continued its spaced, steady cadence.

VIII

THE sun had begun to dip behind the plum thicket, and Kyle Cooper was getting a better picture of the field. He could tell that three of the figures had briefly bunched up and were apparently talking things over. He hoped they were planning a getaway. The anger and rage he had felt a few minutes before had vanished, and in its place a kind of weariness with the game had set in. He had shifted his tune, for no conscious reason, to "On the Wings of a Snow White Dove," firing with the downbeat of each measure, slowing the meter of the song down to accommodate the rifle's bar-rel, which was now too hot to touch. He didn't want to warp his gun over this stupidity, so he diminished the pace of his fire, but he kept it steady, now only working on one telephone pole.

He saw the three figures separate, two of them going back to their former positions, and he expected to see them leap to their feet at any moment and make for the ditch. When they get up, Kyle thought, I'll just wait. Then they'll be gone, and it'll be a cold day in hell before they try to rob old Kyle Cooper's watermelon field again. He chuckled to himself as he bolted in another shell and fired— "carack." God, he thought, he would be glad to see the last of them. He desperately wanted his pipe and a cup of hot coffee.

IX

HERE'S the plan," Rusty yelled at his two comrades when he and Tommy were back in their slit trenches. He glanced back at Kevin's body behind them. He was all business now. The terror,

231

grief, shock he had felt moments before was forced away, down deep inside him. Like a bed of banked coals, the heat of those emotions fed his control, shaped his desire for revenge. For years they had played this game, but now it was serious. He was their commander, their squad leader, their fire team leader. "Assault Number Two. You remember! Fire Superiority! Assault! Fire!" He checked Gary and Tommy, who were already bringing their knees up under their bodies, ready for the first verbal command. "Take your positions and get ready!" Rusty ordered.

It was indeed a familiar plan to each of the boys. In their pre-camping days, they had perfected it with toy rifles and war surplus helmet covers in one of their back yards. Since coming out to the farm they had practiced it, first with BB guns, then with live ammunition against carefully situated dummy targets in the sand hills along the creek.

Gary had been the one to come up with it. His Uncle Calvin had been a marine in Korea, an officer, and when he came home, he gave Gary a battered old field manual. The boys read it cover to cover a hundred times, memorized most of it. Several assault methods in it had intrigued them enough for them to incorporate them into their games. They improvised their own method of make-believe battle, adapting their own limited numbers and absence of air support or mortar crews and grenades to what they could actually do as the "fearsome trio" of imaginary warfare. Assault Number Two was one of their favorites. It offered action, movement, and a kind of built-in competition in the form of a footrace.

The procedure called for them to jump up suddenly from prone cover and to fire a round together—"in battery" as Rusty called it—toward a specified target. Then they would stand in unison, run approximately thirty yards, depending on the roughness of the terrain and the distance to the target, and fire another round as they ran. They then would "hit the dirt," discharging their weapons again in a volley after they were prone and safe once more. They would rapidly repeat the exercise until they were on top of the "enemy" who was presumably cowering in a foxhole or bunker.

In all their imaginary training, however, none of them ever

dreamed that someone would be returning their fire, that an actual human being with a deadly weapon would be trying to knock one of them down dead. But even so, they played the game hard, and when the hunting was poor, the exercise afforded something exciting to do on an otherwise dull campout. Even though this time the maneuvering was real, they felt a sudden confidence come over them that helped push down their fear and anxiety at executing Assault Number Two in deadly earnest.

The key to the plan depended on the commands "Ready?" "Fire!" "Charge!" and "Hit the Dirt!" Rusty, as their leader, would be the one to give these orders. Tommy and Gary busily brushed sand from their .410's and made sure their barrels were clear. Rusty checked his Browning quickly to make sure a shell was in the chamber, then waited to catch the rhythm of the rifle's continual "carack."

"Carack!" He reached up and wiped the sweat out of his eyes. "Carack!" He pulled the OD cap down tightly on his head. "Carack!" He drew a deep breath and held it. He couldn't remember being this anxious about anything before, but the —"Carack!"— thought of Kevin lying back there, dead—"Carack!"—overwhelmed him, and he looked one more time to his right—"Carack!"—and left at his two comrades. They were clearly scared—"Carack!"—too, but he knew they were ready to follow him. He felt the time had come—"Carack!"

"Ready?" Rusty yelled, and without checking to see what they were doing, he came to his knees and braced himself. "Fire!" he screamed and blasted the 16-gauge, barely noticing the echo from the two lighter weapons to either side. "Charge!" he ordered at the top of his lungs and scrambled and sought footing. He ran with his knees high to avoid tripping on the tangled vines and watermelons. He squeezed off another round and felt the satisfying recoil of his new weapon as its "whump" struck his ears. He carried it at his waist, knowing accuracy wasn't a consideration in Assault Number Two. "Hit the dirt!" he gasped, surprised at how hard the going was in the sandy soil, but he fell forward, prone, found the shotgun's trigger and pulled off another round. Then he automatically rolled over onto his back and jerked shells out of his pocket to reload. He checked his right and left flank and noted with pleasure that both Tommy and Gary were still in line. He felt a surge of pride and excitement at the thrill of leading his men into actual combat, and all the years of pretending, all the afternoons of imaginative fighting steeled them in the precise execution of what could only be seen as a purely military exercise.

X

WHEN Kyle Cooper saw the three figures in his field rear up, he suddenly jerked the barrel of his rifle high and took his finger off the trigger. At last, he thought, the sons-of-bitches were making a break for it. He squinted into the final rays of the sun's arch and tried to see if he could recognize the vendor himself among the trespassers, when suddenly he saw small puffs of smoke appear in front of each of them. He opened his mouth to speak, but the distant "whumps" of the shotguns reached his ears and stopped his words in his throat. Then the men were clearly on their feet and running, but they weren't fleeing as he had expected. They were running *toward* him! Another trio of explosions erupted from them as they came.

"What the hell?" Kyle asked in a choking, incredulous voice, but the second report of the shotguns drowned him out. His jaw, still stained with egg yolk, dropped open in surprise and disbelief. "The greaser bastards're shootin' at *me!*" He felt frozen to his chair in panic and sudden fear.

They were too far away to hit him with shotguns, but the very idea that they would come on *his* property to steal *his* melons and then return *his* fire simply would not register in his mind as a logical chain of events. He couldn't accept it, and he sat in his rocker and held his rifle dead in his hands. He was amazed at the sheer gall of these thieving fruit vendors. As he watched, they fired again.

XI

READY? . . . Fire!" Rusty ordered, and again the three boys leaped up and began executing the maneuver they had practiced for so many years. Rusty noticed that the return fire from the porch had ceased, and he decided to gamble and try to gain more ground on the second charge. He heard through his own gasps the blasts of the .410's to his right and left, but he held his own fire for another ten paces, then fifteen, leaping and tripping over the vines and melons, trying to keep from sinking too deeply into the sand, all the while concentrating his gaze on the figure he could now see clearly on the porch, in the shade of the thicket behind him.

"Hit the dirt!" he yelled, firing his weapon almost before he landed, grunting painfully as a watermelon caught him in the chest and knocked the wind from him. His comrades, also breathless and feeling the strain of their mad charge toward the house, fired quickly too, and Rusty realized with dismay, that they still had almost a hundred yards to go before they reached the farmhouse.

Reloading quickly, Rusty took deep breaths to regain his wind. He inspected his troops and noted with pleasure that they were reloading their weapons, rolling back over onto their stomachs, and readying themselves to go again. "Ready?" he hissed at them, and they both nodded back, too out of breath to answer. "Fire!" he yelled, rising and pulling his trigger. "Charge!" he screamed, and they stumbled to their feet and scrambled over the field in the third heat of their race toward the murdering old man on the porch.

XII

KYLE Cooper's mesmerized state vanished as the boys completed the third leg of their charge toward him. Two realizations suddenly occurred to him at once, and a third wasn't far behind. First of all, he discovered, these thieves weren't the men he had seen at the fruit stand on the road at all. These were smaller by a sight, and they were wearing some weird kind of military garb and carrying shotguns. Secondly, he understood all at once that unlike his firing on them, they weren't just trying to scare him. *They were trying to kill him!* This inarguable fact was brought to his attention when he heard the sound of shot pellets hitting the broken-down picket fence that marked the border of his back dooryard. They had closed to within seventy-five yards on their last run, and with their next shots, they could reach the back porch of the farmhouse.

The third notion that hit him was that he had better do something to stop them before someone got hurt, but he didn't know what to do. He had no desire to shoot back, since this had turned out to be an awful mistake in the first place, and he opened his mouth to call to them and explain, but his throat had dried up in fear. His croaking, choking words were drowned out by the uneven "whumps" of the shotguns now coming loudly on the heels of the rattling pellets.

Kyle stood up and moved out to the edge of the porch. His movement upset the Bible and box of cartridges with the rifle's stock. He waved at the boys and lowered his weapon, trying to conceal it behind a skinny leg. He kept yelling, but each time a "whump" flung his words back at him.

The boys—he could see clearly now that they were really just children—dove face forward into the ground once again, and this time, their concerted fire reached the porch and hit Kyle with a stinging sensation that seemed to cover his face and chest. He wasn't hurt, he knew, but behind him he heard the pellets bouncing off the kitchen windowpanes, and he knew he had to do something and quickly.

He continued to wave and yell at his adversaries, seeing that they were up and running again, closing the distance remaining between the house and their last position rapidly, firing as they came. This time windows behind him broke, and shot hit him squarely in the chest, reeling him backwards, but still not penetrating his clothing or exposed skin. As he careened against the rocker, he dropped his rifle, and suddenly he decided he had better get inside and away from the stinging, burning pellets that peppered him one more time before he could regain his balance. The sound of breaking glass was all around him. It seemed that the shotguns' "whumps" came right down his neck.

Just as his gnarled fingers reached the rusty handle of the screen door, something hot and stinging broke out on the back of his balding head. He jerked his hand up automatically, and when he brought it before his eyes, it was bright red, covered with blood.

"Great day in the mornin'! Oh, Jesus!" Kyle's old eyes were wide with terror. "I'm shot! Jesus! I'm shot! Have mercy!"

The pain of the wound passed quickly, replaced by anger which began to well up in his chest.

"Them little bastards," he swore. "They got more balls'n God give a bull." Forgetting safety, he turned around, scooped up the rifle, and tried to aim it quickly where he had last seen the boys. But they were closer now, much closer, and his shot went high. His shell smashed one giant watermelon in an explosion of red meat and seeds. Feverishly working the bolt open and ejecting the empty shell casing, Kyle groped down to the table beside the overturned rocker, but the box of cartridges had fallen on the floor. Shoving the Bible aside into the litter of empty brass casings, he scrambled around until he came up with a fresh bullet. He desperately tried to force his shaking fingers to place it into the chamber. Time seemed to click by slowly. All he could hear was his pulse pounding in his ears. He jammed the bolt home, finally, and raised the rifle toward the boys who were now rushing right up to the broken railings of the dooryard fence less than twenty-five yards away.

"Now we'll see who's the toughest son-of-a-bitch around here," he growled as the bead on his rifle's barrel centered on the middle youth's chest and his finger groped for the trigger.

XIII

THE charging boys had almost given out by the end of the fourth run toward the farmhouse. Their legs felt like rubber, and their feet, unnaturally heavy in the combat boots, sank into the sandy loam of the fields as if it were quicksand. They no longer tried to aim at the skinny figure with the rifle on the porch as they had done when the assault started and they were well out of range. Now they merely pointed their weapons in the general direction of the house and pulled their triggers in jerky, haphazard fashion, pumping out their empties automatically but with increasing effort.

They were out of breath, exhausted, parched, and more frightened than ever now that they were really close enough to hit the porch, for while they knew that continued fire was the key to the plan's success, they also knew that being closer made them better targets for the old man with the high-powered rifle. Collapsing at the end of the fourth leg of the assault, they jerked off their rounds and rolled over to fill their guns, and, without consulting each other, argued silently that another run simply wasn't in them, at least not without a breather and some water.

Rusty, however, knew they couldn't afford to quit or even to rest. Although he was as tired and thirsty as the other two, and although he was no less frightened, he knew that to stop now was virtual suicide. The old man hadn't returned fire since they started Assault Number Two, which meant, according to his understanding of marine infantry tactics, that they had done it. They had Fire Superiority, even though they had weapons of inferior range. The momentum was theirs, and they couldn't afford to lose it, especially now that they were close enough to the porch that he could shoot them like junkyard rats. Adrenaline flowed in him like a hot river of fire, and he readied himself for the next punishing charge.

Like the other two boys, Rusty found that aiming at the porch or the old man with any degree of accuracy was almost impossible as he scrambled over the vines and stumbled through the soft sand, but unlike them, he had made a concentrated effort to do so with each shot. He had seen Old Man Cooper jump up and start to move around after the last volley, and he saw one of his blasts actually shatter a window. As he bounced on the ground after his last "Hit the dirt!" command, he waited a breathless count of three, took as deadly an aim as he could, and fired directly at the man's head. He was gratified and invigorated when he saw Old Man Cooper's hand fly up to his bald pate and then come away to reveal a bright splash of red. As Rusty's hands went through the motions of reloading his weapon, he almost cried out in glee.

He rolled over and looked to either side to check his comrades. "Ready?" he asked, but they didn't move at all. They lay where they were, heaving air in and out of their tortured lungs, staring at the house, and holding their guns loosely in their hands. "Ready!?"

Rusty repeated in a loud, demanding voice, but they remained still, said nothing, and refused to look at him.

At the moment Kyle Cooper's shot came flying just over their heads and struck a big melon thirty yards behind them, and the trio buried their faces in the vines and sand beneath them.

"Ready! Fire! Charge!" Rusty bellowed and came to his knees and pulled his trigger quickly, but his two comrades remained frozen in the sand. "I said Fire! Fire! Fire!! Dammit! *Fire!!*" he screamed at them and raised himself to his feet.

This time they felt his energy and were sparked into movement. They rose and blasted a volley in duet, struggled to their feet, and half stumbling, half falling, they scrambled and tripped over the vines and watermelons toward the rickety picket fence that marked the old man's back yard.

XIV

KYLE Cooper's finger hesitated on the trigger as he forced himself to take his time and pick his target. He squared his shaky legs, but his head was spinning around and around, and sweat—or was it blood? he wondered in a panic—burned his eyes and ran into his toothless mouth and made it more dry and almost unbearably briny. He tried desperately to keep his eyes focused on the boys as they ran at him one more time.

The initial "whump" was quickly followed by two lighter reports that slammed into the porch's support beams and smashed out what was left of the glass in the kitchen window. Somehow, all three shots missed Kyle, and he wavered as he tried to draw a bead on one of the stumbling, running figures before him.

"Which one?" he hissed. "Which one? Dammit!" He had initially decided on the middle boy, but as they ran, he kept changing his mind and waving the rifle between the flanking pair. He couldn't make up his mind, and as he ran a dry tongue over cracked lips, the boys' second volley reached him—"Wh-WHUMP-Up!"—and deafened him entirely. He felt himself being flung back against the screen door, and it took all his strength to find his feet again and raise the rifle barrel one more time, the unfired round still in the chamber.

Dazed and confused, Kyle Cooper shook his head and squinted down the barrel to pick his target. He sensed that he was hurt, badly hurt, but his eyes refused to tear themselves away from the charging boys long enough to inspect his chest and groin, which felt ripped open, exposed to the air. He squeezed his eyes shut and then opened them to try to clear his vision. His head was swimming, his ears ringing, but he could still see. This time the largest of the boys on his near side seemed to attract him, and the old man tried to dead reckon his aim. Bringing the gun to his shoulder was impossible. His arms refused to work. Pain coursed through his thin body, screaming at him from a thousand points of bright, exquisite torture. Even his tongue hurt. He decided to give up. He opened his mouth to yell at them, to tell them this had gone far enough, to stop where they were or he would kill them where they stood.

Then the boys suddenly hit the packed earth at the field's edge and gained speed. They raced up to the boards of the fence and rested the barrels of their guns on the top rail as if the whole thing were some sort of well-practiced, deadly exercise. In perfect unison, they fired in volley with their mouths open, their chests heaving, their eyes wide with fear, terror, triumph.

The last thing Kyle Cooper saw was the rise and fall of their youthful chests as they gasped for air when they pulled their triggers and released their final, explosive blasts, shutting off whatever words the old man was about to say.

XV

For a long moment, the boys stood motionless with their empty, superheated gun barrels resting on the fence's top rail. Their combined fire had lifted Kyle Cooper's body up off the porch and pushed him back into the screen door. He rested in an absurd position, his bony hips sitting in a crude balance on the door's crosspiece, his arms hanging limply in front of him in an empty, pathetic gesture, his head and shoulders supported by the screen's mesh, his legs dangling, one boot on and the other off, resting on the floor where he had planted his feet when he tried to shoot one last time.

Blood was everywhere, splattered with brain and bone all over the outer wall and the doorjamb, splashing onto the cheap linoleum of the kitchen that Bertha once kept so neat. The force of the combined blasts had blown the man apart; what hung in the wire screen was only a shell, its contents gone, blasted out of Kyle's back as if he had exploded from within, the covering held together only by the tension remaining in the screen's wire mesh.

The boys gulped air and leaned against the fence, not really seeing or comprehending what they had done. Tommy fell to his knees in a sudden, helpless gesture, unable to support his own weight on his weak and exhausted legs. Gary lowered his head, feeling vomit rising again in his burning throat.

Rusty gathered what air he could into his lungs and turned his head to look back over the assault route they had just covered. He tried to spot Kevin's body out near the ditch, but the sun was behind the trees now, and the sky was growing dark. The field was covered with a dusky summer evening occasionally brightened by fireflies playing in the plum thicket. Sweat streamed down from his red hair and kept running into his eyes and burning them. He tried to rub them, but sand and dirt made them gritty and hard to clear. He slid to his knees next to Tommy and collapsed by the fence.

"It's over," he gasped. The other two said nothing.

Finally the boys came to their feet slowly and mechanically. They grabbed their canteens and drained them before flinging them down into the dusty dooryard behind Kyle Cooper's farmhouse. Rusty reached into his fatigue jacket pocket and was surprised to discover that only one shell remained. Tommy and Gary checked their weapons. Tommy had a full load left, but Gary was completely empty. He had fired his last round onto the porch. It was a good thing, Rusty thought, he had stretched out the last two rushes. They never would have made it, otherwise. They exchanged looks that said they all understood the wisdom of their leader, but words would not come.

Suddenly, they all turned around together, almost as if on parade, executing an "About Face," and they stared at the porch in the gathering twilight.

"Jesus," Tommy whistled through his teeth softly, "look what we done."

No one else said anything as Rusty led them down the broken fence, through the dangling gate, and on up the weed-covered brick walk to the porch. Chickens, previously subdued by the noise of battle, began clucking again, venturing forth from various hiding places and pecking around the steps. A rooster sounded an angry and indignant crow at the interruption of the afternoon's quiet; the cock's call caused all three boys to jump, then to look around sheepishly. From the distance of the field, the sounds of early evening insects marked a sharp contrast to the dying fall of the cicadas' incessant whirrings, and far off, maybe as far as town, a diesel engine's whining whistle sounded.

The porch was entirely in shadow now, the sun having dipped below the horizon, leaving only the purple outlines of the dooryard in its wake. Rusty slowly stepped up onto the blasted porch, carefully avoiding the brass shell casings that littered the floor. He saw the Bible splattered with Kyle's blood next to the empty boot, and his eyes involuntarily followed the tracing of the splintered doorjamb up to the body of their adversary, the crazy old man who had killed Kevin and tried to kill them.

Tommy and Gary moved up to flank their leader and stood properly behind him just two paces. They didn't dare speak. In spite of their martial bearing, however, they were undergoing an awesome retransformation. They were no longer men, soldiers of fortune, assault forces, combat marines. Now they were only boys, boys who had killed a man. A sickening feeling of being "in trouble" crept over them and drove away their bravado, pushing away everything except fear of punishment for what they had done.

"Christ in heaven," Tommy intoned softly. "Jesus Christ in heaven."

"Half his fuckin' head's gone," Gary murmured. "God! Look at it."

"Yeah," Rusty said. He was unable to take his eyes away from the old man's body perched obscenely on the screen door.

Kyle's face was indeed almost gone. One remaining blue eye stared sightlessly into the gathering dark of the western sky. His mouth hung open in a red gape. A streak of egg yolk ran down his unshaven chin. His chest and stomach were a mass of raw skin and cartilage spilling out of the lacerated overalls and long underwear that also exposed the bloody, crushed bone that had once been his knees.

"He's deader'n shit, man," Gary observed needlessly. "I mean, deader than shit." He felt himself beginning to wretch again. "An' we did it. I *mean* we did it!" He could choke back the reaction no longer, and he moved without shame to the edge of the porch and dry-heaved. Seeing him and hearing his coughing retches, the other two boys found themselves joining him, and the green bile that spilled from their stomachs clogged their noses and burned their sinuses.

Recovering themselves, the boys began walking aimlessly around the porch, picking up shell casings and casting them down again in mindless activity. Chickens began to gather around the porch steps, clucking loudly, demanding to be fed.

"What're we goin' to do, Rusty?" Tommy asked, glancing quickly at the body in the screen door. "What're they goin' to do to *us?* I mean, we *killed* him, man." Gary looked up and nodded. "I mean, we killed the *shit* out of him. That makes us murderers! Nobody's goin' to believe we didn't do it on purpose. I mean, we were trespassin', an'—"

Rusty turned away silently and dropped his shotgun on the sparse grass of the dooryard. He went over and rested his arms on the fence.

"I wish to God he hadn't shot at us," he said quietly. "It was all his fault. God*damn* it! I wish he hadn't shot at us. I wish he . . . I wish he hadn't killed Kevin!" There, it was said. He felt tears coming but fought them back. Then they were too much for him, and a great tearing sob broke from his throat.

"We weren't doin' nothin'! Shit! I mean, we were just goin' to take a couple of goddamn watermelons. What's that? Four bucks?" He yelled his choked words into the twilight. "I mean, *goddamn!* He killed my brother for four goddamn dollars worth of goddamn fuckin' watermelons!!"

He spun around quickly. The hot tears streaked down his face. He could feel the tracks they made in the dirt and dried blood—his brother's blood—on his freckled cheeks. He felt awful, dirty, tired. He looked at his two friends and felt sick all over again. They were just kids, he thought. Dammit! Kids! Just like him!

"What am I goin' to tell my folks? Huh?" He railed at them. "What am I goin' to tell my mom?" His comrades said nothing, staring at the ground. "What am I goin' to tell my goddamn mother?" He was shaking all over.

Suddenly he rushed past them and up onto the porch. He grabbed Kyle Cooper's body by the overall straps and began to shake it. The head rolled hideously on the lacerated neck as it pulled free from the screen, but Rusty continued to yell into the face that wasn't even there.

"You have *kids? You have a mother?*" he screamed. "You'd kill a twelve-year-old kid for a goddamn watermelon, you tight-assed son-of-a-bitch?"

Tommy and Gary were frozen where they stood. Rusty was flinging blood and gore all over himself and the porch. Then he backed off and struck the pulp that had been Kyle Cooper's face with his fist. The force of the blow pushed the entire body through the ripped screen until it fell into the kitchen astraddle the broken door.

Spent, Rusty stood and heaved great sobs into the night air.

Tommy and Gary looked at each other and then turned to study their friend in the dim light of the summer dusk. Rusty was covered with blood. All three boys, as if on cue, sank into themselves. They felt the weight of their exhaustion all at once pulling them down. They longed to move out to the dooryard, to sit on the grass and stare at the sky that was suddenly and strangely illuminated by a giant moon rising behind the house. The night seemed clean, cool, and carelessly unmindful of the carnage in the farmhouse's kitchen and in the field.

"Rusty?" Tommy said, relieved to see his friend's eyes losing the madness they had held during his assault on the corpse. "What *are* they goin' to do to us?"

Gary spoke up in a defensive and falsely deep voice. "Hell, man, we *had* to do it. I mean, he was shootin' at us. I mean—" His words broke off. The argument was silly and useless. They all knew that. Even if they'd only fired in self-defense, Old Man Cooper had been in the right. They were trespassing. They were thieves. That argument wouldn't wash. They all knew it.

Tommy and Gary stared at Rusty, but suddenly they realized he wasn't looking at them at all. His eyes saw past them, and they turned to see what he was looking at.

A car had turned into the road and was bouncing over the ruts and bumps leading up to the farmhouse. In the bright moonlight, they could make out the unmistakable silhouette of the red bubble light atop the sheriff's cruiser.

"Nothin'," Rusty said softly as he watched the car's headlights dip and rise over the tortured road. "They won't do nothin' to us." He stepped over to them. "We're just kids. They won't do nothin'."

Wordlessly, they began to move together out to the edge of the dooryard to meet the sheriff's car. Rusty put on his OD cap and squared it. He spat on the ground. He knew that he was half right. They wouldn't do anything to them, not really. But he was half wrong as well. They weren't kids any more. They never could be kids again.

XVI

A̲FTER a while, the night deepened and gave way to early morning. The moon hit its apex and bathed the heat of the watermelon field in a cold silvery glow now undisturbed by flashlights and ambulance and police car headlamps. The only sounds were crickets and nocturnal birds calling to each other across the˚ dark fields and thickets around the blacked-out house that kept a lonely watch over Kyle Cooper's farm. A gossamer film of dew fell across the vines and sandy paths around the oblong melons, and here and there a rabbit or skunk braved an open patch and scurried in short, jerky races with its shadow between the house and the road, hoping to avoid an owl's sharp vision.

Cautiously, the lumbering shadow of a truck appeared along the road west of the field. It silenced the night's sounds as the engine misfired and the radio sent forth strains of a Mexican polka. The truck showed no light except from the red tips of cigarettes held by men riding in the bed, but it stopped with practiced ingenuity in a familiar spot; the engine's rumblings ceased along with the static-laced music of the radio.

Deftly and silently, the men flung their butts into the ditches before they grabbed the poorly concealed planks and ran them across to the fields. Wordlessly, they moved in among the melons and made selections, chopping them free with long, double-bladed knives. Then they carried the gourds back across the makeshift bridge to the truck where they stacked them carefully, almost tenderly.

The driver leaned against the cab's fender and smoked while the work went on. He kept a constant eye on the distant, dark house for any sign of a light or movement. There was none. He smiled broadly and chain-lit another cigarette, then reached into his cab and ran his calloused fingers through the ink-black hair of the sleeping boy curled up on the seat.

In less than an hour, the workers finished their chore. They re-moved the planks and hid them again, better this time, and climbed over the stacked melons which gave them a perch much higher than the truck bed's walls. They lit more cigarettes and passed around a bottle of whiskey from which each took a large drink. They chatted amiably in soft tones. It had been a good night's work, and they felt satisfied.

After a moment, the truck's engine rumbled to life and again displaced the night's noises. Another polka wafted from the cab's window as the driver ground the gears, maneuvering the vehicle slowly up the road and around a turn beyond which its single working headlamp would be invisible to the farmhouse.

As the noise faded and the crickets and birds reclaimed the night, the moon descended into the western sky, and dawn began to force a pale light into the east. A hungry cock crowed prematurely from a dark perch, and the watermelons in the fields rested undisturbed in their bath of morning dew.

Bluebirds

Pat Carr

I

SHE WATCHED through the observation window as his gloved hand opened the furnace door and drew out a length of pipe knobbed with a red-orange bulb. The glowing red ball was molten glass, and he twirled the pipe warily to keep the honey-thick glass from drooping while he carried it to the workbench. His face was clenched, but his movements were practiced and confident as his other, bare hand grasped the shears, pinched one blade into the throbbing red ball as it circled. A smaller orb rose from the original. With another deft movement of the shears, he poked in two minuscule eyes, drew a tiny beak from the upper knob, then pulled the swoop of a molten tail from the larger, lower globe. In seconds, the unmistakable shape of a bird clung to the end of the hot pipe.

She was continually amazed that she never tired of the process, a process so unerring that each time it was as if the bird form were emerging by itself, as if the same stylized bird would appear whether or not it was urged by the metal clippers.

He grabbed a wooden spatula with a cooler disc of glass, the size and shape of a mint patty, and she watched him snip the red-orange bird free, drop it neatly onto the pedestal of cooler greening glass. He slid the pipe into the water barrel, and steam hissed toward the observation window. He didn't look up as he took the wooden board with the finished bird to the warming oven where it would cool down to green and finally to a brilliant blue. He seemed unaware of the observation window, but she could tell he knew she was there.

251

He tossed down the pot-holder mitten and went out the back door of the workroom, and another, much younger, man came in at once to tie on a leather apron.

She backed away from the window and pretended to examine the shelves of glass bluebirds in the salesroom. They were all exactly alike, and she stood before them for a few seconds before she went to the door and buttoned her coat.

Hugh was already lumbering toward the car, and she went out to where he was getting in on the passenger's side.

She felt herself waddling through the winter air. Only two buttons remained on the coat, near the collar, and although they secured the top, they let the rest of the coat flap open in the cold.

She threw herself into the driver's seat and slammed the door after her to shut out the wind. The coat bunched up behind her back, but she didn't try to straighten it as her cold fingers fumbled the key into the ignition. She glanced at him.

His eyes, the color of the cooled bluebirds, were staring forward through the windshield, but she knew he was aware of her gaze. His jaw was clamped, and thick tendons ridged his neck.

"One of these days I've got to buy some buttons for this coat." She undid one to ease the stranglehold of the collar. "Buttons this size are over a dollar apiece though, and I hate to spend seven dollars on a sixteen-year-old coat." But then, since the VA psychiatrist had cautioned her about guilt-tripping him, she added, to keep him from thinking she was blaming him for her having to wear an old coat, "I've gained so much weight I'm not sure the buttons would close all the way down the front anyway."

Her fingers were iced against the key, but after two tries, the ancient starter slurred on, and she revved the motor carefully before she let the clutch out. Despite her care, the old car jerked forward, the tires spinning gravel against the shop sign: BLUEBIRDS OF HAPPINESS. HANDMADE GLASS.

"This worn-out clutch," she offered while she pushed the pedal in again and tried to control the lurching.

She kept her comments to declarative statements since she was pretty sure he wouldn't respond. He hadn't said anything to her or

252

the girls for nine days, but of course she never knew when he might start talking again after one of his silences. She never remembered from one to the next what she did or said that ended them, or if anything she said or did made any difference. The VA doctor had told her not to worry, assuring her that a lot of Nam vets retreated into silence and that it was a way they handled their experience. "It's better than if they turned violent, isn't it?" He'd smiled at her with such disarmingly straight white teeth that she hadn't been able to question him about what constituted violence. As she'd sat in the tidy VA hospital office looking at the young doctor—clean brown hair in a barber cut, healthy jogging tan, brown-gold eyes behind tortoise shell glasses—she hadn't been able to ask whether Hugh's having struck her the previous week might not qualify. She'd had to tell the young man about Hugh's problems with various jobs, and her shabby coat had revealed that they were low on funds. But to admit to shabby behavior, to admit to the fact that Hugh had inexplicably hit her, was something she hadn't been prepared to do there in that bright office with its wallpaper print of pink lilies. And she hadn't asked the doctor if perhaps Hugh might not be becoming a violent patient.

The car chugged onto the stretch of blacktop that led to their street, a street which was reduced to a dirt road again before it passed their yard, and she didn't try to say anything more as she urged the old car along. She knew the ancient Buick would last longer if she didn't take him to work and pick him up in the evenings after she got home from her job at the Sunshine House, but she had no intention of suggesting that she stop going to the shop. For the glimpse of him behind the polished observation window creating the blue glass birds constituted the few seconds of her life that allowed her to remember what she might have seen in him once. Watching him work and watching the birds appear allowed her to ignore for a few seconds the hovering presence of Van that had begun to claim a portion of her attention no matter what she was doing.

She pulled into the rutted semicircle that was their driveway, and he got out, disappeared into the house before the car had stopped vibrating.

She sat for a moment, feeling but ignoring the bunched wool of the coat, letting her hands curl over the steering wheel and her stomach rest against it, allowing thoughts of Van to surface of their own volition.

Van was the opposite of Hugh in every way. Van was never quiet, would never have been able to maintain a stony silence for nine to fifteen minutes let alone for nine to fifteen days. He was always telling jokes, always flicking his long forelock aside as he threw back his head to laugh at his own anecdotes. He liked long, fact-filled stories that sounded as if he was retelling something he'd read in the *National Geographic* but that ended up in an elaborate pun about some obscure native king who should have had enough sense not to stow his throne under his eaves since he lived in a grass house. "Get it? Stow thrones—throw stones, grass house—glass house," he'd roar. She smiled faintly and rubbed her palm along the steering wheel. She couldn't remember how many times she'd heard that one. The dark lock of hair would whip back, his silver-filled teeth would frame the guffaw while he laughed as if he'd never heard or told the joke before.

Van was tall and loose-joint thin where Hugh had stump legs and a feed-sack chest. Van probably wore a thirty-two long in the pants to Hugh's thirty-eight short. She couldn't quite visualize Van walking—it had been a long time—but she was certain he wouldn't slouch along with a bear gait. He'd been in Vietnam too, and he'd earned a box of colored ribbons as well, but instead of locking him into silence, his overseas experience had made him more vocal.

Of course, that joking, laughing, never meeting anyone he couldn't talk to had caused all the trouble. But if she'd known the other extreme of the Vietnam veteran, the terrible tensed stillness of someone like Hugh when she'd left Van she might have rethought her action.

She sighed without knowing she had and opened the car door to the cold wind.

The metal protest of the door hinge reminded her that she needed to oil the door before it sprang loose from its swivel pin again. They couldn't afford another twenty-two dollars to get it forced back on.

The payment for Hughleen's retainer was due, and the dentist had been so good about repairing it when the dog chewed it that she hated to make him wait yet another month for his check. She'd known when she'd married Hugh that he didn't drive, that he hated machines. She half understood why he jerked back from the sight of a motor as if he'd glimpsed an open wound, why the damaged planes he'd repaired in Saigon had somehow become entangled with the bomb death of his friend Ray, but although she tried to sympathize, she still often yearned for Van's skill at handling engines. Van kept his second-hand trucks whirring, but Hugh let bolts fall off and screws rust shut as if he'd never known motors at all.

She sighed again and walked heavily toward the house, the two sides of her coat flapping.

They were so different. And those differences were the reason she'd been talked into marriage while she was still smarting from Van's betrayal.

II

SHE pulled away from the curb in front of the Sunshine House and checked the lunch list as she drove. No new elderly shut-ins had been added, none had been deleted since Tuesday, and she could follow her usual route to the first stop, a small clapboard house with a yard clogged by stiffened weeds and crackled yellow vines.

She stopped and adroitly slid the foil-covered tray off the rack of the minibus. She carried the still-warm tray through the gate and up the rotting porch steps.

The screen on the door had bulged loose the way hers at home had slacked into disrepair, but she didn't stop to contemplate it. She pulled open the rickety, useless wooden frame and rang the bell.

It sounded through the little house with harsh clarity, but before the echo had died she knocked with a loud rap on the front door panels and then immediately opened the door.

"Mrs. Lasater?" she called as a semi-announcement, but she knew the old woman had been waiting for over an hour expecting the hot lunch van. Once the route had been set and they knew her time, they expected her on the dot. If she was ever detained or a new name was added to the list to delay her, the regulars became peevish and sullen.

"Mrs. Lasater, I've brought your lunch."

She also knew that the old people liked to fancy that the lunch on the metal tray had been prepared with them in mind. All of them were aware that the same lunch was cooked for sixty-eight in the Sunshine House kitchen, but they didn't want to be reminded of it.

The old house had locked in the odors of ancient boiled stews, worn shoes, decayed linoleum, and she always had to shallow her breath for a few minutes each time she entered.

"That you, Amy?" a fragile voice called.

But by that time she was at the bedroom door, and she didn't have to identify herself.

"My, don't you look pretty in pink today," she said instead. She always resisted the temptation to speak with the cozy "we" so many of the workers used. She felt that the old people needed their own individual dignity and shouldn't be merged into a faceless shared emotion.

The papery dry face on the pillow cracked into a grimace of pleasure. "My granddaughter Maureen got this out of my bureau drawer for me last night." The bony fingers covered with faded tissue paper flesh patted the machine lace trim. "I thought to myself, 'What am I saving this bed jacket for? It's about time I got some wear out of it.' Maureen's too old-fashioned to let me be buried in it. Too flimsy and sexy." She cackled a gasp of stale breath. "You notice, Amy, how straight-laced these young people been getting?"

The question was delivered with another gasp while Amy eased her into a sitting position and propped the extra pillows at her back.

"You smell the cedar? I packed all my lingerie with cedar chips. When you take things out, there's this nice fresh cedar smell."

"I noticed," Amy said although the scent of the ancient, un-washed body had taken over long before her arrival. "That's a good color on you."

"I don't remember who gave me this. Must be ten, fifteen years old." Then her attention veered to the tray that Amy was balancing on yet another pillow across her lap. "What's for today?"

Amy never knew since the trays were dished up and covered before she got to work, but she didn't reveal that as she began peeling back the foil. "I think it's something you'll like."

"As long as it's not liver and onions. I don't like liver and onions." The waver became querulous. "I don't know why they think we should eat so much liver. Gives me gas every time."

"No, look, it's chicken and dumplings. Doesn't that look good." The folded silver foil exposed the tray partitions, the glossy dumplings settled on slabs of chicken, the fat carrot discs, and a cube of yellow cake with chocolate icing. "I'll get a fork." She almost slipped and said "us."

She went into the kitchen and located the fork she'd washed the day before. She returned quickly to the bedroom where Mrs. Lasater was poking one finger into the chocolate frosting.

"I wish they'd have strawberry shortcake. Tell 'em, Amy, they ought to have strawberry shortcake. One, two times a month they could have strawberry shortcake, don't you think?"

"I'll suggest that." She put the fork that seemed outsized and too heavy into the frail hand and brought a chair from the foot of the bed. Each of the old people on her route had a favorite dish they urged her to request, and she never tried to explain about the dieticians and the geriatric specialists who planned the joint sixty-eight meals by the month. There were all sorts of changes of her own she'd have made if she'd had the credentials.

She sat down and nodded as the old woman filled her mouth and talked, but she wasn't able to concentrate as usual on the memories the old woman was creating for her. A vague image of Van rose unbidden in the stains of the dun-colored wallpaper, and she had to glance away from it.

". . . since he carried the messages for the battalion. He was a good runner, you know, and his captain used him to run messages back and forth to the general behind the lines. They had that trench warfare, you know, and the men was pinned down and he'd be sent back with reports," the old voice recited.

It was Mr. Lasater's memory, a World War I experience in his words that his wife had incorporated into her own, and Amy had already heard it dozens of times.

Would that have been something that could have happened to her if she'd stayed married to Van? Would he have told her Vietnam experiences so endlessly that when she reached eighty, she'd have heard them so many times that they'd begin to seem like her own? Hugh never talked about Vietnam even when he was talking. But would Van have told . . . ?

"And there he was laying in the ditch not even breathing, and the German patrol was walking right by. He couldn't understand German, but there they was, we called 'em Huns then, there they was, the Huns, strolling down the road while he hugged that ditch."

The soft glazed dumplings had disappeared and the huge fork was attacking the orange carrot rounds. The old people never left a morsel. It was often the only meal of their day, and the supervisor had cautioned her never to stay and have coffee with them no matter how earnestly they insisted. None of them could really afford to share. Besides, she was allotted only fifteen minutes for each after her stop with bedridden Mrs. Lasater to whom she could give half an hour.

"He was never so scared in his life, and he just knew his heartbeat was going to give him away to the Huns."

That was the excuse Van had offered, that he'd never been so scared in his life. That the jungle was the most terrifying place he'd ever been. Some of the men could handle it all right, he'd said, but he never learned to and he hated every minute of it. That was why he'd had to have something to anticipate when he went back to Saigon. It hadn't been any more than that, he'd explained; it was just having someone close in the night when he woke up trembling in the blackness. It was just having someone there to reassure him that he wasn't asleep in the jungle.

Perhaps if she'd heard Mr. Lasater's fear in the parrot voice of Mrs. Lasater, maybe she'd have understood before it was too late.

Mrs. Lasater was pushing gently at the molded partitions.

"Well, wasn't that a good piece of cake?" She scooped away the empty tray.

The dumplings and the rich chocolate frosting had given strength to the old chin and it jutted out stubbornly. "I like strawberry shortcake. Two, three times a month they could fix strawberry shortcake."

III

BLUEBIRDS OF HAPPINESS. HANDMADE GLASS. That was the sign at the edge of the parking lot, but the one over the shop door added HOME OF THE ORIGINAL BLUEBIRD OF HAPPINESS.

It seemed an easy and appropriate title for the blue transparencies of glass, she thought as she watched the thin metallic sunlight glitter on the little birds and pedestals lining the railing before the shop.

Each one handcrafted. Each one an original. A bluebird of happiness. Dozens of them inside and outside the shop.

The glass factory featured other glass items made with the same composition of pure white sand and cobalt, made with the same mixture of copper and silver, but the specialty of the shop was the bluebird. Once when Hugh was talking he'd said that the bluebirds—he'd called them *his* bluebirds—were a big seller in hospital boutiques. Visitors bought them to cheer patients into getting well. But Hugh worked two four-hour shifts a day fashioning the cheerful birds, working eight hours a day five days a week with the glittering cobalt glass, and he didn't get well.

She shook herself impatiently. That kind of thinking didn't do anybody any good.

It was just something he had to work through on his own, the VA psychiatrist said, nodding before his pink lily wallpaper. The young doctor's wife had probably chosen that print. It looked like something a young doctor's wife would select for her husband's office. "Just be there for him and let him work it through." He smiled reassuringly. "You just hang in there."

Did Van have anything to work through? Or had he already worked it out when he found the Vietnamese woman to sleep beside

259

him in the night to keep away the black jungle fear? If only he hadn't had a child by her—a child that might have his dark wing of hair falling over an oriental face—maybe the shock of discovery wouldn't have been so jolting.

The woman merely wanted to marry him to get out of Vietnam and come to the U.S. He'd been too unsuspecting and had married her right after the divorce. Any American woman with half a brain could have warned him, but he was too trusting. It became obvious even to him when the woman dumped him a month after she got to Pennsylvania with her child, but he'd been too gullible to see it earlier.

She knew where he was, of course. She'd known for maybe six or seven years, ever since she'd sent his dad in Detroit a Christmas card one holiday and had got one back that said, "Van's here with me."

Was he working in Detroit? Or had the shell that sheared off the muscles and tendons of his right shoulder allowed him a pension? She did know that the Saigon woman and her child—she tried to remember if she'd ever heard whether that child was a boy or a girl—had disappeared into southern California and that Van and his dad were alone.

The cracked clock in the dashboard had stopped at 12:20 some years earlier, and she'd taken off the plastic digital watch she used to time her old people, but she was sure Hugh's shift was over. Perhaps she should go in.

But she didn't move.

She felt suddenly as leaden as the sky. Her body was a thick packing of fat encased in a frayed aqua blouse, old navy slacks stretched to their seams. Her hands were anchored to the steering wheel.

She told herself she ought to move.

But before she'd willed her muscles to tense and lift her weight, she saw Hugh shambling with his bulky gait around the corner of the building.

The blue glass birds perched glowing, gleaming in their row on the two-by-four porch rail as he passed them. He was staring at the gray gravel under his feet.

IV

Hughleen's failing math and English," she said as she pressed the remote control bar. The late evening news made Hugh anxious. "She may have to repeat the fifth grade if she can't improve."

He didn't look away from his concentrated study of the blue-white after-square of the TV.

"I don't know how to help her. I don't know the kind of math they're doing in school now. It's like algebra, and I wasn't good at that. The teacher thinks we ought to get her a tutor." She paused a second, but his blue eyes stared at the fading TV blue. "She wanted us to come to school and talk about it. I told her we couldn't get off that easy, but she said we'd have to do something pretty quick."

He sat immobile, his hands spread flat on his thighs.

"She said Hughleen's falling more and more behind all the time." She moved deliberately between his gaze and the TV cabinet. "The year's half over already. Don't you think we should follow her advice and get a tutor?"

He raised his head slightly so that his stare moved up from her stomach to somewhere near her throat.

She thought for a second he might answer or at least look into her face, but after a long pause, during which his eyes didn't blink away from her neck, he raised himself in a tensed uncoiling way. His hands hung loosely just below his belt, and he turned to go out the door.

"Don't you think we ought to get Hughleen a tutor?" She reached out and had almost touched his arm when that arm swung so quickly and unexpectedly toward her that she didn't see it coming.

The side of his palm caught her just below the chin. Air was chopped from her windpipe, and the force of his hand tipped her instantly off balance. She tried to catch herself, but her wrist smashed against the rim of the TV and she fell heavily onto the coffee table. It overturned with her. The milk-glass bowl of popcorn hulls slid to the floor, its crash coinciding with the thud of her hip and the table.

The impact reverberated into her skull.

She sat where she'd landed, took a shuddering breath, and let her eyes refocus from the careening sweep of the fall.

The momentary pain in her throat blurred into the throb of her wrist and hip. They would probably both discolor by morning. She tried to separate the sensations of ache as she bent her wrist back and forth to see if the bone had snapped. The pain didn't increase with the movement, and she told herself that nothing was broken.

Yet even as she framed the words, she saw that the glass bowl her mother had given her and Van as a wedding present had exploded into three large irregular triangles and scores of tiny keen fragments.

This second blow was somehow less surprising to her than the first had been. Was Hugh now one of the violent outpatients? Had she subconsciously been expecting it after he struck her the first time? "Just hang in there for him," repeated the straight white teeth. But had the time come for her to stop being there?

She got awkwardly to her feet, favoring the bruised wrist.

Was his second blow the stopping point? What if he had used his closed fist rather than an open hand? Should she draw the line at the loss of her favorite bowl?

She looked down at the shattered bowl. She'd better sweep it up before she went to bed. The girls turned on the TV first thing in the morning, and they wouldn't notice the glass slivers until they ran through them in their cold bare feet.

She'd left Van the very afternoon she'd learned about the Vietnamese woman and her child. She'd packed a box—containing the milk-glass bowl and a few sentimental knickknacks—had thrown her clothes in the old red suitcase, and had walked away. Perhaps if she'd hung in there a little longer . . .

She reached down to right the coffee table.

Tomorrow she'd call Hughleen's teacher and arrange for a tutor. Perhaps she should also telephone the VA hospital and let the doctor know that Hugh's condition was no longer stable.

V

As she hung up the phone from her call to the school she glanced at the kitchen clock. There was still half an hour before

Hugh got off work. Her hand lifted the receiver almost without her willing it, and her forefinger punched the squares of the information number almost before she knew she was going to do it.

"What city are you calling?" the tinned voice answered with methodical boredom.

"Detroit."

"Yes?" the same voice intoned as if she'd accidentally dialed Detroit. "What number do you want?"

"Bert Rutsala. On Evergreen." And her having the name and the street at hand also seemed somehow accidental and involuntary.

"Just a moment." But no more than three seconds elapsed before a recording said, "That number is 288-0699. Repeat. That number is 288-0699."

She silenced the recording with the cut-off button, shifted her finger to press the area code numbers before she dared think about what she was doing.

The long distance chime was alarmingly completed and the ring began.

It was then that the audacity of her action pounded into her temples. She realized she could barely breathe.

If no one answered, she wouldn't call again. But if someone did answer, could she speak through her anxiety?

What if a woman answered? She hadn't thought of that possibility before, and the thumping in her head increased. Would she be able to hear over it if anyone answered the ring that was beginning its fifth repetition?

"Hello."

It was a man's voice, gruff, perhaps slightly surprised.

"I'm calling to locate a Van Rutsala." She blurted it without formality. If the man said she had the wrong number, she'd never try again.

"This is him."

And without planning or premeditation she said, "This is Amy. I don't know if you remember me, but we used to be married." She could hear herself as if she'd been listening from across the kitchen and the voice she heard was calm and faintly teasing.

"Amy? Well, I'll be damned."

But she thought she detected pleased surprise.

"I've been thinking about you and I just thought I'd call and see how you were doing," she lied and heard the light touch of the lie.

"Well, I'll be damned."

"So how you doing?" she said, not letting a silence spread along the line.

"Fine, fine. I been here with Bert for maybe nine, ten years now. Couple a old bachelors. But I'm gettin' to be a pretty good cook."

"How's Bui-lin?" And again a name she hadn't known she remembered was at the back of her tongue.

"Oh, fine I guess. I ain't seen her since I moved in here with Bert. We got a divorce I guess you heard. She went off to California with the kid. I figure I'd hear from her if she wanted anything."

"Bert mentioned something about that."

Her questions had run thin, but before she had to flounder for another he said, "But, hey, how you doin'?"

"Oh, fine. Got a couple a kids now myself. Girls. Ten and five. Got a little extra weight, too, and some gray hairs."

"You always could carry a little extra weight and still look good," he said seriously. Then, "You know, I'm goin' to Arizona in a couple of weeks. Beanie's down there—you remember Beanie, the one with the red hair? It's white now. But anyway, she's got three boys and her and her husband's divorced and she's been after me to come down. She sorta wants me to take a hand with the boys I think. Ain't that a kick? Me bein' a role model?"

She wanted to give him the same kind of sincere compliment and tell him he'd be a fine role model for anybody's kids, but he didn't give her the chance and went on rapidly.

"But like I say, I'm goin' down there. Startin' in a week or so. I'm ridin' my bike and takin' my own sweet time, and I just thought if it wouldn't put you out, I could swing by your way and say hello. You still livin' in Texas? Bert showed me your card. Some little town outta Abilene? You remember how Bert likes to pore over the map. He went and looked up your town right away when he got your Christmas card. He's been figurin' my route to Phoenix. Plottin' it out like he was the AAA. And he'd sure get a kick outta sendin' me down around your way."

"Yes, I'm still in the same little town. Haskell. I live a little way off the main highway through town. Blacktop and then a dirt road, but you can't miss it. 102 Cedar in case Bert lost the address." And she remembered how Van had always talked nonstop, how he'd both entertained and overwhelmed her.

"102 Cedar. Blacktop and a dirt road off the main drag. Got it. I was thinkin' a startin' Wednesday week, so I'll drop you a postcard, let you know when I'll be pullin' in and all. I won't stay the night or nothin' like that. You don't need to worry about me puttin' you out," he added hastily. "But we could maybe chew the fat for a couple a hours or so. Catch up on old times, hunh?"

He abruptly sounded nervous, as if the enormity of her calling and his offering to stop by to see her had struck him in midsentence.

"That sounds great." She felt herself growing uneasy. "I'll be looking for your card. I want to hear all about Bert and Beanie," she said, then added, "Since I'm in prime time, I'll save all my questions until you get here."

"Well, yeah."

"You let me know so I can fix one of those angel food cakes with the strawberry jam and the chocolate whipped cream topping." She suddenly recalled his favorite dessert in a moment of inspired satisfaction.

"Hey, yeah. Haven't had one a them in I don't know when. How long's it been, Amy?"

And the use of her name turned him serious again.

"A long time." But she didn't want the conversation to change into something serious. She was afraid she might start to cry the way she had in all the last phone calls they'd made just before the divorce was final, and she said with forced gaiety, "You plan on stopping, ya hear? and we'll catch up on everything. I'll be expecting you. Bye now." And she waited a brief second for his almost puzzled "Bye," then stopped the sound of his echo and the long distance whir.

As she fumbled the receiver onto its cradle, her heart began to beat again and her numb fingers trembled.

He was coming.

She'd not only talked to him, but she was going to see him. After twelve years and seven months, she was actually going to see him again. It was as if she'd been guided by some outside force to pick up the phone and dial his father's number, she thought. And she'd done it barely two weeks before he'd be passing by her, passing by unbeknownst to either of them without that call.

Her fingers were still shaking as she pulled on the old coat. The bruise on her wrist made her wince as the thick wool cuff pressed against it, but she shrugged and grabbed the car keys.

The call was almost like a miracle, almost like a sign, she told herself as she went outside. Things in her life were going to change.

VI

THE next morning she was no longer certain he would actually come, however, and the uncertainty claimed more than its share of her attention as she fried two breakfast eggs for the girls and poached three more for Hugh.

The call had obviously caught Van off guard, and he'd perhaps without thinking suggested coming by on his motorcycle. That was just the kind of impetuous offer he'd been in the habit of making when she knew him. And naturally he'd still be riding a bike long after everyone else his age had settled down to watching TV in their campers.

But would he really come?

By the end of their conversation he'd begun to get leery about inviting himself to stop and see her. And what if on sober reflection he decided that it wouldn't be a good idea after all? He hadn't asked if she was still married, but he probably guessed she was. He probably knew she'd have mentioned it when she told him about her two children if she and Hugh had got a divorce. And with her still married, he might think he shouldn't intrude on her life. Men were sometimes wary of treading on other men's preserves. She knew that without knowing how she knew. If Van got it in his head that it wouldn't be proper for one Vietnam vet to break up the marriage of another

Vietnam vet, he might change his mind about passing through Haskell after all.

She served the girls' eggs without seeing them.

But did Van even know that Hugh had also been in Vietnam? She couldn't remember if she'd told him that when she'd called him up to say she'd decided to get remarried. It was the one time he hadn't been glib. He'd managed a faint "Oh," and had fallen silent. She remembered wanting him then to talk her out of the wedding, wanting him to convince her that she was rushing into marriage too fast. But he hadn't been able to find any more words beyond his shocked grunt, and after a while she'd been forced to say goodbye and to hang up on his stunned silence. She'd always wondered what might have happened if she'd called back after he'd had a chance to recover. Would he have said the magic words that could have canceled her marriage to Hugh?

She saw that the water was boiling, and she cracked Hugh's eggs into the bubbles, making sure they were centered in the three aluminum rings. Hugh liked poached eggs to come out in precise circles as if he were being served in a good hotel dining room.

Well, if she didn't hear from Van for two weeks, she'd know he changed his mind. Two weeks wasn't very long.

She eased a spatula under one egg at a time and transferred each to the toast before she removed the restraining rings.

"Hurry up now and finish in the bathroom before your dad wants in," she said as she put the plate on the table across from the girls.

Hughleen's blue eyes were watching fascinated while Dawn dragged a sodden stub of toast back and forth through the egg yolk, spiraling a gold design on the plate.

"Go on now. You're both finished eating." She raised her voice to call, "Hugh, your eggs are ready."

She didn't know if the girls were aware that he wasn't speaking to them. He rarely said anything directly to them anyway, and as long as she spoke to them and to him, perhaps they hadn't registered his silence.

"And brush the back of your hair, Hughleen. If you don't get that wad of rats out this morning, I just might give you a haircut this afternoon." She looked after them as they jostled each other into the bathroom.

Not even two weeks. That was hardly any time at all. If she didn't think about it, if, in fact, she actively ignored the question of whether he would come or not, then she could handle it without any strain.

"Hugh, your breakfast is ready," she called again, keeping her tone wifely as she watched the poached eggs congeal into precise cold circles.

VII

You know, he told me he never forgot the day they ordered 'em over the top. That was his phrase, you know, 'over the top.' 'That's something you never forget,' he said. And he remembered it like it was the most important day of his life. September 5, 1918. That was when it was. That was the day his outfit was ordered over the top."

Amy nodded.

"Half the time he didn't know what day it was, but he always remembered September 5, 1918." The old face was creasing and recreasing with the words and her absorbed chewing. "The captain went down the trench and tapped each one on the shoulder to send him up the side of the wall. They was dug in dirt, you know, trenches seven, eight foot, dug right in the dirt. He told me he saw the captain out of the corner of his eye and he was braced. When he felt that tap on his back, his lungs and heart stopped, but he scrambled up that dirt wall and fell flat on his belly out in the open air facing the Huns. That's what we called the Germans, you know, the Huns. There he was facin' the Huns. For the first time since he'd gone to France."

She paused to pursue an elusive cube of liver with the outsized fork. Her face seemed to have forgotten the story completely as she smacked her eroded lips and started on the creamed corn.

Amy hesitated to urge her to continue since the half hour was nearly over, but it was a story she hadn't heard before, and it was easier to keep from dwelling on Van when she could actually listen to a reminiscence.

Mrs. Lasater had guided the final bits of corn to her mouth and was attacking the sugary crust of the apple tart before she glanced up. "He never knew if he shot a single soldier in that charge, you know. They crawled forward and he pulled the trigger of his rifle and crawled and shot again, but he never looked up to see if he'd accidentally hit any of them Huns."

That was something Van had remarked on once. He, too, had fired indiscriminately into the trees without aiming at anything.

"He had nightmares about it, but he never knew for sure." Mrs. Lasater's faded eyes were gazing at the tray as if she'd been the youth inching through the weeds toward the enemy trenches. "That's the way war is, I guess. All of 'em trying to win a spot a land that nobody really wants and that nobody can use."

Amy somehow knew that Mr. Lasater had said that, too. She waited, but Mrs. Lasater didn't rouse herself again from the silence as her bone finger tapped up bits of crust and conveyed them to her mouth.

At last Amy took the fork into the dark kitchen whose walls gave off a rancid, closed winter odor. She was glad the sagging house was more soured than usual. She'd begun a diet the night before, and the house was helping quell her hunger. She was also comforted by the fact that the dieticians had served up liver and onions that noon, the one meal she could barely stand herself.

In two weeks she could drop maybe twenty pounds, and then even if Van didn't show, she'd be looking and feeling so much better that it wouldn't matter. He'd gotten so serious when he'd said her name that if he didn't come, she'd know he didn't want to risk getting hurt.

She soaped the fork and rinsed it, noting that the silver plate of the tines had sloughed off into a yellowed base metal.

He probably had a comfortable life with Bert. And now with his going out to Beanie's . . . She didn't recall anyone named Beanie, and she couldn't visualize anyone who might have been Van's sister, with orange hair or white.

After she lost twenty pounds she could buy a new pair of slacks in a size fourteen. That would be worth it whether Van came or not.

When she went back into the bedroom, Mrs. Lasater was slumped against the pillows.

"You all right, Mrs. Lasater?" She carefully removed the extra propping to let the frail body down.

"Just tired. They shouldn't ought to of done that to our young boys, you know. They don't ever need to fight a war."

"I know." She smoothed the coverlet over the hump of the body that seemed hardly more than a twist of sheets beneath the quilt.

"Too much happens to 'em. They don't never recover from a war, not really."

"I know," she said.

VIII

WHEN she took the postcard out of the mailbox, she knew she'd been hoping for it, expecting it more than she'd let herself admit.

She studied the handwriting on the address side for a moment. The inked script didn't spark any recognition, and there was no physical response as she read the large open letters of her name and the street number again. She no longer recalled his handwriting.

She let herself briefly anticipate what he might say, then she turned the plain, sturdy card—post office issue without an illustration—over to read, "11–12. Be by your way on 11–18. V."

That was all.

She read it again. He'd be coming on the eighteenth. One more week.

But as she reread the terse message she felt no spur of excitement.

Had he written such spare and businesslike letters to her from Vietnam? Was that why she decided so quickly that his betrayal was unforgivable when she discovered the existence of Bui-lin and her child? The postcard projected nothing of Van, held none of his joking laughter that had so charmed her in person. If this was the kind of communication she'd got during those long months he was in

Southeast Asia, no wonder she'd lost the true Van before he could win her back.

She stuffed the card in the pocket of the old coat under a pair of gloves. No use leaving it around for the girls or Hugh to see. She was aware that the girls would be the ones to suspect something if they accidentally found such a cryptic message.

The only other piece of mail was a bulk rate brochure addressed to her from the community college in Abilene. She glanced at its slick foldout and wondered idly how they happened to have her name. NUTRITION SCIENCES. FOOD PREPARATION AND MANAGEMENT. It was probably something the supervisors at the Sunshine House had signed her up for. They were increasingly anxious about the fact that the agency funds were running out in December and that they were going to have to let her go. They kept murmuring about how good it would be if she could go to college, suggesting a part-time job and classes. Of course, they didn't know her circumstances.

She sighed and put the brightly colored ad in her other pocket.

She didn't worry too much about herself since she'd always been able to find a minimum wage job of some kind, but it was the old people who were going to get hurt by the cutbacks. Most of them were too befuddled to understand why no one was going to have time for them anymore.

She didn't like to think about the elderly and their baffled disappointment when none of the remaining drivers could sit and listen to them while they ate, and she took advantage of Van's card to shift her thoughts away from old Mrs. Lasater in her pink wrapper.

Would Van be carrying a little extra weight, too? Doing his own cooking, munching on chips in front of the TV with Bert?

If she could have afforded those Weight-Watchers packets in the frozen food bins, that'd be the way to go. That was real diet management—the calories already weighed out, and the portions arranged in appetizing colors more original than those on the old people's trays. All anyone had to do was take them home, heat them up, and eat them very slowly. She'd read in one of the newspaper-magazines in the grocery line that dawdling and eating in thimbleful bites fooled one's stomach into believing it had had a full meal. And of course if you dawdled standing up, so much the better. That same tabloid had assured its readers that all the thinnest starlets ate while they walked around, and she considered briefly the possibility of eating her cottage cheese standing up in the kitchen.

Hugh might object to her not joining him and the girls for supper, however, and she didn't want to do anything to set him off again. She didn't want to decide anything, didn't want to alter anything just then. Not when she was concentrating on calming herself down and trimming her body for Van's visit.

She smoothed the tail of the coat beneath her hips as she climbed into the car.

IX

As she sat and stitched on the apple green overblouse—assuring herself that she wasn't necessarily aiming for the eighteenth but that she might have it finished by then—she sucked in her stomach and could feel it tighten.

The bathroom scales she'd found for a dollar at a garage sale were hardly exact, but she had no trouble seeing that the jiggling needle had stopped short of the 160 marker. She'd lost fifteen pounds.

Bright yellow credit lines rolled onto the TV screen, and as she glanced up to thread a needle she realized the show they'd been watching had ended. She'd let it slip away without noticing how the couple had resolved the problem of their teenager cutting ballet class. She'd sat sewing and thinking, "Van, Van," like some ritual in her head, and the program had dissolved.

Hugh was studying the TV Guide in the chair across from her.

"There's a new sit-com premiering tonight," he said suddenly in a lifeless precise voice.

It had been so long since she'd heard him speak that she wasn't sure if he was using his natural tone or not.

"You'd think they'd get tired of trying out new comedy shows."

"You certainly would," she agreed. She hoped her surprise wasn't evident. Why had he started to talk just at that moment? Had she inadvertently said "Van" aloud?

"There's a news special on the other channels."

"I didn't know there was anything . . ."

"The president's giving a news conference." He paused and looked at her. "In prime time."

His words were toneless, objective, and she couldn't read his emotions. She said carefully, "You'd think they'd quit doing that unless there was a real crisis of some kind."

He was staring directly into her face. "Did I tell you about Bryan? He was a friend of Ray's brother."

She hadn't heard him mention that name, but then, the only name he had ever mentioned was Ray.

"He just walked up and put out his hand and said, 'Hello, I'm Bryan.' He knew about Ray. About how he . . . died. They didn't find enough scraps of Ray to fill a grocery sack, but they pretended they did and they shipped a body bag home in the coffin like it was really him, did I tell you that?"

She shook her head.

"That's what they did. They did that a lot."

He paused for so long that she thought perhaps he'd finished talking and would clamp into silence again, but then he said, "Bryan's uniform still had the perma press crease in the trouser legs, can you believe that? There he was in the middle of a Saigon landing strip shaking my hand and wearing a brand new uniform."

His fingers were fondling the remote control block, but he didn't push the button to shut off the announcer's nasal insistence that viewers call immediately for an $8.88 cheese pizza.

"Bryan was younger than Ray's brother. Only seventeen he said. He told me about the memorial service for Ray they had at their gym back home. He had thin hands. Hands you wouldn't expect on somebody that played basketball. He was going home and marry his high school sweetheart."

She realized that she was listening to him the way she heard the old people in their feeble rooms that stank of grease and stale dishwater.

"But a sniper got him. The second month he was out there. When they told me about it, I just broke down and cried. I thought I wasn't going to quit blubbering." By then his eyes had lost contact with hers, and his stubby forefinger abruptly pressed the TV off. "I wasn't sure I'd ever be able to feel anything again."

It was late in their relationship for so flat a confession of weakness, she thought as she watched him stare at the blank screen. Perhaps it was already too late. She waited for an emotion of her own, but there was nothing she could untangle from her involved thoughts of Van. At last she said very gently, "Things like that probably happened pretty often in Vietnam when friends were killed, and . . ."

But he got up with bulky weariness and walked toward the bedroom.

She remained on the couch and gazed down at the green puddle of polyester in her lap.

Back then both Van and Hugh had needed to be held. And there she'd been, waiting at home with two good arms that couldn't help either one of them.

X

For some reason Hugh kept talking to her during that week before Van was scheduled to appear, but she found it hard to pay attention to what he was saying. He didn't bring up Vietnam again, and although she tried to listen to his comments on TV programming and on the profits being made with the glass bluebirds, her thoughts invariably strayed to Van.

What would he think about the house? Would it be as nice as the one he shared with Bert? She'd got her mother's household furnishings, and while the pieces were old, they were good and sturdy. She'd put in the stone walkway up to the door herself, and she knew the flagstones gave the yard a bit of class. She'd put down the rocks, and dirt had washed over them, settling them so solidly that no one would suspect the walk hadn't been there since the house was built. If it was spring, the irises would glow blue-lavender alongside it, and

Van would get a good impression, but of course in November there was nothing but decaying brown leaves that made the yard look frayed and tacky.

What would he think about how she herself had aged?

In her mind, there was only a vague recollection of him talking, laughing, stringing out those awful puns, but she didn't really picture him in any definite way. He was just a dark, good-looking man with slightly curling, almost black hair. His hair was probably his best feature, but he was also tall, and she remembered that he was at least a head taller than she was. But since she didn't have any clear vision of him, his image wouldn't be spoiled if he'd put on some weight or had grown a moustache.

The same might not be true on his side, however. If he was carrying a photograph in his mind of her as a thin—and much younger—woman, then he might be disappointed in her appearance. For despite her loss of twenty pounds, she was still fifty heavier than she'd been when he saw her last.

She stirred the hamburger mixture in the skillet and half listened to the TV moderator enthusiastically prodding a couple to review the blind date the studio audience had sent them on.

Hugh had been a blind date, too, and they'd hit it off better than that TV couple. It was only later that . . .

She side-stepped that thought with a memory of the first time she'd seen Van. Not seen him exactly, but been aware of him. She remembered him standing by the lockers in the hall like a movie actor in a high school letter sweater. A great fuzzy red S clung to the right breast pocket. He'd never quite seemed the type to be wearing a letter sweater, however, and after he'd left for Vietnam she had trouble with that first impression of him. Later, she wasn't really sure if the scene had been an actual memory or if it came from some old movie that it reminded her of.

The TV couple was being ushered away with their appliance prizes by the time she poured the hamburger filling in the casserole and spread it with cornbread topping. The girls had been pestering her for a tamale pie since the previous summer when it'd been too hot to bake anything that heavy.

Did those couples on TV realize they were going to have to pay tax on the gift appliances? she wondered. After she'd read that, the afternoon game shows lost much of their appeal. Everyone thinking they were getting something free, maybe something they didn't actually need or particularly want, but at least something free. But then they'd have to cough up hard cash to pay the tax on it.

She fixed a salad for the girls. Hugh didn't eat anything green, and as she set the table, she speculated briefly on his eating habits that might account for his behavior change.

Did Van like salad? Would he eat the scoop of slaw dished up with fish and chips?

When she could tell that the corn topping was almost brown, she called the girls to wash up and stuck her head in the TV room that she liked to call the den.

"Supper's almost ready."

Hugh was jotting down a toll-free number from the TV screen, and he held up a palm to ward off her words.

She hadn't been listening to what item he might be ordering or what information he might be sending for, but she watched him scribble awkwardly with his left hand for a few seconds before she went back to finish the table.

The kindergarten teacher said Dawn was already coloring with her left hand. At least teachers didn't try to change everyone into right-handed students any longer. The girls were going to have enough problems just having Hugh as a father.

"Hugh? Supper's ready."

The girls sat down, giggling at some secret she didn't press them to share, and she dished out the salad.

For herself she'd sliced two hard-boiled eggs into quarter-inch ovals, and as she set them down she thought they gave the illusion of a full plate.

She centered the hot casserole on a pad and slid into her chair. "Hugh?"

He came around the archway with his swaying walk. "What's that?" He stopped behind her chair.

The girls looked up at him.

"It's a tamale pie." She felt his brooding intensity behind her. "Hughleen's been wanting . . ."

He leaned around the back of the chair and swung his palm across the table. The white and blue-flowered casserole dish and hot pad flew off, smashed against the wall.

Hughleen jerked her chair back in an automatic cringe away from the splattering meat sauce.

"If I want fast food, I'll go out to McDonald's."

"Oh, Daddy!" Dawn on the other side of Hughleen stared over her shoulder at the corn mush sliding down the wall toward the broken casserole halves.

He started to reach for the smaller child.

Amy rose quickly to intercept him. His arm hit her in the chest as she stood up, and she fell back into the chair.

She blinked hard for a second, sensed the vibrations of the old floor, then heard the back door open and slam shut as he went out.

She opened her eyes and saw the terror on the two small faces.

"It's just that sometimes men have bad experiences that can cause them to . . ." But then she no longer had the energy to complete the excuse. "I'll fix you some toasted cheese sandwiches," she said instead. She heard that her voice was calm. She didn't look at the remains of the hamburger casserole spread along the baseboard.

XI

A CHERRY pie with a perfect lattice crust shared the tabletop with a chocolate cream frosted angel food cake. Inside the angel layers were two thick scarlet bands of strawberry preserves, and if Amy hadn't remembered that Van was particularly fond of that recipe, she could never have brought herself to combine so much sweetness in a single dessert. Any of her old people would go into a sugar-induced coma after one slice of that cake.

Whatever their excesses, however, the pie and the cake were flawless. She'd set them decoratively on a hand-crocheted runner left over from her mother's things and had surrounded them with polished forks and dessert plates. Coffee was already perked and waiting in a pot on the front burner ready to heat up when Van arrived.

She glanced in the mirror for at least the twelfth time, evaluating the green blouse and the matching eye shadow she'd found in a grocery cart of marked-down items. At only fifty cents, the green powder would undoubtedly streak after half an hour, but for that crucial initial impression, it would probably look good.

A motor was struggling past on the road outside.

The blood in her temples quickened, and she breathed deeply, controlling herself, touching the table with her fingertips. Then she hurried to the door to see him drive up.

But the motor belonged to an ancient tan pickup that labored under a load of wood. The pickup ordinarily would have deposited a film of brown dust onto the stoop, and as she watched it out of sight, she was glad a broken layer of snow had calmed the dirt road.

Suddenly a black motorcycle whirled into her driveway.

She'd been listening to the old truck and had missed the sound of his engine.

And there he was, without warning, braking on the ruts of the drive.

She flung open the door and the splayed screen before she was aware she was doing it, the way her fingers had dialed his number of their own volition. The air was brisk, but she barely felt it as she ran to him.

He'd swung off the cycle and was standing against the sun in his red helmet.

"Van!"

He opened his arms and she threw herself against him.

She embraced the cold synthetic of his ski jacket and experienced a rush of warmth and affection in the blur of the sun.

She thought she heard him murmur her name, but as she hugged him and the blood pounded into her head she couldn't be sure.

She finally pulled back and said hastily, "You must be frozen riding a bike in this weather. Come on in." Yet even as she said it, she was surprised that her mind and tongue were working.

278

"This might not be racing weather, but it sure is bracing weather," he said.

And she knew he'd rehearsed it on his way to have something to say.

"I've got a good fire going in the fireplace. That fireplace was one of the things that was attractive about this old house when we rented it." She grasped his padded sleeve as they went in. For some strange reason, she wanted him to know that she was only renting the house, that he wasn't interrupting a stable, homeowning situation.

"Hey, look at that," he said toward the two flawless desserts as they passed them. He was tugging off his ski gloves, and when they went into the den, he looked around quickly. "Nice place you got here, Amy."

She was certain his glance had been too cursory for him to register anything, but she instantly forgave that. If he was as nervous as she was, he couldn't have seen anything anyway.

"Take off your jacket."

"Yes, ma'am." He exaggerated 'ma'am' with thick irony, and she wondered if he used to call her that. Was the word a little inside joke he remembered about their marriage that she'd forgotten?

He slid off the jacket with a grimace that reminded her of his shoulder wound. Before she'd opened her lips to ask about it, however, he'd put the jacket and gloves on the back of the couch and had lifted off the scarlet helmet.

He was completely bald.

Wisps of dark hair curled at the base of his pink skull, but they seemed to be growing on his neck rather than on any part of his head.

Her face must have revealed a trace of shock, and he snorted with a slightly embarrassed chuckle, "My hair got a little thin, didn't it?" But then before she had to answer, he laughed, "I sure wouldn't want fat hair though."

He threw back his head in the open-mouthed laugh, and she saw that the silver band of filled crowns gapped with missing teeth. He had only seven or eight molars left, and pink gum ridges showed where his lower teeth had been.

"Come have some of the cake before the girls get home and mess it up," she said quickly to interrupt the laugh. "I did tell you I had a couple of kids now, didn't I?"

"You sure did," he said heartily as he followed her obediently back to the table. "Hey, look at that," he repeated.

"How big a piece can you handle?" She took up the knife and scored the frothy chocolate cream.

"Not too big." He patted a protruding stomach under his khaki shirt. "You know how it is after you hit forty. Got to watch it."

She cut a moderate wedge, used her mother's cake server to transfer it intact to the little plate.

"Strawberry jam filling, too," she said.

"Hey." He took the plate, but he looked down at it as if he didn't really remember ever having tasted it before. "Did I tell you I got to be a pretty good chef doin' all the cookin' for me and Bert? Bert ain't doin' too good health-wise, but he's nearin' eighty now. What can you expect, hunh?"

"You want some coffee?" She started toward the kitchen. She intended to join him with a cup of coffee and not have to eat.

"To cut the sweet, hunh? Sure."

As she reached the doorway, he added, "If you got some Sanka or one a them caffeine-free ones, that is. Reg'lar coffee gives me gas. And out there on a motorcycle . . ." He laughed.

"Oh." She hadn't thought about caffeine. It was one of the things she always remembered where her old people were concerned, but she hadn't thought about it with Van. "I got some herb tea."

"Naw." He grabbed one of the forks she'd set out. "Might as well drink hot water I always say."

There was a silence as they moved back into the den and he sat down on the edge of the couch. "Well, tell me about yourself. You're lookin' good." He cut into the slice of cake. "That's a good color on you. Didn't you always wear a lot of green?"

She hadn't, and she said, "It reminds me of spring. You need something like green in the middle of winter sometimes."

"Yeah."

She watched him finally raise the forkful of cake and whipped cream to his mouth. He reminded her of old Mr. Stapleton in his chair spooning out the dessert section of the metal tray.

"What's this about Beanie turning white-haired on us?" She still couldn't dredge up a memory of anyone named Beanie, but he grinned, showing his lower gums, and set the plate of cake down on the coffee table.

He chuckled and launched into a long explanation of his sister's divorce and the three teenaged boys who were out of control in the Phoenix trailer park where Beanie lived.

He was still describing the Arizona air that was helping Beanie's asthma when she heard the school bus outside and the child voices approaching the door.

She noticed as she hadn't before the black rims of his fingernails and the spots of soaked-in grease and oil on the khaki shirt and pants. She suddenly wished the girls hadn't come home quite so soon.

The door banged.

"Come in here and meet an old friend of mine," she called in a voice she hoped wasn't too stilted. She wondered if Hughleen would remember that she'd once been married to someone with the same name.

"This is Van. Hughleen is the tall thin one and Dawn is the short one." She smiled from him to them, bunched together as if they'd been a crowd of six. "They're ten and five."

"Hey there," he said heartily.

They looked at him and may or may not have nodded.

"Have some cake or a slice of pie, but not a very big piece. And only one or you'll spoil your supper." She gave the instructions in her most maternal voice.

They disappeared again.

"Good-lookin' kids," he said in the same tone he'd used to compliment the room.

She could hear them dishing out portions, being quiet and discreet to avoid being called back into the room.

There was a brief silence.

"Think you could rustle me up a glass a water, Amy?"

"Of course." She noticed that he didn't reach again for the fork.

The girls had disappeared into their room, and she was relieved that they weren't in sight as he followed her to the kitchen.

"No ice like always," he said and put his plate of cake on the counter.

She didn't remember that he drank water without ice and she couldn't think of anything to say as she got a glass from the cupboard and filled it with tap water.

To keep from staring at his adam's apple bobbing as he swallowed or the water gathering at the creased edges of his lips, she looked at the glass bluebird in her kitchen window and dusted it with her palm.

"Hugh works at the factory that makes these glass birds," she said.

He glanced at it.

"Reminds me of a bird I ran into in Nam. Did I tell you about the foo bird?" He leaned forward, engaging her.

She shook her head.

His eyes had come alive in the old man face.

"It's a sacred bird they got over there."

He placed the glass beside the cake, the black semicircles of nails curving with the motion of his hand, as he became engrossed in his description of the bird the Vietnamese kept in their temples for special rituals.

"Some real strange customs they got over there. We'd never get used to 'em, not if we stayed in that country for a hundred years."

He told her how he'd become acquainted with a local priest and how he'd been invited to see one of their sacred ceremonies.

She tried to picture him, tall and American, perhaps with Bui-lin, at a temple of Vietnamese worshippers. Would he have been nervous or smiling and tossing aside his dark hair unselfconsciously? She remembered she hadn't yet asked if he was working or if he was getting disability from his wound.

"There was this ugly-lookin' bird, see, kinda the color of blue mold maybe, up on the rafters, and everybody's kneelin' down, prayin' see, when all of a sudden the old bird just lets go and splatters half a dozen a the kneelers.

"When the prayers ended and everybody was filin' out, there was maybe six people covered with bird-droppings. But they came out smilin', lookin' pleased as punch."

His face was beginning to crease into a smile, and she watched it. For a moment he looked like the Van she was sure she remembered.

"I asked my priest friend what was goin' on, what they was so happy about, and he said, just as sober as a judge, 'It is the sacred foo bird who brings good luck. Our saying is that if the foo shits, wear it.'" And his head tilted back with the force of the guffaw. "Get it? If the shoe fits . . ."

Her lips were dry and crackled as she tried to smile.

How had Vietnam really affected him? He'd once mentioned the fear, had once described firing into the green of the jungle. She'd been taken in by his air of sincerity, but she saw now that those moments of honesty had been the excuses for his straying. After all those years, she saw that he was actually as closed as Hugh. His jokes just replaced the silences. Like his terse postcard, he wasn't giving anything of himself.

She glanced away from him to the cake on the plate.

The sight of the angel food cake slashed with dark red preserves made her throat constrict with nausea.

She looked away from it and tried to marshal her thoughts. But before she could come up with a hostessy comment, he had turned toward the TV room.

"I got to be goin', Amy. Sure was good seein' ya."

He gathered up the gloves and jacket, snared the shiny red helmet in the crook of his arm.

"Got to make another hundred miles or so before I stop. Don't want to be ridin' in the dark for too long in this cold. You're lookin' great."

"I can understand that. It's a long way to Arizona." She followed him to the back door. "Was terrific that you could stop by. Give my love to Beanie."

"Sure will."

A hug seemed too awkward as they got outside, and she stood on her rock path to watch him throw a khaki leg over the cycle, settle

283

himself on the seat. The fringe around the edge of the helmet gave the impression of a ratted scarf.

"Well, thanks again." He didn't say for what. "Be seein' ya."

The bike kicked to an instant start and she didn't have to do more than smile.

He zoomed into a wide circle, one foot hovering free for balance. He held up a glove with a backward glance at her.

She waved in response and watched the black motorcycle speed him out of sight.

XII

SHE stood on the rock path until the sound of the motor had faded completely.

Her faux silk blouse carried the chill of aluminum foil, and she crossed her arms over her chest.

She'd put everything on hold, waiting to see Van again before she made any decision, waiting before she considered what to do about Hugh or her life. But nothing in her life depended on the stranger who had just ridden away; the Van she'd just seen was no one she knew.

She turned to go back inside when she saw Hugh walking up the snowy road.

Van must have zipped right by him, the motorcycle engine filling the silence as they passed.

She could hear the crunch of Hugh's work boots on the frozen ground as he got closer. His face was flushed with what she could tell was a combination of irritation, cold, and exertion.

He reached the edge of the yard, and she saw how really short he was. When she'd hugged Van, she'd come to his collarbone, but Hugh was her own height, stocky and barrel-shaped.

"You didn't come after me." Each of his words puffed out in a sharp ball of mist.

She took a deep cold breath.

"If you ever lift a hand to me again, I'll leave you flat," she said. "I know you got things to work out, but you work 'em out with that doctor at the VA. You're not going to hit me. Not ever again."

They were face to face on the stone walk, and she saw his blue eyes understand that she meant it. She stepped aside, avoiding the dead remains of the iris leaves, letting him walk along the settled rocks.

"There's some cake and a cherry pie I made for dessert. But it's not good for any of us and that's the last sweet stuff we're going to have around here for a long time. Besides, I'm on a diet."

She thought she saw him nod as he went toward the door.

"When my job runs out in December, I'm going to start at the community college over in Abilene. I can work part-time and go to school."

He stopped at the screen door and glanced back at her, and she was sure he nodded that time.

He went inside, and she breathed deeply once more.

In the fading afternoon, a dot of light, a miniature winter sun, had settled in the bluebird in the window, as if in the blue glass beat a tiny sun heart.

Second Lieutenants
of Literature

Thomas Zigal

THE PHONE wakes me. I fumble across her sheeted body to lift the receiver. It's my old friend from the Writing Program, twenty years now, a time before the boom. The younger practitioners consider us rugged precursors, treat us with deference, as though we deserve preservation.

"I've got another one for you, if you want it," my friend chirps. For several years he has been the placement director for the Conference Circuit. We once taught together at a woodsy liberal arts college in California (or was it the one in Oregon?), before we both gave up the aspiration. As I recall, he won an O. Henry the same year, though I can't remember exactly what year that was.

"Tell me where I am," I mumble, struggling to open my eyes. The motel room carries the faint stale remnant of past cigarettes, industrial air freshener, roach spray.

"Let's see," my friend says, pausing, it seems, to shuffle through his printout. "Tucson, I believe," he says. "Yes, yes, I'm sure of it. Today's the twenty-fourth. Did you get lucky?"

It comes back to me, slowly, the closing ceremonies last evening, the drinks, the reveling carload at the dark Mission somewhere out in the desert. I think that was last night. Who is this woman sleeping beside me? The young poet so fond of those physics metaphors? No, she was another time. That little town in Vermont, I think.

"Where is it?" I manage.

He names the location, a small denominational college I've never heard of, two flight connections from here and a car rental for another hour's journey. But I'm in no position to refuse. The page eludes me now, has mocked my dryness for years. Putting words on that vicious white expanse is a prior conviction I would prefer to bury deep in another lifetime.

"The gigs are getting more and more remote," I tell my friend on the phone.

"Competition is fierce, old sack, and getting fiercer by the day," he says. "Please don't be offended if I tell you your stock is slipping."

We chat a bit longer, and when I ask if he's working again he mentions polishing a couple of old stories, resubmitting them for a grant. After we hang up, the woman beside me mutters, "Who was that, Robert?"

I believe Robert is the name of the fellow in the black leather jacket from last evening, the one who teaches poetry in the prisons. I am not Robert, but I haven't the heart to tell her otherwise.

Nine hours later a grainy red dusk settles over the flattest hard-scrabble land I have ever seen, the horizon undisturbed by even the meekest ridge. The town itself, an unimaginative grid of flaking woodframe houses and small, slapdash shopping centers, is severed by an ancient rusted railroad line, suggesting the place was once a water-tank stop along that endless cross-country stretch through the dusty wilderness of the heartland.

The campus cannot be missed, its rotating sprinklers reviving a scorched lawn, the clusters of cottonwoods the healthiest growth for miles. I find the registration tables in the shaded portico of the chapel, an imposing stone and stained-glass structure in the center of the grounds. My host is a thin bespectacled English professor with a boyish haircut, several years younger than I, a nervous man sweating through his blazer.

"We're very pleased to have you," he offers a busy wet hand. "You come highly recommended."

He coerced his department chairman into letting him attend a writer's conference in Houston last year, he tells me, "a real battery recharger." "They're all the rage now, you know. Everybody is scheduling one."

At the conference he took a crash course conducted by my old friend the placement director. "What a pro he is," Professor Weeks smiles enviously. "In half a day he covered the territory, stem to stern, on how to run one of these babies. He's put together a very helpful packet."

It was my friend who recommended me.

"Scott tells me you're top drawer. But you'll forgive me, I hope," he blushes, "if I admit I haven't read you. So many new names to keep up with, all those paperbacks with the same kind of cover. Where can I find your work?"

I haven't written a line in six years. There was a time, though, a year or two out of the Program, when I thought I was going to make it. I was picked up by a prestigious agent, a woman who represented Pynchon and Kesey and a few of the hotshots in my class, a dear kind soul who wrote encouraging letters on a regular basis, those neatly typed pages, the distinctive letterhead, now yellowing in a forgotten file somewhere in my apartment. I have for more than a decade committed to memory the words in Viking's rejection letter: "Our committee agonized over accepting this fine first novel, but in the end, alas, decided we could not make an offer." In those days I was consumed by faith and fairness, and I naively assumed that a first rejection so close would surely lead, in the next submission, at another house, to a generous advance, literary gossip, five-figure promotion, unceasing smiles on my proud parents' faces. Eighteen years later it is not a pleasant realization that that first time, with Viking, was the closest I ever got.

"I'm in the little magazines," I tell the good professor. The ones published by old cronies, drinking buddies, the desperate has-beens I've flattered shamelessly and sucked up to at conferences in quaint fishing villages and glitzy ski resorts. Places where the air is sweet with petroleum lubricants.

It is summer now, the dorms are vacant, and Professor Weeks escorts me to a bare room with bunk beds and team decals pasted on the light-switch covers.

"Here are the stories," he says, removing a thick stack of stapled pages from his briefcase.

"Stories?"

"Didn't they tell you?" he smiles sheepishly. "A hundred-dollar prize for best. Registrants only. We'll announce the winner at the banquet tomorrow night. Do you think you'll have enough time?"

I glance at the pile. "Certainly," I assure my host. Over the years I have at the very least established certain infallible methods for judging literary merit.

After he leaves I unzip my suitcase, hang the blond corduroy jacket, my official banquet wear, in what passes for a closet. The manuscript is there on the bottom, underneath dirty socks and underwear. 'Quietly affecting,' my thesis director said, the old silver-haired pedant, dead now a decade, who adored the Brontë sisters. 'Very real promise. Have you thought about a publisher?'

I cannot remember how far along I am in the revision. They say nothing is ever wasted. One day you make a small adjustment, shift the point of view, say, and there it is. I promise myself I will look at it while I'm here.

The door to the bathroom opens and a man emerges with toilet kit in hand. "Oh, hello," he says, a tall handsome athletic fellow wearing a black shirt, the plastic collar unsnapped and hanging loose. "I'm Reverend James Markham," he says, extending his hand. The place now reeks of his aftershave. "I guess we're sharing the room."

This comes as strange news. The professor did not mention this.

"Do you prefer the top or bottom?" he smiles, a muscled face fighting age lines and decline.

"Bottom, I guess," I say, absently regarding the bunks. "I get up a lot."

I have had my share of roommates in these misadventures, but never a minister. There was that time in Santa Barbara, I think it was. The poor sad poet with the wild hair who insisted on reading his poems aloud whenever I was in the room, stood outside the shower and recited while I bathed. He plagued the staff, followed young women around with a thick sheaf of poems tucked under one arm, loomed over tables at lunch, performing. I remember the night I returned late to the room. 'You ditched me,' he whined. 'You deliberately went out without me. You and all those girls.' It was true, of course. He had arranged a reading in our room, passed the word for days, handed out flyers, and yet no one came. Not even me. That night he cried a little into his pillow. Someone told me he killed himself a few years later, jumped from a freeway overpass. The thing is, I sort of liked his poetry. I guess I should have told him.

"I've been looking forward to this conference for weeks," the minister says, tossing a towel on the top bunk. "I read the announcement in the regional bulletin and knew I had to come. Drove down from Emporia, Kansas," he says. "I have a little ministry there."

He is perhaps five or six years older than I, a shy man, for all his physical presence, whose clear eyes dart about without lighting on anything solid. I suspect that, like myself, he has lost nerve somewhere along the way.

"I know your writing," he tells me with a pleasant smile, his eyes ranging just beyond my shoulder. "I'm very grateful they put us together. I have always found, underlying the strange surfaces of your stories, a profound metaphysic at work. I would even go so far as to say I see in them a quiet . . . spirituality."

He must be confusing me with Jay McInerney.

"I would appreciate it," he says, searching through a leather satchel, "if you would do me a great service." He finds a bundle of typed pages on which there are numerous strikeouts and hand-jotted insertions. "This is my sermon for Sunday next. The Temptation in the Desert," he says, bearing the pages in upturned palms. "I would consider it a great honor if you would read through it and give me a critique."

I stare at the typing, at the faint tremble in his hands. I recognize his need for a drink.

"Reverend Markham," I say.

"Jim, please," he offers a weak smile.

"Reverend," I say, "I don't think I'm qualified—"

"Please," he says, his eyes trying to locate mine. "I've read your work. You know how to humanize the holy. My sermons suffer from being too," he struggles for a phrase, "too *abstract*. No one *feels* what I'm saying anymore. You have a talent for that one small human detail that so perfectly captures what cannot be captured. You give utterance to the ineffable," he says, holding out the pages. "Please," his voice thins. "Will you help me? I seem to have lost the touch."

I place the pages on the work desk. In my suitcase there is a small bottle of vodka, half consumed, from the party at the dark Mission. I offer to find ice.

"Thank you, no," the minister says, scratching the back of a dry hand. "In my denomination we abstain."

Someone knocks on our door, a stubby, overweight man with damp curls of hair, his massive girth bulging over a heavy silver belt buckle. He is wearing scuffed cowboy boots beneath plaid bellbottoms, and his tie, unnoosed generously, is clasped to his shirt by a Rotary Club pin.

"Evening, gents," he grins, his slack face beaming with color. "Professor Weeks asked me to check in on you. Name's Allard," he says, "Hard Allard. Either you boys hungry? I got a truck outside."

The minister declines, saying he'd like to do some meditative reading before bedtime. I need an excuse to get away and follow the affable Hard Allard to his vehicle, a jacked-up Toyota chassis floating on oversized tires. Roll bar, twin spotlights mounted on the cab's roof, a Daisy pellet rifle in the rack.

"For wild dogs," he says when he notices my attention on the rifle. "By profession I'm often called door-to-door."

He treats me to a steak dinner at a place called K–Bob's located in a strip center. The decor is early pioneer. Lanterns illumine the tables; the salad bar is arranged in a portable cloth-canopied chuck wagon. The waitresses wear bonnets, long dresses, lace-up boots.

"I'm writing a history of this whole dang region," Hard Allard tells me. "I begin," he says, "when the earth cooled."

"How far along are you?" I ask.

"Late Cretaceous," he says, spooning sour cream into the split of his baked potato. "Would you like to see the manuscript? Professor Weeks says you're the right man to read it. He says there's always a historical whutchamacallit to everything you write."

"Has Weeks read it?"

"The son of a bitch is sleeping with my wife," he says, mushing his potato.

Though it is quite dark, Hard Allard takes me on a tour of the town. He points out the empty lot where once stood the boyhood home of a Hall of Fame baseball hero, and the cinder-block rec hall where a legendary cowboy singing star got his start. We drive past the school building where fifty years ago the basement boiler exploded, killing seventy-three children, a national record. Downtown, a deserted square of weather-worn shops, we idle for several minutes admiring the well-protected façade of his burglar-bar business.

"Would you like to see where I live?" he asks.

"Sure," I say, hoping the accommodating Mr. Allard might stock a healthy libation or two for such desperate occasions as these.

He drives to something resembling a suburb on the rim of the vast outer darkness, a tidy housing addition with brick ranchstyles, carpet lawns, neatly edged sidewalks.

"See this Camaro," he says, pulling alongside a car parked at a curb in front of a quiet house with a birdbath in the yard. "Belongs to Weeks, that reptile. He always leaves it here, a couple blocks away. They think I work nights."

I regard the Camaro's sporty sheen. "Want to torch it?" I say.

Hard Allard thinks this over. "Not till after summer session," he says. "I'm taking his course and need the A."

He cuts the lights and we coast down his street like a raft adrift in the liquid night. At one end of the block several children are playing hide-and-seek.

"That one there is our Dwight," he says, nodding at some kid racing for home base. "His brother's around somewhere. Boyd was born with a murmur on his heart."

He pauses in front of a sprawling gravel-roofed home, the hedges boxed perfectly, a mailbox near the curb. All the windows are braced with vertical bars, the small entry porch enclosed in a wrought-iron cage. The lighting inside seems diffuse and drowsy, as though no one is home. There is no sound but the occasional *zz-zzt* of an insect electrocuted in the trap suspended from the eaves.

"See any sign of movement?" Hard Allard asks, lowering his head to peer out my window.

I study the bedroom windows. My thoughts turn, as they often do this time of night, to Laurel Morgan, the only writer ever to break my heart. She came out of the Hollins program, I think it was, one of the boom years. Her dustjacket drew me to her, the big soft brown eyes, the full lips, the short tousled hair. And of course those eyebrows: thin, dark, delicate. I doubt I would've read her poetry had it not been for the stunning face on the back cover. She caused quite a stir with that first book, the meditations on South Africa, but I must confess I was less moved by the politics than by her passion for suffering, and her vulnerability.

I finally met Laurel at a conference in Tahoe (I remember the lake), where she was scheduled to lead a workshop in "the poetry of commitment" and show slides of Nicaragua, her latest project. I followed her for two days with my eyes, listening to her conversations in hallways, trying to puzzle out who this woman was when she wasn't burying herself beneath the rubble of a suffocating rhetoric. And then one evening, after the bars closed, there was a gathering in somebody's room, an émigré novelist from one of those Eastern bloc countries. He put on music and people began to dance. She was sitting quietly in a corner, drinking, skimming through a paperback, the novelist's most recent English translation, when I approached. 'Screw art,' I spoke to her for the first time, 'Let's dance.' She was not amused (humor was never her strong suit), but she reluctantly rose and offered her arms, resting the liquor glass against my chest. Roy Orbison, I remember. Waltzy, romantic. Her body was so frail, so insubstantial, I wondered how she withstood the constant skirmishing in ravaged lands. She sank against me, her limbs feverish, clothes clinging with sweat. She was a little drunk, a little overheated. When the song ended, she smiled at me and closed her eyes dreamily, then left the room on unsteady legs. I did not see her again for another year, not until Port Townsend. But that image of her moony eyes never went away.

Hard Allard straightens up and slips the truck into gear. "You a drinkin' man?" he asks.

"I've been known to have one now and then."

"Good," he sighs. "I know just the place."

Because this is a dry county dominated by hard-shell Baptists, the only establishment permitted to sell liquor is a private club, an unmarked, windowless lounge where anyone can become a member for a modest monthly fee. Hard Allard shows his card and signs me in as his guest. We sit in a booth upholstered with slick red vinyl, gold-flecked. A man wearing silver bracelets and a leisure suit is playing softly on the piano, the theme from a television show, though I cannot remember which one.

"Hello, Hard," our waitress says, a pretty young woman with a nice figure. "I know what you're having," she smiles cutely, dropping napkins in front of us, "but what does your friend want?"

She flirts with big bright eyes, still smiling, and I order something strong.

"He's here for the conference," Hard tells the waitress. "Weeks says he's a master of the short story."

"Gosh," she glows. "Have I ever heard of you?"

She asks my name.

"Oh god, *really?*" she says, her face delighting with surprise. "Aren't you the guy that writes about, well, you know, ordinary people? You know, court reporters and welders."

"Opal is in my class," Hard Allard says. "Weeks says she's the best he's had."

Opal blushes, then leaves with our orders.

"Nice kid," I watch her retreat, remembering the high school girl in—where was it?—San Diego, I think. The one who'd won the essay contest and insisted on sitting next to me at the banquet dinner. How she managed to escape her chaperone for the evening, I don't know. The next morning, at some silly session in which the audience was asked to describe something unique about the person beside you, the dear foolish girl confessed, before the entire assemblage, her fascination with my long appendix scar. I couldn't get conference work for at least a year after that.

Hard Allard and I have two quick rounds. He tells me about his wife, fourteen years together, how they met on an air force base. Our waitress, Opal, is too busy with other tables to stay and chat, but a couple of times I catch her staring with girlish curiosity from across the lounge. At one point my host's eyes grow wide, his jowls spread into a rogue's grin, when someone approaches our table.

"Hello, dear," he says, standing politely and issuing the woman into his side of the booth as though he's performed this gesture often. "I was beginning to wonder," he says.

Like him she is nearing middle age, a well-dressed woman with matching purse and heels, her face heavily made up, her hair permed neatly, a concealing blond color.

Hard Allard pecks her on the cheek and introduces us, and I realize she is not his wife.

"Connie is writing a book too," Hard says. "Go ahead, honey, tell him. He's with the conference."

"Oh, Hard, darling," she protests.

"Go on, dear. The man's a professional."

Connie orders a wine cooler and, staring into her drink, reluctantly divulges the plot. Twin brothers separated by the Civil War, a shared Negro mistress (unknowingly), her marriage to a European count, the brothers' pursuit of her to France. As Connie describes it, the story concludes with a rather messy three-way duel.

"I get a magazine," Connie says, touching the sides of her perm. "They tell you how to do them. Number of chapters, everything."

I like her very much and wish I could say something encouraging.

"Do you write books?" she looks up, sipping her wine cooler.

"I've written one, yes."

"What category is it in?"

Hard Allard beams at me, his hands folded one over the other on the table, immensely proud he is with a woman who can ask such questions.

"Tragedy," I smile at them both. I wish she could tell me something encouraging about final chapters.

While Connie nurses her drink, Hard and I slosh through a few more rounds. I'm tired. My words begin to slur. I remember that seedy bar in Provincetown. No, in Aspen. Some old hotel. Crutchfield and I had three sexy researchers pinned down about their boss, the great best-selling blockbuster novelist. 'Come on, you can tell us,' Crutchfield goaded them. 'You write his fucking books for him, don't you?' 'No, not really,' tittered the tall leggy one. 'We just provide him with facts and dates.' 'Come on,' I said, 'I buzzed through his last one and I'll bet money it was written by at least four different people.' 'Not a-tall,' countered the British girl. 'We synopsize for him—historical events, that sort of thing. He's quite capable himself.' 'Maybe at one time,' Crutchfield laughed, 'thirty years ago.' 'This subject is boring,' teased the redhead. 'Which one of you is the bloke with the coke?'

In those days, of course, Crutchfield had that reputation in conference circles. All the screenplay money. He never hurt for company. But it's been four years now and no book. I wonder what happened to the one he was working on.

"He's the kind that'll hit her," Connie says, peering icily across the tables.

Some skinny redneck wearing a grungy pearl-snap shirt and steel-toed boots is yelling at Opal near the swinging doors to the kitchen. He waves a gimme cap wildly as he berates her, his straw-colored hair permanently slicked flat in a ring where the elastic presses. It seems to be a domestic spat.

"Do something, Hard," Connie entreats her beau. "That boy's the kind."

Hard Allard watches the ugly disturbance. "It ain't my place, darling," he says, blinking erratically.

Other heads are turning. The bartender saunters over and lays a large hand on the boy's shoulder, addressing him quietly. The bartender is a two hundred pounder with a thick handlebar mustache.

"I think I've had enough," I tell my host.

Hard Allard tries to focus on my face. "Shank of the evening!" he slurs back. "Let's go have some fun."

Connie sits primly between us in the truck's cab while he drives us into the country along a dark two-lane, the warm menacing desert spanning out beyond this asphalt strip like the deep powdery seas of the moon. Small furry carcasses litter the road. A skunk has died somewhere in the bush. Eventually we near lights, a small cluster of beer joints, a convenience store.

"County line," Hard Allard explains. "They're wet."

He slows to avoid the careless drunks merging back onto the high-way. I see a man come out of the convenience store with a brown bag, the collar of his windbreaker turned up, hurrying for his bug-encrusted car. For a moment I'm certain it's the Reverend James Markham.

A mile or so past the settlement Hard Allard pulls off the road into the sand, his balloon tires bouncing airborne over crevices and dry runlets, the doors shuddering as if they might unhinge. We roar through the darkness, my vision blurred by liquor and the rattling heave of the cab. Then suddenly the truck brakes, my face lunging within inches of the windshield. Dust swirls about us. Hard Allard flips on the overhead spots, and in the whirling grit ahead, paralyzed by the piercing beams of light, a thousand frozen eyes the color of bright rubies stare back at us in mute confusion.

"Target time," Hard Allard says, retrieving the pellet rifle from the rack.

The jackrabbits, dozens of them, make no effort to escape the light. Gnarled, stringy creatures, ancient and cunning, their tall, erect gray ears translucent in the mesmerizing glare.

Allard stands beside the truck and begins to pump and shoot, and several of the critters scatter into the farthest shadows.

"Come on, Connie," he says, sighting, pumping. "Don't you want a crack?"

"Oh, Hard," she expels a breath of irritation, her hands latched firmly on the purse in her lap. "You know I'm not my best without a scope."

The pellets zing dirt in the distance. "Hurry up," Hard says, "they're getting away."

Connie leans over and whispers. "Go ahead and take my turn," she says. "It's best to humor him."

Jackrabbits zigzag in every direction, crossing each other, leaping, panicked.

"Don't worry about them," Connie nods. "They're tough as a shingle. That silly little ol' airgun idn't gonna hurt a one."

After they drop me off at the dorm I search the ground floor for a pay phone, fumble through my pants for quarters.

"Hey, Scott," I say, "I know it's late, man, but we've got to talk."

"Jesus, killer," he uses the nickname he gave me in the Program. "Brandi's pregnant, you know. She's a bitch when she's woken up."

Brandi is his third wife, half his age, a secretary he met at the Conference Circuit home office.

"Listen, Scott, you've got to help me, man," I say, trying not to sound mushy and disoriented, though I am. "This place is weird as shit. You've got to get me out of here. We've been pals a long time, man. I deserve better than this."

There is a pause, the sound of static, my old friend grappling with thought. "These are lean times, killer," he says finally. "The boom is over. A man takes what he can get."

"What about Yaddo?" I plead. "Get me in there for a while. Three weeks is all I need. I'll revise the novel."

More hesitation, the empty hiss. "Please don't do this to me," Scott says. "Please don't make me explain your situation."

Back when we were both publishing a few stories in the quarterlies, I always sent him one of my comp copies. He never reciprocated. I had to seek his stories out, in whatever obscure rags, and pay for them myself. Why didn't he ever return the friendship?

"Sun Valley is coming up soon," I remind him. "Get me in, Scott. I need it, man. It's cold out here. The buzzards are circling overhead."

I hear him sigh. "I'll do what I can," he says. "But don't expect miracles, killer. It's a star system, you know. Don't make me explain where you stand."

When I sneak into the dark dorm room the minister is snoring away on the top bunk, the air conditioner apparently broken, the sealed air as sour as flat bourbon.

I am half an hour late for my morning session, "The New Short Story," and the gathering shows signs of restlessness and annoyance. About thirty in all, 98 percent women, the blue-haired ladies you see eating jello in cafeterias, retired schoolmarms, each of them able to diagram a sentence, quote rules of grammar. The waitress Opal is among them, a forty-year gap between her and the others. She is wearing sunglasses this morning, under this cold classroom fluorescence. As am I.

I drink cup after jumbo styrofoam cup of black coffee and outline for these pinched, unsympathetic faces the characteristics of the New Short Story. Weak verbs, I tell them. To be, to have, to go. Avoid joy. Cultivate enigma. Flatness. A knowing deadpan. Create a central metaphor so simple and obvious no one will accuse you of using metaphor. Draw upon brand names familiar to unemployed alcoholics. Never, absolutely never, end a story on a note of drama.

At one point I call for a break and excuse myself to the men's room, where I give in to nausea and diarrhea. In the stall, elbows on knees, what comes to mind is that awful morning in Taos, I think it was, the panel where Sun Wolf what's-his-name, the white shaman, attacked the rest of us for "cultural timidity" in our writing. No one liked the guy; he was something of a joke in the Circuit, a WASP posing as an American Indian seer, an advocate of the oppressed. So I lashed out at him, veins throbbing in my neck, my words a stumble of accusations and angry, inarticulate venting. At the time I blamed it on an atrocious hangover from so much cocaine the previous night, my patience stripped to the bare wiring, my gums afire. Odd, though, the way reputations are made. Sun Wolf was the obnoxious fake, not a soul in the room respected him, but *I* was the one everybody avoided the rest of the day.

When I return to my seminar, more than half of the attendees have disappeared. Those remaining look bewildered, disappointed. I open the floor to questions. Someone asks my position on simultaneous submission.

"If it's between consenting adults," I reply.

No one laughs.

Afterwards Opal is the only person to approach me. "Thank you," she smiles tentatively. "That was very . . . helpful."

"I see you had the same kind of night I did," I gesture at her sunglasses.

"Oh," she says, adjusting one lens. "It's . . . it's just a condition I get. Pinkeye."

With both arms she coddles a thick notebook like a baby against her chest.

"If you were my girl," I say in a quiet voice, "I'd never treat you that way."

Immediately I hate myself for stooping to such a line.

Opal blushes, lowers her chin, turns to leave. After a few steps she hesitates. "Are you teaching in the afternoon?" she asks shyly.

"Consultation," I say, remembering the stories I must judge before the banquet. "They told me to make myself available for private consultation."

She seems to be formulating something behind the glasses. "I could use a little consultation," she says.

Out in the corridor I spot Professor Weeks surrounded by a gaggle of admirers. He sends me a questioning look, vague and disapproving, and I suspect someone has already complained about me. Hurrying to avoid him I turn a corner and nearly knock down the Reverend James Markham.

"Speak of the devil," the minister chuckles at his own remark. He is conversing with a gaudy woman in her mid-fifties, I'd say, her auburn wig teased into an unusual construction from an earlier era. She is fond of heavy jewelry, and the pasty makeup gives her a decidedly cheap aspect.

"I was mentioning you to Mrs. St. Rose," the minister says. "She's just led us in a splendid session on devotional writing, and I've twisted her arm," he winks at no one in particular, "into reading over that darn sermon I'm having so much trouble with."

"Hello there," the woman measures me with her eyes, extending a limp bangled wrist as though she expects me to kiss her fingers. "Didn't you do that story a couple of years ago in *Redbook,* dear, the one about your daughter dying of cancer?"

I shake her hand, a soft, lotiony appendage, the bracelets jingling. The program notes say Ashley St. Rose writes books from a Christian perspective on how to cope with family crises. She hosts her own talk show on one of the cable networks.

"I'm sure you wouldn't mind," the Reverend Markham says, his eyes wandering strangely, "if I turn over the sermon to this dear lady."

"I haven't read it yet," I say, her hand still sticking to mine.

"I understand," the minister says, patting my shoulder. "Too many obligations, too little time. It wasn't fair of me to burden you so."

I'm losing admirers right and left. "It's no burden," I say, surprising myself with such eagerness. "Who knows, maybe I . . . maybe I'll bring a greater objectivity. I'd like to try. I—"

"My own daughter died tragically young," says Ashley St. Rose from a place far away.

The minister nudges me aside. "May I please have my sermon back, please," he says with a hint of force.

Lunch for the conference staff is served in the faculty center, an old, ivy-covered flagstone manse on the edge of campus. Professor Weeks corners me in the foyer.

"How did it go this morning?" he asks, baiting me, the bastard.

"Challenging," I say.

A voluptuous young hostess captures his eye. "Come across any personal favorite yet?" he says, staring at her.

"Beg your pardon?"

"The short story contest," he smiles slickly.

"Still looking," I smile back, tooth for tooth.

White tablecloths, delicate china, stiff waiters majoring in hotel management. Weeks escorts me to our table.

"Do you-all know one another?" he smiles cordially at the three others already seated.

Unfortunately I do. If I had known in advance that Barbara Perry was on the program, I would've refused the assignment.

"Have we met?" she asks, struggling with memory, running my name through her mind. There is more gray in her ringlet hair now but she still possesses that stylish allure she always worked so hard to affect. Once, in the late hours of a poolside party, I watched her crawl along the diving board on all fours like a cat in heat, her clothes coming off slowly, a strange acrobatic of writhing and stretching for no viewer in particular, and yet for everyone there, a woman of fading promise asking gathered peers if she still had the power to arouse.

"I've read your novels," I tell her, a partial truth. I've never made it more than fifty pages into any of them before being repelled by her snotty superiority. There is an icy distance to every sentence, smugness a virtue, those who are in and those who aren't. Her characters frequent the right galleries, own condos in the Caribbean, send their children away to school. But her writing is not why I dislike her.

"We may have to get you a bigger classroom for the afternoon, Barbara," Weeks gushes, grabbing the chair next to her. "Everyone is raving about you!"

Everyone, I muse, except her publisher. A thirty-thousand-dollar advance three years ago but the woman couldn't deliver. The word is her editor turned down what she finally submitted. She threw an ugly tantrum, doused the guy with a drink at a party, and now no one wants to work with her. Why else would she be here, in this godforsaken place, with the rest of us losers?

"I believe we've published you," says the bearded man across the table. I know who he is, the swine, I know his magazine. "That long poem based on Ovid, wasn't it? Some time back."

The only story I ever submitted to him, nearly ten years ago now, he and his parasite grad school assistants held for six months and then returned with scurrilous comments of rejection scribbled all over the outside of the SASE. One afternoon I found the postman standing near my mailbox, reading what they had said, tears of laughter flowing down his cheeks.

Throughout lunch, inclining his mouth to her ear, Professor Weeks speaks only to Barbara Perry, an intimate discourse, hushed and fawning, and she stares often into his eyes, trying to rekindle that coquettish charm that succeeded so well in her twenties and thirties, when she needed jacket blurbs, lecture tours, guest residencies. The rest of us make strained conversation. The editor names the luminaries who will appear in his next issue, boasts about a grant the magazine has just received, tells of discovering an unpublished Pound haiku in his university archives. His companion is an aloof busty woman, neither attractive nor dull, an academic from another university, where she teaches feminist deconstruction, she says with considerable detachment. Impressed by the resonance of her own observations, she lectures to an invisible spot on the wall somewhere behind me. He wears a wedding band, she does not. It becomes clear that this is how they rendezvous, at conferences across the land, once, twice a year, a few nights of illicit romance, shared literary interests, an exchange of letters. So many I know rely on this venerable convention, the special conference friend. Poor Todd, MFA Greensboro '74, always looked for boys. He pampered them in posh suites, bought them clothes, fine meals, told us they were a nephew, a son. One night in New Orleans, only hours after his delightful reading, he propositioned a young undercover cop. His wife divorced him, tenure was denied, and he moved to Salt Lake City, I am told, where he deals in Mormon church documents and writes under an assumed name.

"Why don't you send me more of those Ovid reconstructions?" the editor says, standing, the meal over. "Do you by any chance translate from the French? We're preparing an issue dedicated to Jerry Lewis."

I am halfway down the stone steps at the entrance when Barbara Perry calls to me.

"I know who you are," she says, coming alongside.

"Uh-huh," I say, squinting in the shimmering sunlight.

"You were on the committee, weren't you?" she says, trying to slip in front of me to slow my stride.

"Committee?"

"Yes, damn you," she says, her small wedge of face showing anger. "For the fellowship. You turned me down. I want to know why."

I stop and look at her. In this harsh light she is no longer young. The mascara, the applied blush, seem to crack and flake like old paint. "My dear Miz Perry," I sigh, "I have never been on a committee in my life, and it is highly unlikely I ever will."

Weeks approaches, puzzled by the animosity, his collar damp from perspiration. I continue my way across the brittle lawn. "I know you from somewhere," she calls behind me.

Indeed she does. Port Townsend, two years ago.

Laurel Morgan was there promoting her new book, tanned now from the Nicaragua sun, her hair longer, lighter. There was a healthier glow in those soft brown eyes; laughter came easy. Though we crossed paths several times she did not appear to recognize me from that night, the one close dance in the Hungarian's room. I kept building my courage to say hello, but her presence always tied my tongue, clamped a fist around my heart. One afternoon we were all invited to tour the former army fortress where the conference was taking place, and I went along because I saw her name on the sign-up sheet. In one of the officers' mansions, a home restored to the era when the base was in use, I wandered into an upstairs bedroom and found her there alone, staring out the lacy curtains toward the Strait. 'Hello,' I said, afraid to lose this rare opportunity, the celebrity poet without her followers underfoot. 'Enchanting place,' I said, or something equally vapid. She turned from the window, smiling that same dreamy smile I remembered from the night of our dance. 'The water is beautiful today,' she said. 'Have you seen it?' I feigned interest in the antique four-poster bed, examining the carved headboard. 'We've actually met before,' I said, my throat dry as sand. I asked if she recalled the party in Tahoe, the Hungarian novelist. 'Sort of,' she giggled. 'I think I had too much to drink that night.'

'We danced together,' I said, facing away from her. 'Roy Orbison,' I said. There was a long silence. I felt her eyes on the back of my neck. 'You're the one who's been writing the letters,' she said finally, her voice very quiet in the attic stuffiness of the room. I gazed at framed photographs resting on a dusty dresser. 'I'm not sure what you mean,' I said.

'Listen,' she said, 'I think they're lovely sweet letters and I'm very flattered. But you ought to stop, really, for your own sake. I'm not going to answer them.'

'You must have me confused with someone else,' I said. 'I'm a terrible correspondent. Ask my mother.'

She came and stood at some distance behind me, our eyes meeting in the dresser mirror. 'You've got the wrong idea about me,' she said. 'I do truly appreciate the sentiment in the letters, but I'm not the seductive, courageous heroine you think I am. Look at these hands,' she said, holding them out, the nails broken, knuckles cracked, callouses yellow and leathery. 'Are these the hands of a Madonna?' she said. 'Sometimes, when I read those darling things you say about me, even the romantic stuff, I almost begin to believe you, that the woman you describe is really me. I'd like to think she is, but I know better. So please, for both of us, let it go.'

'Laurel,' I said, touching one of her rough hands, 'you make me wish I *was* the one sending letters.'

She smiled. 'The truth is,' she said, 'I don't sleep around.' And then she left the room.

That evening I sat alone at a pierside bar, drinking, pondering her words and my next move. That's when Barbara Perry appeared and took a stool beside me, ordering a Scotch. 'I'm a friend of Laurel,' she began without introduction, staring straight ahead, lighting a cigarette. 'She asked me to speak with you. She wants you to stop sending those letters.'

'Look, lady,' I said, 'do me a big favor. Tell Laurel she's got the wrong man.'

Barbara Perry raised her notched chin and blew smoke in the air. 'I can understand it,' she said, staring straight ahead. 'She's beautiful, she writes well, she's a quixotic crusader everybody thinks is a goddamn saint. Wouldn't she be an intriguing fuck? Like bagging an airy movie star, or maybe a nun. Am I getting warm? Well listen up, junior. Your little fantasy is common as dog poo. Every MFA clone in the country has the same wet dream. So leave the poor girl alone, will you? She thinks you're disturbed. Go find some star-eyed grad student to harass. Better still, pack your bags, before you get in trouble with the Circuit office, and head on home to Tennessee.'

I stood up and tossed money onto the bar, paying for my drinks. 'I have no idea what you're talking about,' I said. 'I've never set foot in Tennessee.'

Barbara Perry swiveled on her stool, regarding me directly for the first time, her eyes dimly perplexed. She took a drag from her cigarette, squinting. 'Aren't you the guy from Tennessee who writes all that outdoorsy macho stuff?'

I shook my head and pointed to a table. 'He's over there,' I said.

When I return to the dormitory I notice that the minister's sermon is missing from among my papers. Just as well, I think, trying to coax the air conditioner into working and then giving up, opening a window, the noonday furnace breathing into the room. I glance at a few pages of my novel but cannot read them, the words so familiar even after all these years, so painfully wrong. I settle down at the desk and begin to read the short stories, but my concentration is dulled by a rude hangover and the sorry events of the day.

Soon there is a knock. Opal the waitress cracks open the door and peers in.

"Consultation?" I grin.

She enters the room trailed by a small child, maybe five years old, clinging to the back of her leg. The girl has stringy blond hair, a runny nose, bare feet. She buries her soiled face into her mother's jeans.

"I need your help," Opal says, pale and distressed. Without her sunglasses a deep blue crescent shows beneath one eye. "Clifford has gone off his wig," she says. "Work called and said he didn't show up today. Sometimes he gets this way. I don't want him to hurt hisself again. Will you help me find him?"

I put down the story. "Forgive me, Opal," I say, "but I don't get involved in domestic disputes."

She lifts her daughter to her side. "I don't know what else to do," she says, her voice quavering. "I've got to find him before he gets in trouble with the probation man. Clifford goes a little crazy sometimes. He doesn't mean nothing by it. He's a good fella most of the time. Do you have a car?"

I'm reluctant to tell her about the rental.

"He's got our truck," she says, the daughter squirming, wanting down. "I can't find him on foot. Not with Moira dragging along. Will you please help me?"

"I'm supposed to be available for consultation, Opal," I tell her. "Over at the liberal arts building."

"Please," she says, tears pooling in her eyes.

We drive past the old stucco building where Clifford works in an assembly line making "band candy," as Opal calls it, those chocolate almond bars sold by Junior Achievers and high school bands across America. "Since 1911," the sign declares.

"Don't stop," Opal says. "The truck's not there."

We drive to the home of Clifford's best friend, the yard littered with a rusting junker stripped down for parts and resting on cinder blocks. Opal runs inside, returns with a beer in her hand. "Nobody's seen the dope," she says.

The daughter sits between us and plays with a road map from the glove compartment. We cruise the gravel streets, searching for Clifford's truck. I show her where the baseball Hall-of-Famer once lived, the rec hall where the cowboy singing star made his debut. She knows next to nothing about the town's history, so I feel obliged to fill her in. We drive out to the county line and look for the truck in front of the beer joints, with no success.

"Listen, Opal," I tell her, "this isn't getting anywhere. Maybe you ought to go home and wait for him."

She begins to cry. The little girl begins to cry. "Let's check the jail," she sniffs.

He is not in jail. Nor is he at the rifle range, the trampoline park, the putt-putt golf course, the bowling alley.

"I'm taking you home," I tell her, two hours into the ride. "You'll have to work this out yourself."

"Last time, he ate a dozen raw eggs," Opal says, "and urped all over the yard. He gets a little crazy sometimes."

The daughter rolls the radio dial from one end of the band to the other, back and forth, a cacophony of blips and sputters.

"You ought to talk to the police," I say, removing the girl's dirty little fingers from the dial. "He shouldn't hit you."

"He doesn't hit me," Opal responds quickly, defensively.

"Then how did you get the bruise?"

She hesitates, thinking. "I ran into a cabinet door," she says.

I remember the evening in Missoula, that sad quaalude poet hanging all over me, listing the famous writers she had slept with. She thought I was John Nichols and wanted me in her bed. Her husband assured me he was the best writer from Massachusetts since Cheever, though I had never heard of the man. 'I can outdrink Cheever,' he kept saying, 'I can outdrink Mailer.' At dinner the sad quaalude poet passed out at the table and slid to the floor, and her husband sat her up and began to slap her face with loud, stunning blows, one hand then the other, until he had to be restrained. 'I'm going to outlive the bitch,' he screamed as they led him away. Later I learned they'd stiffed the program at Columbia, cashed their fellowship checks one term and then disappeared. From time to time I ask about them, skim the contents pages of sundry quarterlies. I have yet to see him in print, the new Cheever. No one I know, not even Crutchfield, will admit he's shared her bed.

Opal lives in a trailer park on the outskirts of town, and when we arrive at her place, a long aluminum shell without wheels, one among dozens, Clifford is sitting in a lawn chair in the small grassless yard, a scattering of crushed beer cans at his feet. He is pitching darts at a row of targets lined atop a downed tree trunk. Cans of Spam, deviled ham, Vienna sausages, Beanie Weenies.

"Oh god," Opal says, "he's at it again."

"I want my real daddy," little Moira whimpers.

Clifford pulls himself from the lawn chair and staggers toward the car, wielding a sharp-pointed dart like a knife blade. "Is this him?" he shouts. "Is this that squirrelly perfessor?"

Opal springs from the car. "No, Clifford," she says nervously, "this is not him. This is a nice man that tried to help me find you, you dope. Now you better put that thing down."

Clifford keeps coming, the dart's nasty tip protruding from a doubled fist at his side. "I'm gonna poke him in the eye," he says.

"You'll do no such thing," Opal says, heading him off, grabbing at his unbuttoned shirt. "He was very kind to help me."

Moira hides her face against the seat cover and begins to shake.

I wonder if I should get out of the car. Young Gordon Giles was killed this way, sitting on a bar stool in Juarez, twenty-five years old, MFA Johns Hopkins '85, waiting his turn in the back rooms. Some jealous boyfriend flew into a rage and sprayed the place with bullets. Poor kid didn't live to see his novel, one of those anemic Blank Generation confessions, soar through the bestseller ranks. I shot pool with him earlier that evening in El Paso. He was a friendly lad, bought me drinks, asked about the old days before the Circuit.

"You're pokin' my girl," Clifford shouts at me, fighting to loose himself from Opal's grip, "so I'm gonna poke you in the eye."

My lord, I think, watching Opal struggle. She's sleeping with Weeks.

"Clifford, you're scaring the little girl," I say, opening my door. "Get rid of that thing and straighten up, son. I'm not who you think I am." I'm not who anyone thinks I am. "I'm a visitor here," I say, "and so far you're giving a very bad impression."

Clifford stops scuffling with Opal. He shakes free, looks at her, then at me. I'm five inches taller, forty pounds heavier, not much younger than his old man.

His face and hair are dripping sweat. "You're not the perfessor?" he says.

"Dammit, Clifford," Opal slaps his shoulder, "I told you he ain't."

The boy drops his eyes, puts his hands on his hips, quietly fuming. Suddenly he slings the dart at the trailer and begins to sob.

"Cliffie," Opal says, moving close to hold his head in her arms.

"I don't feel so good," Clifford mumbles into her chest. "I ate a whole bunch of old coffee grounds."

While Opal takes him inside the trailer I unload little Moira and walk her to the sandbox in one corner of the yard. We sit for a while, digging with her shovel, Moira singing in a tiny papery voice the sweet innocent songs she has learned from a Miss Ruby, apparently her sitter. I enjoy the time with her, our collaborations in sand, but the afternoon is wearing on and I have much work to do.

"Okay you two!" I raise my voice, banging loudly on the trailer door. "I want you both out here right now, front and center!"

A plastic shutter opens. "Clifford's a little peak-ed," Opal says in a hush.

"I don't care," I say forcefully. "Get him out here right now! You've taken up a lot of my time, and now I want some of yours."

There is a pause. "Clifford is upchucking," Opal says through the shutter.

"I don't have much time left, young lady," I say. "Now I want you both out here and sitting in those lawn chairs by the time I get back from the car."

They emerge slowly, cautiously, Clifford helped to a chair like a convalescent in a nursing home. He folds his hands in his lap, blinks into the sun, smacks his dry lips. I expect her to arrange a blanket over his legs.

"This is how it's done," I say, dividing the stack of short stories, placing some in Opal's lap, some in Clifford's. "Try to get it down to two or three you like best. Then we'll exchange those and cut it down some more. Any questions?"

Opal stares at me, puzzled, drawing little Moira to the arm of her lawn chair. "What the heck are we doing?"

"Judging," I say. "Clifford, are you with us on this?"

Clifford regards the stapled pages piled on his knees, then slowly peers up at me, the bill of his gimme cap tucked low over his eyes. "Do we take points off for spelling?" he asks.

We read in silence, and in a short while Opal brings out a six-pack, refusing to let Clifford partake, offering him iced tea instead. He sulks, turns pages, asks an occasional question: "What does *proactive* mean?" "What the hell's bells is a *a-b-a-double t-o-i-r*?"

At the end of an hour we take stock. I discover that one of Clifford's picks is Hemingway's "Soldier's Home" somebody has retyped and tried to slip through for the prize.

"Too bad," Clifford says. "I kinda liked it."

We exchange stories and read on. Clifford's other choice is a real jewel, the finest of the lot. It is a quiet, moving story, plainly told, about an eleven-year-old girl caring for her dying mother, those last painful days. When I finish I am fighting back emotion.

"No contest," Clifford grins when I ask their final assessment. "The one about the little girl and her mama."

I look to Opal for confirmation. "Well, Opal," I say, "do you agree?"

The young waitress lifts Moira into her lap, squeezes the girl fondly, kisses the top of her head. "I don't think I should say," Opal replies, chewing her lip. "I wrote it," she tries to smile.

The banquet is held in the Coronado Room of the Holiday Inn, an aging, shabby structure out near the interstate, and by the time I arrive I am quite drunk from the accumulation of afternoon beer and the vodka in my suitcase. Weeks seats me at the far end of the dais, next to a nervous little man who writes children's books from the Christian perspective. Beside each water glass there is a crossword puzzle and a pencil. "This is fun," I hear someone say, so I try my hand. For "devotional" the answer is "Ashley," for "prestigious literary magazine" the answer is the name of the bearded editor's rag, for "acclaimed female novelist" the answer is "Perry." I exhaust all the remaining squares before I realize my own name is the answer to "experimental writer."

I collar Weeks near the podium. "I resent that characterization," I breathe liquor on the man. "My work has never looked funny on the page."

The Reverend James Markham is called upon to lead the convocation in grace, and my stolid roommate bumbles through something rather formulaic and uninspired. During the meal, which I have no appetite for and push aside, the children's writer tells me that the narrator of his latest book is the rooster that crowed twice during Peter's denial of Jesus. "Remember this, my friend," he says: "When an animal tells the story, the kids are putty in your hands."

Weeks sits between Barbara Perry and Ashley St. Rose, charming them with his relentless flattery and lame witticisms. From time to time I catch one of them glaring at me warily, expecting me to do something foolish. Hard Allard winks from his table and raises a tea glass in mock toast. His wife, a prettier woman than Connie, seems distant and unamused, her attention turned to the laughter at Weeks's end of the dais. Connie is here too, in the company of several female companions at a far table. Radiant and silky in a revealing summer dress, Opal arrives late on Clifford's arm, her dark hair curled nicely and falling on smooth bare shoulders. Clifford himself appears genteel and stiffly proud, his boots polished to a sharp gleam, the Western-cut suit and string tie presenting him as the model of a country gentleman.

After dinner Weeks acknowledges the president of the college and the department chairman, who nod to perfunctory applause, then introduces the keynote speaker, the piously intense Ashley St. Rose. She breaks the ice with irreverent one-liners about various television evangelists, but I seem to be the only person laughing. In time she works her way to the meat of her message, how she struggled for three years with her dope-smoking degenerate teenagers, both under the spell of satanic rock lyrics, and with constant prayer, God's help, and medically prescribed lithium, they were transformed into productive young missionaries. What this has to do with creative writing, I don't know; but her eyes well with tears, her voice warbles, as she relates the good news of conversion. The Coronado Room is so quiet you can hear muffled sniffling and the catches in understanding throats. Even the uppity editor's face flushes with color. For no apparent reason my thoughts turn to the two lesbian poets I once mistakenly tried to pick up in a Holiday Inn lounge in St. Louis.

Afterwards the awards are presented, and I am brought to the podium to confer the short story prize. I thank my committee for helping me in the difficult task of narrowing the choices, then announce Opal as the winner and summon her to the front. The applause is light, heads lean close to whisper, eyebrows lift. When Opal kisses me on the cheek, Weeks bends toward Barbara Perry to say something under his breath.

Soon after Reverend Markham delivers the closing prayer I am besieged by disapproving ladies from the audience.

"That little girl of hers was born out of wedlock," one woman complains.

"What about *my* story?" asks another. "The one where the grandmother cans all those figs."

They close in around me, the scent of feminine body powder overwhelming, and I consider making a run for it when Opal breaks through their ranks, Clifford in tow, to give me a dear smiling hug. Her presence annoys the ladies, and they slowly withdraw and regroup at some distance, watching our interchange, murmuring.

"Keep writing," I tell Opal. Then I turn to the straight-backed Clifford, his lean face shining with pride for his sweetheart. "You're a natural as a critic, son," I slap him on the shoulder. "If you ever want an MFA, I think I can get you money."

Outside, heat lightning streaks the dark sky. I drive my rental car to the covered entrance of the Holiday Inn, where a familiar group has gathered to gossip about the proceedings. "Hop in," I say to Weeks, who acts surprised by my offer. He exchanges looks with his companions.

"Don't you want a ride back to campus?" I ask. "It's about to rain buckets."

Weeks shrugs, says something to those around him, and they all laugh.

"I could use a drink," says the editor.

"Get in," I say. "I know where to find one."

The editor and his professor paramour slide into the back seat, and Weeks opens the front door for Barbara Perry, who scoots close enough for this excursion to be interesting. As I pull away, the Reverend Markham dashes to my window.

"Mind if I get a ride back?" he says. "I'm with Mrs. St. Rose, but she's been detained by her flock of admirers."

I speed down the interstate into darkness, a mild desert rain speckling the dusty windshield. "That was our turnoff," says Weeks.

"How far is it to Mexico?" I ask, reaching under the seat for the fifth of bourbon I purchased earlier at the county line.

Weeks laughs nervously. "A lot farther than you think," he says. "Maybe 350, 400 miles."

"I have an idea," I say, sipping the bourbon. "Let's all go on a field trip."

I hand the bottle back to the editor, who takes it but does not drink. "I myself could do with a nice smooth Manhattan," he says. "Where is that place you spoke of?"

"Long behind us," I say, pushing the accelerator to seventy, seventy-five, the wipers smearing the wet grime across the glass.

"What exactly are we doing?" Weeks asks, attempting to play the good sport.

"Going for that drink I promised," I say. "In Juarez."

Barbara Perry glances at the speedometer. "I told you he was a little strange," she says to Weeks.

"You're not serious, I trust," says the editor.

"I'm supposed to meet with Mrs. St. Rose to go over my sermon for Sunday next," pipes in Reverend Markham. "I'd hate to keep the good woman waiting."

"We're well equipped here to handle that sermon, Reverend," I look at him in the rearview mirror. "We've got an acclaimed female novelist, a professor of English, an experimental writer, in case you feel like going out on a limb this week, and the editor of a prestigious literary magazine that specializes in thorough response. And when we're all finished, there's someone here who can deconstruct the text for you. What more could you want?" I say. "So go ahead and deliver your sermon, Reverend. We're all ears."

Professor Weeks exhales an annoyed breath. "If this is your idea of a joke, it's wearing thin," he says. "I suggest you turn around and take us back to campus."

"Don't be such a wet blanket," I tell him. "At this rate we should be in Juarez in five or six hours. I bet the bars will still be open."

The rain has picked up, thin silvery strings traced in the headlights, splashing the empty highway. A luminous green sign announces the nearest city as eighty miles away. Barbara Perry's eyes measure the distance to the keys in the ignition.

"Don't even think it," I tell her, smiling, the speedometer hovering between seventy-five and eighty. I hear the editor take a drink of bourbon and pass it to his mate.

"I told them all who you are," Barbara Perry says in a husky voice, staring straight ahead as she did that night in Port Townsend.

I laugh. "And who am I now, dear Barbara?" I ask, glancing down at her bare knees, the tight dress riding halfway up her tanned thighs. "One of the reviewers who panned your last book?"

"I finally remembered," she says calmly. "You're the guy who's been writing letters to Laurel Morgan."

I rub my eye and laugh. The minister taps me on the shoulder with the bottle, and I have another long burning swallow.

"To idolize women is to demean them," the woman in the back seat speaks for the first time. "Eurocentric man has such a repressed desire to create a goddess in his life. The perfect anima. But adulation is just another way of denying our humanity."

This is getting less and less humorous.

"I've published Ms. Morgan on two or three occasions," the editor says. "One poem took a Pushcart, if I recall correctly. A rare strength of the line. Can't see the two of you together."

Barbara Perry takes the bottle from my hand and touches it to her glossy lips, her free hand resting warmly on my knee. "Take us back," she says quietly, her fingers probing a muscle, "before this goes any farther."

I retrieve the bottle and drink again, tasting her sweet lipstick. "Will you recommend me to your agent?" I ask.

She removes her hand quickly and folds her arms. "Whore," she says.

"A word of advice," Weeks says. "I've yet to make my final report to the Conference Circuit, and at this point it's touch and go. We've had complaints about you, but I'm willing to overlook them and submit a fair appraisal if you'll come to your senses, man, and turn this car around."

"I'm often in bed by now," adds the minister.

"If an automobile passes by," says the editor's girlfriend, "I shall roll down the window and scream for assistance."

The rain is heavy now. Gusts of wind shift the car laterally as we shush along the dark puddled roadway. I turn the radio on and dial through the storm static in search of music, other voices. "People, people," I shake my head. "You're beginning to overreact just a tad, don't you think? If anyone is truly unhappy, I'll gladly stop the car right now and let you out."

The windshield wipers struggle against the downpour. Except for the cadenced squeaking, the car is silent.

"Well?" I say.

More silence, the splatter of rain.

"You're a scoundrel of the lowest rank," says the editor. "I will not forget this easily. I have friends at nearly every magazine in the country, you know. . . . Who has that bottle?"

Barbara Perry does not like my choice of music and angrily switches off the radio.

"The trouble with writers today is we've all lost our sense of adventure," I say. "Melville would've accepted this ride happily. And Jack London, Steinbeck, Agnes Smedley, Richard Wright. Kerouac, of course. They wouldn't have fretted over what's at the other end."

"Spare us the pedantry," says Barbara Perry.

The minister leans forward. "He may have a point, Miss Perry," he says. "Myself, I've been thinking I'd do better to get out of the rectory more often and roll around in the clover."

Weeks makes a noise through his teeth. "Oh shut up," he says to Reverend Markham. "This is bad enough without you encouraging the fool."

The rain stops abruptly. We've passed through a summer squall and the worst is over. The tires shish through pond after shallow pond.

"You know, Harry," I say, addressing Weeks by his first name, "you may be the only one here who secretly enjoys a good adventure. I suppose if a man of your talents ends up beneath his station, teaching at a jerkwater college in the middle of nowhere, the only real revenge would be to ball everybody's wife and half the student body."

Weeks begins to cough. "That's an outrageous charge!" he sputters.

No one else seems surprised by my remark. Barbara Perry turns to him slowly, with chilly disdain: "Is it true?" she asks distantly.

"Barbara, darling," he sputters. "How could you ask such a thing?"

"Taking advantage of the father–daughter relationship inherent in your position of authority," the editor's girlfriend says, "is tantamount to incest and rape."

Weeks leans over Barbara Perry to engage my attention. "Listen to me, you depraved toad," he says, his eyes flashing hatred, "I won't stand for that kind of slander. You'll hear from my lawyers!"

Up ahead, spread across the great dark expanse of buffalo plains like a glimmering constellation, the lights of a city appear as a strange and awesome mirage.

"Are you really taking us to Mexico?" the Reverend Markham asks.

"Why not?" I say, glancing at the gas gauge.

The minister inhales deeply. "Who has the bottle?" he says.

My passengers fall into quiet reverie, a somber resignation of spirit, and their silence causes me to drift off at the wheel, numbed by alcohol and fatigue and the monotony of white stripes, my thoughts fixed dimly on those pearls of light drawing ever close. Whether remembrance of actual events or a desperate wish, I don't know; but I slip into a warm drowsy dream of an earlier time, an elegant old home overlooking the sea, sherry in crystal decanters, cigars by the fire. Laurel was staying there, a large open bedroom, faded floral cushions, bay windows facing down upon the port and a huddle of weathered fishing boats. I knocked at her door and she answered wearing a long cotton gown and reading glasses, a book in her hand. 'I stopped by to clear up some confusion,' I said, peering past her to the covers folded back neatly on her bed. She hesitated, pointing out the late hour. 'You're a very persistent man,' she said, finally inviting me in for a brandy. I sat on a plush settee, she on the bed, slender legs crossed underneath her. We talked about Barbara Perry, the conference, politics. Finally I found the courage to tell her the thing that was destroying me. I had lost my vocation. I couldn't write anymore; I had nothing to say, no conviction inside. It had once been there, I thought, but something happened, motives blurred, passion moved to a remote and inaccessible region of the heart. When they came at all, words reeled across the page with no attachment, a wallpaper of meaningless syllables. 'So tell me where I went wrong,' I said to the beautiful woman on the bed. 'You don't have this problem. Your work is getting better and better. I'd like to know how you keep yourself going.'

She smiled at me, her soft brown eyes filled with sympathy. 'I don't have any secret answers,' she said, bringing the brandy to her lips. 'The puzzling thing is, everybody wants to be a writer but no one can remember why. To tell the truth, I'm not much interested in art and the test of time. Maybe that's the key,' she said. 'Don't let it matter so much. Make a good life for yourself. I mean, what do you do when you aren't attending all these conferences and playing the writer game?' she asked. 'Do you belong somewhere? Do you join causes? What do you do for fun? Are you in love?'

The last question hung between us, a cruel blade suspended by the most delicate thread, swinging dangerously near. I was incapable of response, of course, because the answers were so painful and pathetic. She guessed this and let it go, her eyes grazing upon mine.

'I like to dance,' I said finally, trying to smile, trying not to collapse into the emptiness of my life.

'I know,' she said in a dreamy voice. 'I remember.' And then her face softened into an expression of sudden and unaccountable intimacy. 'Are you going to keep writing those letters?' she wondered.

"Oh my god, we're on fire!" Barbara Perry says.

Sure enough, a geyser of smoke is spewing from the hood and a red light on the dash signals that the engine has overheated. Damn these rentals, I fume. I once broke down in the middle of the night outside Mesquite, Nevada, the clutch shot on my rental, 102 degrees in the dark. I had to walk five miles through a plague of crickets to find an open Stuckey's.

"This is just wonderful!" says Weeks. "Just ducky! What do you propose to do now, Agnes Smedley? I'm sure the garages are all closed."

"Let us not abandon hope," says the minister. "Shall we join hands in prayer?" He begins to laugh, tipsy from drink, the gurgle in his throat harsh and unsettling.

By the city's third freeway exit the smoke is so thick it fogs the windshield. I pull off, limping through dark sinister backstreets, what appears to be the barrio, small wooden row houses, the streets unpaved, mangy dogs digging through garbage. Turning a corner the car dies, and we coast to a stop in front of a narrow strip of cinder-block cantinas. Ranchera music booms from competing jukeboxes; long hyena *gritos* peal through the night. Several brown-skinned hookers stare at us from the corner.

"Lock your doors," says the editor.

His companion wakes from his shoulder and squints, massaging her eyes. "Are we home yet, daddy?" she asks, slurping drool.

I get out and raise the scalding hood. Steam belches upward in a ball of heat; the loud hissing noise alerts ears along the dark sidewalk. The smell of burning rubber tells me a radiator hose has melted.

I try to open my door and realize I have been locked out. "Come on, people," I say, tapping on the glass. "This car won't be going anywhere for a while."

They all stare out at me, mute, enraged, unforgiving.

"You can't stay in there forever," I say, watching the hookers saunter over on platform heels.

Barbara Perry is now sitting behind the wheel. Her window lowers precisely two inches. "You're ruined," she says, staring ahead at some fixed point, her voice grim and tight. Then the window whirs again, sealing itself.

"Okay, scouts, suit yourself," I say, patting the roof. Lowriders hanging out in front of a bar have noticed the car and are making their way over. "Get ready to earn your merit badge," I say.

Waving a twenty-dollar bill I ask the gathering hookers if anyone has a car. A short thick girl with willowy black hair and ruby lips drives me back out to the city limits, where a dilapidated, poorly lit filling station advertises itself as "The Last Stop."

"That's all?" the girl asks as I climb out of her car.

"That's all," I shrug.

In a short while a shiny new El Camino rips in for gas, the bumper papered with various stickers: "Jesus Is Lord" and a decal from the college where my suitcase awaits me. Fortunately I am dressed presentably in corduroy jacket and tie. I tell the young couple my car has broken down and ask for a ride.

"You must be new at the college," the young man says as we zoom through the misty night. "What do you teach?"

They have been to the new Burt Reynolds movie in the big city.

"No kidding?" says the young woman. "I'll be darn," she smiles, turning to her beau. "Tell him about your novel, hon."

By the time I reach the dormitory it is nearly one A.M. Ashley St. Rose lounges at the work desk in my room, smoking, a thick manuscript heaped in front of her, the read pages turned over in a shorter stack.

"Well," she purrs, "what a pleasant surprise. I was expecting Jim Markham. Hours ago," she glances at the watch that matches her gold jewelry.

"The good reverend has been detained," I say. It is then I realize the manuscript is my own.

"I was bored so I went looking for something to read," she explains. "I hope you're not angry with me. I'm truly impressed by your writing. It has a kind of . . . of . . ."

"Convincing spiritual quality?" I say.

"Yes, that's it," she smiles.

"An underlying metaphysic at work?"

She laughs at herself, then for quite some time stares me up and down, the smile turning naughty. "You'll lock the door, won't you?" she says, unclipping a gaudy earring.

When the phone rings I don't know where I am. I raise up on the bunk bed and blink at the woman tucked under me, her masklike face unfamiliar, twin scars from plastic surgery concealed along her hairline.

"You're not doing yourself any favors, killer," says my old friend Scott. "I got a call from Harry Weeks. I think the poor guy was at a police station."

There is an auburn wig on the desk by the phone. A scattering of female baubles.

"What the fuck am I going to do with you, man?" he exhales tiredly.

"I'm sorry, Scott," I mutter. "You shouldn't have placed me here. Those people made me a little crazy. You know how much I hate Barbara Perry."

"What's happened to you, killer?" he says. "You used to be so solid. Oh, the publications were never there, but you had a way with people. Charmed their socks off. Best one-on-one critique man in the business, they used to say about you. Could make a seminar full of first-timers wet their pants to get started writing. Now nobody will have you, man. The word is out."

"What about Sun Valley?" I say, panic creeping into my voice. "That's coming up soon."

"Sun Valley is for names," Scott says. "You couldn't get a job there serving hors d'oeuvres."

The woman in bed begins to stir.

"Come on, Scott," I say, "you've got to get me out of here. Twenty years, old sack. Doesn't that count for something?"

There is a pause, the crackle of electrons. "I do have something for you, my friend, but you've got to promise to take this one seriously."

"I promise," I say.

"I mean it, killer. This is your last chance. Twenty years or not, I can't cover for you anymore."

"Where?" I say.

A longer pause. "Minot, North Dakota," he says.

"*Where?*"

"If you leave today you should be there in time for next Thursday."

"I'm *driving?*" I say.

"Trailways," he says.

Once, years ago now, I sent him a story I worked hard on and was very pleased with. He had been a tough critic in class and I valued his opinion. Months went by, a year. He never responded. Finally I swallowed my pride and gave him a call. 'Did you ever get that story I sent you?' I asked timidly, an afterthought, I pretended, at the end of our long phone conversation. 'Remind me,' he said. 'My head is so clogged with trivia.' So I described the story. 'Oh yeah,' he said: *Thin*. His only comment. 'Thin,' he said.

"One final thing," Scott says. "It has come to my attention that you're sending annoying letters to one of our best talents."

He continues with his avuncular admonitions, but the words dissolve into a vacuum of white noise, so I settle the phone quietly on its cradle. The woman, Ashley, rolls over to face the wall, her breathing deep and somnolent. I am tired, my bones ache, my mouth is dry and prickly. I dress slowly and begin to pack. Minot, North Dakota, I think. Minot, North Dakota.

'Make a good life for yourself,' she said.

In a hidden pocket of the suitcase the bundle of carbons is still intact, tied together with string, undisturbed by meddling fingers. I loosen the string and slip free a page, studying my handwriting.

"Dear Laurel," the letter begins. "Are things any better in Nicaragua?"

Notes on the
Authors and the Novellas

Contributors to *Careless Weeds* were invited to comment on their novellas; these comments immediately follow the biographical notes.

JANE GILMORE RUSHING was born in 1925 in Pyron, Texas, a community located on the plains of West Texas. She earned degrees in journalism and English from Texas Tech University and taught at both the high school and college levels. She has published seven novels, including *Walnut Grove, Mary Dove, The Raincrow,* and *Winds of Blame.* Her most recent book is *Starting from Pyron,* a "photostudy," with photographs by Billie Roche Barnard. The book is a personal view of the hamlet where both women lived as children.

"In my early childhood I lived for a little while in a village that in memory and imagination has often appeared to me like the setting of a children's story book. From time to time small events of that period come into my mind—transformed, it may be, by such associations. Something made me think of a traveling show that came to our town once, and I remembered how exotic it seemed, how fleetingly wonderful. But what if those dear, insular, prosaic people had found mysterious outsiders like these show folk camped in their midst for a prolonged stay? I wondered, and the possibilities took shape in the novella *Wayfaring Strangers.*"

MARGOT FRASER is a former juvenile probation officer, librarian, bookseller, and serious gardener. She now lives outside Odessa, Texas, where she is at work on a second novel and a collection of short stories. She is the author of *The Laying Out of Gussie Hoot,* published by Southern Methodist University Press.

"I think of *Hardship* as a tone poem, a meditation in shades of gray, buff, pipe-clay, and rose. It evolved from impressions of the Big Bend country and the people who have prevailed in that landscape—one of vastness and silence, a pitiless climate combined with surprising beauty. While telling the story, I wanted to keep the same muted effect and yet not lose color and movement, so that the whole seems written in one key, a sustained adagio with moto allegro."

DAVID L. FLEMING was born in 1951 and grew up on the farm near San Marcos, Texas, where he still lives with his wife and two daughters. He holds an M.A. degree from Southwest Texas State University and for the past fifteen years has taught English and creative writing at Seguin High School in Seguin, Texas. His first novel, *Summertime,* appeared in 1986. He is currently working on his third novel.

"My maternal grandmother lived in Coldspring, Texas, and as a boy I spent many summer weeks and special holidays there with my family and relatives. It was a small, main street town then, even though it was the county seat, and it was memorable to me, growing up on blackland prairie, for the pine trees and the sand and the curious, obvious separation and almost choreographed intermingling of black and white cultures. In *The Sun Gone Down, Darkness Be Over Me,* I returned in memory to this small town of thirty years ago and set out to write a story about love and prejudice. I wanted to show that Willie was as prejudiced in his own way against Esther Ruth/ Louella as the bigoted Mr. Reynolds was. At the same time, I wanted Willie to love the girl as the singular human being she was without regard to family, marriage, or sex, the way she loved him only for what she instinctively knew him to be. To me, the love of one human being for another, on those terms, is the prettiest and most selfless love there is."

CLAY REYNOLDS is the author of *The Vigil* and *Agatite* as well as short fiction and essays. His most recent novel is *Franklin's Crossing.*

"*Summer Seeds* was born of a story from my childhood. What happened was that a group of boys returning from working one of their father's fields stopped to help themselves to some watermelons on the way home. The farmer, intending to have some fun, shot at them, way over their heads, to 'put the fear of God into them.' That was about it. The more I thought about it, though, the more I realized how easy it would have been for a harmless joke to backfire, to get out of hand. In the late fifties and sixties, my friends and I used to go on weekend campouts. I'm shocked now, as a parent, to recall that we routinely carried firearms and shot at damn near anything that moved except each other—and we might have done that if we hadn't been afraid of getting into trouble. We played 'war,' imitating our uncles and fathers who had been away in Korea and World War II, acting out parts that John Wayne and his contemporaries made famous."

PAT CARR was born in Wyoming in 1932 but has lived most of her life in Texas. She holds degrees from Rice University and Tulane University and has taught in a number of Texas universities, including Texas Southern University and the University of Texas at El Paso. She has published eight books and has been the recipient of several awards and grants, among them the Iowa Fiction Award (for *The Women in the Mirror*), the Texas Institute of Letters Short Story Award, and a National Endowment for the Humanities Grant. She currently teaches fiction writing at Western Kentucky University in Bowling Green.

"The impetus for *Bluebirds* came from my knowing a family that had become dysfunctional because of the father's Vietnam experiences. I also once lived near a glass factory where bluebirds were made, and in telling the story, I found that the blue glass birds were an apt metaphor for the fragile relationships between the characters."

THOMAS ZIGAL was born in 1948 in Galveston, Texas, and grew up in Texas City. In the early seventies he earned an M.A. in creative writing from Stanford University. His short fiction has appeared in a variety of journals and quarterlies, and in 1983 he won the Texas Institute of Letters Short Story Award. He is the author of a novel, *Playland,* and a collection of stories, *Western Edge,* which won the 1982 Austin Book Award. At present he lives in New Orleans with his wife, Annette Carlozzi, and their son, Danny.

"The title of my novella derives from a 1985 *Paris Review* interview with Robert Stone: '. . . there are all these academic writing programs turning out the new second lieutenants of literature, and some of them somehow do manage to get published.' I was amused that he compared the MFA programs to ROTC."

TOM PILKINGTON, editor of this volume, is a native of Fort Worth, Texas. He has been a teacher and critic of Texas, Southwestern, and Western American literature for nearly three decades. He is author or editor of nine previous books and has published dozens of articles, essays, and reviews. He is Professor of English and University Scholar for Literature at Tarleton State University, Stephenville, Texas.